I detected the taint of ammonia in the air as the lock was cracked. Then four strange, bat-like faces peered around the edge of the hatch cover. I had never seen the like of such as these—inhuman creatures that looked to be nightmares personified. Aliens, for certain, and things I was sure that I had never known to exist.

"Screeeeeee," they exclaimed, piercing my ears with their high-pitched speech. Behind them I could see a reddish, dimly lit space filled with dark darting shapes.

"Screeeeeee," they repeated. D'vore slumped, his whole being collapsing into a pitiful heap. "Case, this is worse than ever expected.Qalyub Gudlag," he sighed and pointed at a scrawl of characters at the rim of the hatch; a checkered square and bisected circle. "This is a Penchon ship."

DREAMS OF EARTH

BY BUD SPARHAWK

PRELUDE

The weeks since I recovered had passed quickly as I learned the basics of life aboard *Tollembol,* this strange vessel that had rescued me. I had recovered enough to clean and dress myself, get food when I wished, and had begun to formulate questions about my past.

The accident had been catastrophic, I'd been told. I was the sole survivor, but of what I was not sure, so muddled was my mind. Strange dreams and chance memories filled my head while shooting pains and sudden tremors occupied my body.

"Give yourself time, Case, D'vore had said, using the name he'd given me. "It takes time for mind and body to heal after such trauma. Fill your days with undemanding tasks and let your mind rest." To aid that process he permitted me to help in the ship's surgery.

As I was cleaning a stain from the surgical platform where we'd recently performed another grisly operation, I felt *Tollembol,* our strange star-ranging ship shake. The motion was so unexpected, so like an earthquake, that I became immediately disoriented, no longer so trustful of the apparent gravity that mysteriously gave everything a proper up and down-ness.

Up to this time I had taken the ship's gravity for granted, another miracle among many that I'd encountered since awakening. No one remarked upon it or even found it strange that we should not be floating about free from gravity in this vast gulf between the stars. Somehow I knew that even if someone explained it to me I would probably not grasp the answer until I had once again gained more understanding of this technology.

Without warning, the deck dropped beneath my feet and

then slammed upward with considerable force. My knees buckled under the impact. I threw an arm out to keep from staggering. As I fought to retain my balance I recalled that I'd felt this before, only that time I had fallen under the console.

Console? That must have been what saved me while the others of my crew had been crushed! I must have …

That vagrant thought disappeared as the orientation of the ship abruptly changed, spinning forward, to the left, and rotating simultaneously. A wave of nausea overcame me as I was thrown tumbling against the bulkhead. Somewhere in the distance a continuous, shrill alarm began crying. There were shouts. I could hear voices screaming and the clatter of loose gear. There was a long series of sharp sounds, too soft for explosions and too loud for anything else. More shouts and a few screams followed.

The ship began to creak and groan as the up and down-ness became arbitrary, tossing me from bulkhead to floor to overhead and back again. A lethal cloud of sharp and pointed instruments flew around me, clanging in metallic peals as they clashed. A scalpel grazed my cheek and sent a spray of tiny red globes flying. I realized that if I did nothing this deadly swarm of cutlery would do worse damage than a nicked cheek. I had to find someplace safe, somewhere that I could brace myself against the ship's wild gyrations, someplace far from these deadly devices.

My compartment was a short way down the companionway. There, maybe, I could brace myself beneath the bunk until whatever disaster was befalling the ship was spent. When down-ness reasserted its presence I scooted away from the clatter of falling hardware and, with one hand on the bulkhead, began making my way to the security of my bunk. It was only a few dozen paces, a short, straight run, I thought, but it turned out to be a much more precarious journey than I anticipated. Despite what my eyes told me, the deck quickly became a steep incline that grew so extreme that I knew I would not have the strength to climb by so much as a single step. I braced one foot on the surgery's hatchway so I would not tumble stern-wise.

Suddenly the far bulkhead became deck and I flew across to crash in a heap. Quickly, I scuttled along much like a star-borne cockroach, using hands, feet, legs, buttocks, elbows, and knees to propel myself to a position just below the open hatch of my compartment. I moved sideways in I the next gravitational shift turned the hatch into a yawning hole. I had barely moved when another shift sent me sidewise to crumble on the deck. I recovered quickly and crawled toward the now normal hatchway.

I was on the verge of the entrance when, suddenly, strong arms swept me up, threw me over a shoulder, and carried me backwards and away from my refuge. I could not understand where we were going. I tried to recognize passing hatchways and bulkheads but they looked so different from my upside down position and might have been recognizable had there not been so much debris and dead crewmen.

We stopped abruptly. I was thrown into a strange, cylindrical room, one so small that I could almost reach one side to the other with a single span of arms. I turned just in time to see D'vore turn and slam the hatch shut. "We are safe for the moment," he said.

His words did not reassure me. I was disoriented, confused, and terrified.

"Strap yourself down before the next field shift," D'vore ordered brusquely. He indicated the place I was to lay. I did as I was told. At least the straps would hold me tight and safe against the random movements that had made my earlier movements so fraught with danger. D'vore strapped himself on the other bunk.

Nothing happened for a few beats of my hammering heart. I no longer heard the creaks and groans that had been background noises since that first sickening jolt. There was a series of musical tones and then an inhuman voice announced in cold and clinical terms; "Ejection sequence commences in three seconds, two seconds, one second." A sharp bang followed and my stomach flipped as up and down first reversed and then disappeared entirely. I realized instantly that I was in free fall, just like I'd experienced in training school. That had been another fleeting memory without context–what school, where and when?

How had this come to pass?

PART ONE AWAKENING

After an eternity of agony and pain I woke to find a creature hovering over me. It appeared to be a man, but no hair adorned the shining skull, nor did ears protrude from either side. The eyes were large cream orbs, the nose a slight rise in the center of the smooth ovoid. There was a thin slit where an open mouth should yawn. It was a manikin's head, a minimalist's concept, not something that should sit atop such massive shoulders or control the strong, very human arm that reached out to lift my head and press a cup of water to my lips.

I heard a stream of gibberish before words began to take form. *"Zu conscious, nu? Ista cognizant?"* The speech seemed to come from the head, but I could detect no movement of lips that would form the words, no flash of tongue, nor a glimmer of expression that would add meaning. Yet, the tone alone conveyed concern. It was a very human voice, deep, resonant, undoubtedly male. I nodded, unable to speak through the aches and pains that raked my body, but to acknowledge that I'd heard.

Massive hands brushed my cheek in a gesture too intimate, too feminine for one so heavily built. *"Ser gutt.* Excellent. *Trebien. Du ist nomen haben?* [click] Name *ist?"*

Name? I seem to recall answering to something, but there was a void in my mind around the space identity should live. I strained to loosen the cells that held my identity and, as I struggled, the silver ovoid tilted to one side. *"Recovered non est. Dorme'. Spraken autenlatter."* There was a feather touch on my forehead and, as if on command, I slept and dreamed of seas and mountains, of machines, and glimmering, shimmering landscapes.

The second time I woke there I was no one in the cramped room. My head seemed clearer and many of the aches that had accompanied my previous moments of consciousness seemed to have disappeared. I sat upright and immediately felt the world spin. I was dizzy, weak. How long had I been here, and where exactly was here?

There was a sense of otherness about this place. I sniffed. The smells were unfamiliar, but I could not focus as to what might be so different. The two doors I could see appeared out of proportion. I felt—they should be narrower and certainly taller, but I couldn't remember why this should be. The lights were too bright, too blue and hurt my eyes.

I felt heavy and sluggish; no doubt a consequence of my weakness, but it could equally have been due to a return to gravity after being on the ship. Gravity? I had no way of knowing if I was in one of Einstein's hypothetical elevators or back on … The name escaped me for the moment.

When the dizziness passed, I tentatively stepped off the bed. My legs wobbled, yet I was able to make my way to the commode and washstand, both in pale blue ceramic. They had an institutional look about them, it much like you'd find in a hospital.

A hospital? Was that where I was? Yes, I recalled—there was an accident. I recalled agony and wondered what had happened. A panicked examination of my nude body revealed I was whole, with no missing limbs or damaged flesh. Neither was there operating scars or bandages evident. From all I could tell my body was normal in all respects, save for my weakness, disorientation and parts of me that appeared mismatched in color and hairiness. I must have made a near miraculous recovery unless, of course, the accident had been a fantasy of my unsettled mind.

I noticed a small mirror. I held fast to the washstand with trembling hands and peered into the glass. A bland, expressionless face of a stranger looked back at me. I didn't have the faintest glint of recognition. Before I could examine the strange face further, my legs collapsed and I slipped to the floor.

A slight, short, and muscular woman wearing green garments helped me up. At first I thought her coloring curious, a pale cinnamon tone but, as she wrapped her long arms about me, I saw that she had a fine brown pelt.

Her face was broad and long, bisected by a narrow nose that bracketed close-set eyes above pursed lips. She didn't alter her look of utter boredom as she efficiently bundled me into an olive coverall and half-carried me along a curving passageway, all without speaking one word or acknowledging that I was aught but an object to be managed.

There was something familiar about the way that passageway curved. It was very much like the companionways on the deep space stations. Deep space stations? Where had that image come from? The thought vanished as quickly as it had come.

She stopped before a blue door and spoke a few words that I couldn't understand, then pushed me inside with a strong hand between my shoulder blades.

"*Inkomen.*" a gruff voice announced. "*Velkomen.* Hello dere."

"Uh, hello," I ventured as I looked around. The room was wedge-shaped, narrower at the door than at the far end where a vast window framed a deep black sky filled with brilliant stars. Stars could only appear that bright from space, where no atmosphere dispersed their light. I realized then that I must be on a space ship, or perhaps a space station. But the stars did not move, as they would have if we'd been rotating. It had to be a ship.

"*Sadista.* Sit you down," my host instructed and waved me to a large chair facing the window. He looked nothing like the woman and was much more muscular than the one who wakened me. He was, a brute of a man with broad shoulders and a massive chest. Thick black hair protruded from the neck of his shirt, making me wonder if he too sported a furry pelt. His hands, resting on the desk were large enough to crush my head were he so disposed. There was an overall hint of menace about him, a threat that I could not define.

He gazed at me from dark, deep-set eyes. "D'vore did well,

pasticher. Gutt. Now must pay the debt. What ship *votre* and wherefrom *despache*?"

I must have revealed my confusion at this polyglot speech, for he continued, but slower, his language improving by the moment. "You, we rescued. Much energy obligated to find and recover from wreckedship. How old ship comed so far?"

A shipwreck? Yes, that would explain my memories of an accident. Wait, hadn't he called me "Pasticher." I clutched this morsel of identity as if it were a life preserver. *Pasticher.* It was a start. I had a name.

He frowned. "We found the wreck and D'vore recovered you. We to learn how you came to be so far? How get you here?"

I realized that D'vore must have been the silver-headed man. "I don't know. What did you say about a wreck? Yes, I recall some sort of accident. Sorry, I don't remember anything more than that," I finished plaintively. "My thoughts are so confused that I don't even know who I am."

He scowled and then rubbed his chin with blunt fingers whose nails, I noticed with some wonder, were a deep red color, but whether that was natural or paint I wasn't certain. "Medician D'vore did not do so well as thought. Ship were derelict—unknown design, but no identification. Crew was damaged badly. Had to reconstruct, Pasticher. Took time. Much resource obligation."

This was another mention of obligation. What did it mean? Wait, hadn't he said reconstruction? Since my body appeared to be unblemished he must mean that I had been reconstructed and brought back to health. "How long?" I choked, wondering how long Luella had waited for my recovery. "How long did this reconstruction take? Who else survived?"

"Thirty-six million seconds," he answered flatly. I quickly calculated that he meant two years at least. No wonder I felt weak. I had just lost two years of my life and God only knows what else. But why did I have no memory of this passage of time? Surely I hadn't been unconscious the whole time?

"When can I see my wife?" I asked and, an instant later realized that I had no idea of what Luella looked like. Nor was I so certain of her name. Mary and Cindy seemed equally appropriate. My thoughts churned. Neither of those names seemed to fit the sudden memory of a thin blonde's girlish face. "My wife?" I asked with fading hope, but the captain's expression told me that he knew nothing of my origin. At that moment, I knew that I would have to recover my memories if I was ever to return home.

In the days that followed, I explored as much as I could whenever the D'vore, a title that hadn't been explained, allowed me to leave my room. I observed much but understood little.

Tollembol, whose name I'd discovered, was vast, far larger than any spaceship I imagined possible. I wandered for a full day, never revisiting a single location and still did not plumb the entirety of the ship. Nothing was familiar. Dining halls I recognized, although I was unable to operate any of the dispensers that lined the walls. Neither did I recall how to handle the simplest eating utensil. Rest rooms there were aplenty, but without doors or stalls. Modesty, it appeared, was not something the crew valued. At times I saw pairs coupling in the open, seemingly unconcerned about exposing their most intimate moments.

Much of the ship was devoted to mysterious devices that hummed, emitted a small amount of heat, but had no apparent instrumentation or controls. I once stumbled into an octagonal chamber where five crewmen were engaged in assembling a mechanism of complex design. None of them noted my presence. Neither did they answer any of my questions, much as others had rebuffed my every attempt at conversation.

I watched with fascination as they fitted part to part with nary a word. It was as if all were the fingers of a single hand, so coordinated and controlled were their movements. When they were finished they hugged one another and left the room. The machine did nothing I could detect, although I watched it carefully. No one come to fetch or operate it so I left as ignorant as I had come.

All of the crew, save the captain, D'vore and myself, appeared to be close relatives. They all had the same muscular build, the same cinnamon-colored fuzz, and identically long faces. But there could not be hundreds of brothers and sisters, I knew, so their close resemblance must be due to my unfamiliarity with them. In time, I hoped, I would be able to discern their individual differences.

At the captain's insistence, D'vore took me to view what appeared to be the wreckage of my ship. This was probably in hopes of jarring my memory. In this, all of us were disappointed, for there was nothing familiar about the torn, battered, and shredded hulk in the cavernous cargo bay.

"This is a rendering we can use while we are processing the data," D'vore said as a phantom image of the wreckage flowed around us. I was amazed at the realistic image that allowed us to drift unimpeded through twisted metal. Never could I recall such a flawless method of presentation.

How could I have forgotten such a wonder?

But that was simply another puzzle among many. Everything I'd encountered since awakening seemed so new, so foreign to my numbed senses that I wondered just how much of my memory was truly lost. I was a child again, learning the common, everyday things again, it seemed. How could I have forgotten the objects and machines that everyone else took for granted? Why did D'vore have to explain the operation of a simple clothing artificer or show me how to seal the seams of my clothing, something every child should have learned in infancy?

At the heart of my confusion lay a deeper mystery, one that plagued me whenever I had a moment for contemplation: From what source did I draw the few facts I seemed to recall? It was knowledge, but without memory of how it might have been obtained. Try as I might I could not discover from what well flowed the facts and concepts that floated unconnected on the surface of my thoughts. It was as if there was a wall shrouded in fog between my past and present. It was disquieting, this feeling of separation from my past, from my identity.

I tried to make sense of everything I saw and heard but could not recall more than half of the words used to describe objects and I feared that aphasia was also a problem. How could I have forgotten so many words? It was as if I were an alien from another civilization seeing wonders for the first time so poor was my memory.

Coping with things I did not understand was so frustrating that I focused on the menial tasks I was allowed within the surgery where I had awakened. On occasion I assisted D'vore and quickly became proficient at disposing of severed fingers, arms, and other damaged bodily parts. From the number of patients it seemed that there were many a dangerous hazard on this ship.

I could not understand all that D'vore did, so intricate were the movements of his surgical trade and the assortment of serums and ointments that he employed. The restoration of a limb or digit appeared magical, and the resurrection of an apparently dead crewman miraculous. Despite the gore and screams of the injured D'vore always went about his surgery with calm confidence.

I noticed that the crew behaved strangely toward D'vore. Despite his excellent treatment of their injuries and their rapid recovery, none gave him even a modicum of courtesy. It was as if they thought him a mechanism, an unselfconscious object that needed no acknowledgement for performing its functions.

Their attitude toward me was no better. I tried to approach them but was rebuffed again and again. I had the impression that they loathed the sight of me, but could not determine why they did so. I was certain that it could not be my appearance. I did not have the compact weight lifter's build that seemed so universal among them nor did I share their cinnamon coloration save for my right leg, which was becoming more like the left with each passing day. I was taller than any of them, more slender, and my skin was a fainter hue. I doubted that such minor variations would justify their aversion, but could think of no other reason. After a while, I gave up further attempts to talk to them.

"Many of the sixteen are like this," D'vore explained. "It is a fact of human psychology that others be suspect. Do not concern yourself over this." There were so many questions implied by that statement that I hardly knew where to begin and, in the next moment, had forgotten what they were.

The one exception to universal unfriendliness was the

captain, not that he ever referred to himself as such, nor had I ever heard anyone address him that way. Still, it seemed to me that he filled that position of responsibility and should bear the title.

He called upon me on occasion, apparently for no other reason than to inquire about my health, my general state of mind, and whatever few facts may have surfaced from the depths of lost memory.

"Have your memories clarified?" he asked on one occasion. "Do you recall much of what happened to your ship? For that matter, do you recall anything of where you might have come from?"

In response to his queries I described the flashes of faces with forgotten names, of names surfacing without reference, of so many lost words and the inability to recall any of the ordinary day-to-day activities of life. The scattered nature of my mind showed no sign of cohesion and I was always distracted by some stray image or thought. "I was hoping that you might have some answers for me."

"I expected you to be confused," he answered. "Didn't the medician warn you it would take time?"

"Yes, but I thought ..."

He didn't let me finish. "I'd hoped for better. So, get more rest, to eat well, and keep trying to remember what happened. We'll talk later." I took that as dismissal and walked away disappointed. Still unknowing of my own past and even less informed about this ship.

Despite my persistence on subsequent interviews, the captain never explained how I had come to be on the ship, where we were bound, nor the purpose of this voyage. His unwillingness to share this information, tied to the same reluctance on D'vore's part raised my suspicions.

Was their behavior because the ship was on a mission they were not permitted to talk about? Neither captain nor crew appeared military in behavior or dress. Everyone I saw went about their tasks with an air of bored competence, dressed in clothing so unique, so different from another's that they could not possibly be considered uniforms. No, this ship had no trappings of the military or a mission.

Were they pirates, perhaps? But I failed to see how such a criminal enterprise could be profitable in the distant and empty regions of space? No, piracy made no sense given the advanced technology all around me. Perhaps it was a commercial venture, or scientific exploration.

In the end I decided that I knew too few facts to make any sort of judgment; such knowledge would come, if ever, in its own time.

I mentioned the aversive behavior of the crew as D'vore and I shared an evening in conversation. "One gets used to it," D'vore assured me. His intent, I'm certain, was to relieve my feelings of isolation. "They shun me because I am not a person."

"Not a person?" I asked. He appeared only slightly different from others, other than the silver globe that was his head. The exposed portions of his arms were covered with the same cinnamon hairs and, I suspected, so was the remainder of his body. I had no idea of why anyone might not consider him as a crewmember.

"Yes," he confided. "I have been forced to supplement myself with parts I've salvaged here and there." He flexed an all too human hand and patted his chest. "But I think my basic self is as I was created, reduced considerably, but unchanged where it matters."

I had witnessed many an operation in his surgery and was quite familiar with the medical miracles that could be accomplished in restoring limbs and organs. I had no doubts that the same knowledge he employed could have joined that metal head to his body. He pointed at the center of his silver globe. "Had you been in poorer shape, I'd have acquired a better nose." He must have noted my start of dismay for he added with a chuckle, "I intended that as a bit of humor."

Relief flooded me. I had no references from which to judge such comments, such was my confused mind. "What happened to my memories," I asked. "It's as if all of my past life, my memories of even the simplest of daily routines have disappeared. I keep having these flashes of memory, but nothing focused, nothing that gives me context for the images."

The faceless ovoid tilted in what I took to be a gesture of concern. "Those are the result of traumatic shock, or perhaps there was insufficient perfusion of your brain. As I said before, it will take time before your mind, your memories become fully integrated. My advice is to allow yourself time to see what obtains." He patted my knee in a gesture of concern.

The fluency of his speech was remarkable. I could not fail to notice that both D'vore and the captain's facility with my language had steadily improved and was quickly becoming completely understandable. Both had even lost much of the nasal accent that I'd noticed at first. "Thank God you've learned how to speak to me," I said. "I'd be completely lost otherwise."

He gave a rich baritone laugh. "It is you who have learned ours," he said. "During your reconstruction I installed a few mimetic units for language. When you are more fully recovered I can install others to give you more useful skills."

That he had "installed" a facility for language surprised me. Vague memories of study and lessons before droning professors swam beneath the surface of my mind for a moment. I suspected that these mimetic units had not been the way I had learned in the past, but could not bring the reason to mind.

"What language am I speaking now?" I wanted to know if this mimetic thing was translating his words or was doing something more profound. I felt as if I were speaking in my native tongue, whatever that might have been.

"I think the name of this tongue is *Trade*. It is common among the human spaceborne."

At D'vore's urging and the captain's insistence I made numerous virtual tours through the imaged wreckage. We all hoped to find some fragmentary key that would loosen a flood of memory, or provide something that would trigger a recollection of the fate that befell me.

The torn and twisted metal was so distorted that it no longer resembled a ship. I saw what might have been a passageway, passing my hand with ease through the image of phantom knives of torn metal that projected from bulkhead or deck.

At one point I stood before a jagged, distorted gap that might have been a workstation had it not been squashed to an eighth of its former height? In the crushed space I saw fragments of instruments, bits of electronics, broken hoses and mysterious brown stain that might have been the blood of whoever had been at that station when we emerged.

Emerged? I stood, shock stilled, holding onto that tiny piece of my past as if it were a life ring tossed into the maelstrom of my confused mind. Yes, we had been on a mission of some sort. We had come from some place whose name was .... I struggled to pull forth more facts.

I recalled a sense of anticipation, of working competently, but with an undertone of childish excitement. Something momentous was about to occur and I was a key player. I felt pride and fear over the mission and ...

The slim concept of mission remained, but I could elicit nothing further from the black pit of forgetfulness. Still I was encouraged by this small fragmentary memory. That tiny flashback could mark a beginning and, perhaps, the rest of memory would, as D'vore had advised, follow. So I hoped as I searched eagerly through the remainder of the ship's image, looking for another revelation that might release the floodgates of memory.

But none could I find.

D'vore was upset when I told him that the captain had mentioned my last name. I was "Something Pasticher," I declared.

"That is a cruel joke," he declared. "He should have corrected your misinterpretation at once. Pasticher is not your name. It is what you are."

I slumped in disappointment. Losing even this putative bit of identity was a blow that struck me in the heart. I was so upset by this that I did not ask what the term that I had thought my surname might mean. "So I have no name?"

"I shall call you Case," D'vore said, interrupting my thoughts. "Yes, Case seems right for you." I accepted the name willingly. Having a name, any name, was better than remaining nameless. It would serve until I recovered memory of my true identity, or so I thought.

In other conversations with D'vore I continued my inquiries regarding the ship, this vessel whose limits I had not yet discovered, and was again rebuffed. "At least tell me where we are," I said in frustration after he once again refused to provide a definitive answer.

He took a moment before replying. "I suspect we are far from your home and amidst the Periformus Rift whose shoals are fraught with danger."

The answer confused me even more. "I thought we were on a space ship or station of some sort. What's all this talk of rifts and shoals? Aside from a few thousand cometary bodies in the ring, the space around the solar system is mostly empty." There it was, more facts from my past rising unbidden from the depths to roll off my tongue so authoritatively.

D'vore tilted his silver head to one side. "Which solar system, friend Case ? And why would you think we were so near to a star? The Periformus is a place where reality seems to have faint hold. There are no star systems within two million light years and of those nearer, none of the sixteen have knowledge."

Two million light years? All at once my perception of the universe I thought I knew shifted. For some reason I'd thought there was only one solar system, a system that my ship was trying to escape. Was this one more aspect of the earlier confusion that still preyed on my mind? What were we trying to escape?

With that other unbidden memories surfaced. I recalled the sound of our ship ...

... *as it readied itself, the rising pitch of the generators, the acrid smell of hot wiring, my sickening dread that something would go horribly, tragically wrong, and my confidence that it would not. Then there was the absolute silence, the fuzzy appearance of objects near and far, the taste of apples in my mouth, and a feeling of being swathed in thick cotton battens. Then, after a timeless interval, there was an icy shock, momentary agony, and blackness.*

D'vore appeared to have taken no notice of my preoccupation. "It depends on which star system you mean," he continued.

"By certain clues of its composition we guess your ship to have hailed from somewhere in the Magellan region. That would be several hundreds of millions of light years from here. Strange that so small a ship could come so far."

I immediately suspected that D'vore was a madman. The captain had told me that I had only been in recovery for two years. There was no way that this ship–even a starship, for God's sake—could cover that unbelievably immense distance in so little time after rescuing me. Neither was it reasonable that D'vore could speak so casually about such incredible distances. No, he must be mad, I thought.

Or was I? "What is the date?" I asked hesitantly. Perhaps I had been in recovery longer than I had calculated. The year 2134 stood prominently in my mind, but I could not recall the month or day.

"It is the fifth cycle of the year five twenty-six by reckoning of the ship clock," he replied. "The year seven, seven, eight, fifty-four by our head's counting, and forty ninety and two by my own measure."

Clearly these people measured time by different standards than any I could understand. "I left in 2134." A location popped into my mind, unbidden. "From Earth." The word sounded as if it didn't fit this new language.

"Eart? Never heard of it. What was its universal designation?"

"I don't know," I screamed in frustration. "All I can fucking recall is the name."

D'vore nodded sympathetically. "I can understand the frustration you must feel, Case . I, too, have lost my bearings in an unknown sea." He indicated his body with a sweep of his hand. "Little do I have of what I once was yet I seem to recall that I was far more than this pathetic relic."

"But you know who you are, what you are. You have a name. You have a place on this ship, and an occupation! How can you possibly know how screwed up this situation and lack of memory is making me?" I realized was shouting uncontrollably when D'vore pressed something against my temple.

"Let the drug take hold," he advised calmly. "I'm afraid that all of this information has somewhat unnerved you." D'vore was ever the master of the understatement.

Within seconds I began to relax. My sudden fit of anger ceased. It seemed so easy to simply let go. No more sudden memories plagued me as I slipped into dreams of seas and forest, of fields and flowers, and strangely, of blinking stars.

My feelings of frustration seemed to be gone when I awoke. "How did you come to be on this ship?" I asked D'vore, hoping to elicit more information about this strange vessel and its purpose. The very concept of a star faring ship was a wonder. How could I ever have forgotten such a magnificent machines, such a huge concept as travel between the stars?

"I was transferred from another ship, forty tens of cycles past," he replied. "Skilled in biologic repairs, I am used to fill a role vacated by death."

That raised more questions than I had time to frame. "Where did you come from originally and what happened to your head?" I hoped that such a direct question would not be too rude, but how he came to possess his silver head had intrigued me from my first glimpse.

D'vore's silver face showed no expression, but the tilt of his head and the shrug of his shoulders told me that I had touched no sensitive nerve. "I was told I originated on Gleebor, out toward the Rim," he explained in words I heard but could not comprehend. I did not know of Gleebor or what this rim might be. "I vaguely recall being shipped out on a circular run as a rite of passage and was caught by mischance when only halfway through," he continued. "I was apparently badly damaged and drifted for years as support declined and more and more of my functions decayed. Like yours, my memory faded.

"Luckily a freighter discovered me while only a handful of my functions survived. Little of me remained, I imagine, so they rebuilt me as best they could. So much was lost that I was trained as medician and sold to *Tollembol*. Since then I have supplemented myself as best I could."

"They turned you into a cyborg?"

D'vore shrugged again. "If by that you mean that they turned me into this half meat, half machine form, the answer is yes. It was not a solution I chose, but no one inquired about my feelings on the matter. They severed what was useless and used materials they had on hand to restore functions. In the end I was only a portion of what I had been, a tiny, edited fraction. In fact, I share this with you: that I lost so much that I cannot recall all that I once was, only a vague sense that I had been much more than this pitiful fragment I've become." I half expected to see tears on his metal face, so sad did he sound.

"But, to continue, after I recovered some limited functionality I had an obligation that I could only discharge by using the knowledge and skills they had installed. I became a biologic specialist, a medician. It was a role equally lonely as it has been on this ship, I assure you."

"They shun—are shunning you—you simply because of the way you were reconstructed?" I found his silver orb not entirely unpleasant, now that I had grown used to it. Of course I had not yet glimpsed what lay beneath his many layers of clothing to determine how extensive his mechanical prostheses might be. Yet, to all outward appearances he seemed almost human. His arms and legs were the same cinnamon color as the crew so I could see no reason for them to treat him as they did simply because of a metal skull.

"I could not return home, even if I knew its location," D'vore continued in a resigned voice. "I suspect that most of my kind would find my reduced form and functions too painful to look upon, a constant reminder of what they might face if damaged in some distant place where replacement parts were not on hand." He shrank visibly and buried his face in his hands, muffling his next words. "Ah Case, I have lost so much that suspect I can never return." He sat silent for a long while, thinking, no doubt, of his loss. I could sympathize.

He straightened up after a few moments and whispered. "There is a part of me that longs to know what I once had been, that wants to know what I might have become. But I digress—let us just say that I hoped this vessel would provide a friendlier environment. The crew, I quickly discovered, found my appearance quite distressing, so much so that I altered myself to my present more human form and tried to match as closely as possible the crew's appearance. It was not difficult, a few adjustments to head and torso and a reduction of legs. It took only a few hours of work for one with my skills. But it did no good. They seemed to find me more horrid afterwards for reasons I could not fathom."

His words shocked me. "Just how much did they alter you? I mean, why did they make you less than human?" I tried to picture alien surgeons reconfiguring D'vore's surviving body into a chimera that approximated their own form, using mechanical parts to replace what was irreparably damaged. Since I had no idea of what D'vore originally looked like, shocking nightmare images of snakes and scorpions flashed through my head.

But it was D'vore who reacted with shock. "*Less* human? No, Case, it was the meat parts they added to make me functional. That is where I got my original arms and hands. Not the few human ones you now see, but three more on each side and two below—useful because I needed all eight limbs. Some of them were from other races than human, which may be what disturbed the crew."

I tired to picture what he described, a fantastic Shiva of ravaged parts, a spider assembled by unknown aliens from the raw stuff of other bodies. But this was not so horrifying as the dawning realization that he had declared his mechanical parts as his original body, and those only a part of what he might have been. How many times had he replaced those arms, and from what resources?

I conjured images of him using his bloody surgery as a source for his gruesome transplants, amputating human arms and legs for his own uses. With a shock I recalled his remark about wanting my nose and realized that it might not have been the joke he'd declared.

Another horrid thought seized me: Parts of his present body could have belonged to one of my own crewmates and, if an arm and a leg were no problem, then what else had he stolen from their warm bodies? I felt the bile rising in my throat, a visceral reaction as I realized what a travesty of the human form, what an obscene construct this dreadful ghoul was. It was one thing to use human organs to repair another human, but to have an alien appropriate those for its own purpose was wrong, obscenely wrong to my mind.

At once I understood the revulsion that the crew must feel. What was more repulsive was the fact that D'vore did not understand why a human being would feel this way. That alone made him seem far more alien than anything I could imagine and one with whom I wanted as little to do with as possible.

I stayed away from D'vore for weeks after his revelation, unwilling to speak to him. He had betrayed my trust. He had presented himself as a friend, a confidant and deceiving me the while. He acted as if he were as human as me! What was the purpose for his deceit, I wondered and realized that I had no more chance of understanding his alien viewpoint than him understanding mine.

With the loss of D'vore's false companionship my loneliness became nearly unbearable. I continued to try to decipher the tangled mass of my mangled ship, hoping for another epiphany, but none was forthcoming. Between times I delved through *Tollembol*, spoke infrequently to the captain, and allowed myself to be wordlessly examined by D'vore, wondering the whole time if he viewed me as patient or as a potential source of replacement parts. I always discarded my clothing after visiting him, as if I could rid myself of the stink of death he carried.

Unlike the motley worn by the crew my own clothing remained utilitarian, the artificer's default setting, a drab, one-piece coverall of olive hue that embraced my feet and relieved me the necessity of boots. A slightly oversized drab coverall was all I could make the artificer produce, despite carefully writing down my coefficients so I would not make a mistake in sizes. Apparently there was some art to creating more varied clothing, a skill I had obviously lost along with other memories.

The coverall's material seemed as unfamiliar as everything else I touched. Each morning I found it to be crisp and clean, lying where I left it, as if it had been laundered while I slept. Try as I might I could not recall any fabric in my poorly recalled past that behaved in similar manner.

It was just another wonder among too many to question.

Despite my enmity D'vore allowed me to do what I could to help in the surgery. It was in this role when the ship seemed to turn upside down, inside out, and disoriented me completely.

The confusion was complete as I struggled to find safety only to be snatched by D'vore and summarily deposited in a cramped escape capsule, strapped in, and violently shaken as it exploded from the ship.

This was my worst nightmare. I was in a tiny capsule, light years from any help, and trapped with a monster!

No sooner had the burst of acceleration ceased than D'vore began to wail, a plaintive cry that seemed to come from his very depths. "*Tollembol* is gone. All is lost!" It was a cry of such passionate loss that I felt the deepest sympathy, even for such a monster as he.

After several minutes, D'vore released himself and began floating about, checking various storage places about the small vessel. I was amazed at the number of compartments that surrounded us. From one he withdrew packets of food, from another medications to tend my bruised and battered body. A third provided tools for adjusting his head, a process that left me somewhat queasy and without appetite for the chewy ration he'd handed me.

"We'll activate the beacon when we are far enough away." He pointed at a yellow handle projecting from the bulkhead. "Link with other survivors, we will."

"What happened? Was there a crash? Did we hit something?"

D'vore pulled himself to his bunk and pulled a strap across his lap before answering. "Attacked perhaps, or some mischance too great. The Rift is full of danger."

Attacked? Was this a continuation of a war no one had mentioned earlier or something entirely different? My earlier dismissal of the ship's military mission may have been wrong. Or perhaps it was the Rift, whatever that was, that had caused the violent shaking.

Could that be what destroyed my own ship? Had we foundered on some unknown hazard? Was that same force now crushing *Tollembol,* twisting the remains, and tearing it to pieces? And what of the crew? Had they all being killed or had some escaped?

I was even more confused than I'd been in those first hours after I'd awakened so many weeks before.

We drifted in the capsule for days before the monster attempted to converse. "I do not understand," he said when he noted that I had wakened from one of my fitful naps. "What have I done to make you treat me so? I thought that we were kindred souls, that we could provide each other needful companionship."

I did not answer. After all, what could I say to this alien being that he would understand? I doubted in my heart that he had any concept of the offenses he had committed and was committing with every motion of those severed limbs, those stolen parts of corpses who would never rest whole and entire.

"Have I not treated you well?" he continued. "Did I not do everything I could to make your adjustment as comfortable as possible? Did I not treat you as father to son, as priest to confessor, as psychiatrist to patient? Yet, despite these efforts you have turned on me, you react with revulsion, just as all the crew, save the head. What is there about me that is so offensive? It cannot be my appearance, for I have configured myself as closely as possible to the local human norm. It cannot be my essential self, for I keep that closely hidden from human eyes. Perhaps it is an attitude, a manner that so offends, but I have analyzed my conversations, my actions as thoroughly as I could and can detect no variation from the patterns engaged in by humans."

The simulation of pain in his voice was quite convincing, I thought. I had to admit that whatever this thing was, it was clever. Had I not known of his true nature I could easily believe D'vore to be honestly uncomfortable about his isolation.

"Please Case, tell me what so offends you that I might set it to rights and resume our former relationship." There was no expression on that silver globe, but the set of its body, the angle of arms and legs cried out for an answer.

"It is nothing you do or say," I began. "It is your arms, your legs. You stole these—that is your crime!"

D'vore rocked back as if I had struck him. "But the use of limbs that are no longer needed by their owner is a routine practice. Few there are of the crew who had no parts replaced at some point in their lives.

"When they first restored me I lost so much of whatever I once was and, to be honest, was uncertain of which elements of myself were original and which due to their creativity. Nevertheless I prevailed, I learned to work with what I had been given; this life they gave in return for my obligation to do their bidding. It was a simple surgical gift, nothing more. I do not understand why you feel this way."

There it was, the statement that proved that his alien heart lacked any moral sense. I knew my feelings weren't *logical, but my v*isceral reactions went beyond rational explanation. It was a reaction that went to the core of my being. I knew there was no way to explain this in terms an alien would understand.

"I cannot remove my limbs to please you," D'vore pleaded. "The limitations of mechanical substitutes for my limbs have proven too crude, too clumsy for the fine work that I must do. It is only by adopting others' meat limbs that I came to be marginally functional." He paused as he flexed an arm, as if considering his words carefully. "I am certain that this limb's former owner would not mind my using it to preserve the life of others."

"It does not matter what use you've made of them," I screamed, allowing all of my rage to spew out. "Nothing you could possibly do would ever justify your misappropriation of human parts. You are a travesty, a horror, an assembly of parts stripped from others. You say you are trying to appear human, but what you do is parade your difference, your *indifference* to everything I hold decent. It is not what you say or do, it is what you *are* that disgusts and repulses me."

Unexpectedly D'vore began chuckling. "So you would bestow humanity only on those who have integrity of body and mind? What am I, if not fully integrated? All of my parts function. I am as whole as you."

I could not stand his presumption of our shared humanity.

"I share nothing with you, D'vore. You cannot become human by attaching men's parts to yourself. You cannot be a man just because you shape yourself to resemble one. Being human means having certain values, of sanctifying life, of seeing people as more than an assembly of component parts. Being human is being born of man and woman." D'vore shrank from my words as if each was a missile striking his body.

After my wave of anger had passed a feeling of relief flooded through me. At last our differences were revealed. Now the ghoul understood where I stood and what I believed. Now D'vore knew that he was a monster. Now, he must realize why the crew had shunned him. I just hoped he felt a measure of shame.

At the same time I questioned my sense of moral outrage in light of his logic. From what source, what hidden memory had my reaction sprung? Why should I feel so strongly if I could not even recall my past, those things that must have shaped these feelings of disgust? Were my reactions instinctive or had they been taught at an earlier age? Was my revulsion indoctrinated so deeply that it was beyond mere memory?

"I ?" His quiet voice was querulous, hesitant.

"Yes?" I answered, half expecting some sort of apology, or another attempt at self-justification.

"There is something you should know," D'vore said. The pitch of his voice was somehow different, a voice tinged with very human sympathy. "Something that I should have mentioned earlier, save that the head insisted it would interfere with the recovery of your memories."

I could not imagine what that might be. As far as I was concerned nothing could have made my recovery less unproductive. "What would that be—my real name, perhaps? Or knowing how long the wreckage drifted before you found it? What sort of secret knowledge about me was it that you felt I could not handle?"

"Not about your past—that is still locked inside your head, in your fragmentary and recovering memory. Only you can answer the questions you pose. Only you."

"Then what is it?" I demanded with some heat. "What is it

that I don't know?"

"You must understand what we had to do," D'vore began. "I was working at the limits of my ability, far beyond what the head believed my poor skills could accomplish. There were so many fragments, so many disintegrating pieces."

"Get to the point!"

"We picked up the signal of your ship's collapse and reached the wreckage within hours of whatever misfortune befell you. I was among those who searched for survivors, who searched for someone that might have escaped whatever destroyed your ship."

"And found me," I added. "Lucky for me."

D'vore said nothing so I prodded. "How badly was I hurt? I know it must have been terrible, because the captain said it took two years to reconstruct me. I must have been in pretty bad shape."

"There were no survivors," D'vore said solemnly. "I found only partial, crushed bodies. We gathered as much as we could, but the vacuum. Well, a lot of tissue had degraded from gas expansion and evaporative loss."

"So where did you find me? Was I in some sort of sealed compartment or rescue pod?" The miracle that I alone had escaped the carnage that destroyed the remainder of the ship was beyond belief. How that could have happened I could not remember.

"As I said, there were no survivors. I had to make do with what I had. The brains were the most fragile. I'd only time to recover a fraction before time ran out. Then there were difficulties at the cellular level—the stocks were not compliant, your mitochondria were so different."

I was having difficulty understanding him. "You said there were no survivors?"

D'vore nodded. "Yes, Case . You are not, strictly speaking, a *survivor*. You are a construct—I had to patch you together with the parts we gathered. Your mind was assembled from whatever I could scour from the viable brains. I'm afraid that I didn't have time to be selective—the pressures of deterioration and time, you understand."

I was shocked, barely comprehending what he was saying.

"Little remained," D'vore continued. "A finger here, there organs still pulsing with life, half a leg over here, part of another there. Only eighteen pieces had a trace of life remaining." He shrugged. "I am sorry Case, but I had to make choices."

A number appeared in my head—eight. "There were eight of us who started the voyage, eight who you say are now dead." My voice was wooden, without emotion, reflecting the cold feeling that was growing inside of me.

"You are wrong, Case. All eight survived. They are you, the *you* that lives and breathes and walks and talks. The entire crew is in your wakening memories, in your arms and legs, your liver and spleen, heart and lungs. You too are a man of parts, Case!"

I struggled with this new knowledge and what it implied. If he spoke the truth then I was no better than him in my use of spare human parts. But where he had merely appropriated a few bits of muscle and bone, of skin and ligaments, I had been formed both of bodies and minds. I was no less a creature of nightmare and, in many ways, far worse than ever D'vore had been.

Pasticher wasn't a name; it had been a description! That's what the captain really meant—that I was a pastiche of my crew. I grew numb in the dawning knowledge of what I was. I suspected that none of the eight souls rested easy with their memories intact. I could hardly believe that portions of all were now part of me, whatever I was.

"Yes, Case, you are drawn from many, and yet you are still an individual, a person in your own right," D'vore had correctly guessed the reason for my sudden introspection and then added, "As am I."

Be that as it may, I now understood why everyone on the ship had shunned me. It was that I was a zombie, manufactured from the dead bodies of my comrades, a travesty of a human being, something artificial and undead.

D'vore pressed something to my temple. "Sleep. It will be better when you wake."

I welcomed the bliss of forgetfulness as night closed on my troubled mind. As before, I dreamed of Janice, Pat, Luella, and Mary, of Billie and Cindy, of all those who wandered the corridors of my mind, seeking their lost loves. I dreamed of twisted space and the proud faces of my crew as we departed on our test run. One of them, I momentarily hoped, might have been my own true self.

But I had no self, no unique identity. I was all of them.

I was numb for days, more unsure of who or what I was than ever before. Unable to think of little else but my alien nature and lack of identity, I allowed D'vore to clean and feed me, allowed him to minister to my modest, nearly comatose needs. All the while a jumble of confused and seemingly random thoughts rattled in my mind. I could not determine which pieces of memory had been my own, whatever that might mean, and which had been stolen from another.

"You must reconcile yourself to what you are, what you have gained," D'vore advised as he fed me yet another ration bar. "You must attempt to integrate your thoughts so you can become whole."

"I'm a damned zombie feeding on someone else's happy memories," I replied hollowly. "I am not really a person, not someone apart from those whose memories and bodies I've stolen. I have no self. I have no history, no mother or father save your damn bag of tricks."

D'vore reacted as if I had slapped him. "You are no less a person because of the way you were reconstructed. You live, you breathe, and I have seen that you express feelings and emotions. You have shared your thoughts, and memories so you clearly have an active mind. Even your healthy body says you are as human as any other."

His statement jarred me. Could what he said be true? Was I truly an individual in my own right? That thought was more troubling than expected. Up to the point of his shocking revelation I had imagined myself on a higher moral plane than D'vore. Until his explanation my smug and superior self had looked on his use of human parts with horror and loathing. But I could no longer hold the high moral ground now that I knew I was a constructed thing of parts and pieces.

It was in such self-pity and self-abasement that I wallowed for days. At times I contemplated suicide but was uncertain that I could do it, given D'vore's powers of restoration and the lack of resources within this tiny capsule with which to dispatch myself.

It was D'vore who brought me back from the void as he sat and talked to me. "I extracted what life I could from each of your crewmates," he told me. "There were no coherent thoughts I could find—only random memories resident in the remains of their brains. The speed of deterioration was such that I had no time to be selective, no time to discriminate between those neurons containing valuable information about your ship and what befell it and those of long before. At the same time I had to use whatever cells appeared viable.

"The body was no less difficult. I had one good trunk, assorted undamaged limbs, and not a single good skull. For that I had to use the only one available—my own."

To say I was shocked was to minimize the impact of his words upon me. Not only was I a chimera of crewmates but I had also adopted the skull of someone this alien creature had appropriated years, perhaps decades, before. I stared at him in shocked amazement.

He shrugged. "It was a minor operation. I transferred my own mind to this artificial head and then placed the scavenged memories within yours. It mattered little to me but awakening with such an artificial head would have been too great an emotional shock for you."

"That's unbelievable," I said finally finding my voice again.

"Trust me, I experienced no pain, no sense of loss in the transfer," he chuckled in a rich baritone. "I have considerably less attachment to my extremities than you humans."

That might be true, but that he had sacrificed something of his own for no other reason than my psychic comfort revealed a considerable amount about his moral values. I had obviously misjudged him. I had applied my petty, biased morality to a situation I did not fully understand. I was shamed at my behavior. "I need to apologize," I blurted, nearly choking with shame for the way I'd behaved.

To his credit he seemed to hold no grudge. He never mentioned how deeply it might have affected him or how hurt he might have felt. Of course, my suppositions about his alien psychology might be wildly wrong, but it gave me a working basis from which a relationship could be forged.

For thirty days after we drifted, two assemblies of spare parts orbiting each other. We once again became companions, if not friends.

We passed the days by examining the image of my poor ship that D'vore had salvaged before our escape from whatever disaster befell *Tollembol*. On one such "visit" I glimpsed where the plating had been stripped away to reveal a panel that looked familiar. Had this been the physicist's or the engineer's? Familiarity tugged, but no clear memories emerged. It was difficult to recall that I was actually reclining as I walked about the pile of tortured metal and glimpsed portions of the interior through the rents. "I know your body so well that I can read the involuntary movements of your muscles and move the image accordingly," D'vore said, which was an explanation without illumination. Occasionally there were flashes of something half remembered, but none clear enough to recall afterwards. In sleep the dreams persisted, scenes jumbled together without context.

An older man was speaking at the head of a table. "Why go two light years when distance is irrelevant? I say we try for ten. That's far enough to get a good parallax and still close enough to see the Sun."

There followed random scenes that made less sense; a rocky seashore, a weathered ferry, a man's strong muscular chest against my cheek, and a small child's hand in mine as we purchased a spun sugar treat.

Immediately upon awakening I told D'vore everything since moments later, when I was fully awake, the dreams would fade to forgetfulness. Whether these were fantasies of my imagining or recollections of times past I did not, could not know.

"Give it time," he advised, as always.

There had been no responses when we pulled the yellow handle. Did this mean we were the sole survivors? That I should be twice so lucky defied belief, yet here I was.

Alive.

Our salvation came on the thirty-first day of our escape from whatever misfortune had befallen *Tollembol*. A startling CLANG and a sudden sidewise reorientation that pressed me against a bulkhead heralded our salvation. The hint of gravity regained gave me a rush of panic, half believing that the impact of striking ground after so long a fall could only be moments away. The feeling passed as I struck the bulkhead and reoriented myself to a world of up and down.

Unwarranted relief must have shown on my face for D'vore cautioned, "One should not expect kind treatment, friend I . Until we learn who our rescuers are be silent about who and what you are. Say nothing of how you came to be here. There will be an obligation to repay for our rescue, I fear."

Perhaps he was, I surmised, speaking from the experience of his rescue long before. Nevertheless I was grateful for whatever came next, if only for no other reason than to escape the confines of this tiny compartment.

I detected the taint of ammonia in the air as the lock was cracked. Then four strange, bat-like faces peered around the edge of the hatch cover. I had never seen the like of such as these—inhuman creatures that looked to be nightmares personified. Aliens, for certain, and things I was sure that I had never known to exist.

"Screeeeeee," they exclaimed, piercing my ears with their high-pitched speech. Behind them I could see a reddish, dim-lit space filled with dark darting shapes. "Screeeeeee," they repeated.

D'vore slumped, his whole being collapsing into a pitiful heap. "Case, this is worse than ever expected."

"What do you mean?"

"*Qalyub Gudlag*," he sighed and pointed at a scrawl of characters at the rim of the hatch; a checkered square and bisected circle. "This is a Penchon ship."

"Screeeeeee," the aliens screamed again. "Screeeee, screeee!" D'vore replied with a terrible screech that nearly deafened me. The bat faces drew back, silent. D'vore screamed again, this time it was, I think, his tone was slightly more conciliatory. This was followed such an exchange of high pitched screeching that I feared my hearing would never again be the same, with D'vore's screams replying to their piercing inquiries.

Finally the screeching stopped and the faces withdrew. "They will not kill us," D'vore whispered. "But I think they will extract a steep price for rescue."

"Do you think they might know about Earth?"

D'vore spun about and pressed me against the bulkhead. "Say nothing of your origins. If they believe you are from an unregistered planet all of your kind will be at risk. They would not rest until they found it and, once they did, the population would be exploited in a way you would find horrifying. Be silent and you will have nothing to fear, friend Case."

Chastised and embracing the nugget of fear D'vore had planted, I crawled out of the escape capsule and into the belly of the alien ship. "They will take care of us, I am certain," D'vore said again as two of the aliens motioned for me to follow them.

I struggled to maintain my balance as I shuffled across the deck. Gravity felt strange and I found my legs abnormally weak. The surface beneath my feet felt crumbly, crunching softly with each step. The ammonia smell became even stronger than before.

I had gone a dozen or more steps behind the awkward four-legged gait of our rescuers before I realized that D'vore was no longer at my side. When I tried to see where he might have been taken but my hosts pushed me along and prevented that. I was led to a small chamber, scarcely larger than the small vessel I had just left. It was bare of furnishings and lit by the same dim reddish light that seemed to permeate the ship's interior. The hatch slammed shut behind me as I entered, sealing me within. Thankfully, the hatch reduced the strong smell of ammonia.

There being nothing else to do I lay on the warm floor and slept. That I was able to do so was a mark of how exhausted I, unused to gravity, had become by the short walk. I dreamed of stars and children, of forests and fields of blue and golden flowers. There were views of snow-covered mountains and ruddy canyons, of arid wastelands and deep lakes. As before there was no context, no order, no explanation of what these signified. Whether these were memories or the products of my disordered mind I knew not. Might they all be scenes of my lost Earth?

The opening hatch awakened me. A Penchon crawled into my room and settled on its rear haunches. Loose folds of deep brown skin hung from each of the upper limbs and draped on the floor like the folds of a wet velvet cape. I noticed that each of its four hands had a delicate set of fingers, each pair opposed by another. One pair was on the tips of the fore arms (legs?) A second set emerged from the creature's chest. It was by far the most ugly creature I had ever seen and easily the most odoriferous. The reek of ammonia was strong about it.

It held a strangely limp device in one hand as it screeched softly, barely above a whisper. "Human, you are," the device spoke. "Where do you from?" A close examination revealed that the limp appearance of the device was due to it being only partially mechanical. Behind the device's metal face was what looked suspiciously like a human throat and a heaving bag that might have served as a lung.

"I am from … *Tollembol*," I replied, remembering D'vore's warning at the last moment. "There was a wreck, I think."

"You are obligation. We transport. Needs you what?"

I realized after a moment's shock that this alien was merely being hospitable and inquiring as to my needs. "Something to lie upon, water, food, and information."

The Penchon screeched softly into the device. "Not knowing what information you need."

I was fascinated by the way the organic throat flexed as it produced the words. Was it a construct or had it been cut from some living creature? Too well I recalled D'vore's comments about the Penchon's grisly supply of spare parts and their skill with using them. Could this be another example, albeit a more horrible application than surgically attaching a mere arm or leg?

"For starters where are we and where are we going? How did you find us?" The latter was more than idle curiosity. Had we been in vast intergalactic space, as D'vore had declared so casually, the likelihood of our escape vessel being discovered by another ship was so improbable that it strained credibility. Either that or the density of ships in this part of the galaxy was far greater than I'd imagine possible. Then I had a horrifying thought. Could the Penchon have anything to do with the destruction of our ship?

"We search the Rift for materials," the throat device said without affect. "We scavenge the by-products of those less fortunate. You, we found as well." With those words the creature placed the device back in a pouch at its waist.

The pouch had so closely matched the dark velvet that I had not noticed it before. Was it like a kangaroo's pouch or merely a fanny pack? Not that I recalled what a kangaroo or fanny pack might be. It was another example of those flashes of random knowledge that so plagued me.

After the alien departed the strong ammonia smell remained. I discovered the source to be a small damp spot where it had been sitting.

Later they brought one of the bunks from the escape vessel and all of the rations. Included was the water container, a miraculous device that was somehow replenished regardless of how much I drank or used. They did not bring the sanitation facility and seemed uncomprehending of why I would need such a thing. As a result I was sure that in short order my compartment would equal the stench of the rest of the ship.

Hopefully, when it came to that, my nose would have learned to shut out such smells.

The days passed without incident in my sparse cell. I slept, woke, ate, ruminated on the meaning of my being and the nature of identity, tended to my few personal needs, and grew ever more restive. I could detect no motion of the ship, no sign that I was being taken elsewhere. The deprivation was greater than that in our escape capsule. There, at least, D'vore held my attention. There, at least, was a dialog about how the ships moved through something called seven-space and continual guesses about how my tiny wreck could have possibly crossed such an immense distance to arrive at the Rift. There at least I could explore the image of the wreckage.

More conflicting memories harried my mind during the subsequent days. I recalled soft red hair and glimpsed brief images of a young freckled face that disappeared as soon as it appeared. Other times I remembered classrooms of several types, and apartments, homes, ranches, and automobiles of every color of the rainbow. Of a night I'd awaken to symbols and formulae dancing in the dark, the meaning disappearing as morning mist to my awakening mind. The taste of a bit of ration might cause me to recall a day on the beach with a willowy blonde in a bikini. Stubbing a toe in the dark could bring a flash of babies crying in their cribs. A whiff of burnt oil would bring back candlelit dinners with a graying beauty.

These diverse visions were maddening. I could build no coherent vision of what I had been. Which woman had been the true love that I had lost—one, or all of them? Were these memories from engineer or crew, scientist or command? I tried to ascribe a face to each fragment of memory, positing which crewmate had been which, but was unsuccessful as before. Was I any of them or all? Did I have an identity apart from my components?

After what seemed like an eternity, but was more likely, judging from my sleeps, only five days, my screeching host appeared with his device. "Be well are you?" it asked. "No activity seen so assume unhealthy prevails."

"I am tired of this damned cell," I replied. "I need stimulation. I need to learn something of this ship."

"We must check," it replied. "You follow." I had no choice in the matter and followed its lead down the corridor.

I noted that the vast volume across which I had walked from the escape capsule was bounded on either side by sheer walls, unbroken save for a row of floor level cabin hatchways, one of which was my own. The remainder appeared empty. A little further along there was a series of small projections on a wall that led to an opening some five meters above my head.

My host seemed to have no problem scurrying up the wall and waited as I painstakingly and carefully followed to stand before the entrance to a tube with a bar running down the center. The walls of the tube were festooned with handholds. I watched in fascination as my host grasped the handholds and swung its lower extremities to the bar, which it clutched with both feet. I as quickly used hands and feet to scuttle crab-like along this passageway.

At the far end of the passageway we entered the ship's central cavity. I stopped, looking in amazement at a mighty spine-like column in the ruddy darkness. At intervals along the column I saw banks of instruments and controls; each surrounded by a circular bar on which perched several Penchon. I had difficulty focusing in the dim red light. At times, parts of the controls seemed to flow, change shape, and color. None had the sharp edges one would associate with machinery. Obviously the Penchon used a very different technology than any I could understand.

This, I surmised, must be a control center of some sort. It might have been engineering, navigation, or even the ship's bridge. I had no way of telling, so different was its design from anything I might have known or remembered. I was absolutely certain that I had never seen anything remotely similar.

The next chamber was terribly warm and covered with soft hide not unlike my own skin, but colored dark brown, nearly black. No, I realized, the chamber had to be some sort of animal. There were several orifices, large sphincters that pulsed open and closed and emitted a flow of warm air. As I entered the chamber shuddered, nearly tumbling me off my feet. I glanced up and to my utter surprise, discovered a very human eye, but enormously large, staring down from the ceiling. When it blinked I shrank back, afraid of what the existence of this room implied.

"No harm," the Penchon screeched and motioned me forward. We passed through a vast aerie where dozens of individuals hung slumbering from their perches above a pit of abysmal stench so overpowering that I could scarcely.

Our destination looked to be either a workshop or abattoir,

so bloody was it and filled with assorted torsos, arms, and legs, among the unfamiliar mechanisms. I recognized a human arm but had no idea of what species the others might belong to. My stomach was unable to resist the impulse to void while my horrified mind fought to reject the implications of what I saw. If ever I needed reinforcement of D'vore's warning, this was it. I too horribly recalled that these creatures harvested human bodies.

Two of the creatures seized me and before I could react and strapped me down. They ignored my screams as they explored my body and every crevice. One even forced something thick and slimy into my mouth. It went down my throat without making me gag. I felt another thing slip into my anus while something moist enfolded my crotch, causing an unexpected and involuntary erection. Something nipped my earlobe while I felt hairs being plucked from head, nose, legs, and chest.

Somewhere along the line I, overcome with horror over being rendered into component parts, I fainted.

I was back in my cell when I woke. A quick examination of my body indicated that I was whole and unharmed. My relief was complete. I was alive.

My host entered and squatted without preamble, as usual. "Much puzzling. Where from to be so variant? Carhera discovery?"

"Carhera? What does that mean? I told you I was from that ship–*Tollembol.*"

"Is not true. WOAFT says no one like you on board."

The conversation was rapidly becoming incomprehensible. "WOFAT?" I repeated. "Was that the captain's name?"

"Why were you on board? What role you had?"

"I was just helping D'vore in the surgery. I don't know anything about how I got there or what *Tollembol* was doing."

We continued in this vein for another hour; my host bringing up one incomprehensible term after another and me demanding that it explain what it was talking about until finally it stormed away, probably thinking me the ship's fools–and in that I could not honestly disagree. I really was ignorant of practically everything.

Apparently my lack of information made me seem harmless. Thereafter, my door remained open so that I had the freedom to learn more about the Penchon.

Days later, when my daily explorations had taken me far from my cell, I discovered what I believed to be an engine room. The throb of power than emanated from the machinery implied that we were indeed proceeding, but to where and why I still had no clue. The smell of ozone and warm insulation were a welcome relief from the ever-present ammonia stench that so abused my nostrils elsewhere. While I was at a loss to put a name any individual part in the mass of pipes, cables, and cylinders, I nevertheless felt a familiarity about the arrangement.

The novelty of the ship and its strange fittings took my mind off of my own situation for a time. But, as the ship's strangeness faded to familiarity the question of identity and my scattered memories returned to haunt me. Try as I might I could not wrest meaning from my tortured dreams. Worse yet, as I thought about D'vore's revelations about my reconstruction I questioned whether I was more of a person or less?

I finally realized that it was D'vore who might hold the answers to my questions. Despite our strained relationship, he was the only being within the ship with who I shared a history, however brief and tumultuous it might have been. I needed to find out where he had gone. And why.

My repeated inquiries about my companion met with apparent confusion. I described him as best I could, given the restrictions of our alien orientations, to the Penchon who looked after my needs, but it did no good. It was as if the Penchon were unaware that there had been two of us. In fact, it acknowledged only that I was the sole alien in the capsule, an obvious lie to my mind but I could think of no reason why they should do so.

To distract my mind from the recurring unexplained memories I continued to explore, ever looking for distraction and this, in time, eventually led to what I believed were the cargo holds.

Within these spaces I was surrounded by what I believed to be the stuff of interstellar commerce. There were containers of every shape and size, from vast black, brown, or blue globes—it was hard to tell the exact color in the reddish light—to thousands of small boxes the size of my palm. None of these small boxes had an obvious opening or control. All gave off a pulsating heat when I held them in my hand.

In another hold I discovered mechanisms of such strange design that I doubted that I could ever understand their purpose. Some were clearly of recent manufacture while many of the others showed the wear of long and hard use. Many were scarred and dented, showing scorch marks and torn metal as if they had been taken from their places with unseemly force. None featured the organic technology of the Penchon. The third and fourth cargo holds were much like the others, an mélange of assorted machinery, containers, and bins of loose materials whose composition and purpose I could only guess.

It was in the fifth chamber, at the end of one row of huge orange dodecahedrons, that I found D'vore.

"It has been very lonely here," were his first words. His silver head sat atop a dull, dappled metal cylinder that seemed too small to contain his body. "It is good to see you once again."

"Likewise, I'm uncertain. I must say that your accommodations seem less comfortable than mine." I was not sure that such humor was fitting in his present circumstance.

He shrugged. "The confines do not bother me. In fact, it is rather restful, now that they have removed those parts requiring exercise."

With a start I realized what had seemed so wrong. The cylinder was several feet shorter than my own height, and that was at least a head shorter than D'vore's had been. Neither was the cylinder wide enough to accommodate his muscular arms or his legs.

"How did they ..." I began, wondering how to broach the subject. "I mean ... It's so small!" I blurted in confusion

"I should think it obvious that only multiple amputations would allow me to wear these new clothes," he replied with wry humor.

I felt like gagging, such severe editing was even harder for me to emotionally understand than knowing where those now absent arms and legs had originated and where they might now reside.

Apparently D'vore sensed my discomfort. "Do not worry, Case. There was little pain associated with the removal of my extremities. Believe me, the Penchon's skills quite exceed my own surgical prowess."

"But to do this to you," I began, grasping for the words to express my outrage. "How could they even consider abusing someone like this?"

"Ah, but I am no longer a 'person' Case. I have once again become property," D'vore said simply. "I am now merely another device they may adapt to their own uses," D'vore continued. "But this is not so bad. As property, I might be sold, much like before. Who knows, perhaps I will eventually serve on another ship, human or otherwise."

"That was what you offered them when we were rescued," I said, recalling that complex exchange of screams and screeches during our rescue. D'vore must have struck a bargain to protect me. That was what the Penchon meant about bringing them a present. This travesty of my former companion was the price of my passage.

Much as I'd abhorred the source of D'vore's limbs I was even more offended by the Penchon's ill treatment of him. "I will ask them to restore you," I declared. "I will offer to purchase you."

D'vore laughed. "It will cost you an arm and a leg."

I shuddered. My brief experience in the abattoir left no doubts in my mind as to the truth of his words. So this was the price at which my freedom, my continued existence, had been paid? I felt shamed. This abhorrent creature, this chimera that I had so long despised, had sacrificed his own future that I might live. "Why?" I asked. "Why would you do such a thing?"

"You are my creation," he replied simply. "And you have treated me far more decently than any human I have ever encountered, even when you were repelled by my augmentations. For that I owe you a debt of gratitude."

A wave of emotion passed through me. I patted his casing gingerly. "I will be back," I promised. "I will not abandon you."

Over the following days I returned time and again to talk to D'vore. The Penchon, had they even noticed, did nothing to stop me. In fact, they seemed ever more intent on completely ignoring my presence.

I continued to struggle with the emerging memories, trying to force them to do my bidding, to fit into a pattern that I could understand, that I could reconcile with sanity. But at this I was unsuccessful as ever. I expressed my frustration to D'vore.

"You are fighting the process of integration by trying to force your memories down a path," he advised. "Do not resist where they take you and accept them as a part of your being. You cannot exclude one or another any more than you can cast off an arm or leg. They are, and will remain forever a part of you."

Even as I accepted his wisdom I was at a loss to understand how this alien being could have such insights on my very human problem. I tried to do his bidding and, in some way, perhaps his advice helped. I began accepting those random images without restriction, as a part of me, as a part of us. Eventually, I prayed, the accumulation would start to make sense.

When I was not speaking with D'vore I continued to explore. I found the variety of cargo, the puzzling shapes of containers, and the tantalizing and unknowable contents, fascinating. It was on one such expedition that I came across some twisted and torn fragments that I instantly recognized as parts of a workstation. It still had familiar lettering above where the screen must have been. This was no image carved in air but hard, solid, sharp, and real. Solid evidence that all D'vore had said was true: There had been a wreck.

Neatly stacked not far from the fragment were sealed, transparent boxes that contained human remains of cinnamon flesh and muscular build. Among the mass of parts was a familiar head, the captain's, with a neatly burnt hole in his broad forehead.

I had assumed that *Tollembol* had run into mischance and its destruction had ejected our capsule. But had that been true the crews' bodies would have been frozen in the absolute zero of the vacuum, or burned in some flaming holocaust. Those were deaths I could fathom, deaths I could understand. Instead these parts looked as fresh as if they had been butchered and carefully placed away.

I ran away as quickly as I could, wanting no more of this new horror and what it implies about my hosts.

D'vore didn't appear to be surprised when I informed him of my grisly discovery. "The Penchon are known to be scavengers of the shoals," he said. "Just the same, be cautious about your discovery, Case. I cannot predict what they might do should they discover that you know of it. We cannot assume they are responsible for the deaths. Neither can we disprove it. Caution is advised."

That was good advice; which I intended to follow. Yet, after a few days I felt compelled to return to the fragment of my ship to see if it would elicit any further, and hopefully more specific memories.

Unlike the virtual explorations I had formerly conducted, examination of this object was far more difficult and dangerous. The sharp edges of its torn metal could sever a vein if I were not careful. I carefully walked around it and cautiously placed my hand within the openings with exquisite care.

I spotted a splash of green and recalled that the panels had been painted with this bilious color, something that we'd joked about endlessly during training. It was yet another fragmentary memory, but this time with some context. Perhaps, as D'vore had promised, the integration of my memories was progressing.

Despite these and other recalled fragments from my past, I still had no inkling of where the ship had originated and even less of how we arrived. Was I truly, as D'vore contended, millions of miles from the Earth of my memory or was it somewhere near where they found me? I did not have the faintest idea of which direction was home.

I posed the question to D'vore and, after much thought, he produced a theory. "As I told you earlier, your gross physique is different from the norms of the sixteen human races I know. I would suspect that your ancestors departed from the mainstream of humanity at some point.

"The most likely explanation is that your planet of origin is hidden in some forgotten backwater. Perhaps it is not far from the rift, hidden by a dust cloud, circling a sun too dim to be seen or orbiting in loneliness. If so, it has evaded the cartographers and explorers for all of human history. I doubt any of the alien races would keep such a place secret."

None of these concepts sat comfortably in my mind. Sixteen human species seemed unlikely when only a single one seemed to fit the memories in my head, which could substantiate the lost planet idea. At the same time I recalled starry nights, hardly possible if Earth had been inside a dust cloud. No, nothing he suggested seemed plausible. More likely it was that these memories were as scrambled as my mind.

"We are approaching Toril," D'vore informed me. How he had learned this I did not know. I'd noticed no change in the ever-present murmur of the engines, no change in the reeking atmosphere, no outward indication that anything whatever had changed. Either his senses were much more refined than mine or had some secret access to the ship's business.

"It is imperative that you must get off this ship," D'vore warned me. "From what you have told me, the Penchon have become too interested in your presence on *Tollembol* and that, I fear, is not in our best interest."

That they continued to have an interest in me was no surprise. Hardly a day had passed when my interrogation had stopped, and always with the same mutual frustration by my ignorance and their incomprehensible language. "There's no way they are going to let me leave. They'll probably lock me in my cell when we arrive."

"The hatch will not be locked," D'vore assured me, although how he would know this was as mysterious as the arrival announcement. "I have certain connections to the ship's systems." That seemed a strange capability for him to have, but I let it pass.

"Now, you must open the top of this carrier. I have something you must deliver to some parties on Toril."

After fumbling with a catch designed for the Penchon's tiny hands I managed to partially open the face of the container and behold what looked like a segmented, blue leather vest with five sections, one above another.

"Lift the top flap of my carapace and remove the core," D'vore instructed. I gently pried it apart and found, beneath the leathery flap, a gray box, scarcely wider than my thumb. It came loose from the flesh behind it with a sick, sucking sound. The base of it felt slimy. "You must take this to the blue hats," he said. "They will know what to do."

I had no idea of what a blue hat was or how would find them.

True to D'vore's prediction the ship noisily docked a day after our conversation. I felt the sudden change in pressure as the ship equalized atmospheres with the station. That also implied that somewhere there was an open hatch.

I slipped down the companionway and toward the hatch where we'd first entered the ship. Before I could reach it I noticed a slight breeze from my right. I turned in that direction and shortly found myself facing a large open hatch where the Penchon were busily transferring cargo from ship to dock.

I waited until none were near and ran across the open space and onto the dock, ducking behind a stack of containers so I was not exposed. A few more strategic dashes took me well away from the ship and finally gave me a chance to look around.

Nothing I saw looked familiar. The air was bitterly cold on my face and hands. Bewildering smells carried by a slight breeze assaulted my nose and made me sneeze. The din of moving machinery and shouting assailed my ears. I could make no sense of what was before me. I felt a surge of tears come to my eyes from the sensory overload after so long restricted to the stark utilitarianism of the Penchon's interior. "Toril Station," D'vore had said, but if this was a station then it was far larger than anything I had imagined.

I looked around with wonder. The station was so vast that a haze obscured the far distance. The cold wall behind me was, I realized, the side of a ship and, a hundred meters to my right, was a yawning opening through which a stream of cargo was being passed and, beyond that, another and yet more. Each was an opening on the cargo holds I had explored during our journey.

Penchon and other things swarmed among them, moving pallets and containers. Everywhere there was the bustle of workers. Farther away, barely seen through the haze was another ship, equally as occupied with loading and unloading. Beyond that and fading into the mist, the walls of the station curved ever so slightly, an indicator that the station had to be tens of kilometers across. This was a structure of such immensity that I could not imagine how it could have been constructed.

But the size of the station was unimportant to my immediate situation. I knew nothing of this station or where I was supposed to take D'vore's I . The air was so cold that my immediate concern was to find warmth. Perhaps, beyond the wall there were facilities where I could find some sort of help. There had to be a stationmaster, a traveler's aid, anything that would service crew and passengers. I took one last look at the alien script above the hatch of the ship and slipped away.

I wandered aimlessly for hours. Nothing I encountered seemed familiar. I saw aliens far stranger than anything I ever imagined. Some were enclosed in environmental suits, others swathed in layer upon layer of fabrics. Most appeared roughly bipedal and erect, of heads larger and smaller than my own, with arms differently articulated, and whose gait was decidedly un-human. Sealed within their suits I could not tell whether any of these might be my own kind or of some close relative— one of D'vore's sixteen, perhaps? I caught a momentary glimpse of a tall, thin brown human in the distance, but the figure disappeared before I could reach him.

With some surprise I once again found myself near my starting point. I was famished. As much as I disliked the idea I wondered if I could get back aboard and find one of the food packs in my previous chamber.

I saw no Penchon about as I entered through an open and unguarded cargo hatch. Neither did I encounter any of the crew as I wandered among the goods stored within. It occurred to me that, since I had no knowledge of departure schedules, any attempt to reach my compartment would be foolish—what would I do if the *Qalyub Gudlag* were to depart while I was inside? No, safer for me to look among those boxes close to hand.

In my hasty examination I found nothing that looked remotely of human manufacture. The octagonal containers looked somewhat familiar, so it must be a cargo hold that I had visited. Yes, now I knew—it was the one adjacent to that where D'vore rested.

I raced through the hatch and onto the dock. To my right another hatch yawned open. I raced to it. There were no Penchon standing guard or wrestling with the loading so I entered unimpeded. It took only a short search before I found D'vore.

"I didn't know what to do," I admitted after explaining my aimless wandering. "I have no idea of where to go."

"I can direct you," D'vore said.

"But what of you?" I asked. "I can't leave you here with these butchers."

"I am hardly able to follow you," D'vore answered calmly.

"No, I can't accept that. There has to be some way." The idea of D'vore being used as nothing more than a machine by these hateful creatures appalled me. Freedom was only a few steps away. "They are murderers. They killed the captain and crew. Maybe they even destroyed my ship."

"That they've stored a fragment from the wreckage proves nothing, Case. As I stated before, the Penchon are scavengers. They might have simply discovered the crew and saved what they might be able to use," D'vore replied.

I doubted that. I clearly recalled the neatly executed captain. It seemed certain evidence that he had been alive when he was dispatched so efficiently. From that could only assume that these Penchon were pirates, murderous pirates, and any theft from them was fully justified. I had to act on what I felt was right and proper. D'vore might not be able to move, but I could try to help. "You are coming with me," I insisted over his protests.

My only problem was how to move D'vore. His cylinder was far too heavy for me and I did not feel right in rolling it along on one edge as you would a drum. There has be a hand transporter somewhere close by that I can use, I thought and wondered what it would look like?

I heard a sharp sound close by and felt a start of fear. At any moment I might be discovered and that might mean that D'vore would be lost forever. There was no more time to delay. I searched about, rejecting the half organic transport devices I'd seen the Penchon use until I found a small sled-like device. It had a single handle and a broad blade that lay flat on the deck. I hoped it was some sort of gadget I could use it to lever D'vore along.

When I grabbed the handle, the blade floated a few centimeters above the deck. The cart might be deceptively simple to use but I knew it had to be a far more complex mechanism than it appeared. I pulled it effortlessly back to D'vore's resting place, slid the blade under the base of his cylinder and pulled the handle again. Without any other effort the cylinder lifted easily from the deck.

I carefully maneuvered the cart toward the hatch, D'vore protesting the whole time that I was being foolish. I was within a meter of the hatch when we were spotted.

"Screeeeeee!" the scream set my nerves on edge but motivated my feet to manic motion. There was a flash and I felt a burning sensation in my shoulder as something grazed me. The fabric on my shoulder was smoldering. There was a second blast as we reached the dock and a red spot appeared on D'vore's cylinder.

I needed no further encouragement and pounded among the stacked cargo as fast as I could move, glancing back to ensure myself that D'vore remained on the cart while desperately attempting to steer around the fleet vehicles and static boxes of stacked goods, striving to keep from coming into physical contact with any random being or equipment. At any moment I expected to hear the screech of pursuit close at my heels or the flurry of wings above my head.

Apparently, somewhere along the way D'vore had decided to become an ally. "Turn right," he shouted. "Head toward the central pillar."

Until that moment I had not paid attention to the singular feature looming dark and vast through the haze. From this distance it appeared to be merely a vast rectangular mass but, as we came nearer, I could make out its cylindrical shape and size. The structure had to be at least a kilometer wide.

I was exhausted by the time we reached the base of the pillar. My lungs were burning, the muscles of my legs felt like hard, leaden lumps, and my heart was threatening to jump completely out of my chest.

"Can you see the designator?" D'vore asked and when I did not reply he added, "Look above the entrance." He could not, I realized, articulate his own head to look upwards. "Tell me what you see."

"How the hell should I know," I finally wheezed with what little breath I could muster. I could make no sense of the strange symbols. "It looks like a couple of boxes and a horizontal stroke."

"Close enough. Go through the portal. There should be a red doorway somewhere. Go straight through and talk to anyone yellow."

A cross hallway was several hundred meters from the entrance and a red doorway just a few paces more. The door was a massive plank that swung upwards instead of to the side. I had no way of knowing whether D'vore had led me to surrender to the local police or to get the help we needed. But there was no other place to turn.

I came to a halt as soon as I stepped inside. There were four horse-like aliens in the room, each three times my size and covered with blindingly bright yellow fur. They had four lower limbs and two upper, but there would be no mistaking these for the mythical centaurs, for the head of each was mounted amidships and resembled in no way any animal with which I recalled.

"*Tsu nu D'vore pillie nut horso,*" D'vore warbled as soon as we were inside. His voice grumbled in low bass tones that made my teeth rattle. "*Nunch Case !*"

The aliens rumbled something in reply and again D'vore responded. A discussion among the centaurs followed after which they seemed to come to some sort of agreement.

"These Carhera wish to know your origin," D'vore explained. "I told them you were of the Magellan, who should have enough credit here to cover our expenses."

"*HOALLA NU Case*!" shouted one of the aliens in a booming voice that momentarily deafened me.

"*Larso horso*," D'vore replied more quietly and then, in an aside, "I just told them that you were my owner and that I was collateral for their help."

I was shocked. No sooner than I had rescued him from years of slavery but here he was offering himself once again. It had to be some sort of personality defect, incipient insanity or something similar. "You cannot ..." I began.

"It is nothing, friend I , compared to the price we've paid for the enmity of the Penchon. I can serve them for a few hours and be done with it. Rest easy. It will be a trivial obligation."

Before I could argue further two of the aliens leaped toward the door and thundered through with a scrabbling of claws. One snatched D'vore from the cart with one arm and held him at its side. The other creature lifted me off my exhausted feet and pinned me likewise to its furry flank. Thus carried, we thundered out the door and along the hallway.

They were moving at such speed that I almost heard the wind whistling in my ears. We raced down the corridor and made several confusing turns before stopping at an open bay.

Ten diminutively sized aliens scarcely the size of small cats and clad in green, surrounded me. The centaurs deposited me on a hard slab where several of the small aliens scurried up my chest and peered into my eyes and ears, chattering the while in a swiftly flowing stream of musical syllables.

"We are safe now," D'vore told me. "The Pittul will ensure our safety and health. Just remain calm and let them work."

Easy for him to say, I thought as the tiny creatures became more and more personal in their examination. By the time I had been stripped and fully examined they had D'vore's cylinder opened.

I had imagined D'vore's leather-clad torso to be more or less human. Instead I saw that what I supposed to be a leather vest was a hard, segmented shell of darkest blue.

What was revealed horrified me. Until that moment I had believed that the Penchons' removal of his limbs had been a clean, delicate surgical procedure, not unlike unplugging an extension from a machine. Instead there were bloody stumps where his arms had been hacked off and ragged edges of his upper legs, bone projecting from the clotted mass of dried blood. Had those crude amputations really been as painless as he'd reported, I wondered and marveled at D'vore's stoicism. Somehow the trivial pains of my aching legs faded into irrelevance.

"We are safe now," D'vore sighed. "These Pittul are medicians. They ensure safety and health. Let them examine, please." He might have said more before his brutally edited body was whisked away, but the Pittul were already swarming over me.

I was quickly stripped and lifted onto a gurney as the Pittul continued their incessant chattering. The tiny creatures became more and more personal in their examination. When I tried to struggle something feeling much like a warm blanket enfolded me and rendered my arms and legs immobile. The warmth let me relax despite my determination to resist. "Rest now," the Pittul ordered as the world immediately faded into black.

There were no troubling dreams.

"Well you be, but body confused," one of the tiny Pittul mused when I awoke. "Mitochondria not compliant." I realized that I must have had another mimetic implant that allowed me to understand the high-pitched chattering. Understanding the words, however, was the easy part—understanding the content in context was more difficult without any cultural references.

"D'vore," I croaked through parched lips. "Where is ..." I could not go on. Attempting to match the high register of the alien sounds hurt my throat too much. I was shivering.

"Will adjust for comfort, but must research more fully." It said mysteriously as it bustled away to concern itself with a bank of instruments. "Sleep now."

When I awoke I was once again clad in my coverall and feeling none of the chill that I'd felt before. As I sat up I noticed a tall olive-skinned thing nearby.

It had four thin legs with feathers on their back. Above that was slim body enclosed by a pink mantle. The head was vaguely insect-like with both large and small eyes. What looked like a feathered cap adorned its head.

"Feeling more comfortable?" it asked. "The Pittul adjusted your body when they realized that you had no natural adaptability to this environment."

"Isn't it the other way around," I asked and got a puzzled expression in response. "I mean; it seems warmer now."

"It matters little to me," it said dismissively. "Where did you come from?"

"I wish I knew." The question evoked memories of clear warm days, of parched dirt and scraggly cattle. It brought the feeling of heat to my tongue and fire in my belly. Try as I might I could not trace the reason for those associations, but that lack was not discomforting. Integration must be proceeding, I supposed. "Texas?" I answered.

I got a puzzled look in reply

"There is problem," one of the nearby Pittul cautioned. "Body is not well. Much has been repaired from live tissue. Some confusion at cellular levels may create problems. Need more research. Cannot release until complete."

"What sort of problems?" the alien asked. "It appears to be human."

The little alien pondered this. "Cannot be. Library has no record of this cellular makeup. Mitochondria differ by five sigma from human norm. DNA with similar shifts. Is puzzling," the alien continued. "Almost subhuman. Could be old offshoot?"

"Perhaps a lost variant, one of the early lost settlements," the alien suggested. "How far back would that place the deviation?"

"Much drift. Minimum one or two thousand generations," the tiny alien replied after a moment's consideration. "Maybe many more."

"Over half a million years separation," it said as he turned to me. "Obviously some ancient offshoot, probably one of the lost colonies of prehistory."

"I find that hard to believe," I replied. "Nothing I've recalled suggests that there was anything other than a single world and only one human race. No, I am sure there was no history of ever being a colony. You are right. My ship must have traveled where we did not intend. Either that or we drifted for years," I choked at the thought, "before we were found."

"Not possible for a wrecked ship to have drifted for long. Human tissue does not survive long in space—hours at most, minutes or less would be usual. No, this entire recovery of viable tissue argues for a quick recovery."

"In that case Earth must be close to where they found me," said joyously. "Our ship couldn't possibly have traveled very far."

"Perhaps," it promised. "Meanwhile allow the Pittul to care for you. I think that since you are such an interesting specimen they may waive any obligations."

"And you are?"

It made a gargling sound that sounded like "ThripoBlastenav" before it abruptly departed.

The Pittul swarmed over me all the next day, collecting samples, measuring every aspect of my being until I thought no orifice, no fluid, and no organ remained to be examined in detail. That I was unconscious much of the time saved me from knowing what else they had done to satisfy their apparently insatiable curiosity.

Every time I woke I asked the Pittul if there was some way I could find out the where and why of this place, the reason for so many aliens, and how to operate the damn toilet instead of pissing into a bottle all the time. Finally, one of them brought me a tab to orient me to the station and applied it to my forehead. A deep stupor immediately overcame me.

When I awoke I knew the how and why of most of the human features of this place—simple things such as using the toilet, operating the clothing fabricator, and even how to bathe in the narrow cylinder I'd taken to be a support pillar. How could I have forgotten such simple tasks was beyond me, but I was relieved that I now felt I had some control over my world, slight though it might be.

Other facts had crept into my mind during the training or

whatever the tab had done. Contrary to my initial belief about human construction, it was some group called the Carhera who had built and continued to operate the stations. I also learned that the centaurs and the Pittul were merely two of the alien races chosen to deal with humanity. Quite a larger assortment of races were more than trade partners and allies, less than mentors or friends, but I could not grasp what their true relationships to mankind might be. I assumed they must be the sixteen races D'vore had spoken of, with humans being just one.

The Toril station's assortment of "histories" turned out to be worse than useful, providing great detail on recent local events, mostly about the verdant and under-populated planet that this station circled. I discovered some sketchy descriptions of external politics that were ever less informative the further I went back into history. The earliest "local" event seemed to be the settlement of Toril several hundred thousand years before, when the Carhera brought humans to settle.

The people, places, and motivations described down the pages of history were completely foreign to me. I could find nothing on how today's people amused themselves, how they related to one another, or whatever they did in their everyday lives. None of what I could gather meshed with my emerging memories of a far different society and politics.

As D'vore had predicted, the integration of my mind appeared to be progressing. While random unanchored thoughts continued to plague me those fragments were not entirely without context. Instead each memory brought with it other, deeper memories, other references, other faces and other times. I could now recall fragmented scenes instead of flashing images. I recalled laughing children, beautiful women and, sometimes I recalled the scent of one wife, sometimes another. One disturbing memory was of a husband whose warm hands and probing tongue strangely excited me. Apparently not all of my component predecessors had been men.

Occasionally I basked in recalled scenes of warm seas and cloudy skies. I remembered prairie and snow-capped mountain, the yellow sands of seacoasts, and snow-chilled plains. Earth,

I finally decided, must be a wondrous place to hold so much variety. As I embraced these memories I became more and more at ease with what I was. Although I remained a man of many parts, I was becoming a man unto myself and would, I hoped, grow my own hopes and fears, dreams and desires.

I could live with that.

"I am here," D'vore announced.

He once again had his normal height, but was longer in the torso, with a small hump in the middle of his back. Stockier as well, I thought. I was glad to see that his arms had been restored and, although one was quite human, the other appeared to be made of metal, but metal that flexed like skin at the four joints along its length. A mechanical version of a human hand was attached at the wrist.

Where had these arms come from, I wondered, and at what price? A pair of stocky legs emerged from the bottom of his tunic. At first I thought they were clothed in patterned cloth and then realized with surprise that the pattern was a coating of iridescent scales. I could not imagine what sort of creature had formerly owned these and pointedly tried to ignore the startling changes in his appearance.

I was confused. "Why? Why should anyone want to help us?"

"There is a question of where you might have originated. I suspect the Pittul revealed the facts of your background and this aroused the interest of certain Carhera who would like to exploit lost colonies. Since your physical appearance is unique in many respects, they believe that your Earth may be one of them"

"That's very altruistic," I said. "I should think that anyone who could help us, like "ThripoBlastenav"–I hoped I got the gargling sounds right—who was here earlier ..."

He did not let me finish. "ThripoBlastenav? You have no idea of what its interest might be nor even if it would help you or your home."

"And this is better than what the Penchon want?"

"ThripoBlastenav is more interested in a possible market for *squotreui*," D'vore added.

I had no idea what this squgery stuff was nor was I particularly anxious to find out. Just being reunited with D'vore, my guide to this weird universe was welcome. I did not need to understand either the or why of it.

"Quickly now. We have to leave," he declared. "The Penchon are still searching for us."

"Leave for where? I have no place to go, no resources, no idea of what this crazy universe of yours has to offer. Nothing is as I recall it—star ships, aliens, strange humans and this crazy-assed station or whatever it is. It's all too much for me to absorb."

"In time you will get your bearings, I am certain," he replied. "Your mind is still unsettled as you integrate your memories. Until then I will guide you. After all, you are the reason I was freed from a prolonged Penchon indenture. I owe it to you to help you get back to Earth."

I wondered whether his obligation was preferable to the Penchon's, but lacked any basis for judgment. "Then let us go," I said as, together, we stepped into this strange new world.

"I have obtained berths on a small ship that will arrive shortly," D'vore informed me as we headed for the docks. "It will eventually take us to Oroenoe, a planet where we might some record of your type or maybe even a hint of where your colony might have settled."

That seemed improbable. I failed to see how anyone could fail to mention an entire species, much less keep an entire system secret. "That's a lot of trouble when he could just send an email," I said and realized that I had no idea of what an Emale would look like – a messenger of some sort, I imagined. As usual the word had come from the depths without meaning.

"The voyage toward the Magellan sector will give you time to gain balance in your mind." Somehow that didn't sound convincing. "Besides, I think it best we do not remain on this station and in such proximity to our former hosts."

Now that sounded like a better reason. Getting out of town and away from the grasp of the bloody Penchon was a damn good reason. But there had to be a cost for this. "What did your benefactors demand as collateral for passage—our souls?"

D'vore appeared impervious to my barely concealed

sarcasm. "On the contrary, space on the ships is too valuable to waste on passengers. No, Case, we are to be crew members and earn passage through our skills and labor."

"My skills," I sneered. "The most advanced skills I possess are probably as useless as chipping flint arrowheads or weaving baskets of reeds. I just learned to use everyday items like a child and still have no idea of how most things I use work. Those things, those ordinary chores were lost to me. You, above all should know how much I've forgotten."

"Ah, but you are wrong, friend Case . I am certain that your mind retains some innate ability to navigate." He held out a tiny tab, no larger than the nail of my little finger. "We will build on that capacity to create a narrow set of skills that you will need. Yes, I assure you that you will be a capable navigator when the ship arrives. I am also certain that skill will be most useful in your quest."

Was this how easily training could be achieved in this strange civilization? I had no reason to doubt that small mimetic implant would give me everything necessary to navigate a starship. Yet, while it seemed too easy, too facile to be real I shortly discovered that I had beome conversant with the texts on seven-space navigation and eager to learn more.

This acquisition of new skills did not come, I discovered, less easy than I expected. There were no free lunches at the counter of knowledge. The days-long headaches and constant terrible, obsessive hunger that burned the knowledge into my brain was the price I had to pay. Still, despite the cost of this newfound knowledge, I found that I thirsted for more.

There was a feeling of familiarity as I went over the principles and methods, yet I recalled nothing of why that should be so. I found myself driven at every opportunity to scribble notations for geodesic routings across seven-space's multidimensional surfaces. My burning curiosity also drove me to learn all I could of a dozen navigational engines of various designs and how to operate them. I could not shut off this drive to absorb knowledge, to gain ever more insight.

The mechanics of travel in seven-space became clear to me after the grueling lessons. In layman's terms, a ship rotates out of the three dimensions of space and then translates along the vectors comprising those four dimensions that have folded themselves within our perceived three and contain them as well. In this translated region location is merely a parameter of being and a slight thrust along one vector is all it takes to move a ship to another location. Mathematically speaking, it is simply inverting a seven dimensional matrix.

Only after the drive to learn all I could of navigation did I apply the processes of seven-space mathematics to my own situation.

Seven-space travel requires vast energies and sheer mass. Because of this I realized that the engines in my original ship, based on what I had seen of them in the wreckage, could not have been anywhere near as powerful as those in use on this or other ships and consequently, the distance I traveled therefore could not have been great, just as D'vore contended. I was reasonably certain that my Earth had to be within a few hundred light years, probably less, from the location of the wreck.

"If Oroenoe is near that region then maybe we can search. It should not be difficult to backtrack." I argued, unknowing of the distances and difficulties involved.

"That will not work," D'vore stated after a second's hesitation. "There are few systems close by the rift and all of them are known. It would be improbable that so many surveyors and explorers missed an entire star system containing your Earth."

"But what else can we do?"

"Perhaps the Library at Oroenoe might have a record of your type. Some trivial mention that has evaded everyone's notice."

That was mighty thin. Had D'vore actually arranged the positions on this arriving ship or had some unknown agent done it for him? Was it they who were directing us to Oroenoe, where records might still exist? I did not know what position they, or any other alien, might have in this station nor could I even guess as to their motives and objectives. Those were as opaque to me as everything else I'd encountered upon awakening for my resurrection.

Although D'vore protested that he was obligated to help

me find my way home, I continued to suspect that he was also trying to find his own way. That was all right with me, for I also felt a need to help. I was equally certain that this desire to assist him arose from my own thoughts and was not some drive imposed from without.

As the time grew close for our departure I found my random memories growing so strong that I often teetered on the edge of losing my own self and surrendering to the crowd of those who owned them. The flashes of memories, of my women and children always drew me back from the brink. It was the love I held for each, the loves that I cherished as surrogate for the twenty who died and the eight who live inside me that kept me going. So long as I lived and held them in memory they would not be lost. That, I prayed, will repay my debt to those who sacrificed themselves so that I could become my own self.

Now, I had only to find Earth to be complete.

PART TWO THYS NOR

To my eyes, *Thys Nor* appeared to be incredibly old and poorly used at that. Whatever paint had adorned its hull was long gone; its name little more than a faded suggestion above the main hatch. Portions of the hull were adorned with pockmarks, scrapes aplenty, and large, deep dents that might, had there been a micro joule of energy more, have become a disaster.

I hoped that the interior was in better shape.

"That must be Jaycea Lapin Horl, *Thys Nor*'s Master." D'vore indicated a large woman chewing on a stick and scowling at a reader held out to her by what looked like a hulking industrial machine. He had mentioned the Master's name earlier, but not that it would be a woman.

"Freaking robbery!" Jaycea bellowed. "I'll be damned if I'll carry cargo at that rate, Syl. They can obligate themselves to the Carhera if they want charity. Tell them I said hell no!"

The machine ponderously turned to nearby group of tall, thin individuals that somewhat resembled humans and were clad in thick furs and who were huddled protectively around a pile of small crates. A loud stream of consonant-rich invective poured forth from the machine as it loomed over them. Only one appeared upset over the Master's abrupt refusal and made a rude gesture of defiance as they departed.

"What are you two freaks staring at?" Jaycea demanded as she noticed. "Never seen a real woman?"

I didn't know how to answer that. I was certain that I'd never met a female quite as heavily padded. Her thick legs supported a heavy trunk; with an overly generous bosom that thrust her tunic forward and so concealed any stomach bulge. A sleeveless tunic exposed strong arms, both easily as large as my thighs while her neck supported a surprisingly lovely, delicate head. She appeared to be perspiring heavily despite the penetrating chill of the loading dock.

"We are your new crew, Master Horl" D'vore said in response. "I am D'vore," he gestured at himself with his human arm and pointed at me with the mechanical. "And that is your new navigator, Case Pasticher."

The Master took the stick from her mouth. "The name's Jaycea. Horl's my sept." She examined the chewed stick as if it had suddenly become distasteful. "I thought the contract I signed was for two humans, not a pair of—what the hell are you two freaks, anyway?"

It was easy to understand the confusion about D'vore, especially considering the unadorned silver orb of his head. His right arm was human, his left arm was mechanical, and his legs were covered with yellow, alien scales. What she could not see was that, hidden beneath his cloak was what remained of his leathery, segmented body. "I was a Centul," he answered. "But now I am reduced to what you see–a thing of parts."

"And I am as human as you," I added for good measure, lest she have any doubts. I was pretty sure that he had a claim to humanity, even if I had been pieced together.

"Damned if you are; not with that scrawny body, not like any decent human I've ever seen," Jaycea replied. "And I've seen all kinds; Spix, Daggoners, Flitzheads—you name it. Wouldn't have a one of those deviates on my ship—lazy, thieving bastards all. That's why I only want real humans, people I can trust."

"Am I to understand that you no longer have the need for a medician and navigator?" D'vore said smoothly.

Jaycea spit out another piece of stick. "Didn't say that." She chewed on the stick a bit more before she spoke again. "Said I wouldn't like to have anyone aboard my ship but humans; certainly not any damned freaks." With that she put the stick back in her mouth, swirled it around a few times, looked around the dock, and then sagged in defeat. "Crap," she spit at last. "I have to have a medician and navigator before I can clear for departure. Truth be told, there isn't anything but you

two available in the Registry. I don't like it, but I can't afford
to be choosey." She sighed. "I guess you two will have to do."
She turned to me. "I don't want any trouble, you hear? And as
for your ugly alien friend," she tilted her lovely head at D'vore,
"keep it out of the way."

"I don't know if ..." I started to protest after a glance at the
scarred sides of the ship.

Jaycea guessed what I was about to say as she grabbed the
handle of the hatch. "Think *Thys Nor's* too good for the likes of
you; is that what you're thinking? She's a good ship. Solid as
a rock." As she pulled, the hatch's hinges squealed in protest.
"Damn, that's another thing we have to fix. Either of you good
with a torch?"

The ship's interior was clean, but as worn as the exterior and
colder than the dock. Unlike the large volumes of *Tollembol* and
the Penchon ship, *Thys Nor* seemed cramped. The passageways
were narrow and the hatches barely wide enough to permit
D'vore passage. The bridge was buried amid ships, as best I
could judge from the route they had taken. The only controls
I recognized from my rapid navigation lessons was an old,
but reliable Herclue model at the navigation station. I flipped
the viewer into ready mode and checked out the encyclopedic
register.

"Careful there," Jaycea remarked sharply. "I don't want you
screwing up my equipment."

I shook my head. "Don't worry. I know what I'm doing." My
hands manipulated the Herclue as if I'd used one for decades,
even though, until this moment, I'd never physically touched
one. The mimetic navigation skill D'vore had implanted a
few weeks before, coupled with the manuals and extensive
simulations, had given me all the knowledge and skills he
needed.

The encyclopedia's data weren't current. "You need to get
this updated," I remarked.

"Can't afford it. Thing's only a century or two behind and
there's not enough stellar drift to give us any serious positional
errors. You'll have to make whatever corrections are needed
when we get close to our destination. I'll take responsibility for

the route changes if you're not comfortable about reliability."

"I appreciate your confidence," I said dryly, trying to hide my sarcasm. "But it isn't a matter of my comfort; it's the safety of the ship that worries me!"

"So add whatever safety factor you need, boy. Just be sure you get us close to where we're going." Jaycea replied. "It's your ass as well as ours. But that's enough talk; Let me show you where you can bunk." She started off without looking back.

She led us past several places that looked like crew quarters, past the galley, and through the first cargo deck. This part of the ship seemed even colder than the bridge.

"Word of advice, boys. Stay clear of our cargo master. She was the one I was talking to on the loading dock. Sylvestra doesn't much like freaks or aliens and makes no bones about it. The rest of the crew went on leave, so I'll warn them about you before they get back." She stopped and slapped her hand against a panel set in the wall of the passageway to reveal a cramped compartment. "You bunk here, Pasticher. Lots of room for your things." Her lack of a smile said it wasn't an attempt at humor. All I held was a bag with a few personal hygiene items.

"We'll put you in the other cell," Jaycea continued as she led D'vore further along the passageway. I watched as they disappeared before examining his compartment more closely.

The cramped space had a bunk that might be too short, but certainly wide enough, near the overhead. Beneath it was a locker and a large blank panel. A fold-down seat was on the wall opposite the bed. I realized that, if I stood on the seat and spread my arms I could touch both bulkheads.

The locker operated much as they had on the station and, when I pressed a hand against its face, it popped open. There were some shelves inside for personal items. After storing his few possessions I sat on the seat and stared at a narrow panel that ran half the length of the compartment. A panel unfolded when I touched it and revealed compartments, instruments, and a small lavatory. As I looked in vain for something that would control the temperature a small yellow square began blinking. I touched it.

"Welcome aboard, crewman," a melodious voice announced

as an image appeared. It was a face of unbelievable beauty. No, not an attractive woman, I realized, but one with an exquisite symmetry of perfect features.

She had large lustrous eyes, full lips, and flawless, unblemished skin. Her lips parted slightly when she spoke, the tip of her red tongue appearing between rows of perfectly white teeth with each sibilant. A crown of gorgeous hair framed her narrow face and tumbled down her shoulders, leading my eyes to a lush, partially exposed figure that promised so much. "I shall need certain information," her delicious voice continued.

"I ... I ... I'm ..." I didn't know what to say. Some strange feeling was washing over me and twisting my thoughts into unfamiliar configurations.

"My name is Halo," the image continued without a pause. "I shall need your designation." She paused, looking expectantly and, when I didn't reply, added: "Your name, please?"

"I am..., uh, Pasticher," I volunteered. Goddess she was: a walking dream, a bit of heaven, a lovely angel to his eyes. I felt a rush of lust, of desire, of yearning that I could barely contain and I knew I was in love.

The goddess seemed unmindful of my riveted attention. "Please state your skills and classifications, be specific as to ship or home designation."

"Navigator, second level. Earth," I croaked weakly. I could not take my eyes off her large eyes, perfect nose, finely chiseled cheekbones and chin, and the arched eyebrows all framed by her shimmering hair.

"Home or ship?" she replied in the same sultry tones. "Please clarify."

"Home," I replied, trying to burn her perfect features into his memories.

"Data recorded. Thys will know you now," and the screen blinked off.

I could scarcely believe she had been real. No real woman could be that perfect. Her image must have been enhanced but, even so, could there really be a goddess such as she aboard? I hoped so, but what if they should meet? If her image had so filled him with lust, how would he react if he saw her in the flesh? No, I shouldn't be thinking like this, not on so little information. There had to be something going wrong. I needed to be checked by D'vore, and quickly.

There was no way to open the hatch. I searched the wall on either side for concealed controls, checked the desk, and pressed against the sealed hatch, hoping it would spring open. When nothing seemed to work I sat frustrated and fuming until the hatch suddenly opened.

"I'm here to fix the cell door," an individual who looked as if he might be Jaycea's brother, so alike were they in general configuration and so unlike the beautiful woman who had spoken over the link. "The usual residents aren't the types we want wandering around," he laughed as he disassembled the locking mechanism and rigged a switch that he fastened to the wall. "Press it to open, press again to close," he remarked and demonstrated.

"My name is Case . And you are?"

"Vladda. take care of the ship," he replied tersely.

"Could you give me a little more warm air? It's awfully cold in here."

"Need warmth, navigator? I'll warn you now, this is as temperate as Jaycea allows, but I guess it's still too damn cold for you weak types. Word of advice, freak; don't let Jaycea hear you bitching. Better you bundle up instead." He fiddled with the overhead vent. "There, that should help."

The air grew slightly warmer, but still too cool for comfort, as it flowed from the overhead. "I am in your debt," I said dryly.

"No obligation necessary," Vladda replied gruffly, as if offended. I immediately felt he should apologize, but could honestly think of nothing I had said that might have been offensive. Instead, I decided to speak of other things, such as the location of the nearest artificer where I could get warmer clothing, and the galley. "I'd also like to know what the crew does to pass the time."

"You make your own choices," Vladda replied. "Pleasures on board are games and such. I wouldn't play cards with either Jonn or Brews, lose you will. Sylvestra's all right, but she does tend to get a little upset over losing—holds a grudge, too. On second thought it might be best for you to look to your alien friend for entertainment. Not all of the crew are as tolerant of freaks and aliens as me. Besides, most of us are pretty tight— we're all practically family, after all."

"I'll keep that in mind," I answered, inwardly seething at the insult.

"That's good," Vladda boomed and slapped him on the shoulder. "Was afraid you'd be one of them thin-skinned freaks and take offense."

"I do, but I try not to let it show."

The sarcasm seemed to be lost. "Well, no worries from me. Friend to all the Spix, Spines, and Butt-heads, that's me. Don't mind mucking about with the lower orders. Hell, I guess some of them are almost good as us Eglaners."

"I'm glad to see that someone on the crew has an open mind," I replied, which gained me a smile.

"I can see we're going to get along just fine. I like them what knows their place. Wasn't your fault you wasn't born an Eglaner."

"I wanted to know ..." I began, but was interrupted before he could repeat his questions.

"The artificer's forward, near the cleaner, but it don't give many choices in what to wear. Galley's amidships, but most of us eat alone, except Halo and the Master."

"Halo?" I said, brightening at the mention of the goddess.

Vladda smiled. "Seen her, have you? Well, bound to happen– you two looking so much alike. Best stay away, though. She's trouble," he added so sadly that he might have been speaking from bitter experience.

The discovery that Halo was a real person and not simply a manufactured image raised exciting possibilities for me. Perhaps we could meet, get to know each other, and find out why, considering the Master's apparent aversion to non-Eglaners, another human like me was among the crew. If the lovely Halo were as isolated, wouldn't it be likely that she needed a friend? Yes, all I had to do was arrange that initial meeting and ...

"Were I you, I'd stay away from the Perf," Vladda barked, catching my thoughts with uncanny insight. "She's not for the likes of you."

I was shocked at the vehemence of the response. "You don't want me to get friendly with her, is that it?"

Vladda snorted. "Are you that stupid? She's a freaking Perf! Didn't you hear me? She wouldn't come near a crippled freak like you."

Crippled? I didn't understand. "You can't be serious. What's a Perf?"

Vladda slumped. "I can't believe you don't understand. Her kind claims they're the end of human evolution, the perfection of the human genome, the ideal form. For generations they've pushed every damn physical characteristic to their ideal— perfect teeth, perfect bones, perfect every-fucking-thing, and their damned eternal, all-knowing smiles like their shit don't stink. To a Perf, the rest of us are the results of bad decisions and random evolution."

He paused for a moment as I absorbed this fantastic claim. "For the most part I agree with their opinion that most freaks aren't worth a bottle of warm piss. But to Halo even us Eglaners are insignificant animals." He grinned at me. "I imagine to her mind you'd be like a Spix, or probably lower. That clear?"

I noted that Vladda was not handsome with his large, hairy ears and thick, powerful-looking legs. That he might have once had designs on Halo and been scorned was completely believable. Love is often blind to discrepancies of size and shape, but if what Vladda said was true ... "I understand," I answered, hoping that I really did. In this strange universe I'd learned that it didn't pay to make assumptions.

Vladda immediately calmed down. "Ah, she's all right. Not her fault for what she is."

D'vore's small surgery had been set up amidships, just aft of the crew quarters. The small operating room had barely enough space between the edges of the operating bench and the faces of the many drawers, lockers, and instruments that lined the bulkheads. There was barely enough space to allow D'vore to move. He had just finished going through a complete inventory as I entered.

"Will you need my help? Maybe my brief acquaintance with

surgery on *Tollembol* might be of some use."

"I think not," D'vore replied. "Your duties as navigator should keep you quite occupied. Besides, with so few crew I expect that there should be little need while we are in transit. But I will be better able to judge that after my baseline examinations—Ah, here is my first patient."

Another of the large crewmembers of indeterminate sex squeezed into the surgery. Part of the problem of determining whether it was male or female was the shrouding clothing the crewmen wore. I wondered if it was to protect them against the chill that permeated the ship. It was a practice I would have to adopt if Jaycea maintained this "temperate" clime.

"Name's Brews, master of engines, adventurer, and expert at seventeen schools of love-making," The rotund fellow remarked in a gravelly voice. "What the hell are you two?"

"I'm Case and he's called D'vore," I replied with a wave as I took the measure of this new face. Brews was a head shorter than Vladda and sported a bushy beard that hid most of his face. His fingers were short, thick, and covered with callus.

Brews noted the direction of my glance. "Ah, the result of too much need and not enough luxury. But those times are behind me and now I enjoy life to the fullest." He turned to D'vore. "So, what will you with me, medician?"

"I shall need only an assessment of you," D'vore answered. "So that I may be of service when, or if, it becomes necessary."

I excused himself as Brews began to disrobe. The surgery was far too small for the three of us to be comfortable and I had no desire to see what the clothing concealed.

I was trying without much success to cajole the artificer to produce clothing of sufficient warmth when I heard a disturbance near D'vore's surgery. Someone was shouting loudly.

D'vore faced an individual with an excessive amount of hardware hanging from various parts of its body. There were sockets at each joint, pendants of connectors hung from its major muscle groups, and its head of smoothly artificial, sexless features was encircled with a wired crown of extraordinary complexity. The left-hand had been replaced by a mechanical prosthesis that seemed to have twenty or more tiny fingers while the right was quite human, down to the gaily-decorated fingernails. There were no obvious indications of gender.

"No bloody damned alien is going to touch me, especially some blasted ghoul. Who the fuck let this thing on board anyway?" It grated in a toneless mechanical voice.

"Calm down, Syl," Brews answered, "Jaycea hired it."

"Well, that fucking thing is not going to touch me. Sylvestra takes care of herself, you hear me, ghoul. I take care of myself—always!"

"Nevertheless, my services are at your disposal," D'vore replied smoothly. "I assure you that I am completely competent to service all forms of humanity regardless of the degree of injury. If you have any doubts …"

"Doubts have nothing to do with it, ghoul. I just don't want your filthy alien hands touching me. Is that clear?"

"You'll change your mind if a cargo shift flattens you," Jaycea said as she came up. "This thing's our medician. Accept that. There's no one else available."

"Now, Jaycea," Sylvestra whined. "You and me been together too long for that kind of threat. You should have spoken to me before you …"

"You were too wrapped up with your fellow mechs to talk about personnel. Now let the medician check you out—I want to make sure you haven't gotten yourself pregnant again."

"I take precautions in a tangle," Syl said defensively. "Come on Jaycea. I've got issues here."

"Forget the war, Syl. It's over. Now, let the thing do its job. I'll hold your hand if you want." A slight smile played on Jaycea's lips, a smile that was not, could not be reflected on Syl's rigid countenance.

Syl stood silent. Her mechanical hand clicked open and closed, as it marked a twenty-note cadence. "Fuck it; I'll take my chances," she said at last and walked away, fingers still clicking.

Jonn, the *Thys Nor*'s communicator, showed up scant minutes before the ship began disengaging from the station and jumped aboard as Jaycea was sealing the ship. "What the hell is a freak doing on the ship?" he demanded when he spotted me at the navigation table. From the smell, I could tell that Jonn's brief leave had been a sodden affair.

"I'll explain after I get him sobered up," Jaycea said as she sent Jonn staggering away. "You won't have too much of a problem when he's sober."

Her prediction proved true when the now sober Jonn returned. He even helped locate reference points and identify routines that I needed to guide them toward Hammasod station, their first stop on the way to Oroenoe.

In those intervals when *Thys Nor* drifted slowly between navigation beacons marking the way to departure, I attempted conversation. It was a difficult undertaking and doubly frustrating since while Jonn had a thorough knowledge of the ship's data stores he was unwilling to share anything that wasn't directly related to the job at hand. Consequently, I learned little of him and less of the rest of the ship's complement.

It was an indication of what the voyage was going to be like.

The ensuing weeks would have been long and lonely were it not for the continued exploration of the massive twisted and tortured pile of wreckage's image that D'vore produced. I still marveled at the fidelity of the image. Despite the realistic seeming sharp edges of torn metal he was able to pass through unharmed. I often wished there were some way I could bend the metal back to a semblance of what it had been. If that was possible I might be able to wrest more sense from it.

The futility of these examinations frustrated him, but each time I mentioned giving up, D'vore would convince me that only by continuing would I have any chance of remembering the truth of my origins. "Only by evoking the ghosts of your crew will you be able to find your Earth," he advised.

Try as he might, I never seemed able to synchronize my trips to the galley with the elusive Halo. On occasion I managed to catch glimpses of her slender form in the passageways, but always with the forbidding Jaycea hovering nearby.

Mindful of Vladda's warning I tried to not think of her, but found that nearly impossible. Her face was always in my thoughts. I felt a physical yearning I could not seem to quench nor, to be honest, wished to do.

"I notice you appear distressed," D'vore said as he touched my forehead during one of his checkups. The adaptations of my piecemeal body had still not stabilized.

"Could you salve the ache in my heart?" I asked and, after assuring that he had only been speaking metaphorically, explained my physical lust for Halo. "What should I do? How can I stop these thoughts?"

"I suspect a hormonal imbalance of some sort as a result of your healing. Do you wish me to make a glandular adjustment?"

I started. Did I want these feelings to stop? Could it be possible that the cure could be so simple? "No, I don't want my feelings manipulated. Let me work this out myself."

D'vore hesitated before replying. "Since your revival you have been without the companionship of your own kind, Case . I suspect that Halo's appearance fits some mental template that represents an ideal female. Since she is close to you in appearance I suspect that you are having a visceral reaction. In other words, since she appears to be unobtainable, you are driven to want her the more.

This is nothing more than a few physiological and psychological adjustments as your body heals and asserts its base demands. A lowering of testosterone levels seems advised. I ask you again, allow me to make a few adjustments of your body chemistry so you will be more comfortable."

"No!" I shouted and drew back. "This isn't a matter of body chemistry that can be treated as if it were an upset stomach or bad rash. I know there's an emotional bond, something so personal that no amount of medical mediation will excuse it. Do not touch me."

"As you wish,. I want only to help. However, I am concerned that these imbalances may interfere with recovering your fragmentary memories."

"Are you talking about my dreams?"

"Yes, and you need to concentrate on how to better bring those memories into play during your examination of the image. Perhaps you will be more focused without this distraction."

"Distraction? My feelings can hardly interfere more. I wake up from these crazy dreams confused and frustrated. Nothing makes sense. Do you seriously expect dreams to produce useful memories? God, I feel like I'm going crazy. Nothing I recall seems to make sense!"

D'vore listened quietly, offering no judgment or guidance.

"You're saying I have to find my own way. Is that your sage advice?"

D'vore did not reply, which was an answer unto itself.

A few days after departing Torii I brought up D'vore's curious hump. I had let the matter pass earlier but felt that e had attained a level of familiarity that allowed him to ask.

Any thoughts that D'vore might prove intractable were dispelled when he threw open his cloak. A small container was affixed to his back. It was length of a forearm, nearly as wide, and half that in depth. "ThripoBlastenav has obligated me to carry this to Hammasod."

"Aren't you curious about what might be inside?" I asked.

"This is no simple container, Case. The device is intimately tied to my body and draws energy and nutrients from it. You may think of me, in your terms, as a nursemaid to this."

"I see." Fantastic as the explanation sounded, D'vore's puzzling hump seemed no more incredible than any other wonder.

"But, please Case, do not speak of this to the others. I do not trust them with this knowledge any more than we do your origins."

"But I am sure that Master Jaycea ..."

D'vore stopped me. "Especially Master Jaycea. I am certain that she would not look kindly upon me transporting this without paying the tariff and believe me, the cost for what I carry would be very, very great."

I thought that caution excessive, but saw little harm in this small subterfuge. He nodded. "Agreed."

In the periods when the navigation console was not otherwise employed, I used it to search the encyclopedia for his home and quickly realized the futility of such a search. Names of stars, systems, and worlds appeared to be slippery terms, often changing and seldom singular, varying by language and disposition of the system's governing class. To eliminate the necessity of frequent changes in place names, the encyclopedia was organized by universal designator, quadrant by sector, globe by quarter—none of which he knew well enough to gain any facility. In the end, I was reduced to making random guesses of similar names and at various pronunciations in hopes of eliciting some clue to Earth's location. When this proved of no avail, I decided to ask Jaycea.

"Ert?" Jaycea said, mispronouncing the name. "I was there once, I think. Close to a blue giant, hot as hell. Had to stay within the containment field all the time. No fun at all."

"Hot as hell" in Jaycea's terms probably meant that the temperature had been anything above freezing. I was certain that the Earth sun had been a pleasant orange, not the scalding blue-white monster she mentioned.

"Why are you so interested in this Ert place, anyhow?" she asked, trying unsuccessfully again to match y exotic pronunciation.

I explained that, since the accident, my memories had failed to jell into anything that would present a coherent picture of my past and how I'd had difficulty sorting out his memories. I was careful to hide the truth of my reconstruction; fearful that since she thought so little of me to begin with, I hated to think what her reaction might be of she knew my fractured nature. "The name of Earth is the one constant that everything else revolves around. It's a name, a place. It's my home," I concluded with a catch in my throat.

Jaycea nodded sympathetically. "Ah, home. I can understand that. Seen quite a few places in all the years I've been traveling. All of them are home to somebody."

It was the first time I'd heard her speak so gently, so wistfully. Perhaps, I hoped, this was an opportunity to penetrate her gruff armor and mentioned a strong image that had occurred more and more of late. "It might be a planet I've visited or an image carrying a great deal of emotion. It's a simple thing; a mottled blue sphere hanging against a dark field of stars."

"Planet, probably." she grunted. "Sounds like."

"Or it might have been a piece of art. I have no way of knowing," I replied. "But that particular image is usually followed by one of sailing on a golden sea with a lovely, smiling gray-haired woman at the helm." I continued talking, speaking of floating weightlessly in a large cylinder and watching the twinkling lights of massive cities passing below. I spoke of large cities and small, of towns and villages, of blue skies and towering mountains, of seas and streams.

Jaycea was quiet for a long time after he finished. "Sounds like every place I've been. What about your ships?"

"I only recall three ships, all the others were simulations during my navigation training." I replied. "This one, the one that rescued me, and the Penchon ship that recovered us when *Tollembol* was destroyed."

Jaycea jerked back. "Destroyed? Was there an accident?"

I tried to explain and how I'd no time to assess what was taking place before D'vore threw him into the escape vessel.

She was silent for a few moments before she next spoke. "I find an accident near the Rift damned strange and even if one did happen, how could the Penchon have stumbled upon the wreckage? No, space is too empty, too vast for coincidence. Do you recall *Tollembol's* purpose or place of origin?"

I expressed ignorance on all points. "My mind had been so befuddled that I could scarce take care of myself let alone learn anything about the ship that rescued me." Still, I described *Tollembol* as best I could, focusing on the remarkably homogeneous crew.

"Heinies," she spit when I described their furry hides. "Cinnamon color says Heinies." When he looked puzzled, she explained how a single individual could be cloned and replicated to staff an entire ship. "Cheap labor," she finished. "I imagine they cloned female versions as well, the damned perverts."

I nodded. "I saw a lot of men and women. I idly wondered if their couplings had been a form of incest?

"I don't understand why they'd have an alien medician on

board. One of their own would be better."

"He said he was traded from a Penchon ship. They trained him as a surgeon."

Jaycea chewed on that for a while. "Even more improbable, but something the Penchon might do—especially if they thought they could make a profit. I assume they give him that weird appearance, like that hump on his back?"

"I suppose," I replied guardedly. There was no need to tell her the entire story so I quickly changed the subject. "Can you tell me why Vladda seemed so upset when I thanked him for adjusting the temperature in his compartment? I don't want to offend him again."

"Yes, he mentioned that you offered to be in his service, boy. Hell of a thing to say."

"All I said was that I was in debt for his service. Is that so bad?"

Jaycea laughed. "Whew, you're either dumber than a Farker or really did lose a chunk of memory! Obligations are currency, Case. Better than precious metals or accounts with banks that might not be around when you come to collect. Obligation's a promise for a trade of service, of loyalty, balancing the scales."

She noticed my perplexed look and continued, speaking much as she would address a child. "Look here, back at the station I took on cargo. They paid by letting me use the obligations they had so I could get fuel, water, food, and raw materials for the artificer, and even entertainment for the crew.

"The same thing will happen at the far end: Those who receive the cargo take on obligations to the shipper and to us. On a larger scale there are vast enterprises who manage obligations on a much grander scale, turning entire systems, races to service to achieve some objective."

This seemed very strange. If such a system really existed, and it seemed this one did, it seemed nothing more than simple bartering—hardly a sophisticated system and one clearly fraught with problems, especially on an interstellar scale. "There has to be some portability, some way of changing obligations from one purpose to another," he protested.

"Of course," she snapped. "Each ship carries a set of records with it. The WOFAT of the last station loads a record for the next station we reach and that station reads it to balance accounts. Since there are thousands of ships, the accounts are constantly being adjusted and shifted. It's highly complex, but it works well enough."

I was skeptical. There were obviously subtleties here that I did not understand, such as who or what might be a WOFAT. But the hour was late and Jaycea had ceased being amused by my apparent ignorance.

The conversation with Jaycea had raised some interesting questions. If, as she declared, it was unlikely that the Penchon had "stumbled upon" the rescue pod, how much more unlikely was it that *Tollembol* had been so near to his own "accident?" The only knowledge he had of those events were D'vore's statements of what had transpired and he had no way to validate those.

I slept fitfully that night, as I dreamed of the blue ball, russet sails in the sunset, the gray-haired woman, Halo's lovely eyes, and the possibly deceitful D'vore.

A starship's imminent arrival at its destination is a time of exquisite torture for crew, but more especially for navigators. In preparation for emerging into three-space the ship encounters a seeming resistance, as if it swam in a sea of treacle instead of empty vacuum. In preparation for arrival, a ship would be rotated, the orientation bent, and its attitude adjusted. Although such position altering terms have atmospheric referents their equivalents have other, less restrictive meanings in the seven-space universe.

The ship's preparations produce many assorted grinding noises, pings, and groans, as if it were an old man awakening from a cramped nap. During this period the navigator is ever plagued with doubt that the resulting adjustments are appropriate or correct, that is, if the routing to *Thys Nor's* destination had been correct to begin with and it wasn't arriving where no station or system awaits.

During a lull in a clamor of ship maneuvers I overheard the Brews and Vladda arguing whether their new navigator had been completely sober when the destination had been first calculated, whether the proper navigation tables had been used, and whether Jaycea had foolishly overridden or shaved one or more of his careful calculations at midpoint to save fuel or adjust arrival time.

At some point in the argument bets were placed, with Jonn ridiculously betting on the ship's emergence inside a star. How he expected to collect if this turned out to be true eluded me.

For all of these reasons, arrival at Hammasod, Jaycea's first destination, was preceded by hours of nerve-tingling anticipation and punctuated by microseconds of sheer terror. I knew that even a minor navigation error en route could place the ship and crew far from anything familiar, far from any known star where, without knowledge of position and time, all aboard would be doomed to a slow and distant death–and my own would no doubt precede all others.

A precision error likewise could place the ship seriously at risk of collision with Hammasod itself, the station, or just some tiny piece of intra-system junk that would impact at close to light speed and turn *Thys Nor* into a brief, but very bright star as mega joules of impact energy were released.

The ship's clock counted down, the drive did its seven-space magic, and the stars of three-space appeared once more. Thankfully, the ship had emerged near its target and along the right vector to proceed to the destination.

I had not needed my brown pants after all.

Within microseconds after emergence *Thys Nor* was caught in the web of detectors and beacons, ship sightings, and guidelines so that, by the time she fell below relativistic velocities, the choreography of the system had been adjusted to accommodate her headlong dash while she was days distant from the station. Hours later, after *Thys Nor* emerged from seven-space, the station's electromagnetic wave front reached the ship with the route and docking instructions.

Jaycea met us at the hatch. "Changed your mind about continuing, I hope?"

"D'vore said you were taking us to Oroenoe," I reminded

her. "That was your obligation, wasn't it?"

Jaycea looked around. "I told that thing that I'd take you as far as I could, which is the first station where I can find decent replacements. Not that you two haven't behaved, but I'm sure you'll be more comfortable among your own kind."

I realized that Jaycea meant she'd be more comfortable with a crew of her "own kind." Her prejudice rankled. Still, it was not his place to tell a ship's master how to think, especially since I relied on her good wishes if he were to reach Oroenoe.

"We shall see, Master Jaycea." D'vore appeared less willing to concede her point. "We shall see."

Hammasod station's dock seemed much the same as Torii's save that the atmosphere was a bit warmer, the light slightly more blue, and the scents exotic—sweet, with overtones of cinnamon. "Is this the exciting life of an interstellar trader," I mused as I breathed deeply of the air. "Did we just fly between the stars only to stand on another stinking cargo dock?" D'vore was moving with some deliberation and did not answer.

"How do you know your way around this station?" I continued as we shifted back and forth through the stacks of cargo containers.

"The human portions of these stations have a common, boring design," he responded. "It makes finding one's way easy." I looked around in as much confusion as before and hoped he would discover what this boring design might be for no other reason than to become independent.

"I'm getting hungry. Can we get something decent to eat?" The matter was one of taste rather than hunger, no doubt driven by the scents that assailed his nostrils. I'd grown bored with the limited selection of meals offered by the galley on Jaycea's ship and wanted to experience a broader range of flavors. Who knew what delights might be found where the cuisines of interstellar cultures combined with those of alien worlds?

"I have little need at the moment, but there are many eating places in the hub," D'vore replied and indicated the central pillar. "There might be someplace there to satisfy your needs, but I suggest you buy only from the human vendors. The others could prove fatal to the unwary." There was no trace of humor in his voice, so I took it for sound advice. "In the meantime I will study the WOFAT copy of our contract to ensure we can use it as leverage!"

I was fascinated with the swirl of activity as I walked toward the hub. On Torii I had been so preoccupied with escape that I hadn't noticed the station's details and variety.

There were many human-like aliens, although some of their features and shapes were strange to my eyes. D'vore scarcely reacted when we encountered those that had me gaping in astonishment. At one point a hulking giant of a man, a mountain of muscle that stood nearly half again y height on legs of tree trunk girth advanced on us. His proportions were odd; body more broad than long, of greater hip and smaller trunk in proportion to his legs. His hands curled at knee height and had huge black fingernails. Of greater interest was a head of abundant, coarse brown hair, each tuft of which was tied with a brightly colored bow.

"*Hrunfgh. Da spuk wista?*" he said with a resonant bass voice. "*Da spuk?*" he repeated with a gesture of one of those huge hams toward me .

"High caste merchant, married, ship owner from Windrow," D'vore whispered. "He is a believer in Chironism as well,"

"Do you know him?" It was astonishing that we should encounter someone known. The chances against this had to be astronomical.

D'vore laughed. "Not at all. His place in society is marked by his adornments. It announces to all who and what he is, which is a necessity in Windrow's rather formal culture."

That the giant should wear badges of identity so plainly only appeared strange by degree. I vaguely recalled having done the same with uniform and manners, with choices of clothing and behaviors in y previous lives. Perhaps the Windrow merchant's way was much more civilized in that it eliminated much of the guesswork.

"Bow," D'vore instructed.

When I did so I was surprised to see a bright smile appear

on the giant's face. The giant bowed in return. *"Spiknuck. Thys Nor Na whish du?"*

"His name is Spiknuck. He is asking if you are of the *Thys Nor*," D'vore advised.

"How would he know?" I asked, not understanding how this stranger could know of the ship. "How did he know that?"

"Du cit," D'vore said, which sounded like an agreement and, no sooner than the words were spoken, the giant became clearly upset.

"Spiknuck! Na dik! Na dik!" the giant responded with great agitation when D'vore translated and then followed with another long and serious discourse to which D'vore responded only briefly and occasionally.

"List harth," the giant said as he gently touched my forehead with a huge finger, apparently a Chironist blessing. Then, without another word, stomped away.

"Wait," I yelled, but it did no good. In moments the giant disappeared among the stacks of cargo. "I don't understand. What made him so upset?"

"Who can tell?" D'vore shrugged. He said nothing of the long conversation they'd had. "I would advise you to forget this incident."

I was certain that D'vore knew the answer, but wasn't going to share that knowledge. It was just another mystery among so many.

Shortly after the encounter with the giant and after having narrowly escaped being run down by a variety of machines, we entered the hub and proceeded along one of the spoke corridors. On either side I glimpsed bays in which aliens and things that looked almost human were working. But there was little time to dwell on the specifics of their work as I tried to keep up with D'vore as he turned this way and that, seemingly at random, until I was certain that e had lost their way. Finally, just as I was about to protest this aimless wandering, we entered a broad and open area. I was stunned as my eyes roamed the array of sights. It appeared to be a marketplace of exotic items of unknown purpose and constitution. I was so overwhelmed that I didn't know which way to look as we walked into the confusion.

The market was a delight to the senses, a challenge to the mind, a cry for exploration and experimentation. Each step revealed a surprise. Each inhalation carried a scent of mouth-watering delicacies. I detected perfumes at once repugnant and enticing. The sensory overload nearly overwhelmed me. Tears came to my eyes.

"Breathe deeply," D'vore advised when he noted my distress. "The emotional surge will pass in a moment." I took two deep breaths and closed my eyes to shut out the sights. It seemed to calm me.

A few moments later, as I was staring at a selection of orange fruits or vegetables that had the texture of peaches and a faint smell of vanilla, all thoughts of tasting them fled my mind. There, a few paces away, in front of a jewelry display, stood Halo.

She'd wrapped herself in a diaphanous cloak of pale blue that covered most of her body and head, leaving only those lovely eyes and her delicate, long-fingered hands exposed. I recognized her instantly, despite her translucent disguise. It was the way she held herself, her perfect proportions, the graceful way she moved.

I looked around, half expecting to see Jaycea, Halo's ever-present protector, nearby. Apparently the goddess had freed herself, for the master was not to be seen.

This was an opportunity not to be missed yet I struggled to think of what I might say; how I might best use this opportunity.

It looked as if Halo had decided to purchase the brooch she'd been fondling, for she pinned it upon one perfect breast and brushed it with her hand before turning to leave.

"Hello," I murmured as I fell into step, so close that I could feel the warmth of her arm. It took every ounce of restraint to keep from reaching out and touching her.

When Halo turned those perfect, large, wonderful eyes upon me, I fell silent, drowning in their beauty. My awareness of the market disappeared like mist as I, enraptured by the fact that we were so close at last, drank in every detail. It was a precious moment, a priceless moment. "I ?" she asked in a wonderfully melodious voice.

I found that despite his intentions, I could not speak. Up to this point my sole objective was to be with her, to gain her attention. What I might say at this point, how I might tell her what I felt had not occurred. "I ... I," I stammered, feeling as if I were once again an adolescent summoning up courage to ask a girl for a date. My mind was blank, my intelligence paralyzed. I hated myself for remaining mute.

Halo stared at my dumb form for a moment more, shrugged, then moved to a nearby eatery, and flowed into a seat, perching so prettily that I wondered if it were a pose. No, she was so naturally graceful in all her actions that her posture would not be pretense. Her thin cloak settled on her slender, perfect body, concealing much but hinting at the riches beneath. I sat nearby, unwilling to force myself on her, yet unable to venture far away.

When her food and drink appeared, I asked to have the same. At least they'd be sharing a meal, even if she did not realize it. When my own bowl and glass appeared I absently spooned a large portion into his mouth.

There was an immediate reaction. Suddenly I could not breathe. My mouth was aflame. Tears rolled down my cheeks. My tongue felt as if burning acids had been dripped upon it. My heart raced. I could feel the flaming morsel travel down my throat and into my stomach where it ignited a blaze that I imagined would shortly consume me. Somehow I had mistakenly ordered one of the alien dishes that D'vore had warned me about. I had been poisoned for certain!

I reached for the cylinder of liquid and gulped greedily, hoping to quench the flames, and drank so quickly that I didn't notice the taste. All I wanted was something to cool the fire, to stop the destruction of mouth and stomach.

The drink was terribly sweet and flavored of licorice and mint. It burned my tongue and throat as well, but in a far different way. Overwhelmed by the disaster occurring I struggled to take a breath, knowing I was surely going to die from these two alien poisons.

Halo calmly watched me. While I was still gasping in agony

she delicately spooned a tiny sample from her own bowl and followed it with a delicate sip of her drink. She seemed quite unaffected.

Her kind must, I concluded through my tears, have evolved some sort of digestive insulation to be so immune to the effects of this wicked dish. Then, as the fire abated, I noticed a wonderful, smoky, piquant flavor on my tongue. The flavor wasn't something I'd paid attention to during the shock of that first bite of hellfire. The residual taste was delightful.

Carefully, I followed Halo's actions and ventured another, albeit smaller bite, following it immediately with a sip of the strange drink. Taken that way, the heat was manageable and, I hoped, minimized permanent tissue damage.

We ate the remainder of our shared meal in silence and, while I stole frequent glances at her, I detected no similar interest on her part. Was her feigned disinterest a rebuke, or an invitation?

At several points during the meal Halo touched the brooch but did not look at it when she did so. Perhaps it had some tactile qualities that she found pleasing, I thought and tried, without being too obvious, to examine it.

The brooch was circular, a ring of gold surrounding a blue stone. The face of the stone had an intricately woven pattern of silver lines across it that glinted in the bright overhead lights. I could not tell if the lines were raised above the surface of the stone or incised within.

Before I could discover more she unexpectedly rose and spoke. "Jaycea has decided to retain the two of you for now." Hearing her address me so abruptly broke my chain of thought. "You will accompany *Thys Nor* on the next leg." She moved away before I could rise from my seat.

I hesitated, wondering if I should pursue her. No, maybe I could build a relationship from this small, and somewhat embarrassing, beginning. Yes, there was no need to rush now that I remained among the ship's complement. Other opportunities would present themselves.

It was only then that I realized that in my focused desire to be with Halo I had completely lost track of D'vore. Had the

D'vore absented himself when he saw that I was drawn to Halo? Had he taken the opportunity to go about his own business, unencumbered by a novice? Either way I was grateful; certain that D'vore's presence would have made a difference in our intimate meal.

I wandered the market for hours; entranced, mystified, confused, and sometimes alarmed. The market's delights appeared to be endless but eventually I was able to note variations on common themes that had probably been ever the same in every marketplace on every world. In the end, when all my senses were sated and burned out by the novelty, I found myself yearning for the plain, unexciting ordinariness of *Thys Nor*'s confining walls.

The corridors were not so confusing once I noticed that the directions to the docking areas were clearly marked at each crossing. I soon found myself striding on the docking bay, but wondered if I was in the right sector.

After a brief study of one of the many station diagrams with their locations clearly marked, I realized I'd emerged a quarter of the way around the rim from where *Thys Nor* was docked.

Instead of doing the sensible thing and going through the hub to emerge on the correct radial, I decided to take a circuitous route along the periphery of the station to give myself an opportunity to see what the other ships might carry.

Not surprisingly, they all appeared to be doing much the same cargo unloading routine. Oh, the size and shapes of the containers varied enormously, as did the methods of handling them. I marveled at the variety of the humans and aliens but was becoming jaded to the variations. Each new one was less shocking. In time I wondered if I would soon begin accepting D'vore strangeness as normal.

I was within shouting distance of *Thys Nor* when a familiar ammonia scent tickled my nose. At the same time I heard a distant Penchon's screech. Curious, I followed the sound and soon came upon a ship that looked remarkably like the one they had left at Torrii station.

"Screee!" a Penchon to the right shouted. "Screeee," came an answering cry from the left and, in moments, I was surrounded by at least a dozen of the ugly aliens. At the same time the nearest cargo hatch slid noisily shut.

"Screee, screee," the coven of Penchon cried. As I took a step to move away they closed ranks, blocking the way. Another Penchon, somewhat larger than the others and just as smelly, appeared with one of the partially organic translators in its hands.

"What you doing here?" the device said in a very human voice as its red bellows blew air across what I suspected could have been a human larynx.

"I lost my way," I replied. "I was looking for *Thys Nor.*" I tried to explain that I'd emerged on the wrong radial and had decided to walk back.

"Screee! Not near our ship. No humans need be here," the translator groaned in reply. "Are you trying to find what we carry?" Clearly his curiosity had alarmed them, which was puzzling. The Penchon on the *Qalyub Gudlag* had not barred my examination of their cargo. Why, I wondered, were these being so protective?

"No, no. I was just curious," I explained. "I've never seen a Penchon ship up close before. Can't blame me for being curious, can you?"

"What you doing here?" Obviously his excuse was not convincing. He spread his hands wide to indicate that he could provide no further information. "What did you see?" the large Penchon pressed. It stood close enough that I could see the fine hairs that covered its body. The flaps of loose skin that hung from each of the major arms rippled ominously. "Why are you so interested in a Penchon ship?"

I didn't seem to be making any headway and began sweating profusely, wondering if the large Penchon, who looked a bit like the same officer who had spoken so frequently while I had been aboard, would recognize me. No, that could not be possible. They had left *Qalyub Gudlag* and its crew far behind. This had to be a different ship.

"I really have to get back to my ship," I repeated as I stepped toward the encircling ring of Penchon. "Been a pleasure talking to you, really." I moved toward the nearest edge of the ring and, when the Penchon hesitated, was afraid that bluster would not work. I was bracing himself to charge when the large one let out an authoritative "Screeee," and the circle parted.

I moved away as swiftly as I could, not wishing to give them another excuse to interrogate me.

"Where the hell have you been and where is D'vore?" Jaycea asked when I encountered her a short distance from the berth. "Of all the damned luck, there's not a cleared navigator or medician listed at the Registry. Second time in a row that's happened, damn it, so now I have to keep the two of you on my ship." Jaycea was clearly not overjoyed at having to haul them on another leg.

"I am glad to see you once again," I replied with a smile.

She looked around. "Where's the alien—the medician?"

"We parted company earlier," I replied but didn't go into the details of my interlude with Halo. Some things are best kept to oneself. "I assumed he had some business to attend to." I thought it best not to bring up D'vore's search for the contract.

"Well, I didn't see it. Damn, just like an alien to wander off, instead of keeping its ugliness hidden. What sort of business could it have here, for God's sake?"

Did she suspect the truth about the contraband D'vore had hidden on his person? "What do you mean? I really don't know that much about his affairs."

Jaycea looked at him sharply. "You're not the only one. Reclusive sorts. Keep to their own mostly. Usually run into them as ship."

"You mean on a ship, don't you?"

She sneered. "Said what I meant, boy. That kind has a real intimate connection with their attachments. Don't make much distinction between mechanical and organic parts."

"Like Sylvestra," he said.

"Hardly," she spit. "Syl's just got a few more prosthetics than most, but she's still an Eglaner. Don't know if D'vore ships are part of them or vice versa. Like I said, really alien."

"But D'vore isn't like that. He doesn't seem that strange."

Unmentioned was my opinion that every individual I'd encountered since awakening had seemed equally odd. In fact, D'vore at times had seemed far less strange than many humans I'd met.

"Some say they steal souls," Jaycea added knowingly. "Along with the organic parts they use."

"That's probably just superstition," I replied immediately, driven by an impulse to protect my friend. At the same time I wondered how much credence to place in her words. That any being could evolve half machine, half organic seemed wildly improbable. At the same time, the ease with which D'vore adopted body parts seemed to support her comments.

"Damn!" At first I thought her exclamation another expression of pique at D'vore's absence and then saw, just twenty meters away, a group of Penchon gathered about a broken cargo container where an avalanche of spilled yellow-green globes were scattered about the deck.

"Get away from there!" Jaycea yelled and ran toward them, shaking her fists in the air. "That's my cargo, you bloody be damned alien bastards!"

The Penchon scurried away. Jaycea took a swipe at one particularly laggardly one but didn't make contact. "Look at this," she said as she kicked one of the globes. "What a mess. Where the hell is Syl? She's supposed to be unloading, not letting aliens steal us blind."

"Perhaps something has happened to her." I pointed at one corner of the container where a smear of pink fluid glistened on the deck. It could have been blood, lubricating fluid, or a mixture of both.

"Syl!" Jaycea exclaimed and raced for the hatch, shouting as soon as she was inside and heading toward the surgery.

Syl was on the table, her arm dangling loosely from her shoulder. A jagged tear extended from the center of the shoulder and down her left bicep, exposing the muscle beneath. Thankfully the flow of blood had been stanched by a bloody rag. Two of her connectors had been torn loose and hung on shreds of skin from bicep to wrist. I could see where the silvery connecting wires had been woven into the muscles of her upper arm.

Brews was attempting to treat the damage with one hand while holding D'vore at bay with the other arm. Syl flinched each time Brews shifted his grip, making her loose arm dance. A steady stream of curses poured from her lips in an obscene mantra of suffering and pain.

"Move aside and let me treat her," D'vore insisted as he was opening a locker with his mechanical arm and removing a device that looked much like a staple gun.

"Don't touch me, you filthy Beast!" Syl yelled and tried to pull away, dislodging Brews' grip. The movement caused the wound to open and a fresh flow of pale blood to gush from her injuries. "Leave me fucking alone!"

Ignoring her words, D'vore easily pushed Brews to one side, lifted the gun, and applied it to the base of Syl's neck. "This will eliminate the pain," he told her. "Now, let me repair you."

"Brew can do what's needed," she answered softly as the painkiller did its work and the tension flowed out of her. "We humans can fix ourselves, beast," she said, her voice barely above a whisper. "Don't ... steal any ... meat."

"I can handle this," Brews interrupted. "I just need to get her to a decent medician, is all. It's not as bad as it looks. All we have to do it run the implants and apply new skin."

"New skin takes time to adhere and more time to heal," D'vore countered and turned to Jaycea. "Let me repair her. I can have her operational in a few watches at most."

"Syl's the best judge of what she needs," Jaycea interrupted, supporting her crew. "Why don't you find something else to do while we get her to a decent medician."

The rebuke was pretty crude and D'vore wisely backed away.

She helped Brews lift Sylvestra from the table. "In the meantime why don't you educate your tame human about yourself?"

"It is much the same everywhere," D'vore said sadly. "Always there is this barrier, this suspicion, this hatred of his kind, of those who differ. Why are humans this way, Case?"

I immediately recalled my immediate revulsion when I first learned how D'vore's had acquired his human arms and legs. Did the Eglaners' objections arise from similar prejudice or had their feelings some basis in fact? Was there some instinctual reaction to anything that appeared different? "I don't know," I answered.

I hadn't noticed the change in D'vore's appearance in the close confines of the surgery during the excitement. The hump was gone from his back and he seemed slightly taller. Less apparent was his increase in girth, which was somewhat hidden by his enveloping cloak. What could not be ignored was the extra set of eyes placed slightly above and to the outside of D'vore's former set.

"The new optics provide me with greater depth perception and visual acuity," he explained. "This will greatly enhance my usefulness aboard the ship. I will be able to perform much finer surgeries than before."

I found that candor interesting. The D'vore who had left the ship would hardly have willingly provided an explanation, nor would he have been as assured of its reception. Whether this indicated an acceptance of me as confidant or simply greater personal assurance I could not tell.

Was this the same creature that left, or had he mutated into someone, something different? With Jaycea's distrust still present in y mind I began to wonder about his relationship to the alien creature that had given him life and realized that my trust in D'vore might be mistaken.

Syl returned to work on the cargo loading four watches later, but her movements were restricted and tentative. The delay in returning to work, and her inability to use her appliances to maximum effect meant that Jaycea had to employ other mechs to handle cargo. That, in turn, meant that one of the crew had to always be present to "keep the thieving bastards from stealing me blind," as Jaycea so charmingly put it.

Jaycea called me away from my watch duty to plot a course to Uropygi station, our next stop on the way to Oroenoe. I began searching *Thys Nor*'s century-old register for Uropygi's possibly outdated coordinates. That *Thys Nor* had not yet met with disaster gave me some assurance that Jaycea had been right about the register's ancient entries not being critically incorrect.

When the optimal plot was complete I presented it for approval. "I plotted the shortest path," I explained. "That will shave the most time off the transit and allow you to collect a bonus for early delivery.

"What's the 'but'?" Jaycea demanded. "Why the hesitation?"

I squirmed. "Well, this plot has the disadvantage of requiring added fuel—about a quarter more, in fact."

"Hmmm. I want two more alternatives. Give me a minimum energy route that will conserve fuel, yet meet our scheduled arrival window, and then plot the most economical; one that's neither the fastest nor the most fuel-efficient but will get us there no later than the outside period of our scheduled arrival window. When you get those done I'll look them over, consider our options and make a choice."

"Including this one?" I asked, still hoping for speed, but got no answer.

After working the plots for several hours it became clear that the shortest and the most economical alternatives were equivalent in cost. That they also took the ship quite close to the Rift and the area where they found me was a pleasant coincidence. Perhaps, I hoped, Uropygi was the place where he would find a hint of home.

During my free time I tried to learn as much as possible about the Rift, but what I discovered left me more puzzled than informed. According to what I could gather, the Rift was a long and narrow volume of discontinuity pointed directly at one arm of the galaxy in one direction and at the Andromeda galaxy in the other. When it had first been detected it was little more than a curiosity—a visual disturbance that distorted the background stars. Later exploration discovered that the volumes around the Rift were a veritable Sargasso, scattered with wrecks of ancient twisted and torn ships.

How such an accumulation of ships came to be became obvious when one of the probes sent into the Rift disappeared, only to emerge half a light year away as a crumpled mass of torn metal. No one ventured near after that.

There were many theories: was it a vortex of strange matter, an extended superstring, or perhaps a holdover from the origins of the universe when forces beyond understanding reigned supreme? Measurements of every conceivable kind had been attempted, all of which increased the confusion, for few of the resulting measurements were stable. At times the magnetic field strength measured hundreds of thousands of Gauss and at other times there was none. Electrical fields wove out and about, ever changing, waxing and waning in chaotic rhythms. Light was bent as if there were a core of super gravity at the Rift's center, an elongated black hole whose event threshold impossibly formed the Rift's boundary.

There seemed to be no answer despite centuries of research by dozens of races and so, in time, interest had waned. As far as I could learn, only scavengers and a few dedicated researchers now patrolled the vicinity, hoping to salvage what they could or discover an elusive clue as to the Rift's origins or destiny.

After checking my seven space calculations several times I took the alternatives to Jaycea and recommended the course I had originally plotted. "Looks too close to the Rift," she said absently and placed the plots to one side. "I'll check the arrival dates on these later, after Halo's finished tallying the manifest," she said. "Right now I want to know more about that *Tollembol* ship that rescued you."

I thought the change of subject surprising but shrugged. "What more is there to tell? They found my damaged ship and resurrected me." I did not want to pursue this discussion further since I'd already told her all that I recalled.

Jaycea cocked her head. "Bullshit. You're holding something back. You never said anything about before about a damaged ship."

"That's because I don't remember anything about what happened. All I was told was that something pretty well smashed my ship. The captain of *Tollembol* said we must have hit the Rift."

"Nobody could have survived that," Jaycea said and then

slapped her forehead. "Your name—Pasticher. Damn, should have known. Reconstruct, aren't you?"

"How did you know?" I asked with alarm. "What did I say that gave me away?"

"Nobody survives the freaking Rift. Lucky they found you quickly. How much reconstruction? Twenty, thirty percent?"

"One hundred," I replied and was satisfied by her look of amazement. "D'vore is a very good medician." I felt relieved to finally talk to someone about my awakening and the strange events that followed and found that I couldn't stop until I'd recounted how D'vore had assembled me from what viable remains they found and how the D'vore had gathered the residual memories from the brains of the crew and integrated them so imperfectly.

Jaycea listened calmly. "I don't understand," she said when I finished, "why *Tollembol* would reconstruct you. Can't see the profit of it."

"The captain kept asking me how my ship, a very small ship, came to be so far from any known human location. Perhaps he hoped that by reconstructing me with those stolen memories I could give him a clue as to my origins."

"Finding new human worlds isn't exactly a priority. Lots of the early human colonies were lost. They encounter a few every century or so. No, there has to be another reason they had you reconstructed. Perhaps D'vore knows," I suggested.

To be honest, the reason for the captain's intense curiosity had never occurred before she mentioned it. That was certainly a sign of how unstable my mind had been.

Jaycea grunted. "All right then, let's get D'vore up here and see what it can tell us about you. Maybe he knows the reasons."

D'vore protested that he was unable to explain the captain's reasons either. "I was instructed to reconstruct a human. That was my job. It was not my place as a ship's medician to ask the reasons."

"Sound suspicious," Jaycea said sarcastically, "Clone ships usually have their own kind as medicians. What was that ship doing? Clones are only used on long haul transports."

"I think it was a scientific expedition," D'vore opined and shrugged. "Perhaps they were collecting data on the Rift."

"Nothing they could collect that hadn't been done a thousand ways," Jaycea exclaimed. "Besides, a bunch of Heinies couldn't do decent science if they tried."

"Nevertheless, that is what I assumed," D'vore answered. "As I said, *Tollembol* obtained me for my surgical skills. I had little interaction with head or crew. Much the same as now," he added with a measure of bitterness.

Jaycea ignored the barb and dismissed him. I had something else to say. "There is one more thing about the crew of *Tollembol*," and quickly described my grisly discovery of the crews' remains and the burnt hole in the captain's head. "I think they were murdered," I concluded.

Jaycea was visibly shaken. "Penchon are bloody bastards," she replied, "but careful executions aren't their way. More likely they'd butcher the crew for parts. Must have been saving the head for something. Evidence perhaps."

"Evidence? Of what?" I could not follow her thinking.

"Murder. Evidence that someone on that ship killed him."

"But if they were all clones than who would ..." her implication was clear. "No, it can't be."

"Why not?" she replied. "Wouldn't surprise me that D'vore killed the crew and then abandoned the ship with you. You said you didn't know what was happening just before you escaped. Sounded like an impact, but that's unlikely, Case. I'd say some random mischance is improbable. There's more to this than what you've told me. I can feel it."

I did not believe her conclusions. "But D'vore sacrificed himself to buy me passage to a human station. That he's a murderer is completely at odds with everything I know about him. For God's sake, Jaycea, they abused him like he was a piece of equipment."

"Maybe that was to immobilize him so they could deliver him to the Carhera?"

That was the second time I had heard the term. "Carhera?"

Jaycea looked up. "They run things, like this station. Keep a tight rein on we humans, they do and make sure we don't get too damn close to their advanced technology. Bad situation if they're involved."

"But they didn't deliver him," I protested, thinking that reason too easy.

"Maybe that's because you stole him?" Jaycea nodded. "But the point that they didn't leaves my theory in doubt, I'll admit. Just the same, you need to watch out!" She appeared to be deep in thought. "More going on here than I understand," she finally said. "I don't understand the why of D'vore's involvement, but he's got to see some profit from helping you."

I didn't know if I agreed, but then, I was having trouble putting all of the pieces together myself.

As I huddled in the galley waiting for my dinner, Jonn, the ship's communicator, mentioned that Jaycea had decided about the Uropygi route. He'd had little as possible to do with me except when work forced us together, but that was more contact than he'd had with the rest of the crew. I decided to take advantage of the opportunity to talk to someone new and asked Jonn to explain the system of interstellar obligations, figuring that to be a neutral but informative subject.

As soon as Jonn began to use terms like "peer handled bipolarities" or "leveraged dichotomies" I lost the thread of the explanation. Nor could I attach any meaning to such adjectives as degil, runorton, or supercalic when applied to nouns such as head, extension, or reposit. I let Jonn continue as I realized that I simply lacked the cultural background and knowledge necessary to understand even the simplest explanations.

Nevertheless, I continued to listen intently, hoping to glean some nugget from the dross of words. Jonn finally ran down from a subject he clearly cared deeply about.

"I have to see Jaycea about the route selections," I said as I departed. "By the way, thanks for taking time to explain the degilizing of head bipolarities."

That sent Jonn into a paroxysm of outrageous laughter. His guffaws followed me along the hall. Apparently I hadn't even understood the easy parts.

As I turned the corner to reach Jaycea's cabin I collided with

Halo. "I'm so sorry," I blurted instantly. "I wasn't watching where I was going and …"

Halo stepped back, brushed her gown to smooth the folds into perfect alignment. "Of course you weren't." There was no hint of amusement in her voice, no criticism either. It was a simple, dispassionate statement of fact.

I looked around and saw no one else. "Are you as lonely as I?" I asked hastily. "You must be, among these chill Eglaners."

Halo blinked. "Excuse me. I must return to my cabin."

"Just a moment," I said and placed a cautionary hand on her arm, hoping to delay her departure. "Don't I deserve an answer?"

Halo moved away. "I do not appreciate your intentions, navigator."

Were my motives so transparent? "But surely you must be lonely among this chill crowd."

"Lonely? Oh, you have no idea of what loneliness is." With that she hastened away while I stood gape-mouthed, wondering what her remark might have meant.

Jaycea looked up as if I'd startled her. But it was my turn to be surprised when I spotted Halo's blue brooch with the silver filigree at Jaycea's breast. How had it come into her hands and what did that imply about her relationship to Halo? That one such as the goddess would give a gift like this to the gruff master was beyond imagining.

"Here," she said without preamble and tossed a data thimble at him. "We'll use the third option."

That choice was completely unexpected. I had checked the other routes against the manifest to measure the degree of profit each would provide. Jaycea stood to make a substantial bonus for early arrival, and, using the route I had recommended, use the minimum of fuel, further improving the ship's profitability. Her refusal to take the most logical route defied belief. "There must be some mistake," I protested. "The second option's better."

"No mistake. Passing close to the Rift's not a good idea. D'vore suggested we go the longer way. Safer and the date's better."

I couldn't imagine what criteria made a later date better, but was certain that had nothing to do with profits. "Safer perhaps, but the danger of the best route is slight," I said with some heat. "It's well clear of the edge of the Rift."

"Talk to D'vore," Jaycea replied with a wave of dismissal. "He'll give you reasons."

"How could you recommend such a route?" I demanded as I forced my way into D'vore's compartment. I was seething. "Why did you talk Jaycea out of the best route we could follow? Isn't that why we are on this ship; to get ourselves to Oroenoe as fast as possible?"

"You are angry," D'vore said calmly. "One cannot think clearly when angry. But to your question: I did not advise the Master, but she did question me about what I knew. The route you recommended would have put us in grave danger."

"Danger? I know that the Rift presents few dangers so long as you avoid contact," I shot back.

D'vore sighed. It was such a human action that I almost forgot just how alien he was. "What you do not know is that the entire volume is under Penchon control," he explained. "That is dangerous for humans in general, but of particular danger to us: You have stolen from the Penchon. As far as they are concerned, I am an escaped obligation slave. They would risk much to restore their honor, therefore venturing near the Rift would be personally dangerous, Case—that is why Jaycea has chosen the path of lesser profitability."

What he said made little sense. What did Jaycea care about their safety? No, what D'vore said about personal danger made no sense at all.

His explanation did not satisfy me, convincing as he tried to make it sound. Jaycea's warning about D'vore's possible motives came back and I found my trust of D'vore diminishing. I was certain that the alien had motives beyond helping and vowed to discover what game he was really playing.

And why.

A few days before the scheduled departure from Hammasod, D'vore left the ship, thus presenting me with an opportunity to examine his compartment, which, I hoped would contain some clue as to the alien's objectives. I did not know how I would recognize such a clue, how it might manifest itself, or whether such a clue might exist at all. Regardless of possible outcomes I had to take advantage of the opportunity, if only to satisfy my curiosity.

D'vore's compartment was clean, with everything carefully secured. I lowered the desk and examined the locker. I peered into each nook and cranny, trying to find something, anything that might tell me something, but all I found was a worn cloak that had not yet fed back to the artificer, a small black brush, some bottles of an odorless, oily substance, and a set of tiny surgical instruments.

"What are you looking for?" D'vore asked suddenly. I stopped, my hand halfway back to the place where I had removed the bottle of oil. I wondered why I hadn't heard the clicking of boots upon the deck that would have given me a few seconds warning.

"I was curious at what you might have," I replied. "I was curious about what a Centul might think interesting."

D'vore closed the hatch. "You are no accomplished liar. You have a far deeper interest than mere curiosity."

"I want to know what you know about my ship. Why you don't want the ship near the Rift." Confronting D'vore directly might be the best approach since I had, after all, been caught rifling the place.

"I have not lied to you, Case . There is a Penchon presence near the Rift that is extremely dangerous for humans. Believe me, I have nothing but your safety in mind." He loosened the bindings of his cloak. "I know that asking you to trust me in this is strains your credibility."

"It does," I replied honestly, wondering where this conversation was now going.

D'vore was holding the folds of his cloak closed. "Not telling Jaycea of the canister showed me that you are worthy of trust. Now I show you this to demonstrate my own trust in you." With that he threw wide the cloak.

Earlier, when we had been in the Pittuls' care, I'd glimpsed the dark blue, segmented body from which D'vore's organic limbs and silver head had been severed and a small array of appliances. Since that time D'vore had acquired even more, all carefully folded close to his trunk. The additional eyes had hardly changed his appearance, compared to what had happened beneath the cloak.

A wide ring encircled his waist and gave him the increased girth I'd noticed earlier. Above the torus, and just below the joins where his human arms were attached to his blue trunk, were folded a pair of tiny limbs with pincers much like a crab's.

"Acquisition feels like the proper way to grow. I think am regaining portions of what I once might have been," he said. "Like you I am impelled by some drive I do not fully understand. I only have a vague memory of what I once was, before I was brought back to life. Since then, I feel the need to enhance myself, to become more complete, to develop a fuller understanding of what I might become."

This was more frankness than expected and made me uncomfortably aware of my own situation. It also made me less confident that D'vore was the knowledgeable source I had supposed.

"What is the purpose of this?" I pointed at the torus. "What does this do for you?"

D'vore shrugged, a movement that made the tiny arms twitch. The claws clicked open and closed with the sound of sharp shears. "The arms are obviously more useful in certain situations than these crude organic and mechanical substitutes." He flexed his human and metal hands to demonstrate. "I'm afraid an explanation of the purpose of these augments would not make sense to you, however, given your current understanding."

I'd had enough trouble understanding Jonn's economic explanation and didn't care to strain my limited understanding against something so completely alien. "I assume, as before, you wish me to remain quiet about these."

"Yes. As I said, I showed you this as a matter of trust. Sadly, I am afraid that knowledge of these changes would only cause Syl and the others to mistrust me even more than they already do."

"How did you come by these, D'vore? Did it have anything to do with the canister?"

"I delivered the canister as promised, thus removing that obligation. However, I obtained these augments by exercising certain skills that local authorities might find distasteful." I wondered about that, but thought it best not to ask.

"We have protected and supported one another since the ship's destruction and I wish to continue to do so," D'vore continued. "For that reason I have placed my trust in you, Case. Trust that I believe I have earned."

That sounded fair enough, given what we had been through. We had saved one another, although the margin between saving and stealing was thin. Even so, I struggled, divided between supporting my own quest with D'vore's help and my continuing doubts about the D'vore's motives.

In the end I decided that my best course was to continue to heed D'vore's council, but henceforward I would trust only those things I could verify.

The next morning, I was summoned forward. Jaycea was clearly angry. Very angry. "Didn't you understand my instructions, freak? Didn't I explain that you were to keep away from the rest of the crew, that you were to mind your own damn business? Didn't you hear me explain those simple rules to you in language even you could understand?" With each question her voice rose in volume and pitch until, she practically screeched the final rhetorical; "Didn't you say that you agreed?"

"I assume this is about Halo," I replied calmly, assuming that Halo had reported my crude advances. "I do not consider that a violation of your explicit orders—she is no Eglaner. Surely she must be as lonely as I in this unfriendly ship." My tone left no doubt of what I thought of the Eglaner bigotry.

"From now on that proscription means every damn soul on this ship and especially Halo. No contact, no words, no notes— nothing! Is that crystal clear?"

"As you wish, Master Jaycea," I bit out. A master's word is law between the stars, I reflected as I left.

"Not so much as a nod," she said to my back.

I reflected on the ennui of an interstellar journey when one cannot converse with another human? I ate. I slept. I spoke only with D'vore, but only of mundane matters. With the crew there was only work-related converse, for most kept to their own, protective of their privacy, wary of the outlander and his alien companion, no doubt.

In the privacy of my tiny cabin I had fantasies of Halo along with the now familiar dreams of a past that was growing more distant and hazy by the day. I did not know whether to be happy or not. On the one hand it was a relief not to try to force understanding on the confusing and often conflicting fragmentary dreams that never quite came into focus. On the other hand, not fretting over those same troubling images might represent a slow severing of my connection to something real, to loves lost, to a world unknown, to my precious and receding Earth. Where was a middle ground I could live with?

Some days I reversed the orders of my daily life. I slept. I ate. Such is the pulse of life on an interstellar freighter. One day becomes indistinguishable from the previous.

Or the next.

Upon arrival everything seems to happen at once, It is all too quick, too soon, and too abrupt to absorb. As the universe swims into reality the comms are alive with curses and directions, beacons appear, vectors require adjustment, stars crowd in unfamiliar patterns, and the screams of the engines become screamingly noticeable.

Thys Nor was fortunate. They'd chosen a good course to Uropygi. The ship did not hit this star, missed the planets, and, so far, hadn't run into another ship.

Some days the navigator is lucky.

Exotically named Uropygi turned out to be another damp and smelly station, only fractions of a degree cooler than the interior of the ship and still too chill for me, who was clad in many layers of clothing in an effort to keep warm. I could see my breath in the crisp air.

"Feels good to get back to comfortable climate again, eh Case?" Jaycea exclaimed as we emerged onto the dock. She wore a sleeveless shirt that exposed both arms to the frigid air.

"Simply bracing," I replied and imagined Jaycea's home world to have been some barren, ice-frozen wilderness where the temperature never, if ever, rose above freezing.

Using the knowledge of station layouts I'd gained earlier, I easily found the market in the same relative location as on the other station. It was slightly warmer in the market area so I was able to shed a few layers as I took in the sights, scents, and sounds.

More than those, I found the variety of human forms fascinating, but several stared at me, as if I were some rare curiosity. I doubted that I could be as interesting as the various mechs congregated near a hardware vendor, the exceedingly tall and thin or short and bandy-legged, the occasional hulking giant and other types of human forms among the crowd of even more outrageous aliens. No, all colorations, configurations, and body types appeared far more fascinating than my rather ordinary body.

I was partaking of a sweet treat offered by a woman with webbed fingers when I noticed Halo making her way through the crowd. My heart caught as she walked toward me, certain that she'd noticed me. She was so lovely.

My astonishment was confounded when three individuals of equal beauty and grace appeared behind Halo. The three were nearly identical in appearance, although the female's face, like Halo's, was slightly more narrow and her eyes somewhat larger than those of the men. All three moved with a fluid grace that was half dance, half floating. All eyes turned to them as they passed.

The effect of seeing so much beauty was nearly overwhelming. These were, I realized as I recovered from my surprise, Halo's people–the supposedly perfected humans!

Halo must have noticed the crowd's attention and turned. One of the handsome men noticed and began to smile. Then, as he drew closer, the incipient smile turned to one of distaste and he stumbled to gracelessness.

I realized that, in that single glance, the man had judged Halo appearance as repulsive. Although I could not understand why this was so, I resented it. How dare he judge her! How dare he think that she was unworthy!

It was as if scales had fallen from my eyes. I looked closer and saw that the proportions of his face were subtly wrong; his cheekbones were too high and his eyes too wide-spaced and large. His nose was a sliver bisecting his face and punctuating a narrow slit of a mouth. When taken a single feature at a time each feature was far too refined, too abstract to be human.

All of this flashed across my consciousness in an instant before my attention was drawn back to the continuing tableau of the marketplace encounter.

The group's woman had also noticed Halo but instead of expressing distaste her face softened to pity. "Poor thing," she murmured and hastened to catch up to her rapidly departing companions as Halo drew the hem of her cloak across her face and ran in the opposite direction. I thought I'd seen a glint of tear. Certainly the way she carried herself denoted utter shame and rejection.

With that, the strange encounter was over. I turned to the vendor and was amazed to see her staring at the trio's receding figures. "So graceful," she murmured. I snorted in derision. How could she not see them for what they were?

Somewhere in the back of my mind an idea formed that I might purchase a bit of jewelry to replace that brooch Halo had given to Jaycea. II hoped the present would salve the pain of rejection and hoped it would also be interpreted as an offering of my affection, a sign that I wished their relationship to go further.

Yes, maybe such a gift would gain me a quiet visit, absent of Jaycea or crew. Fantasies of where that might lead filled my head to such an extent that I lost track of where I was walking and stumbled into a hairy mountain.

"*Da spuk wista?*" the mountain boomed. I realized it was a beribboned giant, like the one I'd met at Hammasod. I recalled the protocol and bowed. "Excuse me," I said, doubting the giant would understand me.

The giant bowed in response, grunted and turned back to his companions. I bowed to them as well, a slight bend at waist that they acknowledged. The assortment of bows twisted into the hair of one of them looked so familiar that I was certain it was the one we'd met. "Spiknuck?" I cried.

Spiknuck started and stared. *"Du visha parad?"* he demanded. *"Du visha?"*

"D'vore," I said, gesturing with my hands to indicate the dimensions of my companion, hoping that would jog Spiknuck's memory but the wild gestures only produced more confusion. The giants rumbled among themselves for a few moments and then one of them came forward.

"Uh, ve you to know how?" he said in a thick accent that was barely understandable.

"We met before, at Hammasod station," I stammered. "Don't you remember? You blessed me." I patted the top of his head to make the meaning clear.

"Not have gone Hammasod yet," the giant cried. His alarm was obvious as he turned to the others. *"Mukch devon na vish Hammasod parad! Clush! Clush!"*

With those words all three raced away. Spiknuck glanced back over his shoulder with panic writ large in his face. Clearly something had been said that alarmed them enough to send them scurrying away, but for the life of me, I could not figure out what it might be.

How could Spiknuck deny having met? There was seeing no sense in it. Nor could I understand why the giants refused to acknowledge that they had been to Hammasod. It was one more mystery among far too many that he needed to add to his every growing collection of questions.

When I returned to the ship I mentioned the strange behavior of the giants and their obvious panic to Jaycea. "Unfortunate," she replied absently as she pored over the plots to Oroenoe. "Time shifts aren't usually that noticeable."

"Time shifts? Nobody mentioned the shifting of time. I don't understand."

Jaycea let out a sigh. No doubt my continual expressions of ignorance were wearing on her. "Size of shift depends on vector. We get ahead or behind each trip." She shrugged as if the matter were inconsequential. "Doesn't matter anyway, simultaneity's not measurable over interstellar distances. In the long term it all evens out."

I was appalled that she could speak so casually about jumping backwards and forwards in time, and even more that she could discount the implications. "Do you know this for a fact?" I asked, hoping that there might be some mistake in his understanding of what she had said. "I mean, how can you tell?"

"WOFAT," she said, and then, noticing the puzzled look on my face, continued. "It's the Write Once for All Time repository. Ships carry copies from station to station. Sometimes the record we bring is ahead, sometimes behind. It's all adjusted and corrected so we hardly ever notice."

"The register," I suddenly understood the seemingly senseless adjustments in orbits and plots the Herclue had insisted I make. Of course, the routes had been adjusted for the time shifts. How could I have not noticed that?

"That's the reason we keep track of our own time," Jaycea explained. "Helps when you change ships and jump on a new set of vectors."

I recalled the strange manner in which the current date was always expressed; personal and ship time. No wonder; in this mad environment absolute time, the steady progression of days, weeks, months, years only had meaning relative to the individual and the ship, not some external standard.

In a flash I realized that I had not been keeping track and, consequently, did not how much time had passed since my rescue. Neither did I have information about any ship save *Thys Nor*, which was continually compensating as she moved about.

Terror rose in my breast as the implications of the seven-space time vector were clarified. If they were moving ahead in time, following a universal time arrow, days; months, possibly years ahead as she declared, then what hope had I of ever returning to my home, to the people held in memory? The places recalled might have vanished in the mists of time.

The more I learned of the malleability of time frames the more likely it seemed that I would become a man lost in time as well as space.

In the long days between the stars I'd occasionally and surreptitiously conversed with Vladda, the one crewman who seemed to tolerate me, so as not to raise Jaycea's ire. In one of these conversations Vladda revealed that he was also afflicted with the desire for home.

"There's a beauty to the long days of winter," Vladda said, speaking of his own home. "Cool crisp breezes across the snow fields, the scent of blood from the hunters, the crying of birds as they rise from their nighttime roosts, the clear, clean skies above. Gods; how I miss it.

"But the summer heat, when the ice breaks and the snow melts, is unbearable. When I was a child my family would always head south to the pole when the seasons changed. Pole was where the climate was more hospitable. I would race my sled across the ice fields from dawn to dusk, never concerned of danger or harm. I was free from care, free from responsibility. Ah, those were the good times." He subsided into silence.

"So how did you come to be on this ship?" I asked.

Vladda shrugged. "I was the second son, the one who would not pick up the holdings so I had to leave my homestead. I decided to travel and crewed on a ship. That was long ago, Case . I have now been traveling for over two hundred thousand watches by my personal clock."

His answer was astounding. If he was to be believed then Vladda was easily ninety years old, perhaps more, although he appeared a person settled into his early middle years. Surely there must be some misinterpretation.

"The years must be hard for all of you," I said. "I am sure everyone aboard yearns to return home some day."

Vladda shook his head. "Hardly. The ship and stations are home to many. Syl and Brews were both raised among the spaceborne. They are already home among the stars."

"What about Halo and Jaycea?"

"Jaycea's like me. *Thys Nor's* her adopted home, her life. Halo, well, she's got no choice." This last was said with deep sadness, as if he were speaking from personal experience. "I'm sure she aches for home as much as I."

"But she didn't act as if she wished to be with her people

when she saw a few of them back on the station." I described the encounter in the marketplace and the chilling effect that it appeared to have on Halo.

"Bastards!" Vladda spit. "Yes, they would act like that. I hate them."

"What did she do to earn their enmity?"

Vladda stared. "She didn't earn it, she was born with it. She's a defective, a misfit, and an ugly duckling born among swans. That's probably why they sneered at her, as if she were a hunk of shit."

This was unbelievable. Halo was perfect in all respects. Defective? Surely Vladda was speaking out of pique for the loveliness that he could never possess.

"I imagine it's hard for you to believe, but it's true," Vladda continued. "The Perfs weed out defectives as ruthlessly as our brute ancestors probably did cripples or those with retarded mental abilities." He reddened, "No offense."

"None taken," I said automatically.

"It would have been better had Halo's deformities been apparent from the first, but I heard they weren't noticeable until puberty, an age when even the Perfs hesitate at murder."

"Deformity," I repeated. Had she some hidden flaw beneath those robes, or was she incapacitated in some subtle manner not apparent to his casual observation? If so, then why had this supposed deformity led to banishment, disdain, and estrangement from her home, her people? "But even so, she is an astoundingly beautiful woman."

Vladda snorted. "What if you were raised among animals, Case? Wouldn't you adopt their ideas, their standards, and their perceptions? When those animals forced you to live among people wouldn't they look strange with their features, their movements, even their bodies so different from the standards you'd known?"

"Yes, I understand the analogy, but it isn't reasonable that she wouldn't accept normal human standards of beauty."

"The problem is, Case, that isn't her situation. It's the other way around. You see, she was raised among Perfs and then forced away to live with us, the ugly, brutish animals that must disgust and repel her sensibilities.

"We found her on an out station where she'd been abandoned as an ugly, wretched, disgusting creature. She'd been trying to commit suicide when Jaycea found her, brought her back to health, healed the damage, and gave Halo an opportunity to travel to the stars. *Thys Nor* became a refuge, and she grants Jaycea friendship and service in return."

"Might I ask what this deformity might have been?" Maybe the deformity that so plagued Halo had been corrected by whatever medical miracles Jaycea performed.

"Her nose," Vladda said. "It's too long. Her irises are too violet. Her face is too narrow and, if you did not notice, her lips are far too full."

"You must be joking. Those are just minor variations. They couldn't possibly be considered deformities."

"How far would you press those differences? Would Jaycea be as attractive if she had D'vore's metal arm? Would you see Halo as so lovely if she had a face like Brews or mine?" He grinned. "Don't bother answering with some lie. Your expression tells me your answer. The difference between your reaction and the Perfs is a matter of degree. It's just a human trait for physical conformity taken to extremes."

Chagrined, I returned to my compartment to ponder the implications of what I'd learned. In Vladda's words were truths I did not like, that I wished I could deny, but had to accept. One thing was startlingly clear; just, as I would not consort with an animal, so Halo would never lie with me. Like everyone else, Halo carried her ingrained prejudices, and that meant that she would never, not ever, consider me as other than a beast.

I was having problems. I simply could not understand how to program the cleaning machine to avoid devouring the scraps on which I recorded my most puzzling fragments of memory.

When I complained about this, Jaycea stroked the machine with a few deft passes of her thick fingers. "You're a strange one, Case. Able to navigate between the stars but can't do a task any three-year old could perform blindfolded."

I reminded her of my faulty memory and how I had still not

recovered fully from the accident. "I admit that it is puzzling,' I answered. "I can't remember these normal, everyday things but easily recall complex scenes. For reasons I cannot understand I can't recall ever using these machines."

"Maybe you came from some place cut off from modern civilization. Even so, I can't understand how your people were able to build a ship that could reach the Rift and still be unknown."

"D'vore suggested that I might have come from an unknown world near or even inside the Rift."

Jaycea made a rude noise. "Then D'vore doesn't know much about deep space mapping. There's been a pretty thorough sweep of the entire anomaly. Hard to believe anyone's missed something as big as a system." She smiled. "Look, there isn't a star within a thousand light years from the Rift that hasn't been catalogued and explored extensively. Everybody's already found every place nearby where they could study the Rift and there isn't a one that has people looking like you."

Seeing my crestfallen face she continued after a moment's thought. "Maybe you came through a wormhole; a tiny wormhole that squeezed your ship into a mess of twisted metal. Or maybe you're from a parallel universe where humans evolved differently. Or maybe," she added, in a soft voice, "you were built by a Penchon organ farm to puzzle whoever sent *Tollembol* out there." Her smile might have indicated that she was joking. At least I hoped so.

The remark about being a construct came too close to possibility to be comfortable and I discounted her wilder explanations: The mathematics of seven-space proved that wormholes could not exist and that accessible parallel universes were fantasies. "But what other explanation could there be for me not to know about all these other worlds, about aliens, star travel, or a thousand and one things that everyone seems to take for granted? I must have come from some backwater, someplace modern civilization never reached."

"I doubt that," Jaycea answered. "War touched every human planet. Those who wouldn't get involved were taken over. Most humans captured ended up as parts for the Penchon organ factories, I hear, and those that weren't killed outright probably wished they had. It was a brutal war.. Damn near wiped out both humans and Penchon. If it hadn't been for the Carhera intervention, there's no telling how it would have ended."

"War? Intervention?"

"Yes." Jaycea explained how the huge ships of the five hundred senior races had neutralized the Penchon and human forces and then established a sphere of influence in which humans and Penchon were constantly monitored. Even a slight indication of bellicose activity was quickly and decisively squelched. "But some day those damned Carhera will be gone," Jaycea finished. "Then we'll wipe those filthy Penchon out once and for all."

I was stunned into silence by the mention of five hundred senior races and realized how provincial my viewpoint had been in thinking there were only sixteen, as if that number were less astounding. I had seen alien worlds mentioned in the encyclopedia but nearly that many. Apparently it only listed those of concern to the human ships and those where stations had been established.

Her words opened a great chasm. This galactic civilization was more than human, D'vore, and Penchon, more than the few pitiful races and strange technologies I had so far encountered. It made me feel more lost than ever.

Jaycea continued to complain about carrying us to Vizzon, but with the apparent lack of qualified replacements for our berths, there seemed no alternative for her. "It's almost as if I was being blackballed," she groused. I wondered how much truth there might be in those words.

Since the incident with Syl, D'vore had become so withdrawn that it took considerable prompting to engage him in conversation and even then his comments were short and curt. Still I persisted. D'vore was still my guide and perhaps the only one who could help me uncover the mystery of my origins. Also, he probably had the chronology needed to fix them in time and space.

Throughout the next leg of our journey I tried to gain an understanding of how much time had passed since my awakening. The chronology was strange, relating not at all to the time divisions by which I recalled counting my life. Nevertheless I managed to assemble a rough equivalency between time frames. By my personal reckoning, about six months of personal time had passed since the awakening on *Tollembol*. Before that, and according to D'vore and the captain, there had been about two years during which I'd been reconstructed. That meant it had been at least two and a half years since the accident. It was close enough to let me keep track from that point onward.

Thys Nor moved on. More sleeping and eating, interspersed with eating and sleeping, occupied the long hours. Time passes but slowly between the stars.

The arrival at Vizzon was nothing out of the ordinary. There were the normal delays in berthing, the endless prattle of bureaucratic language regarding origins and destinations, routings and cargoes, the negotiations with lighters and tugs, the cursing of ships on conflicting paths, the jostling and juggling of mating their small ship to the human portion of the moon-sized station.

The scent of ammonia hit my nostrils the instant I stepped onto Vizzon's dock. There were Penchon all about, screeching a discordant roar that made my ears ring and head ache. For a moment I was afraid that some mistake had put us into an inhuman sector but then noticed, in the distance, human forms and was reassured. The ship was in its proper place.

The reason for the surfeit of Penchon was that *Thys Nor* was berthed directly between two Penchon ships. The disparity in sizes was overwhelming. Jaycea's ship, a mere toy in comparison, had been squeezed into a convenient gap created by the Penchon ships' curved hulls. "The station must be crowded if control was forced to do that sort of packing," she remarked.

I did not like the intense way a nearby Penchon glared, or the suspicious manner in which they appeared to be watching my every move.

"It is your imagination," D'vore replied when he aired his suspicions. "I assure you that we are a long way from the *Qalyub Gudlag*, a very long way. There is no way these Penchon could know of your theft."

Perhaps he was right. The Penchons' perceived suspicion might simply be the product of an overactive imagination, or guilt. I tried to ignore the staring aliens as I helped clear the last of the red tape that would allow Sylvestra to begin cargo operations. The final piece of nonsense was a declaration that no contraband was on board, a certificate that he signed as Jaycea negotiated regarding delivery of the Uropygi station's WOFAT data.

"Will you grab this data so we can clear," Jaycea pleaded to control. "I've got priority cargo to unload!"

There was a bored response from control. "No need to off-load the WOFAT, Master. We already received a copy with that timestamp." That revelation startled Jaycea. The probability of another ship departing Uropygi at the same time as *Thys Nor* and arriving at this station was improbably small.

"I thought we had picked up all of the Uropygi cargo," Jaycea muttered. "What ship?"

Control answered with an untranslatable screech that set my nerves on edge. There was no mistaking it—it could only be a Penchon name, a Penchon name that I recognized, with a sinking feeling in my stomach, immediately.

I glanced at the nearest Penchon hatch, hoping to see the distinct markings, but was disappointed. I tilted my head toward the Penchon to be certain that Jaycea would catch my meaning. "One of these might be the same Penchon ship that was docked at Uropygi and," I added with emphasis, "at Hammasod!"

Jaycea raised an eyebrow. "Mighty uncommon to see the same ship at three stations in a row. So improbable that I have to assume they've been following us." She was silent for a long time, pondering the possibilities. At last she spoke. "*Thys Nor* was never involved with the Penchon butchers so it could only be you two they're after. What's so important that they'd do that?"

When I didn't respond she said, "More than simple curiosity, I'd say. Let's find out." So speaking, she thumbed into the station's WOFAT and began searching cargo manifests, deliveries, and acceptances. "Just as I thought, the filthy beasts haven't unloaded or accepted any cargo." She contacted Brews.

"Get D'vore up here. Maybe it's got the answers I need."

Brews reported that D'vore had left the ship moments after berthing. "Just sit tight until he gets back," Jaycea suggested and posted crew to guard Syl as she unloaded cargo under the watchful eyes of the Penchon.

Hours passed and D'vore did not return. Neither was Jaycea able to locate him anywhere within the station. Given the extent to which the communications net reached, she could only conclude that he must be aboard another ship and therefore, shielded.

"It's the Penchon," I said, voicing what Jaycea must have been thinking. "They've taken him back."

"Don't jump to conclusions. Damned difficult for Penchon to overcome something the size of D'vore. They're pretty weak, you know."

"But they might have strength in numbers," I countered and wondered if perhaps they might have used some other form of persuasion to get him back into their ship, such as an appeal to his strange sense of obligation. I shivered when I recalled how D'vore had initially protested against removal.

D'vore had been his guide since awakening and the only one in whom I had any sort of allegiance. "We have to get him out of there," I said at last, positive that the Penchon had taken him. "I can't let those creatures turn him back into a slave." Unsaid was that he was needed to aid in the search for Earth. "Besides, I have a moral obligation to aid the person who gave me life."

"There's no proof he's aboard one of their ships," Jaycea answered. "Besides, too dangerous to confront the Penchon directly. We first have to find out what's going on."

"He's my friend and I have to find him," I replied bravely. "It is an obligation."

Apparently that convinced Jaycea to relent. "All right. We'll check out places it could go if it didn't want to be found—the non-Penchon ships first. After that, we can figure how to deal with the butchers. Understand? Only then!"

"But what if their ship leaves? The opportunity of rescue would be lost. I might never see D'vore again." I implored Jaycea to reconsider, but she remained adamant.

"Can't understand why you are so concerned about an alien. More than I'd do, that's for sure."

She got assurance from departure control that none of the Penchon ships had filed to leave for at least a day. That gave us some time, but could they depend upon the Penchon to keep to their schedule?

As he followed Jaycea I discovered that the station was far more extensive than I'd realized. They crossed the corners of vast warehouses whose enormous capacities I could only guess at, so lost in mist were their farthest reaches. We wandered through life support areas and passed refineries and factories, where goods from a thousand systems were no doubt processed, as well as more living quarters, market places, and assorted industrial spaces than seemed possible in a space station. Since all these places were within reach of the net Jaycea knew that D'vore could not be in any of them or she would have known.

Jaycea eventually squeezed through a narrow section far off the main deck where we brushed frost-wrapped hulls dripping with condensation. "Sometime it's best to ask a local," she said. "I figured the tugs might know something."

The interior of the tug was a nether world of dim light and the noisome smells of closely packed humanity. A pervasive, low-pitched hum rattled his teeth and set my ears to itching. The atmosphere was thick and humid and I soon felt as if every exposed bit of skin had been coated with a thin layer of damp grease.

"Here we are," Jaycea said at last loosened the dogs of a small access hatch. When the hatch opened a golden light poured forth and threw Jaycea's shadow against the far wall. She immediately motioned for me to follow.

"Stop right there," a gruff voice announced before she had taken two steps. Beyond Jaycea was an individual who had roughly the same contours as Jaycea, but sported a thick black beard. But it was not the beard that drew attention; it was the small weapon he held with obvious competence.

"I'm Master Jaycea Lapin Horl," Jaycea said calmly.

"Eglaner—as you can see."

Blackbeard grinned as he lowered the barrel. I suspected that the gleam in his eye was not entirely without self-interest. "What about the freak—what's he doing here?"

"This is my navigator." Jaycea tilted her head to one side and smiled. It seemed ludicrous for someone of her girth to act so coquettish, but Blackbeard seemed to soften somewhat. "I brought him with me to explain things."

"What sort of things?" Blackbeard moved closer to Jaycea but his weapon remained fixed on me .

"Such as why are there so many stinking Penchon around all of the sudden, and why one of them seems to be following my ship and whether they've kidnapped my medician, that's why!"

Blackbeard snarled. "We should have wiped them out when we had the chance." He seemed to consider the situation for a moment and then reached a conclusion. "Come along. Let's see if the others know what's going on."

Several hours later and after much discussion with a small crowd of local Eglaners Blackbeard had gathered, we learned that the Penchon ships had all made stationfall within a few hours of each other, and closely scheduled each other's departures.

"Sounds like fleet maneuvers," a burly Eglaner with a barely healed facial wound that extended from eyebrow, across his nose, and concluded in a scarred pit at the corner of his mouth.

"The Carhera would never let damned Penchon gear up for another attack," Blackbeard insisted with paranoid certainty and glanced at me, "unless some of the stinking freaks are helping them. The freaks always seem to stick together wherever we Eglaners are concerned, you know." I was suddenly aware that I might not leave with a whole skin.

It was obvious that they knew as little as Jaycea and, with a few smiles and a hug that seemed to go on for too long, they departed for the station's dispatch office.

The human behind the counter was fair and pale and wore his official bright blue hat of soft fabric tilted rakishly to one side.

"I need to see the logs on who's visited the other decks,"

Jaycea said as soon as she had his attention. "One of my crew is missing."

"Probably drunk," the blue-hat replied with an ill-disguised sneer as he backed away. I realized that the two of s must smell fairly ripe after their trip to the tug. "And I think I can understand why."

"The station can't find him in the human areas so we think he might have visited another deck. Can I see the logs, now?"

"I can't imagine," blue-hat replied with another sniff, "why one of you Eglaners would care to leave the human areas. Did you check the other ships?"

Jaycea's patience was rapidly coming to an end. She leaned over the counter and put her face not a handbreadth from his. "He's my medician and if you don't show me the damned logs immediately I am going to stuff that ugly hat of yours up your pale asshole!"

The logs were produced, accompanied by much muttering about uncivilized barbarians and the lowering standards of the station. Jaycea ignored the droning complaints as she pored over the latest entries. There was a great deal of traffic between decks, much of it Penchon. This was not surprising; their tolerance for atmospheric differences meant they could park at the station environments above and below the level reserved for humans.

"No indication that he's left this deck," Jaycea concluded as she flipped through the final set of entries.

"That means that the Penchon did grab him," I blurted.

"What did you say?" blue-hat exclaimed as his ill-concealed expression of superiority was replaced by genuine concern. "Kidnapping is a serious violation. We could insist on a search if you have any evidence." He looked at Jaycea expectantly. Obviously humans hung together, despite their dislike for one another, where the Penchon were concerned.

"My navigator thinks that one of the Penchon ships kidnapped our medician. Personally I believe otherwise, but you can never tell where those organ-grubbing butchers are concerned."

"If you have no proof ..." Blue-hat looked disappointed that he could not storm the holds of a Penchon ship. "Well, if you do find any evidence that he might have been kidnapped inform me immediately." He flashed his id tag at Jaycea. "We're on call at all times, Master."

"I'll keep that in mind."

We exited the hub ninety degrees from *Thys Nor's* berth and then began walking the periphery on a route that would take them past a half dozen Penchon ships.

I thought I was becoming rather jaded at the fantastic variety of human genotypes they encountered. Only a few turned my head, usually one of the outrageously beautiful perfected ones who moved like living jewels among their grubby relatives. Although I hated their attitude toward the rest of humanity I could not resist the impulse to find them unbearably attractive.

Were these manifold human forms separate species or merely adaptations over a wider range of environments? If the former, then what did that bode for the race's future—that humans should eventually become ever different, ever less able, ever less willing to interact until they became as alien to one another as human to Penchon? Even as I hoped that would not be true, the vast evidence of prejudice I'd experienced spoke otherwise. Somewhere in the back of my mind I was certain that the meaning of race had once had a different meaning.

The Penchon were not happy to have two humans walk among them and made their displeasure evident by screeching at ear-shattering volume. Were they mouthing obscenities or were they plotting on how best to carve them into component and useful parts? Perhaps the screeching aliens were taunting one another to make the first aggressive move or warning that such would not be a good idea in this open, public space.

A particularly vocal group was engaged in a cacophony of shrill cries as they gathered around something in their midst. I wondered what they might be hiding and tried to see what lay beyond that wall of leathery wings and hairy bodies.

A sudden shift of position, a momentary gap in the crowd revealed a small animal in the center of the circle, half the size of a Penchon and without the usual flaps of dark skin hanging from its limbs. Its coloring was slightly lighter and the hair looked more luxuriant. As I stepped closer to get a better view I wondered if it could be a child.

A dozen more Penchon flocked to the group to form a thick barrier around the small one. Their cries increased in intensity and frequency. Nearly every Penchon in sight was rushing to join the group.

The noise grew deafening as their screeches echoed across the deck. I wondered if they saw me as a threat and, if so, to why? I doubted that they could think I would attempt to harm their little one, not when they outnumbered me by so many. Prudently, and since the Penchon were acting so terribly protective, I began to back away. Every Penchons' beady eyes tracked me the way a herd would watch a predator. I looked around for help and noticed that Jaycea had disappeared.

A hand grasped my shoulder with a tight grip. The hand was far, far larger than any human hand had a right to be.

"What seems to be the problem here?" growled one of Spiknuck's giants who wore a blue hat identical to the one the pale agent's, although this one was considerably larger to fit on his enormous head.

"The Penchon seem to think I'm some sort of threat," I explained as I put the giant between me and the threatening Penchon. "All I want to do is get back to my ship." I gave the berth number and pointed.

The giant grunted and glanced at the Penchon who seemed even more agitated at the arrival of human reinforcements. "Move away," he ordered as he pushed me back.

The farther we retreated the less agitated the Penchon became until, uniting in some fashion, the entire crowd slowly moved sideways and into the hatch of their ship, not once taking their eyes away from the human pair.

As soon as the clutch of Penchon reached their ship the hatch slammed shut. A few seconds later, the other hatches closed as well. Clearly the Penchon were taking no chances that a human might approach.

Did those closing hatches meant that Jaycea was trapped inside? With the Penchon already so deeply upset she could be in grave danger. For all I knew they might kill her on sight. "I think there are two crew members trapped inside that ship," I said. "We've got to get them out of there!"

"The Penchon never let humans on their ships," the giant replied with absolute certainty.

"That's not true. I was a passenger on one of them."

"I find that hard to believe. Never heard of any human being aboard as anything other than spare parts." He cocked his head to one side. "Why were you so anxious to get at that Penchon female anyway? Where's your ID?" The giant's attitude had suddenly changed from friendly helper to antagonistic and suspicious policeman. "Let me see what you have on you."

He ran his hands over me , a bruising examination that probed every possible hiding place, but all he found was a ship's ID. "I'll escort you to your ship" he said after he'd examined the tab.

"That's not necessary," I replied, but his tight grip on my shoulder indicated that he was stating a fact, not offering assistance.

"What set them off?" the giant asked as they strolled along.

"I just wanted to get a closer look at a small animal they had with them," I explained and described it.

The giant swore in a guttural language for a moment and then said, more understandably; "You are damned lucky I come along. They would have killed you for sure if you'd pressed any closer."

"Killed me for just being curious? You can't be serious."

"Very protective of females are they. So few and precious after the war, after what we humans did."

That the Penchon females were so different in appearance was a surprise, but then, why not? Perhaps only humans had single body type and that had biased him.

The giant gave a terse description of the lengths humanity had taken to defeat the Penchon, including a graphic description of the genetic weapons humans had employed. "Figured that by keeping them from giving birth to females we could reduce their population quicker," the giant said. "We nearly succeeded before the Carhera interfered, damn them! Now any human looking cross-eyed at one of them Penchon females is seen as a threat."

The concept was difficult to grasp. Up to this point I had shared Jaycea's dislike of the Penchon, thinking them soulless, brutal ghouls who dealt in scavenged human parts. But it appeared that the cruelty was not so one-sided. That my fellow humans could contemplate the total eradication of another race was difficult to believe. These humans were not the type of people he recalled, not at all.

Or were they?

That gruesome knowledge altered his perception of the Penchon and made me wonder what other unrevealed facts were influencing my view of this universe?

As soon as I was released from the giant's grasp I looked for whatever crewmembers might be on board. Sylvestra and Jonn were the only two available. I quickly explained what had happened. "I think Jaycea and D'vore's in serious trouble. We have to do something before we lose them."

"I don't give a damn about that monster of yours," Sylvestra replied, "but Jaycea's another matter—she's family."

Syl and Jonn debated what actions they might take, wasting minutes while Jaycea and D'vore were being rendered into spare parts, their arms and legs winding up in the abattoir where he been examined. I could picture D'vore once again being placed in his carrying case for later resale.

Syl suggested several wild ideas, most of which involved heavy equipment, brute strength, and confrontation. That the Penchon were within their ship and outnumbered *Thys Nor's* crew did not seem to dissuade her from this straightforward approach.

Jonn could only suggest that they summon the authorities to intervene but I knew that approach wouldn't work. "I couldn't explain how Jaycea had entered the ship to the blue hat that brought me back," I said, and then had to explain how the giant has thought he'd "threatened" one of their females.

Worse yet, further inquiry into why they had D'vore might reveal to the authorities his initial theft and create an even more serious problem, one that might end up with both of them jailed, that is, if they had jails.

Rather than debate the issue further I walked away. "I can't argue any more. I've got to do something." As I passed through the hatch and onto the dock I glanced right and left, just in I the blue-hatted giant was waiting around to ensure that I stayed out of trouble, but there was no one in sight.

Nor were any Penchon. The hatches on their ship remained closed. That bothered me at first, but then I assumed that all the Penchon ships were in constant contact and probably protecting themselves against predatory human.

Out of the corner of my eye I saw D'vore strolling toward the ship as if nothing had happened. As he drew closer I realized that this was not the D'vore who'd left the ship the previous day but a Centul once again changed. Had it not been for his familiar voluminous cloak and the silver pate he might have been mistaken for a stranger.

The heavy legs that propelled D'vore from the ship had been replaced with smoothly articulated mechanisms of eight joints and cables and six or maybe ten legs—they all moved so quickly and independently that I couldn't count a consistent number. They made a soft clicking noise against the metal floor that echoed loudly in the now quiet dock.

He seemed to have gained bulk, but the reason for that aspect of his expansion was hidden by his cloak; a cloak that draped along a more curiously globular contour of his body. His head, the familiar silver globe, bristled with new augments and he realized that the former pair were barely noticeable among the array of tendrils, scoops, and feathery appliances. The only features that remained of his original configuration were the bare, muscular, and very human arm and the matching mechanical one.

"Where have you been?" I demanded, relieved that my companion had not fallen into harm's way and guilty that our suspicions of D'vore being in the Penchons' grasp had put Jaycea at risk.

"I attend my own business," D'vore replied obliquely. "Why are you so concerned?" How he so quickly ascertained my state of mind was remarkable. But that was a question for later, when I had time to ask questions.

I quickly explained the entire sequence of events leading up to Jaycea's being trapped within the Penchon ship. "We've got to do something. Their ship might depart at any time!"

"Are you certain she entered the ship?" he asked.

"She must have. She disappeared while the Penchon were focused on me." But was his assumption correct? "Where else would she have gone?"

"Forget your own feelings.. We must now address the issue of how to extricate Jaycea without causing further harm." D'vore paused. "I have notified the station guards. They will arrive shortly."

As if on signal a trio appeared, all wearing floppy blue hats but otherwise dressed in a wide assortment of apparel. The tallest was a man so thin that he looked emaciated, a stack of thin bones draped with little fat and accompanied by another of the pale men. Rounding out the trio was a hairless man with black, nearly blue skin.

"We believe our ship's master is imprisoned on that ship," I announced as soon as they were close. "She was taken prisoner by the Penchon earlier today."

"Have you direct knowledge?" the blue-black man asked in a curiously high-pitched voice.

The thin man had been staring at me with unabashed curiosity. "Did they by force take her?"

"I said she was trapped inside," I repeated. "Perhaps she was trapped unexpectedly when the hatches closed." Would they find out about my encounter with the giant, I worried.

"Have the Penchon acknowledged her presence?"

I wondered if D'vore had queried the ship or spoken to them, much as he had summoned the trio, silently and without his knowledge?

The pale man put finger to ear. "They declare no human presence on the ship."

"They are mistaken," I countered as he stepped closer. "I am positive that Master Jaycea Horl is on board and possibly in grave danger. What the hell do I need to do to prove it?"

D'vore pulled him away. "I will handle this ."

The thin man disagreed. "I suggest you not interfere further, medician. This is a human-Penchon problem. Stand aside."

After D'vore complied, the blue hat asked a few direct questions to capture the events of the afternoon, save the circumstance of her walking on board while the Penchon focused on his "threatening" actions.

"We will request a customs search," the pale one said. "The warrant will be served immediately and they will ... Ah, there we go!" The hatch opened and a quartet of Penchon emerged.

When they were within reach the blue-black man announced; "We wish to ensure you are not carrying contraband in accordance with ..."

"Enough!" a human voice said from the limp translator similar to the one that had provided his dialog through the long trip in the Penchon's hands. "There is no contraband on our ship," it replied.

"We have a valid warrant," the blue hat said. "Let us board."

None of the Penchon stepped aside. "There is no need for humans to enter."

"More likely the alien bastards are lying," the pale man whispered to his companions. "Do you think we can trust their word?"

"I am certain that Jaycea entered the ship and did not come out," I said as I noticed that D'vore had disappeared. I doubted the Penchon would recognize him in his new guise, but perhaps D'vore felt otherwise.

"We have a proper warrant," the blue-hat repeated. "Your ship cannot depart until the warrant has been satisfied."

The screech from the Penchon deafened me as it went on and on, an undulation that the soft machine did not translate. Finally, it spoke: "Not to enter the breeding quarters. We will accompany an inspector, no more than one."

"I will go," the thin man said. "I can squeeze into areas where a human might be hidden."

For hours, the three of us waited patiently for the inspection to be completed. D'vore appeared once more, but stood apart from the others and well away. He said nothing.

At last the inspector reappeared and walked toward us. No Penchon accompanied him. "I could find no trace of a human on the ship," he said simply. "Neither did I find any contraband that would justify the warrant. I'm afraid we have incurred an obligation for false interference."

"Your ship has placed an obligation on us," the thin one said angrily, turning on me. "Reckoning for our time and efforts will be applied to your ship's obligations." He scowled. "I'd advise you to look to the pleasure bars for your crewmate." The trio stalked away without looking back.

Before I could claim that the Penchon had probably disassembled Jaycea, D'vore took me by the arm and forced me toward our ship.

"Jaycea's in danger," I protested. "We have to get her away from those creatures!"

"There is no live human on board that ship," D'vore replied.

"Oh my God. They've chopped her into parts!" Despite their differences, I regretted that Jaycea should suffer such a fate. "How will we tell the crew? How will I break the news to Halo and how best could I comfort her?" I kicked myself for thinking to turn this tragedy into advantage. "Poor Jaycea."

As soon as they were inside the hatch D'vore turned away, stooped, and then stepped aside to reveal Jaycea coated in a transparent sac of white slime. She appeared to be dead, but no, there were faint movements of her chest. She was still breathing, still miraculously alive.

"As I said," D'vore said emphatically, "there was no live human remaining on the ship."

Jaycea struggled to rip the sac apart, gasped, and began coughing, spitting up gobs of slime. "What the bloody, be-damned hell did you do to me?" she demanded, looking directly at D'vore. "I could have gotten off that ship without your help, you alien bastard."

"Had I not found you and taken precautions," D'vore answered without emotion. "You could have been rendered within hours. You may thank me by honoring the obligation I incurred on your behalf."

"I'll honor nothing from the likes of you freaks," she shouted. "What the hell did you do to me?"

A question I wanted answered as well.

There was considerable muttering among the crew about Jaycea's rescue, or mishandling, as some held true, no doubt fueled by D'vore's unsettling new appearance. Even those few who had been not previously been openly antagonistic toward the medician were now deliberately keeping clear.

Jaycea admitted to hiding on the ship and described how she'd felt a momentary decompression before D'vore appeared and scooped her within his cape.

"Penchon rarely change the codes on their external hatches," D'vore injected. "Getting aboard was a simple matter. Finding Jaycea was not. I had to think like a frightened human–a painful exercise, I assure you." That remark got a stunning stream of invective from Jaycea that left me unsure of which of his adjectives she'd objected to the most.

Jaycea grumpily honored the ship's obligation to the Guard and acknowledged, but only to me , that she was thankful D'vore had gotten her away safely. "I've learned to live with you," she admitted. "But I'm not sure that the ship will be well served if I keep D'vore on board, despite that damned contract. Nobody knows what all these changes in its appearance might mean. We don't know what it might be capable of doing now that it has changed."

"I am certain he can be trusted," I replied. "He has never done anything that would make me think otherwise." I did not mention how my suspicions had been raised on more than one occasion. Nor did I remind her of what D'vore had revealed by the rescue–that he could leave the station and enter the Penchon ship from the vacuum-facing side without any artificial assistance, such as a suit.

"But can we trust you?" Jaycea continued. "Sorry, but I can't go by what you think or say. For all I know you and D'vore are engaged in some scheme that may put my ship and crew in danger. Or maybe that thing has manipulated your thoughts so you honestly believe it harmless when, in truth, it's otherwise.

"Listen, I have a larger obligation to this ship and crew than to either of you. These latest changes have got everyone spooked badly. I can't risk losing my crew."

"But you are accusing D'vore of having motives that you admit you don't understand," I argued. "You are assuming that just because he is different, he is dangerous. Look, we signed on to this ship under a bond of mutual trust and we've done nothing since then to violate that trust. I think we deserve the same from you."

"Everything you say makes sense," Jaycea answered slowly. "But I'm only the Master. The crew thinks otherwise and I've got to listen to them if I want to keep them." For a moment I thought I'd lost the argument but then she added. "But for now I'll do nothing. Let's see if things settle down and go from there."

Matters remained unchanged for several days. There was a slight softening of attitudes among the crew after D'vore treated a few minor injuries without incident. In fact, he seemed more efficient and faster with his new augments, much to the satisfaction of his repaired or revitalized patients. Hopefully matters would return to their former balance and continue as before.

But disaster struck.

Sylvestra and some hired mechs had been shifting a particularly large and unwieldy cargo container on the dock when a few Penchon darted nearby, startling her. That moment's inattention was sufficient to allow the load to become imbalanced, shifting to the right. Syl immediately exerted more force on that side and, in so doing rocked the container, shifting the contents drastically. When the container wobbled Syl pushed on the other side, which shifted the contents again.

It became a feedback loop. The more she tried to balance the load, the less stable the container became. Syl understood finally, but it was too late to do anything to save her. The container tilted and slipped, faster and faster, to fall with crushing force upon her leg.

Several crew and some bystanders leaped to help. Two other mechs lifted the container while Brews pulled Syl free. Her leg flopped uselessly when he lifted her. The framework was bent and, from his vantage at the hatch, I could see that broken bits of her exoskeleton had penetrated her flesh. Blood poured from a dozen places and made the deck slick beneath her.

They carried her to the surgery. Syl had not made a sound at this point, not since a single muttered, "Oh, shit," when the container had started to fall. She had to be in a great deal of pain, but she'd not screamed.

Her stoic silence ended when D'vore stepped into the surgery. Syl cried out and jerked backwards, causing even more blood to gush from her multiple wounds. "Stay away from me you damned ghoul!"

D'vore ignored her and began to clean the areas around the broken framework to better see the extent of the injuries. Syl screamed again and lashed out.

"We have no time to remove her from her mechanisms, nor could we without the possibility of further damaging her," D'vore said calmly as he leaned closer.

She slashed again. It was only her weakened condition that kept the slashing movement of her amplified arm from ripping D'vore's human arm from his body. Her heavy metal claws raked his arm from elbow to wrist ripping skin from muscle and bone.

"Oh, my God," Someone exclaimed when they saw how she'd flensed his arm. The skin hung in tatters from D'vore's wrist, a loose drape of tanned flesh. There was blood, exposed muscles, veins, ligaments, but the wounds were not so deep as to expose bone. D'vore did not seem to notice. He merely shrugged and continued working as if the obviously painful damage were mere scratches. Whenever he moved his arm the muscles flexed and contracted amidst a sea of bloody tissue. It was sickening, but there was no gushing flow of blood that one would expect. I wondered just how real was that apparently human arm?

D'vore paid no attention to the reactions and moved more quickly than eye could follow to immobilize Syl. Working quickly, he removed the broken metal from her leg, stanched the flow of blood, and began applying the techniques he'd performed so many times before.

Finally he was finished and Syl lay, sans framework and leg, in the surgical field. The sight was sickening for everyone knew how much Sylvestra valued her strength of body and the perfection of her interfaces. Now she was one leg the less and possibly damaged forever.

"Keep watch over her," D'vore said and dashed from the surgery. I suspected that he was rushing to repair the damage to his arm, his non-human arm that had fooled everyone for so long.

Jaycea arrived shortly. One glance at the wreckage of Syl on the table told her what had happened. "Where is D'vore?" she demanded. "Did he have to do this to her?"

"He said that the pulped bone and torn muscle was too damaged to repair," I pointed at the smashed framework outside the surgery as proof "It was all he could do."

"Damn, damn, damn," Jaycea cried and took Syl's limp hand in her own. "We'll do everything we can," she promised the unconscious cargo handler. "Everything."

It was doubtful Sylvestra could hear or understand in her comatose condition. Usually D'vore merely immobilized and cut off the sensation only in the area where he worked. This time he had sent Syl into a deep slumber that had relaxed every muscle in her body. She lay as a limp manikin, bereft of animation save the slow and deliberate movement of her chest as she breathed.

A short time later D'vore was back, holding a large container that he set upright on the deck. He stripped off his cloak to reveal four spidery arms and a flower-like orifice open at his waist. "I need space," he said ungraciously and pushed everyone from the surgery. The hatch slammed shut behind them.

"What the hell does he think he's doing?" Jaycea protested. "If he harms Syl any more I'll have his ..."

"He is a good medician," I reminded her. "I am certain that he would do nothing to harm her." At the same time I wondered at what I had seen, the awful array of limbs and devices that seemed to explode from D'vore's exposed body. What was their purpose and what did it have to do with Sylvestra? The other nagging question was what had happened to his earlier bulky appearance?

Jaycea attempted to open the hatch to the surgery but it had been locked from the inside. Even when she demanded that Jonn override the lock she still could not open the hatch—D'vore had somehow sealed it shut.

"There are some Penchon at the hatch," Halo's voice announced from overhead. "They demand to see the Master."

"What the hell?" Jaycea hastened off and I, not knowing what else might do, followed.

There were four of them, including the one with the soft translator. Standing before the massive Jaycea and with the crew at her back the Penchon did not look nearly so menacing as before. They shifted nervously, but who can tell where alien species are concerned? Finally one of them screeched. "We are here to receive the rest of what is owed," the translator moaned. "A thousand weight of water will be sufficient."

"I'll be bloody damned if you'll get a drop of my water," Jaycea cursed. "We have no obligation toward you."

"For spare parts and good will," the translator responded immediately. "We shall not press the incident of assault on our species when you give us our due."

Jaycea raised an eyebrow as she realized what they meant by assault but appeared as puzzled over the spare parts claim. "There's nothing I can think of that would extract such a high price. Certainly we've done nothing to …"

I suddenly made a connection between the quartet and the container D'vore had been carrying. "I saw containers like D'vore brought earlier, on the Penchon ship. D'vore got something from them."

"Yes, spare parts," they nodded. To the Penchon, with their biological technology, that could only mean human parts. "A fresh leg, do you think?"

"He wouldn't." Jaycea was clearly horrified. "He didn't."

Despite her protest, the evidence was all too plain. D'vore had returned with a Penchon container, Syl was in need of a leg, and here were this foursome demanding payment for "spare parts."

"I will make the arrangements," Jaycea said bitterly, accepting the facts before her. From the dark expression on her face the value of that payment would be extracted from D'vore.

Sylvestra's relief that she was not going to be a cripple somewhat overcame her repugnance over her new leg. The repairs were phenomenal, down to the replacement of the hardware interfaces. Certainly D'vore's skill in the surgery had exceeded anything he had done before.

The day after after Syl was returned to duty Jaycea called us . "The crew are threatening to quit because of you," she began. "I'd lose Syl, Brews and my engine crew, and, worse of all, my purser." This last surprised me . Halo was the last one I would have suspected of harboring ill feelings toward D'vore.

"I can't afford to recruit a fresh crew any more than I could afford all that water I had to use to buy back a piece of one of my friends," she continued.

"There are many crew available at the Registry, I am sure," D'vore said. "Humans abound in this station."

"Huh, damned mongrels, most of them!" she spit. "I certainly am not going to let any more non-Eglaners aboard *Thys Nor* again. You two have taught me the folly of that!"

"But D'vore saved Sylvestra," I protested. "She would have been a cripple if he hadn't intervened."

"We could have found a human medician in time," she sneered. "So now she's a damned thing! Who knows what agony the original owner of that leg went through before the bloody damned Penchon bastards took it from him? Gods, every day Sylvestra is going to have to wonder what those filthy animals did just so she could walk. She's going to have to live with that guilt, Case. How does that make you feel?"

I did not fully understand the source of her anger but supposed it sprang from the same source as my initial reaction to D'vore's human parts. Just the same, wasn't it better to save a crewmate than to bear a grudge for a war long over and done with? "Nevertheless, she walks," I said at long last. "She walks."

Jaycea sighed. "I'll give you that, but it doesn't matter. Contract is damned! I can't let you remain on board any longer or I wouldn't have a crew to operate the ship. Sorry, but you have to find some other way to get to Oroenoe."

I gathered my few belongings, including the jewel I had not given to Halo, and joined D'vore at the hatch. There was no one to bid them farewell as they departed in silence to the cold, empty dock.

I felt ill used by both D'vore and Jaycea. Both of them had betrayed my trust at some level and I feared being so used again. At the same time I realized that, like it or not, I had to depend upon D'vore to orient me in this strange universe. Perhaps the alien was sincere in wishing to help me find Earth, or maybe he had some scheme of his own, as Jaycea suspected. I had no way of knowing if I was using D'vore or vice versa.

"Perhaps we will find a more compatible crew on our next ship," D'vore said cheerily. Had I not known him better I would have sworn my companion was actually skipping with pleasure.

Their situation was dire. They were still amidst numerous Penchon, but no longer had a ship affiliation, no means of supporting themselves, no idea of where they might go or with whom, and worst of all, no plan to get to Earth. I could think of no reason for D'vore's buoyant optimism, for he certainly had none.

"Never fear," D'vore said when they were well away from the ship. "There is much we can do at Oroenoe."

I prayed that he was right.

PART THREE—PROVANCE

"Yes, I am confident that this busy station offers us endless opportunities," D'vore continued in his ebullient mood as they wandered. It was a mood I did not share. Without *Thys Nor* we had no way of reaching Oroneoe and the old records about his long-lost Earth.

The expulsion from the ship disturbed me less than the loss of my beautiful Halo. I felt as if my heart would burst from sorrow, my soul shrivel without the warmth of her presence. But no, I warned myself, she was never for me, no matter how much I might wish it so, no matter how I approached her, I would remain in her eyes, as unappealing as an orangutan. The image of a fat old man covered in red hair sprang to mind and immediately disappeared. Was that what an orangutan looked like, I wondered? The connection had faded as abruptly as it came.

This infuriated me. "What are we to do now? We have no ship, no means of supporting ourselves, and we still have to travel to this supposed planet where they have the records of my home."

"For the moment," D'vore continued ignoring my outburst, "I think it best that we keep out of the Penchons' way until their ships depart. That means that we cannot register as crew on a departing ship else they will realize we are not longer among Jaycea's crew."

I recalled what I'd glimpsed within the cargo hold of the *Qalyub Gudlag* and, as much as I wished the creatures away, I did not want to lose that single, solid link to my past or the ability to continue to examine the physical wreckage.

When I'd explored the wreckage earlier I could make no sense of it nor remember the details connected to it. Now, with my mind more stable and my short-term memory improved, who knew what a detailed examination might reveal? Who knew what memories might be evoked by a closer examination of the actual metal instead of D'vore's virtual images? "I wish we could get my ship from them," I said wistfully.

"The Penchon still hold you to be a thief," D'vore reminded him. "And me, their stolen property. No Case, best you let them go on their way and be out of our lives forever. Besides, since I am still working on the images we captured of the physical wreckage, which makes any study of the actual wreckage unimportant."

I was glad to be reminded of the images, but wondered what good they would do without the equipment to analyze them, "Working on it?" I failed to see what else could be done.

"You will see in time," D'vore replied mysteriously. "Let it be for now."

It was bitter advice, but probably wise considering their current circumstance. Let the Penchon depart, I thought, wishing to make no contribution to the Penchon's spare parts bin.

D'vore stopped and looked around. "This location seems acceptable. I suggest that we seek shelter while we wait. Since we have earned a good deal from our work for Jaycea I suggest that you use some of those funds to amuse yourself—drinks, good food, and whatever pleasures you may find in the market."

"Where can I stay? I know nothing of how to find accommodations."

"According to the station plan there should be human resting places not far from here. You can seek accommodations there while I ..." he paused. "While I see to my continued welfare."

I entered the place D'vore had mentioned with some trepidation. The facility looked nothing like a hotel, although for the moment I could not recall what a "hotel" should look like. To my right was an open doorway, through which I could see familiar washbasins and refresher facilities. They were much like those I'd encountered elsewhere save for the pair of orange-wrapped legs extending beneath a stall's door. They were easily the thinnest, longest legs I had ever seen.

Thinking that something might be awry I tried to knock on the stall but my knuckles produced only a dull thud from the soft surface. "Are you well?" I waited for an answer and when none came, shouted louder, "I said, are you well?"

The legs stirred, crossed, crossed again and then withdrew. "Mrwhght," a high-pitched voice replied.

"I don't understand," I said, thinking that perhaps this was a language I had not absorbed as yet.

"I said, what do you want?" the voice replied. "Who are you?"

"I wish I knew," I answered honestly. "I've been trying to figure that out for some time. Say, do you need help or anything?"

There were some shuffling sounds and then the door opened a crack and, far above my head, an eye peered out. "Are you real?" the voice sounded puzzled. I did not understand; I was standing in bright clear sight. Should there be any doubt?

"Are you," I responded, no longer sure that the voice belonged to a member of my own species.

The door opened and an unusually tall, thin woman dressed in orange and blue clothing stepped out. She had a voluminous cape draped over one arm and carried herself with regal bearing. "Provance al Klye l'postu, at your service," she said with a graceful nod of her head.

Her face was remarkable; all angular panes that set off huge green eyes astride a narrow nose and full lips. She was so thin that I realized that although he could easily encompass her waist with my hands, she did not appear emaciated or even skeletal. It was as if her bones and muscles were composed along a lighter, more airy frame.

"I am," I replied. "Case Pasticher." The name rolled off my tongue so naturally that I wondered if I was indeed growing into the name/descriptor I'd been given. Yet, what were my real names–those of each of my component partners or something else entirely? Was I one, none, or all of those who dwelled in memory?

"Pleased am I to greet you, Case," she said with a dazzling smile as she looked down at me. My eyes were level with her chest, so different from the overly ample Jaycea's or even Halo's ripe form. Was there room enough for two breasts on that narrow chest, I wondered idly?

"Where bound?" she asked, breaking my idle reverie. "Are you in transit or, like me, taking a moment's convenience in this poor place?"

"A little of both. I was just dismissed from my ship and looking for a place to rest my head for the night. I am afraid I don't know much about this place or its customs. It is all so strange to me."

"Alas," she said sadly. "I wish I could continue on y own journey but was beset by thieves of the worst sort who took my identity and tabs, leaving me abandoned, without means, and without hope. Like you, I know not what fate will befall me in this cold, unfamiliar place." A tear rolled down her cheek. She did not attempt to wipe it away.

"Have you told the blue-hats?" I asked. "The police or whatever they are who guard the station?"

She drew back. "Blue hats? Why, I cannot trust those in service of the alien Carhera. Who knows but they may secretly support those who assaulted and robbed me of everything I held dear, even images of my father, who is no doubt wondering when his darling daughter will return to his holdings and my poor mother, ill with a wasting disease and not long for the world." Another set of tears poured forth, cascading like a flood of sorrow.

I doubted her tale of woe—too much, I thought—yet felt a surge of immediate sympathy. I'd learned the bitter lessons of abandonment and loneliness all too well since awakening and, like her, did not completely trust the unknown Carhera. In fact, now that I thought of it, I wondered if I had already been too trusting. Unlike my situation, she could return to a loving family when she left this station, something I feared that might never happen for him.

"Is there anything I can do?" I said, assuming that even if I were unable to do anything, a simple offer of assistance would be a small comfort.

"Would you?" She ran her finger along my jaw. It was a

delicate, sensuous touch of the sort I'd longed to feel from my ever-lost Halo and very different from that of D'vore's gentle touch during his examinations. She stooped to bring her face to my level. "Would you really help me?"

I realized that since I had made the offer, I was somehow obligated to do something. "Do you need funds?" I asked and when she seemed confused, said; "Do you need obligations?"

"If you help of course I will be obligated," she replied testily, as if it were obvious. Once again I became confused at the economic principles guiding this exchange.

"You can share my room," I offered, hoping this beanpole would not confuse my intentions. "That would at least give you accommodations for the night." I wondered what had sparked me to make such a generous offer to a stranger.

"I would be very grateful," she replied warmly, stirring my fears that she had indeed misunderstood his offer.

"Just an offer for you to stay; nothing else," I said emphatically wondering what had brought about my sudden generosity. "I have no interest in taking anything in return."

"A gift freely given and well intended is to be cherished," she replied and touched my cheek again. For a moment I wondered if I had been too damn noble with my denial and then discarded the thought. She was nothing like my glorious lost Halo–too thin, too tall, too everything Halo was not.

She was not even faintly attractive.

The "accommodations" D'vore had somehow arranged turned out to be a narrow tube barely wide enough for two but three times as long as necessary. We arranged ourselves foot to foot, which might lead to accidental entanglements through the night but little else of physical intimacy.

"What are you?" she asked in the dark after they had settled. "I cannot understand you at all. Were you in some sort of accident, perhaps a brain injury? Where are you from?"

As carefully as I could I told her of my peregrinations since the accident, and a little of D'vore, my companion and guide to this strange universe. I said nothing of his makeup, the dead clones, or the problems with the Penchon and his wreckage.

Some things are best kept from strangers.

"That is a sad tale, indeed," she replied after I finished. "Perhaps I can be of service to you in return. It sounds as if you are unfamiliar with almost everything. What could I explain to you that would help?"

I thought long and hard. "There was so much I do not know, so much that I don't even realize what I don't know. How does one inquire about the unknown?" I paused to think. "Just talk to me about anything at all. I will ask questions when you touch on something I do not understand."

"Fair enough," she replied and fell silent making me worry that perhaps I had stumbled onto another social misstep.

"Why are you so thin?" I prompted when the silence persisted. "I don't believe I've ever seen anyone like you."

"My people," she replied, "were space borne for so long that we feared we would never find a planet with a gravity field suitable to our diminished bodies, or so we believe. None of our records go back more than a half million years, and those records over most of that time are few indeed, so we cannot be certain.

"Eventually we found a suitable home albeit with more gravity than we wished, but it was such a beautiful place that we adapted, settled, and grew." Her voice became more animated. "You should see my father's forty million hectares of rolling grassland and misty blue mountains. He has three houses, one in each of the villages he established for the natives–those who operate the factories, manage the herds, and till the fields. Ah Case, you have not lived until you've watched the double sunset shining over our fields of larghberries."

"Large berries?"

"Larghberries, a succulent orange fruit," she replied, emphasizing the consonants. "I thought everyone knew what they were. It's our biggest export item."

"I've never heard of them. If your family is so rich why don't you contact them to help you out?"

"I did not leave Graasilet with my father's permission," she replied sharply. "There was a youth he did not trust, a man with whom I had fallen deeply in love. Against all good advice, and without seeking permission, the two of us set out for another place where my family's influence would not prevent us from being together."

"What happened then?" I asked, suspecting what was to come. It seemed a familiar tale and one I might have been a participant in.

"He," her voice cracked. "He abandoned me once the value of my jewelry and purse were exhausted. Said I had no talents of value save that of my body, a body he refused to touch when I gained all this weight."

I suppressed a gasp of surprise as I tried to imagine what this emaciated woman must have looked like prior to that "weight gain."

"One morning he was gone and I ejected from the place we had rented with the last of my rings," she continued. "I had retained a return ticket, one that I kept secret in case my father's opinion proved true. I was about to use it when I was beset by those ruffians who stole my belongings.

"Without my tab I could not use the communications facilities to contact my family nor purchase another ticket. I did not know what to do and took refuge in the only public place I could. That was when I met you, my hero and savior." She rubbed my foot with hers.

I blushed, feeling less like a hero than one who'd stumbled into a situation and allowed my sympathy to override common sense. What business did I have of saving people when I could not even save myself?

There was no more conversation before I fell asleep and into dreams.

There were strange smells and the acrid sting of ozone in my nostrils as we readied the ship for the jump. I glanced right and left at the others, all sitting at their stations and concentrating on their screens. A whisper of conversation drifted through the still air, barely heard over the steady conversations in my earphones.

I heard voices chanting numbers and words I hardly recognized while other disembodied voices echoed their litany. I saw my fingers dancing over a set of switches recessed into a panel and hesitate over one bright red toggle. A bright white candle blinked above the instruments.

I felt fear as I touched the toggle, thinking of the failures to date and the singular success that encouraged us to attempt this long trip. "The stars and back," I recalled someone whispering in my ear as my finger caressed the toggle. The candle flickered and then disappeared.

I somehow knew that although this vision had little resemblance to the ships I had known, they did not seem that outlandish. There was no corridor, just a hatch leading to the rear of the ship. The rest was a long compartment with stations along its length.

I woke drenched in sweat, shivering with fear. Why that toggle had been so frightening was puzzling, as were the fine details of the dream. Had it only been a dream or was it a recovering memory?

The question lay heavy on my mind as I returned to a fitful sleep.

With morning came D'vore and news of Jaycea. "She has two new crewmembers," he said. "A check of the registry shows them as Navigator and Engineer. The medician has enough training to satisfy the inspectors but not, I fear, enough to perform even rudimentary limb recovery."

"What the devil is this?" Provance said as she joined them.

D'vore turned toward her and swept his arm wide. "I am D'vore, a Centul but much reduced, I fear."

"Provance al Klye l'postu, at your service," she replied with a graceful nod of her head. "Companion to Case and grateful to make your acquaintance."

Had D'vore had a face he might have smirked at her remark. She'd said "companion." I wondered when we had established that relationship? My intent had only been to provide her temporary relief from her situation, not encumber D'vore with another refugee.

"I assume that you have been taking care of poor Case and helping him with my problem," he continued. There it was again, the problem, the poor crippled Case, the pity on everyone's faces when they saw me. Was there some aspect I could not perceive that cause this? "What is so wrong with me?" I cried.

Provance looked embarrassed. "Oh, Case, you needn't be ashamed. It's probably not your fault you're this way. I didn't mean to upset you."

"She means your *chaura*," D'vore added. "I had not realized that you lacked that capacity until she mentioned it."

I could stand it no longer. "What in twenty bloody damn hells is a freaking '*chaura*?"

"I am told that it relates to an ability to … er … understand another person's state." D'vore said and turned to Provance. "Is that correct?"

"I can no more explain *chaura* to you than I could explain colors to a blind person, hearing to one deaf, or love to those who have never felt it," she replied. "It is understanding, appreciating, grasping the other's point and knowing truth from lies."

"As D'vore seems to know how I feel.".

"I merely interpret your heart rate, your respiration, facial expression, and body language. You are usually very transparent, Case."

"Most likely because I haven't learned to hide my feelings," I replied. Up to this point I had not realized how closely D'vore maintained a watch over me and how intimately they were connected. No wonder D'vore appeared to be reading my mind on so many occasions.

But that didn't answer the basic question. "What am I feeling or thinking now?" I challenged the thin woman to prove what she said.

She laughed, a light, high-pitched trill that sent shivers down his back. "You are a wounded soul," she replied. "You have been hurt and need human companionship. You distrust both the D'vore and me, but are hoping for some sort of resolution."

Was all that written so plainly for her to see? She was absolutely correct about the trust issue but until she mentioned it, I did not suspect, did not feel the pain she mentioned until she spoke and I knew—knew for certain the truth of how much

I had needed Halo and how deeply the loss affected me. I felt naked, as if my clothing had been ripped away and a cold wind was blowing.

"I did not mean to offend," Provance said soothingly. "Look at me. Can't you see my genuine concern for you?"

All I could see was her narrow face, sharp features, and her pitifully thin body. She had a bit of a smile on her lips and a slight squint of eyes, but I could read nothing from those.

"No, all I can hear are your words."

She stroked my cheek once more; that same, sensual, gentle touch that she'd used before. I accepted it as an affirmation before a new concern revealed itself. Did all these humans have this *chaura*? If so, what hope did I have to survive when my thoughts and feeling were open to all?

More importantly, how did the rest of humanity survive this constant surveillance?

Provance and I spent another night together, but again at opposite ends of the lodging tube. I did not know if her *chaura* ability depended on proximity, but thought it best that we keep our distance. That she might intuit my dreams and nightmares was a possibility I did not want to entertain. She seemed to accept this arrangement with good grace.

In the morning, or at least at the time we had both awakened, we made our way to the market. Provance stayed close by my side as I selected something to eat from the placard outside of a vendor's kiosk. I offered to share my meal since she obviously had no resources and I could hardly let her starve.

She ate hardly more than two bites, but whether that was sufficient for her needs or done out of desire not to impose I did not know.

We were lingering over the remains of the repast when D'vore found them. "Jaycea's ship is scheduled to depart later this morning," he said as he settled onto a broad bench nearby. "I suggest that we confirm her departure and see what happens as a result."

Despite his circumlocution I realized that D'vore wanted

to see what actions the Penchon ship would take when *Thys Nor* departed. While there might be some doubt that the Penchon had been following, the fact that they had arrived at the same station twice made it more than coincidence.

I was puzzled as to why that Penchon ship had continued to follow Jaycea? The expense of such an enterprise certainly outweighed any satisfaction they might have gained from revenge for his rescue of D'vore. No, that was too self-centered. It had to be connected to either Jaycea's cargo or crew instead. Perhaps they had been pursuing her all along.

D'vore found a perch for the three of us between cargo pods and miscellaneous ship parts. It was a spot where we could watch our former ship without exposing ourselves to the nearby Penchon. A large Penchon ship departed soon after we began observing and, after another half hour, Jaycea's ship closed its cargo hatches and blew the station connectors. "*Thys Nor*'s filed a route to Toril," D'vore announced.

Once again I wondered at the resources D'vore seemed to have at his disposal. Without obvious effort he was able to pluck information about ship schedules, cargo, and destinations from the very air. I tucked that query away among a dozen other questions that I needed to ask when we had time.

"Well, that does it," I said when Jaycea's ship cleared. "We are now officially on our own."

"Wait a moment more," D'vore said calmly. "I wish to see the next move of this game. Did you know that our," he emphasized the word, *our*, "Penchon ship has not yet specified a destination, yet it has filed to depart within the hour."

I puzzled over that comment for a few minutes as Provance sat uncomfortably close to my side, hip touching hip.

"Ah, here we are," D'vore finally announced. "They have also filed to go to Torii, the same destination."

The thoughts of losing the fragment from my former ship still lay heavy on my mind. Once the *Qalyub Gudlag* departed the wreckage would be lost forever. Yet, despite my pangs of loss there was little I could do, even if the ship had remained at dock I had no resources, no way to convince them to surrender it. Neither would he have any way to explore it more than I'd already had. Still, losing that one solid touchstone of my past filled me with sorrow.

Provance put her hand on my shoulder and squeezed. "Do not be so sad," she said. It was nice to have a bit of sympathy at that point and I, so deep in my own misery, did not feel at all violated. I wondered momentarily if she thought it was my thwarted adoration for Halo that saddened me or did she think it was something different?

"I fear that a small mistake has been made," D'vore said apologetically. "Someone neglected to remove our names from *Thys Nor's* crew roster after we were so rudely dismissed." He said nothing more; leaving me to wonder once again what resources had been brought to bear to affect such a "mistake." Bribing the drunken Jonn was a good possibility, since he was responsible for maintaining the crew records, but it could be otherwise.

"You think the Penchon still want you back," I said, immediately understanding the implications that they must still believe D'vore was on *Thys Nor.* But, if that was true, why hadn't they not snatched him off the dock, when they had more than ample opportunity? I could think of no reason for their failure to act.

What madhouse had I fallen into, that there were more questions than answers, that every turn of events posed ever more puzzling reactions and behaviors? Was this entire universe insane or was I?

"We now must move quickly to procure transport," D'vore said. "Time is of the essence if we are to reach Oroenoe."

Provance threw us a puzzled glance. "I did not know you would leave so soon." Was there a note of sadness in her voice?

D'vore answered. "Our departure is not so immediate, I think. There are some matters I must attend to before we can make arrangements." He abruptly departed, leaving me standing awkwardly too close to my erstwhile companion.

"Your alien friend appears to be rather secretive," she said. "Do you know where he is going?"

"I seldom understand his actions," I replied. "But circumstances have forced me to trust him. It's kept me safe so far."

"But still, you do not trust him completely." She said it not as a question but as a declaration, mirroring my doubts. "You wish to carve your own course."

"If I had any idea of what to do, how to do it, and where to go, then I would." That summed up his dilemma; I could no more act independently of D'vore than he could run without legs. "And neither is he operating independently." I told her about the packages D'vore transported, and how they had managed their travels thus far.

"So you do nothing but wait for this alien to dictate your moves? I find that hard to believe for someone as intelligent as you appear to be."

I was still amazed as how easily she read my thoughts, but she was right. Why did I have to follow D'vore's every twist and turn? Why was the alien dictating every step of my way? "I know," I replied with a surge of independence, followed immediately by bitter realization. "But I don't have the faintest idea of how to make travel arrangements."

"I owe you for your kindness," Provance said tentatively. "I think I know how you might find a ship and could check, that is, if you would like me to do that?" She smiled quickly and then grew more serious. "I assume you would want someone who didn't document your passage?"

I couldn't recall having said anything about traveling anonymously, but realized at once that it might be a good idea. If they weren't in the WOFAT, the Penchon would not be able to track them. "An excellent idea."

"Of course, there might be a substantial obligation required."

"I'm sure that we have more than enough left from *Thys Nor* to afford passage," I replied.

"Yes, but there might be more than just our passage," Provance answered. "I suspect we'll also need false ID tabs. Some idea of our destination would also help, I would imagine." Once again she had understood my need for finally being in control of my own destiny without me saying so. It was uncanny how her mind seemed to run in the same groove.

"Oroenoe," I replied. "I need to get to Oroenoe."

D'vore was less than pleased about change of plans, but did not seem upset at my sudden burst of independence, which might indicate that I was wrong about the trust factor. If D'vore was willing to go along with traveling anonymously on a ship of my choosing then he could have be no ulterior motive. Or could he? "We will do as you wish." He turned to Provance. "We will provide the funds, but any payment will not be authorized until I feel that the arrangements are what we need."

Provance's sudden frown disappeared as soon as it formed, or had that flash of irritation been a trick of the light? "No need to worry," she replied cheerily. "I am completely honest."

"Your woman appears to be quite resourceful," D'vore mused after Provance departed. "Perhaps there is more depth to her than I suspected."

I resented the implication. "She is *not* my woman!"

D'vore shrugged. "How did you come to acquire such a resource?"

"Look, she was in trouble." I quickly explained the events of their meeting. "It was a spur of the moment offer. I felt badly for her situation and offered her a bit of help." I wondered how truthful that was about my spur of the moment decision and was still puzzled as to why I'd been so magnanimous. "I expected nothing in return."

"Is that so?"

I hoped that he had not leapt to the same conclusion that she had … No, I could not let that idea stand. "I expected nothing from her," I repeated. "We merely shared a bed for the night." The instant the words left my mouth I regretted the implication, but said nothing more.

I questioned my embarrassment. Would something as alien as D'vore understand human sexuality? Would his alien companion appreciate the deeper meanings behind such a relationship? On the other hand, I reflected, perhaps it was me who hadn't grasped the finer points of sexual nuance in this culture? I decided that further protestations would be fruitless and concentrated more on how my apparently helpless female companion had suddenly become so capable. If she knew enough to obtain passage for them then why hadn't she done so for herself?

There was more going on with Provance than met the eye and I intended to find out what that might be.

Emerging memories continued to plague me whenever immediate events failed to occupy my mind. As we awaited Provance's return I described my recent dreams and mentioned the discordant object on the console. "A candle on a spaceship? How rational is that? What could it mean?"

"Or portend," D'vore answered. "I am told that some humans think that dreams forecast the future, although not so precisely."

"How so?" This was an aspect of humanity that I could not remember having heard before.

"Humans are victims of their subconscious mental processes," D'vore explained. "Often these processes pick up details the conscious mind might not be aware of. In sleep, when the barriers are down, these details might manifest themselves as ideas, objects, or feelings that symbolically represent actions we might unroll at some future point."

I tried to focus on the elements of that frightening dream. "So the red switch and the candle might not be what they seem?"

"Perhaps. On the other hand you should ask yourself why a candle would be on the panel. It seems so incongruous that I suspect it was a dream, not a memory."

I had to admit to the truth of that. Yet I could not shake the feeling that although the candle and the red switch seemed to have significance, I was at a loss to understand what that might be.

"Give it time, Case," D'vore said gently. "You are not fully healed. The reconstruction of your mind has still not achieved sufficient integration. Until it does, you cannot be your own person. Time, Case, you must give your mind time."

I did not need to be told the state of my mind. I still struggled to hold a memory for long, to focus on one thing alone before some other memory drew my attention elsewhere. Only by isolating myself from distractions was I able to think clearly for more than a matter of minutes. Memories from the time I had awakened remained fresh. It was the older ones, the memories that might give me a clue to my identity, to my home that remained elusive.

"Do you have the same problem? Do you fully recall what you were, where you came from, and what your purpose might have been?"

D'vore was silent for a long while before he spoke. "I recall some of what I once was," he began. "That is, I can recall some of what I might have looked like and how I might have acted. What I cannot recall are the motivations and control processes I employed when I set forth with my brothers. Perhaps when I regain my full mind ..." He paused for a long time before continuing. "It is a peculiar affliction, this inability to recall the essentials of my being. That is why, at every turn, I seek to restore elements of what I once was so that I can regain my purpose and motives. That is my quest, Case, and for the time being, yours."

I thought that a curious remark. "Can't you contact others of your kind—call another D'vore to help you?" Surely, D'vore's kind could not be so singular as to be unwilling to help one of their own, much as he had extended a hand to Provance.

"There are few in this crowded region," D'vore answered. "The stars are too close and warm and the swarms of lesser creatures too numerous. A Centul requires the deep dark, the beautiful silence where contemplation sits uninterrupted and discourse can proceed on a stately course."

"But you are here, not in some distant vacuum," I protested.

"I am here only until I regain the full capabilities misfortune stripped from me," D'vore answered. "I gather a bit here and there, a slow process, this accretion of possibility, but I am confident that I shall eventually succeed. Then, when I recover the fullness of myself, I shall leave these terribly close places and return to my proper realm. Until then," he added with wry humor, "you are stuck with me."

I hoped that I would find Earth long before that came to pass.

True to her word, Provance returned the next morning with a broad smile on her face. "The good captain of *M'ntode* has agreed to convey us to Vizzon, even though it is an imposition and unproductive of interesting cargo. Nevertheless, I managed to convince him of the urgency of our need to depart this place." She extended a small tab.

"But we want to get to Oroenoe."

"Vizzon is halfway there," Provance replied. "There are no ships bound for Oroenoe from here. At least, not any that would provide the type of accommodations we wish." It was less than I wanted, but again, I was not in a position to change plans now that a commitment had been set.

"I see that the extra value he requested will more than make up for my loss of 'interesting cargo'," D'vore added dryly, as he fingered the tab she'd handed across.

Provance bristled. "The arrangements are quite reasonable. In fact, he reduced the price when we offered to travel as cargo instead of crew." Provance tossed her head. "I am surprised that you would bother with such petty details when your pressing need to reach Oroenoe are at hand."

"I note the arrangements include passage for you as well," D'vore said after pausing a moment more. "That was not what I requested nor something we need."

Provance drew herself up. "I merely assumed that Case would need my services at Vizzon. After all, the l'postu name is well known there because of my family's extensive trading ventures."

I was taken aback. I'd believed her father was a large landholder somewhere else, but then, I was not so confident in my memory that I would swear to it. "If she indeed has contacts she could be useful to us," I suggested.

D'vore looked at me and shrugged; "Since you insist . For *your* sake she can come." I thought that was a strange way to put it, but was glad to see that D'vore agreed.

The captain/master/owner of *M'ntode* was a squat and broad creature whose crown was barely chest high to me. Eyes ringed its periphery and six elephantine legs supported its bulk. It had two muscular limbs in front and a quartet of feathery "hands" bracketing its maw that constantly twitched.

"Mastaxshaw," it introduced itself with a peculiar clucking sound in the middle of its name. "About time. Move quick, quick. Keep to cargo hold. Better for all." With that brusque introduction he scuttled away without turning or reorienting himself and, at the wide cargo hatch, abruptly moved sideways into the ship.

We followed, although not in the same manner, into the ship.

"Small toolplace, uninspected," Mastaxshaw said as it opened a panel just inside the hatch. "You must here stay."

"That seems terribly cramped," I said. "Why can't we move about? There's no danger of someone seeing us once we are traveling."

"Must stay here," Mastaxshaw insisted. I was offended, thinking his unwillingness to let them mingle with the crew as another case of prejudice and wondered if this dislike of anything different was a universal trait instead of simply the human ones attitudes I'd encountered?

I looked into the space the alien captain had indicated. It was barely larger than the life pod on which we'd escaped. In one corner were a stack of threadbare blankets and a box of ship's rations. "There isn't enough room for the three of us," I complained.

Provance protested immediately. "Three? Certainly you don't expect me to sleep with that … with D'vore? I thought I had made myself clear. Since he needs no creature comforts he was to travel as cargo."

D'vore placed a hand on my arm to forestall an outburst. "It is all right, Case . She is quite correct–I have no need of either food or sleep. In fact, while you two sleep together I can continue the processing work."

I started at the "sleep together" comment. Was that what Provance had in mind? Had this ridiculously thin pole of a woman actually imagined that I found her attractive? I determined to make it very clear that while we might share the space, we would share nothing else.

Mastaxshaw's apparent prejudice against having humans

mingle with his crew turned out to be a wrong assumption. The ship's main passageway began at one end of the cargo hold. The hatch was twice as wide as a human doorway and only half its height. One glance inside revealed that the entire passageway shared this same dimensionality. To wander those halls I would have to stoop painfully or crawl on all fours, something I was reluctant to do for the sake of simple curiosity. Since any turns or ladders might offer additional challenges I would be reluctant to try.

I was disappointed at not being able to explore this ship more fully and learn more about the aliens who piloted it. Equally important was that exploration would enable me to get away from Provance, not that I found her company unpleasant, but her constant chatter did pale after a while.

She stated that she'd traveled widely, which I thought at odds with some of her earlier statements, as was whether her family were traders or farmers or engaged in several other pursuits. Every time I brought a discrepancy to her attention she produced a perfectly credible reason for misunderstanding. Yet there were so many occasions that I began to have doubts.

I mentioned this when D'vore had a few moments of privacy at the far end of the hold behind some stacked containers. "I have learned," he answered after hearing my doubts, "that humans are not always truthful. Somewhere in your mind is a rationalization engine that always crafts a tale not to reflect truth but to serve some other agenda."

"I always tell the truth," I replied haughtily.

"Not true, Case . You denied that you were attracted to Provance when all your vital signs said otherwise. If that was not a lie, then what is truth?"

I was upset that D'vore could so casually read my vital signs and gods knew how many other indicators of my state of mind. It was almost as bad as Provance and her *chaura* thing. Then again, was I being truthful or was D'vore teasing?

"No, I am telling the truth," D'vore said quickly, which was an even more disturbing remark. "There is no reason for you to be angry. To me such ability is no different than humans reading another's *chaura*, the set of their eyes, or posture to surmise their intention. It is simply the truth. I am more amazed that you lack this common human ability."

"Either you misunderstand my feelings toward Provance or you're making a joke at my expense."

"Your elevated heart beat, dilation of the eyes, and increased blood pressure whenever she touches you reveal more than you admit to yourself, Case . None of those signs indicate indifference, fear or loathing."

"It must simply be what a human touch does to me," I replied. "It is a purely physical reaction having nothing to do with my emotions."

"As I said before, the human mind is wonderful at rationalizing what they wish to believe, regardless of the facts. You need not be ashamed. I constructed you as a complete human, not a machine.

"Look to your own feeling; you have been without human companionship for months and were spurned by one you so desperately yearned to embrace. Now, suddenly you have a companion of your own kind. It is natural for you to react as you do."

"She is not of 'my kind' and definitely not my damn companion. That's what she said. I didn't even want her to come along!"

D'vore chuckled. "A wonderful example of what I said about rationalization, Case . Bravo for proving my point."

That night I slept beside D'vore, unwilling to substantiate the alien's unwarranted and preposterous assumptions.

Mastaxshaw visited occasionally to check on us, or perhaps it was another of his kind. Having seen only a single example of this alien race I had no basis for determining any individual differences that might have existed among this race.

"Is comfort giving, all?" it inquired with a wave of an appendage in the direction of the cramped closet of a compartment. The creature's voice seemed to be coming from between its legs.

"It's far too small for me," Provance replied with some heat. In order to lie comfortably in the small space, she'd had to fold her legs, and move closer to the center of the compartment. I always slept with my back to her, fearful that any other contact that might be misconstrued.

"Three people in room could fit," the alien replied.

"They sleep standing as they are," D'vore said casually. "Shar does not understand the horizontal nature of your nocturnal behavior."

Shar? Was that the alien's name, gender, or something else entirely? I noted that I would have to ask later, after the matter of sleeping space was settled.

Provance put her hands on her insignificant hips. "Of all the stupid ... Look!" She dropped to the deck and stretched out to illustrate how cramped the compartment seemed.

The alien jumped a meter into the air and screamed while running backwards toward the opening to the corridor. D'vore intercepted it and hummed loudly for a few moments.

"It is all right," D'vore explained after he had calmed the alien. "Shar was going for medical attention. I explained that Provance was not dying and that it was perfectly normal for humans to leave their feet."

Provance sat up and reached out a hand to let me pull her to her feet. I was amazed at how very light she felt and how warm her hand. "I did not mean to alarm you," she assured the alien. "This is how I, how we sleep," she swept her arm to include me. "Together," she added, being unclear whether that was a comment on the space requirements or something more.

I hoped it was the former.

Several hours later a pair of aliens, little different from Mastaxshaw and "Shar," save for their tool pouches and constant humming conversation, entered the cargo bay and began cutting the walls of our cubicle. They enlarged the space by two meters and welded the wall back to the deck and bulkhead. "Done is," one of them croaked and scuttled away. Typical engineers, I thought.

That adjustment gave Provance the length to stretch her long legs so they could lie side by side, but they had done nothing about the width.

D'vore mentioned the arrival at Vizzon long before I noticed any change in the atmospheric pressure. Less than an hour later, I heard the clatter and crash of docking and, soon after, Mastaxshaw, at least I assumed that's who it was, instructed us to climb into a large container resting near the hatch.

If I had thought the sleeping compartment was cramped, this was worse. D'vore entered first and occupied more than half the volume. I followed and pressed against one side with an arm across D'vore's back. Provance came last and pressed herself between my legs so she could bring knees to chin and fit into the remaining space.

Mastaxshaw sealed the crate, which cut off all light and sound. As Provance wiggled a bit to settle herself her hair brushed my face. I put my head next to hers and placed my other arm around her to provide us a more comfortable position.

"A most interesting arrangement," D'vore said. Apparently he could see, even in this absolute darkness.

I felt Provance's heart racing but could think of no reason; her efforts to fit into the crate had not been strenuous. Even as the minutes passed, her heart rate showed no sign of diminishing.

The crate began moving. "I think we're being offloaded as cargo," Provance whispered. Her breath smelled of spice; a very pleasant aroma considering that they'd had little of the hygienic comforts during the voyage. I was sure my own breath was considerably less appealing. Her heart continued its rapid pace.

"We are moving laterally at a walking pace," D'vore said. There were two heavy bangs on the side and then silence. "Customs stamps," D'vore whispered. "We are safe now. There will be no entry into the station's WOFAT regarding our arrival."

"Without being registered how can we move about," I whispered. "How will we be able to afford what we need to find Earth or others of your kind?"

"There are resources I can call upon," D'vore answered, mysterious as ever. "I suspect that Provance has also secured the means to help us."

Provance started. "How the hell did you ..." she began. "Well, perhaps I have," she added quickly.

As before, this oblique exchange left me baffled, not only at D'vore's ability to snatch vital information from the very air, but also at Provance's endless resourcefulness. She was proving to be far more sophisticated than she'd appeared at their first meeting, so much so that I doubted the initial story she'd related. How did they both know and why hadn't either of them mentioned it? After all, I was part of this accidental trio and should have been told.

"I believe we are ready to leave," D'vore announced soon after the crate was moved into place with the most gentle of bumps. "Shar will be along presently."

True to that remark, Mastaxshaw, or one of his identical crewmates, opened the crate and allowed us to tumble out. "Tabs," it exclaimed abruptly and thrust a packet into Provance's hands, she being the first out of the box. It then scuttled away on all sixes, changing direction abruptly and without turning. Despite their recent exposure to their multidirectional mode of walking I still found such movement unsettling.

"A little surprise I asked the good captain to obtain," Provance admitted. "I suggested that we'd need some new identification."

"I apologize for misunderstanding the additional draw on our resources," D'vore said. "Thank you." It was the first time he'd acted surprised; that he could act surprised amazed me even more.

My tab indicated that I hailed from someplace called Jinglan and was of the human Farrakine species. I had no idea that the differences in the humans I'd seen represented different species until now. Did that mean Provance was of a different species instead of just being an unusually thin individual? Just how far did our differences extend?

"I have no idea of how a Farrakiner should act, dress, or what custom they follow. I don't even know if I remotely resemble one. Do they have horns and wings, for God's sake?"

Provance smiled after a quick glance at my identification. "We will have to cover your hands." She ran a hand through my hair. "A little color will also be needed. No Farrie would sport such dark locks. Yes, I think a more subdued shade would work." Her hands lingered at the back of my skull a microsecond longer than necessary.

"We also must put you in decent clothing," she continued. "Why must you wear that hideous olive coverall? You look like a damn deckhand."

"He wears what he chooses," D'vore replied haughtily. "I am not an expert on human manners of dress."

"I haven't figured out how to use the artificer very well," I admitted, trying hard not to sound like a petulant child admitting to an indiscretion. "This is the best I can get any of them to produce."

Provance's grin exhibited a row of astoundingly bright teeth that were at once too many and too small. "I'll need to dress appropriately to my new identity as well. Come Case, we will clothe ourselves as properly fitting for our assumed station."

"You cannot so easily hide your own Gladeshide background," D'vore mused. "Nor can I hide my rather unique appearance." He turned the tab over in his hands. "This declares that I am a chimera created by the Penchon and freed as independent by humans after the war. I imagine none who sees me will doubt the truth of that. How is it with you?"

"Dorish Tallet," Provance responded without glancing at her own tab. "Not a name of my liking, but common enough. It appears that this Dorish also hails from Chanlis, the continent of my own family."

I thought that remark jarring. Hadn't she mentioned another location for her family's holdings, but again, perhaps I was mistaken. I was certain that she'd have an explanation if I asked.

"Farrkinites and Gladesiders? What the devil are those?"

Provance's eyebrows rose. "What sort of backward place are you from? Everybody knows of the Jinglan Farrkinites."

"I only remember one kind of human! They come in various hues, but were all of a type as best I can recall."

Provance shook her head. "The sixteen, Case . There are sixteen species of humans." Ignoring my expression of amazement and disbelief she continued. "No one knows exactly where or when the cladogenesis from the original stock occurred. There are four or five races that claim the title of founder, of being the primal species from which all others derived. All of those claims are patently false. Whatever root group created humanity's many forms has long been buried under adaptation and alteration."

"But, but," I sputtered.

"Six of our species, if you wish to call them that, are clearly close relatives according to both their DNA and mitochondria and can even interbreed, that is, if any might choose to do so." I sensed a note of disgust in her voice. "Three others have some common parts of code in the human code sequences, so there is suspicion they are also related, but not to the six. The rest of us are problematic, similar in appearance save for minor environmental adaptations, but vastly different from one another in the way our minds and bodies work."

She stopped so abruptly I wondered if there had been something she was about to say before she thought better of it. That thought was driven out when I realized that she'd said nothing that I could not understand. Obviously I must have known about the different human races even if I couldn't recall the details.

"So you say," I replied with some anger. "But why can't I remember anything about this, this supposed diversity? Damn it, I'm frustrated with having more questions than answers; at always having to ask for explanations over things everyone else seems to know."

"He was in a terrible accident," D'vore explained before he could say more. "I'm afraid he lost most of his memories. I've been guiding him back to an understanding of what he was and will be, but it takes time. You must be patient with him."

Provance seemed to accept that explanation at face value. "Yes, he mentioned something about an accident, but little else." She put an arm across my shoulders and pulled me close. Had she breasts I might have been excited. As it was, I felt stifled. "You poor, poor man," she crooned as she gently stroked my head.

Despite my aversion to her appearance, I was so touched by this simple act of humanity that I returned her embrace.

"Later, when you are alone you can continue your affections,"

D'vore said dryly. "We do not have time now." For the first time I did not feel offended at his presumption of my feelings.

Resplendent in our new clothing: bright motley for me and a refined beige shift for Provance, we left the artificer appearing every bit the persons our tabs declared. I picked at the uncomfortable six-fingered glove whose extra digits projected like second thumbs from the opposite side of my hands.

"Don't fidget with them," Provance scolded. "And be careful not to pick anything up or you will belie your identify." She thought for a moment. "Perhaps later D'vore can give you a more functional thumbs than those false digits."

I blanched at the thought. I would never submit to such a strange addition. Still, I heeded her words even as I wondered how a race of six-fingered Farrikiners could arise. On the other hand, I could easily imagine the advantage of having extra thumbs.

"About D'vore, your strange companion," Provance began apropos of nothing. "Are you certain that he has your best interests at heart? It seems a strange relationship."

"I don't fully understand him much of the time," I replied. "Still, he has ensured that I have come to no harm. He talks to me and seems to sympathize with his struggles with memory."

Provance said nothing for a while. "I would not trust it, Case . For one like that to take an interest in a repaired human seems unusual. It must have other motives than your welfare."

That she should have perceived my doubts so quickly amazed me. Nevertheless I took this as further evidence that D'vore's objectives might be other than finding Earth.

Vizzon was a bustling station with its own unique blend of scents and sounds, although the loading docks themselves had the dreary sameness as the other stations. Away from the hustle and chaos of the ships the station was swarming with aliens and, now that my eyes were open to them, strange humans. Provance pointed out some as they strolled the dock area. "Homo Gravis," she whispered after seeing a heavy-set pair looking entirely too much like Jaycea's crewmates. "And those over there by the fresher are Adulescens."

I glanced at the three individuals. They appeared to be ten or eleven years old. One of them was clearly pregnant. "My God," I exclaimed. "They're children!"

"Children?" Provance sounded genuinely puzzled. "They might be small, but I'd hardly call them children."

Memories of a tow-headed boy running through a field after a thrown ball, a dark-haired girl in a pink dress, and a pair of brown-skinned girls dancing on a stage flashed through my mind. The fleeting images faded as quickly as they'd come. "It doesn't seem right," I mumbled as the trio disappeared into the crowd.

There were a handful of people looking like *Tollembol's* cinnamon saviors, another woman with webbed fingers, and a pair in swaddling environmental suits. "Spikenas have weak immune systems," Provance explained when I noted them. "Fatally allergic to certain proteins that others carry. A very difficult group to deal with."

Slowly, and mostly in response to my naive questions, she schooled me in the variety of humanity, at least those who had not drifted so far apart that they were entirely different and perhaps fanciful creatures, such as the Homo Benthic, who lived deep in the cold, deep oceans of watery planets or Homo Decorus who flitted through the dense atmospheres of gaseous giants on gossamer wings of gold and turquoise.

How such diversity could arise, how the human race had exploded into so many types from some long-lost parent was a puzzle no one had yet solved. "In some cases, genetic manipulation was the reason," Provance mused. "But mostly it's been simple adaptation to local conditions over the years."

"Nonsense," I countered. "Evolution doesn't work that fast. These vast differences must have evolved over millions of years." I didn't know how I knew that bit of information but was absolutely certain that none of this amazing variety had been known on my world.

Were my people so far removed from the development of humanity that they had been unaware of these greater riches? What would have been different had someone, anyone, from the greater human races made contact to bring my people into humanity's fold?

Or was that simply my poor memory and I had simply forgotten?

The non-humans at Vizzon were endlessly fascinating in their diversity, ranging from the diminutive Pittul to the gigantic Zhangii. When I expressed surprise at their small number Provance laughed. "These aliens are only those who share our biome and breathe air suitable for humans—they're practically relatives. Let's see, I know of only six or seven alien races that could walk these decks without artificial aid. That's six or seven out of over five hundred that we humans can trade with. There may be many more, but the Carhera haven't allowed those contacts as yet. 'Humans are too immature,' they tell us. More likely keeping honest trade to themselves, say I."

I was about to ask her to explain more when, emerging from a cross-corridor a dozen meters ahead of them, were five Penchon. I thought I could smell them, but that might have been my imagination.

"What is the matter, Case ?" Provance asked. "Are you ill?"

I stood mute as the Penchon drew abreast, afraid to speak, afraid to look into their cold black eyes. I held my breath as the quintet parted to either side, passed, and went on their way. Only then did I relax. "I'm fine," I replied. "Just a momentary faint. I'm all right now." That was an understatement. I was still quivering inside from being so close to those creatures and fearing that they too might somehow be pursuing D'vore.

"More than that," she said. "You are fearful, worried as well as hungry. I think we need to get some food in you," Provance glanced my way. "Yes, and something to drink. Perhaps you are dehydrated as well."

In short order she found somewhere to eat and ordered our meals. I kept glancing about, fearful that the Penchon would return. Intellectually I realized they were not the same ones who'd pursued Jaycea's ship, but that did not quell my reaction to their sudden appearance.

Her choice of eatery seemed to a hangout for humans. Each

table held two or more of each of the types seen on the docks plus one of those with the blue-black skin. None of the tables but theirs held mixed groups, which was puzzling. Why should like cling to like among so much diversity? Was this behavior yet another expression of their prejudice? I realized that I shouldn't make unfounded assumptions. Too many of those had proven false already.

Two platters were rudely placed before on the table, spilling part of the food from the plates. My plate held a generous portion of chopped fruits and nuts while Provance's held only a tenth as much. In odd contrast, her drink was easily twice the size of mine. Earlier I had noticed earlier that her diet was minimal. A few bites of ration were all she ever seemed to need. I imagined that her paucity of appetite was somehow related to her extraordinarily thin frame or a highly efficient metabolism.

I was about to pick up a fork when Provance glanced about with an alarmed look and stayed my hand. "I warned you about picking up things," she hissed.

"Well, how the devil am I supposed to eat then?"

In answer she rose and came around the table. "Put your arms around me," she instructed. "I will feed you as a proper lover might. Just don't try to use your hands."

I wondered if she was doing this to protect my identity as a ploy to further cement our non-existent relationship. I could feel her rapid heartbeat as she pressed close.

I allowed her to lovingly place morsel after delicious morsel in my mouth, trying to act appreciative and not act like a petulant child. At one point she startled me with a soft, lingering kiss. I assumed that this was more subterfuge and smiled. I licked my lips, surprised that a taste of spice lingered there. She giggled girlishly and stroked my cheek. "That was very nice."

A pair at a far table made a rude noise, immediately rose, and hastened away, the woman throwing an angry scowl at us while her companion kept his head down as they hastily exited.

"Damned whore," an individual at the next table bellowed. Another mumbled something and its companions burst into coarse laughter, no doubt at Provance's expense. I angrily pulled away from Provance and began to rise.

Provance pulled me back. "It's all right, Case . Our tryst can be part of our new identities. Let it pass. I am not offended by their thoughts."

Her remarks did little to mollify me, but I wondered if I had become angry over the supposed insult or the insinuation that the two of us were engaged in an unsavory commercial relationship?

We finished our meal while ignoring the angry glances from the other tables. "It is not only our behavior that so offends them," Provance whispered in my ear as she placed another morsel between my lips. "It is that we should share the same table and, worse, that I should feed another in public that more deeply offends them."

I couldn't understand what was wrong with either of those things. Why should feeding someone be scandalous? Why shouldn't they share a table? Once again I had more questions than answers, which seemed to be the on-going script of my new life. Was I to be forever and continuously puzzled by every nuance of this human culture?

D'vore had stated that he had some business at the repair docks. How he could so quickly arrange "business" upon arrival and with a new identification was yet another puzzle for my already too full inventory and one that I felt unwilling to pursue. "I am sure he will return when he is finished."

Even with that assurance, she grew restless after several hours of waiting. "I don't like standing around waiting for who knows what," she said. "We have no place to stay, no means to support ourselves, and no plan on what we might do next."

Aside from his sudden initiative in having Provance procure transport I had depended entirely upon D'vore to state what our next move would be. The only other initiatives he'd taken were the escape from the Penchon ship and asking Provance to arrange transport. I couldn't recall why that had seemed so logical at the time, but there was nothing I could do about it now.

"I say we try to find him. The repair docks are that way," Provance said as she pointed at a glyph-encrusted signpost.

After a glance I wondered why reading hadn't been part of my language implant?

The repair docks were a quarter turn around the station, a fair distance that had him working hard to keep up with Provance's long strides. By the time they neared the facility I was breathless. Provance seemed not to have noticed the strenuous pace she had set.

It wasn't difficult to identify D'vore; he was so different from everything else as he stood in rapt attention, staring through a port at a strange asymmetrical ship, its battered design quite different from the few star ships I'd seen. All of those shared the characteristic of being surrounded by spars and booms, outriggers and pods, cable hitches and lateral planes that paid no heed to atmospheric resistance. But those attachments and adornments were peripheral to the general purpose of the ships, which was to enclose and keep safe the crew and cargo.

This ship shared none of those features. Instead it appeared to be a wild array of rods and brushes, of random plates and awkward planes dotted here and there with random splashes of color, no two of which agreed in hue or tone. I could see no place where an atmosphere could be contained, no central structure for cargo, nor even a place where someone or something could control it. There was no apparent pattern or organizational concept to this wild array of hardware.

"Is it not beautiful?" D'vore said. There was a sense of awe in his voice that I had not heard before; a reverence perhaps, although whether he could experience such an emotion was questionable. I couldn't see how I could honestly agree with D'vore's esthetic judgment; it was the farthest thing from beautiful that I could imagine.

Provance sneered. "Looks like a machine of some sort, I'd guess. Certainly doesn't look like something anyone could use."

D'vore turned. "It is registered for sale by a master who declines to state where he obtained it."

"Alien to be sure," Provance answered. "But what is your interest in this thing?"

D'vore hesitated. "I am not sure, but the design calls to me. It is an irrational idea to be sure, but one I cannot discount."

"It certainly looks like nothing we can use," she countered, "and it surely isn't putting any operating capital in our pockets. I say let's forget it and move on to more practical matters."

D'vore pulled away with obvious reluctance. "We still have some funds remaining after paying for the voyage and," he added with a glance at the distressed ship, and other things. Provance," he continued with a cautioning glance at me, "you mentioned that your family held reserves here, did you not?"

"Perhaps I might have mentioned that," Provance replied curtly. "But it will take time and possibly a little more investment."

"Then let's stop talking about it and get something done," I exclaimed. "I'm getting tired of the oblique statements you two constantly toss at each other. Why in hell can't you just say what you mean for a change?"

That outburst seemed to offend them. Neither said another word as we left to find accommodations for the night.

That night we lay apart, although I could not say whether that was Provance's preference. It certainly was mine. I had no desire to become more than friends with this pitifully slender woman.

"Do you think I am lovely?" she asked in the quiet of the night just as I was on the verge of deep slumber.

"For your kind, perhaps," I replied groggily but gallantly. "I am hardly one to judge."

"Ah yes, your disability and mental problems," she replied slowly. "I was wondering if the accident impaired you in other ways."

"I seem to have all my parts in working order, aside from these damned puzzling memories that seem to relate to nothing else." My abject ignorance of the most trivial things, and a complete lack of knowledge as to where or how I knew some things and not others continued to plague me. "Aside from that, there seems to be nothing else wrong with me." I tried to keep the sarcasm from MY voice. "Why do you ask?"

She didn't answer for a while and then, very tentatively said; "That was a very nice kiss." She paused, and then I heard the rustling of clothing and soft footsteps. "Can I have another?"

I was shocked to the point of not knowing what to say or whether to say anything. I'd thought that by my actions and lack of willingness to engage in any but the most innocuous of exchanges I'd made it obvious that I had no physical interest in our relationship, at least not in the terms she had suddenly and without warning made embarrassingly clear.

While I delayed, she slipped into the bed, took my face in her hands, brought her lips to mine, pressed her sparse form against me and sent her tongue exploring deep and wet. Once more I tasted the spice of her lips and drank in the sweet smell of her hair. I didn't want to respond but her need was so obvious that I had little choice but to answer back with the same spirit. Neither did I object to the rise of my own needs as we tangled in sweet bliss.

We spent the night locked in each other's arms, a pair of souls relieving their loneliness for a few brief hours.

D'vore was waiting at the entrance. He had become elongated the torso, which pitched forward slightly. "Why has your shape changed once again?" I was worried that I might lose track of exactly what D'vore looked like.

D'vore shrugged. "My need to become myself cannot be resisted. I found someone to help and now I am closer to my goal, even though I do not know where that end might be."

"Surely you must have some idea, some plan to achieve your ends," I protested. As much as I was curious about these changes I was a little upset that D'vore had gone to someone we were hoping to avoid. Didn't he have any concern about protecting our new identities?

"I grow unknowingly into my fate, I fear," he replied. "As do you, friend I. As do you."

After we acquired more permanent accommodations D'vore opened a small dispensary near the docks. "It establishes a basis for my new identity," he explained. "It would look odd were I not to be in character."

After making certain that his skills were available, D'vore began the messy business of repairing the daily mishaps brought. I assisted as best I could, which consisted mainly of cleaning the floor and instrument and tossing away the occasional spare part.

In the first week we aided a few Xingu, beings that I could not differentiate from the erstwhile Master Mastaxshaw, a Lajjoya named Cnaeus, a Gladesider that the diagnostic aid identified as a member of the Levidensis sort, and a squat human female Dimorphus whose shoulders barely reached my waist.

Their injuries were all less than fatal, such as Cnaeus', who'd suffered a broken anterior spine achieved in a encounter with a chair being swung by one of its crewmates during a dispute involving a bit too much pfalg, or so I understood it to say, without any knowledge of whether pflag was food, drink, or some alien drug, nor did I wish to know after getting a single whiff of the alien's loathsome breath.

The Gladesider's leg had been crushed so badly that D'vore had to attach a mechanical prosthesis. "This will hold you until I can negotiate a spare leg from the Penchon or some other reliable source. Check back next week."

The little Dimorphus female had suffered multiple blows about the head during a domestic dispute and needed only a few stitches. When her two-meter tall husband arrived to claim her, D'vore strongly suggested that perhaps a minor maladjustment of his chemical imbalance was at fault for the assault. The corrective chemical injection was easy, despite the husband's frantic struggles to escape D'vore's steel grip.

They left a happier couple.

And so it went, an endless parade of cripples made whole, the ill cured, and the injured succored. I never failed to be amazed at D'vore's skills in the surgery, nor the willingness of his variegated patients to succumb to his ministrations.

Provance created a bit of extra income during the time we worked at the dispensary, but was quite evasive about her activities. "It does not concern you, Case, nor affect our new relationship. There is no need for you to be jealous."

I still felt no physical attraction to her except when she was too close to be ignored. Which is why I wondered at my twinge of jealousy and, worse yet, how she had known?

"I found a place where they play a game of some complexity and skill that offer rich rewards for those who have the luck to win," she grinned. "And I seem to have been blessed with that luck. Here, let me explain." Suiting action to words she described the five-suit deck of seventy-two cards and a complex set of conventions that guided the game.

I begged her to teach me the rudiments of the game, but I quickly discovered that the cards were too small to manipulate easily. Provance, however, handled them with amazing dexterity, so much so that I wondered if she were doing something more than I could detect. I lost consistently as we played for favors and I started to wonder if the few times I did prevail were truly won.

After a while I realized that I had become fond of Provance's company despite my continued lack of appreciation of her dubious physical charms. I felt more of a brother than friend, less a companion than a sleeping partner.

Provance seemed to reciprocate the attraction, demanding little save occasional attention to her physical needs. "You remind me of a friend back on Parras," she said one evening, as we embraced after a satisfying session. "Not physically, but in personality and behavior. He too was reserved and calm, never speaking of his inner self."

That comment hurt more than I thought it would. "Am I so cold and unfeeling?" I wondered if my internal self-image had little to do with how others might perceive me? But that was only a momentary distraction. "Wait, did you say *Paris*?"

For some reason a strong memory of a past wife brushed my mind. I could picture her oval face, black hair, and green eyes as she turned from the rail of a tall tower overlooking a river. She held a chubby child in her arms. I recalled her ruby lips parting as she started to say something and … As quickly as the memory had come, it disappeared, leaving behind no clue as to its source or context.

"Are you all right" Provance asked, clearly alarmed.

A second memory appeared, this one of a statuesque blonde holding two infants and smiling insincerely. The light glinted for a moment on the single tear falling down her cheek as a different me walked away to board. With startling clarity I remembered the appearance of our ship, whole and complete, as yet untouched by disaster. I almost grasped the reason for this scene before it too faded away.

"This is so damned frustrating!" I pounded on the wall. "Why can't I remember for God's sake? Why do I get these little snippets of memory with no continuity, no context?"

"There, there." As Provance wrapped her long legs around me I tried to think of what might have triggered this latest assault? Was it her past lover; a friend or someone back on, where was it when she said "Paris."

"Did your Paris have bright lights and crowded roads?" I asked, as more memories brushed the surface of my mind. "Did your Paris smell of fresh bread and excellent wine? Could you buy roasting chestnuts on the boulevard and eat them in the rain?" The memories of a vast city, of museums, and restaurants, and bars, and dancing, and music, and wonderful sights and sounds drummed through my head so fast that I could hardly grasp one before another replaced it.

What was astounding was that these memories did not immediately fade. Instead they remained as a continuous tapestry of images, a memory of an experience long ago with a redhead named Francine, whose face I could not remember.

"Don't be so sad," Provance murmured.

But I was unable to stop the images flashing through my head. Tears poured down my face as the memories became tinged with despair, sadness, and a sense that my Paris, as well as a large part of my heart and soul, had been lost forever.

Provance continued to hold me as I continued to cry until, finally, exhausted and drained of emotion, I fell into a deep, dreamless slumber.

Provance was gone when I woke. She'd left no indication of her destination or when she would return. I'd become so used to this behavior that I wondered why I felt so much irritation at her absence on *this* morning. Perhaps it was because, after sharing so much of my emotions, I'd expected her to feel an obligation to reciprocate.

I helped D'vore prepare his surgery by pulling instruments from their charging booths, lining up poultices and ointments on the shelves, and placing a sterile arena where D'vore could treat who—or whatever next came along. Each day presented different issues and challenges.

"You did not sleep well," D'vore observed. "You walk with heavy steps."

I described the troubling memories of the previous night and the emotions they'd aroused. "These weren't fleeting images, not like the others," I explained. "These were more or less continuous, like linked scenes. Each one invoked emotions, smells, tastes, and sounds. It was almost as if I were remembering something from a few days ago, a year at most."

"That is a very good sign," D'vore answered. "It indicates that your mind is finally knitting up the raveled ends of retained thoughts. Did you happen to remember anything about your ship?"

I almost mentioned the single vivid image of the undamaged ship, but hesitated. Why would D'vore associate my random string of memories with the ship when I'd said nothing connected to it? Was he more concerned about the ship than my mental well-being? I decided to not mention the ship, not now.

"I can understand why my string of long-term memories is so poor, but my near-term memory seems affected as well," I said to redirect the subject. "I find it hard to properly recall things Provance told me about her past. Every time I think she's said something different it seems I've been mistaken."

"Very interesting. I also have noted some inconsistency about her statements." I thought that a strange remark coming from someone who never seemed to forget anything and had such mysterious access to facts. Perhaps it was just his way of expressing sympathy.

By the fortieth day after our arrival we had amassed considerable savings owing in equal parts to D'vore's skills as a medician and Provance's as a gambler, although I suspected that there was less gambling than skill involved else she wouldn't have won so consistently. Her winnings varied in amount and frequency, but were fairly level over time.

"I never win enough that should bother anyone," she said with a wicked smile as the three of us took a short walk across the docks. I no longer cared about her honesty but was more worried that she should fall in harm's way, that she should be doing something that would once more get her in trouble with the station's blue hats. I was about to mention my concern when I recognized the glyph emblazoned above the hatch of a recently docked ship. "That's *Qalyub Gudlag*!"

"You are correct," D'vore answered quickly. "However, I doubt that they could have traced us here. This might simply be a coincidence."

"We can't be certain. I think we should stay out of sight."

"Why are you worried about this ship?" Provance asked. "What did you two do to them?"

I quickly explained the two previous improbable coincidences and my assumption that these Penchon were in pursuit.

Provance tilted her head to one side. "Surely you don't expect me to believe that you have a Penchon ship chasing you? That's a really expensive effort unless there's a reason, a really important reason." There was a hint of mischief in her expression, as if she were making a prolonged calculation. "What aren't you telling me?"

"I'm shocked that you don't believe me. Haven't I always been truthful? I might leave a few details out here and there, but on the whole I've been as candid as I thought necessary."

"I am not concerned with your feelings, Case . Why are they after you?"

"They think we hold the key to a wrecked ship they have on board," D'vore interrupted. The unexpected statement shocked me . I had been thinking that this was all about my theft of D'vore. The thought that it might involve the wreckage had never occurred to me.

"But what's so important about a bit of wreckage?" Provance continued. "The Rift is littered with wreckage. Why should Case's be of particular interest?"

I thought she sounded a bit too interested for my liking. "I don't know," I admitted. "What's more, I didn't even think of the wreckage before now."

Provance stared. "You didn't trust me with that knowledge." It didn't sound like a question.

"It isn't that. It's just that explaining more would take too much time and we ..." Provance stalked away before I could say another word,.

"I do not fully understand her motivation for leaving in such a state," D'vore said.

"Perhaps she simply wanted some time away from us," I replied defensively. "I was not exactly candid and she probably did not want to start an argument over something I was obviously sensitive about."

"Perhaps that was a reason," D'vore answered. "However, I did not think that the entire answer. Not to be too direct, Case, but she is not that enamored of you to do such a courtesy. I would be careful about trusting her too much, despite your misperceived affection."

He said it with such conviction and lack of emotion, as if it were simply a fact and not an opinion, that I immediately became defensive. "How can you say that? You know we've been intimate, have shared our lives, and that she displays her affection quite openly. Of course she cares for me and I resent your saying otherwise."

"For one who denies any attraction for the woman, you appear to have more emotional involvement than you've admitted."

It was true, I finally had to admit; I had developed strong and quite unexpected feelings for Provance.

I did not reply to the question.

Where had she gone? As the hours grew long and since Provance had still not returned I wondered if she decided to amuse herself without me? Had some other fate befallen her or, darker still, had she fallen afoul of the bloody Penchon? "I'm going to look for her," I finally declared and made to leave.

"She is probably safe, if that is your concern," D'vore said.

"The Penchon have no reason to connect her to us. Unless, of course, she has chosen to inform them."

"She would not do that." I shouted, angry at the implication she would betray us.

"Of course," D'vore replied smoothly. "But I can see that you have other reasons to find her."

I stomped from the surgery without another word.

There were no Penchon lurking about, which I took to be proof that Provance had not betrayed us. There was a trio of humans staggering toward their ship, arms linked and chanting unrecognizable songs with either slurred diction or the use of some unknown language. I dismissed them as of no importance.

There were not that many places where humans congregated, so I proceeded to visit them one by one, always looking for someone tall and thin.

I had just about given up hope when I entered Gelan's Refuge. Provance was sitting in a back booth with her arms draped around two muscular men.

Unlike those people in that restaurant weeks before none of the people here appeared to act appalled at her being with humans of different species and, from the casual familiarity in which they were acting, I immediately suspected that the three had been intimate. I could practically picture the three of them sharing one another's bodies. The thought titillated and disgusted me.

How could she, I thought with rising anger? How could she take our relationship so casually and ruin it by behaving like this? Didn't she understand how much I cared? It was too much to bear. I turned on my heel and left, unwilling to confront her in such a public place and afraid of making a piteous spectacle as the jealous lover.

My angry retreat from the bar eventually brought clarity. Why had I felt that insane surge of jealousy? Why did I feel betrayed when Provance had given no overt commitment? She had pledged nothing, nor even deluded me that our physical relationship was anything more than responding to the bodies' physical needs. So why did I feel so hurt?

Was D'vore right? Had I unwittingly fallen in love?

"I'm glad you remain safe," Provance gave me no embrace, made no contact, and didn't even smile upon her return.

I examined her carefully, as if the evidence of infidelity would be written on her face, as if her guilt would reveal itself in words or actions, but there was no sign that I could detect. Was the tryst I'd imagined been a phantasm of my jealous imagination? Even though it was possible that nothing sexual had taken place—that this had been innocent companionship—I could not ignore my feelings, or stem my emotions. "What did you do?" I blurted, unable to contain my anger. "I saw you at Gelans! I saw you pawing those men."

Provance raised an eyebrow. "Is it so important to you what I do while we were apart, dear Case? I do not understand why you appear so upset. I would expect to see you concerned over my absence, relieved at my safe return, or even angry at not knowing where I had gone. Instead you seem filled with this puzzling rage. Please, tell me its source?"

Once again I had forgotten how easily she could read the emotions that boiled inside. I was defenseless against whatever emotional games she wanted to play and debated what I should say; how I could explain this rage that even I did not fully understand.

D'vore relieved me of the burden of responding. "Case is merely expressing his relief at your return."

"No," Provance replied sharply. She had never stopped staring. "There is more, much more to it than that."

"Yes, there is," I tried to restrain my voice. "I don't believe that your behavior with those me was simply companionship. I think you had sex with those men. Don't deny it. I could tell what had happened. I know how easily you give your favors. You are nothing but a whore. No, worse than that, a whore who makes no pretense at love."

Provance tilted her head to one side and smiled. "Is that what you think of me, Case? Why should such a simple thing as sex with others bother you so much? By doing what I want with my body I take nothing from you. In fact, I have never denied you any favor, even those you did not voice. Why would you demand more from me?"

That gave me pause. Was what she said true? Was there truly no rational reason for me to feel jealousy? Was my emotional reaction another manifestation of some attitude buried so deeply that it wasn't even a memory? I said nothing as I turned away to honestly examine my feelings and sort out whatever strange relationship I had forged with Provance.

I kept trying to rationalize the source of my feelings of betrayal, but could not think of a logical basis for the emotions that welled up, no reason that I should have expected any more from Provance than what she'd given. As she said, she'd promised nothing, yet, tearing at the corners of my heart, at the base of my soul was an empty feeling that my very core had been torn, leaving a shell of loneliness behind that no amount of rationalization could erase. Why was I feeling this sadness, this overwhelming sense of loss when, despite my deep feelings of betrayal? I still wanted to return to that comfortable friendship we'd had. I wanted her to share my bed. I wanted to taste her lips, smell her hair, and hear her sweet voice whisper passionately in my ear. At the same time I wanted to hurt her. No, that wasn't what I wanted. I wanted to tell her how deeply she'd wounded me. No, I couldn't do that. I had no right.

Around and around these conflicting drives tore at me I longed to feel her long legs wrapped about me yet knew with certainty that I would only be thinking of the others she'd had. I felt trapped between desire and hatred, adrift between the pillars of lust and principle. Trapped in an emotional quagmire, I struggled mightily as the hours and days passed, feeling physically sick–hating and loving her at the same time. I spoke no more of her supposed infidelity that she neither admitted nor denied. That I could see no trace of similar conflict on her behavior or conversation only made my misery the worse.

D'vore woke me with a whisper. "Someone has been making inquiries about a medician with a human partner."

"Penchon again? Why are they following us? I can't remember anything about the ship or my origin, that is, if that's their real reason."

"I said nothing about Penchon," D'vore answered. "Nevertheless, they do not know of your memory loss." Was he telling the truth or trying to mislead? D'vore had always been the ballast of my voyage and my one stabilizing influence. I had to believe that D'vore was indeed trying to help reach Earth and was not, as Provance suggested, simply using me for his own unknown and alien purposes.

"I suspect they did not immediately connect you to the wreckage," D'vore continued. "Or maybe they did not discover the odd circumstance of your ship until later, after we departed. Whatever the truth others may think you have vital information about it, Case, information they want to possess.

"Another possibility is that they were the ones who killed *Tollembol*'s crew to gain possession of the wreckage and did not realize that you were the sole survivor. After all, few would suspect anyone being left alive after examining the condition of your ship and fewer yet would attempt what we did to restore you."

"Yet, you did save me," I replied. "Or rather, the captain and you together brought me to life." Their reasons for that effort had not been apparent before; thinking that simple humanity to rescue a shred of what remained had been their only motivation. Now I realized that no one I'd met had done anything altruistic. What had the clone captain hoped to gain from having D'vore piece me together?

Perhaps D'vore was right that the pursuit was really about the twisted pile of metal that had once carried my ship's crew to their deaths. Yes, I thought with rising certainty; that must have been the captain's reason for examinations of the wreckage, for insisting that I pursue my memories to shed light on where it had come from and whatever drove it.

Somewhere, locked inside my head among the scattered memories, among the multiple lives and loves, among the detritus of several lifetimes must be the bald facts of the ship and its origins. Could that knowledge be sufficiently valuable to justify pursuing those memories across light years, so important that it cost the crew of *Tollembol* their lives, and so precious that it would probably cost my own life as well? "We've got to get away!" I concluded and, only when Provance rushed to my side did I realize how loudly I'd screamed.

D'vore seemed unaware of my inner conflict. "I agree. Flight is the only reasonable course. We cannot hope to hide our presence for long. I will see if I can make arrangements. You two stay here until I return."

While he was gone Provance and I traded impossible scenarios of how to prevent being discovered, how to escape to another station, and explore possible ways to discover the memories that everyone, including D'vore, so desperately sought.

When D'vore returned I immediately took stock of his appendages, the size and shape of his torso, and the location of his head to see what, if anything, had been altered during his absence. The examination could only be cursory since so much of D'vore remained hidden beneath his enveloping cloak. There was a slight bulge on his back, a lump that I might not have noticed had I not been so attuned to past changes. The lump appeared to be the same size and general shape as the previous cylinder.

D'vore gave a slight bow. "You are quite correct, Case . I am being forced to make another delivery."

"But why? We have enough problems facing us already. We don't want to be burdened by yet another obligation." I cared not a bit for this continual dependence on unknown parties, who themselves might be using D'vore.

"It is the price of immediate travel," he replied. "We must go to Solifugoe on board *Schyys*. That station is another step closer to Oroenoe."

"*Schyys*?"

"A ship due to arrive in three days," D'vore responded. "We will replace a few crew members when they discover that their second navigator, medician, and watch officer must answer certain questions by the blue hats–questioning that will keep them occupied until long after *Schyys'* scheduled departure."

Once again he had plucked a miracle from thin air. What access did he have to ship schedules, station management, and things like these sudden questions? Until now I had assumed that D'vore had been sold to *Tollembol*, but perhaps there had been earlier owners or some other arrangement. Neither did I know how long D'vore had been apart from his own "accident."

Questions, always questions and more than I could ever hope to have answered, it seemed, and every new question added to the complexity of the situation without a hint of resolution. There were too many agendas at play, too many possible players, too many motives, and most of them probably beyond my pathetically weak understanding of this strange human culture, let alone hope to grasp alien motivations and behaviors?

We tried to be as unnoticeable as possible as we waited for *Schyys'* arrival. The Penchon seemed to be everywhere. Had they learned of our false identities? D'vore's cover as a failed Penchon experiment from the war certainly would alert them if nothing else. When they connected that identity and the medician services he'd performed, a suspicion was sure to arise. Best that we shut down the surgery and disappear.

While D'vore closed down, Provance and I agreed to never venture forth in each other's company and be ever wary of watchful eyes. It would only take a small slip to disclose who we really were. To prevent even a small disclosure we decided not to return to our room, frequent familiar restaurants, or follow any earlier patterns of behavior.

"You are correct," Provance agreed. "The best course is to assume that our identities are already compromised. I can't accept that we dare not move about the station, feed ourselves, or even risk a place to sleep. I don't know about you, Case, but I have no desire to spend the next two days scuttling about like a damned rat." With that she stalked away, head held high, and striding as if she had not a care in the world.

"We will have only the possessions we carry," D'vore said as we slipped away. "No doubt whoever seeks us is waiting to pounce should we try to access our funds."

Our funds in hand were a pittance compared to our savings. "What about ThripoBlastenav? Would it help us so you can deliver that container?"

"They will not," D'vore responded. "Demonstrating support for us at this juncture would be likely to reveal certain activities they wish to remain secret. Why else would they choose me as courier?"

I had no desire to become more deeply involved in these machinations, whatever they might be. I had problems enough on my own without being sucked into their realm. "So what can we do?"

"We will move only during the Penchon's sleep cycle," D'vore suggested. "There is a storage facility near Bay 12, not far from where *Schyys* will dock. It may be somewhat cramped, but sufficient to keep us hidden until they sleep. We should be able to move safely then."

I hoped that this one would be more commodious when memories of the small crate we had arrived in popped into my head. I also wondered how Provance would accept "scuttling like a rat."

The hiding place was more spacious than expected and Provance did not overtly complain, despite her earlier remark about rat holes. After a while D'vore announced that *Schyys* was docking. "Let me make certain the way is clear," he said and slipped away.

I worried at his prolonged absence. "Do you think something has happened? Could the Penchon …" Fear that the aliens had wormed our location from a captured D'vore grew in my breast with every passing moment.

Provance laid a hand on my arm. "Best we leave before they find us, Case . Come on. I know the way to where *Schyys* is docking." She tugged me along.

The route she chose took us along narrow and indirect passages that I thought would be difficult for Penchon bodies to navigate should we be mistaken about the aliens' sleep cycles. For all I knew those cycles might not be synchronized across ships or even followed equally by an entire crew.

Provance carefully peered around the first corner to ensure there were no watchful eyes to see us dart across the wide corridor, just in case the Penchon had enlisted others in the search. Provance's long legs quickly took her across the open space. "Should I carry you the next time?" she asked with a smile as I caught up.

"I'll try," I panted, certain that those damn legs of hers would outmatch mine no matter how fast I ran. We darted down another passage, climbed stairs, and leapt from one platform to another as quickly as we could. Some of the places were just barely wide enough to pass.

"It's down here," Provance whispered and pulled me around a corner to face with two muscular men from the cafe. I was unsure of who screamed louder, the startled men or me, but I was quicker on the uptake when we lunged at them. I spun Provance around and pulled her back the way we had come. "There may be others after us," I panted wondering why she seemed so slow. The encounter could not have been an accident.

"We've got to split up," Provance shouted and pointed at a ladder. Splitting up might be a good strategy, I imagined, but it possibly meant that one of them would be captured. I had no idea if the ladder was an escape route or if it would lead me into a dead end. Still, I clambered up as quickly as I could once Provance raced away. At the top a walkway extended to right and left. I raced along the walkway, looking for a route that might take me out of danger. One glance back told me that one of the men was ascending the ladder with fluid ease.

I reached a branch and took the left one without thinking. It ended a few steps later at a tiny hatch, half my height. I removed the dogs from the handle and crawled inside, hoping that perhaps there was some way I could lock it from the inside. No such luck. Once inside I discovered I couldn't even turn around to reach the hatch, which now yawned wide and revealed my escape route.

Panicked, I scurried forward on hands and knees into darkness, extending one hand after another, feeling for another hatch, or some yawning chasm I might fall into. It seemed I'd crawled for hours, but it could only have been minutes when I heard someone scrambling behind and crawled faster, no longer mindful of what dangers might lie in my path. Abruptly there was no floor beneath my hands. I fell hard, striking my chest on an edge as I flailed about, trying to stop my headlong momentum and touching only air.

The descent was narrower than the passage and friction of my body against the sides impeded my fall. Nevertheless I struck bottom so hard that it took my breath away.

I looked around and noticed a dim glow to one side. It was a grate and, on the other side of it was an area filled with cargo bins and scurrying loaders. I painfully turned about to kick at the grate, hoping to dislodge it.

The first kick seemed to do nothing except send a sharp pain up my leg. There was a little give on the second and on the third I definitely felt the grate loosen. Unmindful of the damage I might be doing to my leg or the noise I was making, I continued to kick until the grate finally fell away with an alarming clatter to the deck below.

I turned and backed through the opening until I could grasp the edges and lower myself. My hands slipped. The fall was about ten meters and snapped something in my already screaming leg. I tried to ignore the pain and tried to rise. When the leg wouldn't support my weight I had to crawl away using arms and my one good leg to find refuge among the containers. All the time I kept an eye on the huge loaders racing around, moving cargo about, afraid that one would run over me.

I wondered if my pursuer had followed? Would he emerge from the yawning grate? The probability was all too certain as I continued to look for a hiding place. Then I heard a cry of frustration or a call of victory at finally trapping his prey. I knew it would only be a matter of moments before others entered the space to take me into custody.

Where could I hide?

I spied a the loaders' entry portal just twenty meters away and increased my frantic efforts to propel myself along with hands, elbows, knee, and sheer will, hoping that, if I could only reach the portal I might find help or discover some other way of evading the creatures who could only be moments away. I heard faint, dull thuds as multiple feet hit the deck, followed by sounds of rapid footfalls. The portal was less than ten meters away, a distance I could not possibly cover in the remaining time.

Then, to my right, I saw a small space between containers sitting on a wide pallet. The space was barely wide enough for my body but I pushed into it, straining to fill every available space. From this position there were no options, no escape routes. In this narrow space all I could do was await the inevitable.

I could feel the drumbeat of my heart as two men passed by, so close that I could hear their soft footfalls. I held my breath, afraid that they would hear even a faint exhalation of air from my tortured lungs as I strained to retreat further into this refuge.

An automated loader approached, stopped, slid its tongues under the pallet on which I rested, and smoothly lifted it. Turning about, it carried the pallet, and more importantly, me, away. I didn't know where the loader was bound, nor did I care. The fact that it was moving me away from certain capture was sufficient.

The loader made several turns. My limited view through the narrow opening was flashes of bulkhead and doorways, corners and corridors. I had no sense of place or position in relation to where I had been. Finally the loader passed through another portal and trundled into the dim recesses of a room containing dozens of shipping containers where it finally halted, set the pallet gently down, backed away, and departed.

I listened for the slightest sound that might betray someone or something nearby. Certainly the loader had shifted the pallet at someone's direction. Even in this strange station it was unlikely that loaders possessed any volition where cargo was concerned. I wondered what purpose had been served by the move.

My leg was throbbing, not only from the fall but also from being compressed into this too small space. I struggled from the refuge and tried to straighten up. Agony screamed from foot to knee.

"The pain must be considerable for you to grimace so much," D'vore said calmly from a few meters to my right.

"How?" I gasped. D'vore was the least probable individual I expected to encounter, but before I could frame another question, the D'vore replied.

"It was a simple matter of paying attention to the maintenance alerts and watching the surveillance cameras. Once I located you I merely ensured that certain cargo be shifted." It was yet another revelation of his astounding capabilities.

"Provance," I gasped. "We split up. Do you know where she is now? Could they have … ?" I began, fearful of what the answer might be. "We have to find her."

"We must stay here a while longer," D'vore advised. "Certain events must unfold before we can move."

I tore free of his grasp. "We have to find Provance! We can't just sit here."

"We must. Besides, there is nothing you can do for her, not with that bad leg. Best we remain where we are."

But I refused to listen and immediately broke into a shambling run, favoring my damaged leg, looking for some sign of Provance as I raced toward the dock, ever alert for sign of the Penchon.

As I approached the bay I spotted her standing near *Schyys*, scanning the dock, no doubt waiting for me. "Provance," I cried and stumbled toward her.

She broke into a wide smile and spread her arms in welcome as she moved toward me. "Case . At last!" Dark figures emerged from the shadows behind her.

"Watch it," I yelled, but the Penchon had already surged forward past as she smiled at me.

I stood dumbstruck as a huge container flew past and struck the racing Penchon, sending them tumbling to the deck. "Quickly," D'vore cried. "This way, Case ."

I was trying to understand why Provance merely watched the struggling Penchon with an expression of disgust. "I don't understand," I cried as D'vore quickly dragged me away to leave Penchon far behind.

Or so I hoped.

The two of us sat for what seemed like hours as I struggled to work out some reason for Provance's betrayal. Perhaps she was unaware of the Penchon's reasons for capturing us and thought their only concern was my theft? That was most likely–better than that she'd been captured and used as bait–but then, why no warning? There had to be a better reason for what she appeared to have done.

Suddenly there was an incredible explosion. "Quickly," D'vore ordered and lifted me off my feet. Alarms were clattering from all sides. Smoke billowed for a moment further along the row of berths and disappeared as a fierce wind roared through the corridor. There were screams, the pound of racing feet, and the clatter of equipment.

D'vore, keeping a firm hold on me, darted to the right and then immediately changed direction, avoiding direct contact with figures racing toward the ships. We cleared a hatchway just before it slammed closed and ran through another door to return to the docks. Ahead, just a dozen meters away, was a ship's hatch. People were streaming toward it from all directions. D'vore pressed our tabs to the portal as we entered.

Moments later a thin and harried crewmember who strongly resembled Provance rushed up. "Navigator! I just saw you tab aboard. You've got bridge experience, haven't you? Listen, captain needs you to help us leave."

"What is happening? Why do we need to leave?" I wailed as she raced away, providing no answers to my questions. I looked around and found that D'vore had disappeared as well. People were streaming into the ship, clearly panicked. There was clearly some sort of emergency and, although I did not understand what it might be, I clearly felt their need for urgency.

As I entered the bridge the captain, a small imp, was screaming at departure control. "Listen to me, damn it! I need a clear outbound lane immediately. If you don't clear me in the next five minutes I damn well will depart without one and the hell with the consequences." He turned. "Can you find a route to take *Pletopf* away from the station without running into something? I need it in minus ten minutes!"

"I'll try," I stuttered and did my best, given the short time I was given. "It looks like we can take a clear lane between two others waiting to dock if we leave now." *Pletopt* was not the ship we intended to be on, but considering the emergency I was not going to dispute that detail. Maybe we could find *Schyys* later, when the emergency died down.

In the background I could hear the cries of the crowd pressing to pack *Pletopt* with far more than the vessel usually carried. Immense and complex as these interstellar ships might be they had little room for passengers since all crew on board were required to do their part to ensure safe and profitable passage of the cargoes. I wondered how the captain was going to handle these extra passengers and how they would affect *Pletopt's* mass? But the likelihood of *Pletopt* leaving the system was slight. More likely we'd just move a safe distance for a while.

Most likely.

The captain, an imp with a withered limb, was named Lustal. It had a staccato manner of speech and tended to slur the longer words when it was in full rush. "Blessings for helping, navigator. I hope we can return soon. Leaving a lot of cargo on the dock." he muttered as he reviewed my proposed outbound route.

Pletopt finally got clearance in the form of being roughly disconnected and ejected from her berth. There were no formal preliminaries as the pilot fired the impulse engines without waiting for the gentle administrations of a tug and immediately began the long climb away from the station and away from Provance.

"What happened?" I asked the first person I saw after being dismissed from the bridge. "Why did we have to leave?"

"I heard an explosion," a woman cried, "and somebody pushed me onto this ship. I don't know where my husbands are or what happened to my ship." She began crying.

"Listen, I need to know what happened. Do you know anything at all?"

She acted as if she hadn't heard and continued to wail. "My husbands are tall, dark. They were wearing red. We were looking for a restaurant. Have you seen them?" When I shook my head she raced away, still looking for her lost mates.

A man dressed all in gray utilities said there had been an announcement to move people off the station by any ship available, but was no more knowledgeable about the nature of the emergency than the woman. "There was an explosion–some ship, maybe Penchon I'd guess. In their docking area, anyway." Although that was no confirmation of the explosion's cause or the location I knew in my heart that it could only have been the *Qalyub Gudlag*. Worse, he suspected that D'vore or his associates had been behind the explosion.

The crew had herded the crowd into *Pletopt*'s nearly empty hold and let the others find their places. Was Provance now safely aboard a Penchon ship or had she been on the *Qalyub Gudlag* when it exploded? Even if she had not, could she have been close enough to be killed?

The image of Provance's burned and bloody body, her vacuum-frozen form, her torn and broken limbs, grew steadily more graphic in my mind and nothing I could do would drive them out. It was a torment, a burden—pain so real that I grew physically ill. Growing with the pain was the certainty that D'vore had a hand in whatever had transpired to kill her. The very ship that was pursuing us exploding as we tried to escape was too great a coincidence to be ignored. How or why D'vore had done this was beyond my understanding, but I was determined to get an answer from him, one way or another.

D'vore had set up an emergency clinic in one of the cargo holds when the ship's small surgery proved unable to handle the number of injured and distressed. There were aliens and human of every shape and description crowding for attention. Many of the humans sat in stunned silence as they waited D'vore's ministrations as the similarly distressed aliens sat among them. None of them seemed to have life-threatening injuries, although with an alien, that was ever in doubt.

I waited patiently as D'vore took care of the wounded and disturbed, one after another, doling to each their measure of aid, patching their wounds, or giving them some medication, until all were served. "What did you do?" I nearly shouted as D'vore tended to my injured leg. I was filled with the rage that had been building as I waited, filled with the certainty of D'vore's complicity in the disaster they'd fled, and frustrated that there was nothing I could do to make the medician share my agony and loss.

"I can understand your feelings," D'vore answered. "Despite her obvious deception, your feelings are only normal considering the degree of infatuation the woman engineered."

"You bastard!" I flailed at him. "Infatuation? Engineered? How could you know the love I felt for her? How could something as alien as you hope to understand the depth of our relationship? She must have been forced to help the Penchon. That's the only explanation!"

"I can assure you that she did not reciprocate your emotions," D'vore continued as he held me at arms' length until, impotent against his strength, I slumped in dejection. "Provance is likely on another ship," D'vore continued quietly. "I am certain that she was not injured."

"How do you know that? How can you know that?"

"I don't, but we can assume that since she was so close to the hatch, she probably boarded *Schyys* safely. You need not worry for her welfare. She is highly capable of caring for herself, as we both witnessed during our brief acquaintance."

I had no way of knowing if D'vore was merely saying what I so desperately needed to hear. I knew that the alien had the ability to read my body, if not my mind. Even knowing this I welcomed the balm of his words and felt the some of the rage diminish even as the sadness and loss remained.

I still refused to believe D'vore's assertions about Provance's affections—certain that we'd shared something that the inhuman bastard could never understand. No matter what it might have looked like, I was certain that Provance wouldn't have willingly betrayed me, not after all we had together, the way we felt, and our love.

I fumed: D'vore's deception about *Schyys* had been more than a simple lie and, as a result of his acting on completely unfounded suspicions, Provance was now racing away. "Why were you so intent on separating us?" I screamed. "Why did you lie?"

It would have been humane for D'vore to pause before answering, to show some sign of reflection, but he did not. "I lied for your benefit, Case . I was forced to do so when I noticed how easily Provance was reading your emotional state and twisting you to her advantage."

"That's a damned lie! It's not true! Our relationship wasn't like that. We were in love, for God's sake!"

D'vore continued as if he hadn't heard the protest. "I clearly understand that you did not realize how she was using your emotional vulnerability."

I could not believe my ears. Was D'vore trying to recast his duplicity as something he'd done for my benefit?

"Perhaps I share some of the blame for the sorrow you are no doubt experiencing," the medician continued. "I did permit this attachment to develop, but only because you obviously needed human companionship to become emotionally settled. In that the relationship appeared successful and was very beneficial to your physical well-being. You must admit that your emotional outlook improved."

"Emotionally settled? We fell in love!"

"No, you were maneuvered into feeling you were in love, but it was a fragile relationship at best. Have you forgotten your doubts when she was absent? Don't you wonder about your reactions whenever she came near? Be honest with yourself, Case ; you were a victim of someone with no investment in your welfare."

"Impossible. I know that I loved her, damn it! Nothing you can say will change that." Easy words, but the questions remained on my mind for days and, gradually, some doubts began to form, not the least of which was the question of her apparent betrayal.

Could D'vore have been right? I suspected, but had never admitted that Provance's inconsistent stories were not, as she contended, evidence of my confused memory. Worse, now that I remembered in the cold harsh light of the ship, I could not honestly recall when she had voluntarily expressed her feelings toward me. Always, it seemed, such statements were in response to my urging.

Her suspected deception became constant question, as was the agony of loss. All I had was a circumstance that might mean that she'd betrayed me. All I had was D'vore's word that she had boarded *Schyys*, if that was true?

Despite the rising certainty of her duplicity, I nevertheless longed for Provance's touch, her smell, and the wonderful taste of her on my lips. I loved her, missed her, and distrusted her in a confusing tangle of emotional contradictions that I could not reconcile.

Thoughts of my lost love were occasionally pushed aside as my earlier suspicions returned. "What did you do back there?" I demanded of D'vore. "Don't deny your hand in this–there's too much coincidence surrounding the explosion. Did the accident involve *Qalyub Gudlag?*"

"There is no evidence that a specific Penchon ship had an accident," D'vore assured me. "Quite a number of Penchon were arriving, as we noted earlier. Whatever happened could have been caused by one of the arriving ships accidentally rupturing the station's walls. Or perhaps some volatile cargo was placed too near a heat source. There are so many possible reasons for the apparent explosion that we cannot guess at the correct one. I would suggest that you ask the captain to look at its most current WOFAT logs. They should have been updated as we departed and probably contain the answers you seek. You will also find no evidence that I was involved."

"Yes, it seems an implosion occurred near a cargo storage volume quite close to the Penchon berths," Lustal, the captain, confirmed after scanning the last download. "The massive decompression imperiled the pan-human level of the station's life support systems. It was that failure that forced the evacuation, not damage to any ship."

I wondered if D'vore, with his control of the cargo handlers, have shifted more than the pallet where he'd hidden, such as a container that would explode when placed near heat? He'd even admitted as much when he mentioned possible reasons so I no longer had any doubts of his hand in this, even if I could not understand the reasons.

Pletopt stood apart from the station for long days and nights until whoever took care of such emergencies restored the station. When not preoccupied with further explorations of my wrecked ship's image or mourning the possible loss of dear Provance, a supposition that I debated explanations for the accident.

Had D'vore created this situation to throw the Penchon off our trail? In the confusion they'd have no way to tell which ship we had boarded and, even if they could ascertain that fact, they may not have known who we were.

If D'vore's objective had been to prevent the Penchon from continuing their pursuit, then he had also severed the only link I had to my past. Without the physical touchstone of my ship, the twisted pile of metal in their hold, I had only my scattered memories and the realistic images retained by D'vore to jog my memories.

Regardless of what I might suspect, I had no way to force a truthful answer. Neither could I sever my relationship with D'vore. I had no other resource. Like it or not, the two of us were tightly bound until sufficient memory returned to allow me to act independently.

D'vore was as ever solicitous as the days went by. "You remain distraught," he said. "Is it still about Provance?"

I didn't want him to know how heartsick I was. "No. I was just thinking that when we evaded the Penchon we also lost all possibility of finding something in the wreckage that might yield a clue to my past."

"Not lost, Case . Nothing of your ship will ever be lost. I finally finished processing the image. Look at this." I started as the shimmering image of the wreck appeared before us. The sudden appearance of the wreckage inside this cramped space was impossible. That huge mass of tortured metal and plastic could not possibly fit into the crowded cargo hold. It had to be an illusion, a trick of the eyes, or some aspect of virtual presentation. I glanced around. No one seemed to have noticed the huge ship floating in their midst. D'vore must have done some mental trick so that I was the only one who could see it.

"You can explore the ship if you wish," D'vore said gently as I gaped wide-mouthed in amazement.

I started to step forward but D'vore held me back. "No, don't move. All you have to do is think of moving forward and I will manipulate the image to your wishes."

"You can read my mind?" I wondered again if D'vore's

control went far beyond the simply reading my body's signs.

D'vore laughed in a rare display of amusement. "No, that is beyond my capabilities, but I can detect the tiny involuntary muscle movements that precede thought and action and adjust your view of the image accordingly."

I had to take him at his word for acceptance of the alternative, that D'vore could control my mind, would be too uncomfortable. The idea that he could put this image into my head was disturbing enough, but if all he was doing was manipulating a few optical nerves ... Best not to pursue that thought too far.

The sharp projections of torn metal were as I recalled, as were the stains upon the decks in the few visible areas. "This is as frustrating as before. There is so much I can't see, so many hints of what might bring back more memories."

"I note that you do not seem as emotionally disturbed as you were on earlier explorations."

D'vore was right. On earlier explorations, as I'd walked through the wreck, every turn had flooded me with strong feelings of loss and sorrow, each stain a reminder of a crewmate that I might have known. But now I only saw the wreckage as an artifact, a cold inanimate object with nothing left of the life that had once filled it.

"Do you feel you feel stable enough to see the original ship?" D'vore said. "I've reconstructed the way the ship might have looked."

"I don't understand."

"Whatever befell your ship folded, bent, and distorted it," he explained. "But nothing became detached. Even the torn edges of metal remained close so that much remained connected."

"That is interesting, but what does it have to do with ... ?"

D'vore didn't let me finish. "Since the accident I have been working on the complex topological problem of the wreckage. Part by part I've unfolded the images of the bent portions, reconnected torn metal, and separated all that had been forced together. I can now show you my assumptions of what the original ship may have looked like."

I was stunned that such a feat could be possible as I looked at the compressed mass of metal. The sheer processing power that it would take to do what D'vore said was immense and that he had done this himself was nothing short of astounding.

My amazement faded quickly as the possibility of once again walking the corridors, virtually touching the controls, and sitting where one of my crewmates had sat overwhelmed me. It was almost too much to bear. What memories, what emotions would be brought about? What feelings would flood my mind? Would there be revelations and associations that opened the gates on my past? Would these actions finally provide me with the answers I had so desperately sought since awakening in *Tollembol*?

Even though I was excited at the prospect, I was uncertain if I was prepared for whatever emotions those images might bring. "I … I," I stuttered, unable to complete the sentence, unable to force words through my lips.

D'vore winked the image away. "I understand, Case. Think about this, give yourself time to grasp the idea, and, when you are ready, I will let you visit your ship."

Once again my alien companion had shown compassion without me giving voice to his confusion.

For days afterwards I struggled to resolve my burning desire to know more of my past with an undefined fear as to what I might discover about my ship and destiny. I could not put my finger on the source of my fears, the gnawing unease that I might find the reconstituted ship too much to bear. It wasn't rational to feel this way, not after struggling for so long to recall what I once was–that is, if "I" had any real meaning, given that I was an amalgam of the entire crew.

Could it be that I feared that my parts would call out to those departed crew, that my sense of self would be torn asunder by an emotional flood my carefully restored personality could not withstand? Were all my fears groundless, meaningless to the reality of today? There was no rational reason to fear the ghosts of my crew. Rather I should rejoice that they, through me, still lived and would once again regain our home.

After chewing the possible gains against more dire outcomes

I resolved to put my fears aside. Although I couldn't ignore my reactions, I would not let them control me. With that resolve, I faced D'vore. "I am ready," I said simply as we huddled together in one corner of the cargo hold, an arm's length from a family of four.

The wreckage appeared as before; a twisted pile of metal far too immense for this small hold. Slowly, as I watched with rising disbelief, a metal panel atop the pile bent back and fused along one edge with another. Other panels below it now did the same, building the exterior of the ship. If I thought the wreckage itself was too large for the hold then this transforming vision went far beyond as the reconstituted hull stretched far beyond the confines of the entire ship, dwarfing me with its growing immensity. I again started to rise to step forward. "As I said before, do not move but merely think of moving," D'vore cautioned with one hand on my arm. "Wait a moment more until I am finished."

Through an open hatch I glimpsed pieces moving about, sliding into place, bent areas becoming smooth, healing tears and softening sharp edges merging into bulkheads, decks and equipment. I waited impatiently, wanting to see the interior so much yet reluctant to take that first step, fearful of what might be revealed.

"It is done," D'vore said too soon and, with some reluctance, I stepped inside and discovered a small, cramped space and facing a second hatch. The words "air lock" came to mind. I marveled at how natural this virtual movement felt for only an instant before the wonder of what I was seeing overwhelmed me to acceptance.

On either side were large hooks just above head height. A panel of switches was beside the inner hatch. Portions of whatever had been printed above each switch were still evident, although not enough to make out whatever words there might have been. The inner hatch swayed open. I stepped through and into a corridor so narrow that I had to twist sideways. The deck was bare metal, embossed with tiny crosses for traction. Handholds were placed at intervals along the bulkhead and, strangely, on the overhead. Here and there I could read embossed symbols adorning latched covers; "HiVac," "Release A," "Compart B," and "43567Ab Inverter." I was tempted to open one compartment, but didn't know if D'vore's simulation would support such efforts and set that thought aside. There would be time to test that possibility later, after I'd explored the length of the corridor.

Ten virtual steps along the companionway widened to contain a chair surrounded on three sides by instrument panels. The chair appeared formfitting and was mounted on a slight track, most likely to allow side-to-side movement. Curious, I sat down, or at least thought I could. The mixture of virtual and real seemed to have faint hold for the moment.

"Do not over-analyze. Relax," D'vore whispered from behind my left ear. "Let your mind wander. Perhaps associations will form."

After a moment's hesitation I allowed myself to become immersed in the experience, letting whatever memories might emerge take hold. The name David floated into my mind as the chair embraced me like the familiar arms of a lover.

It was a beautiful night off Bermuda when I was trying to relax from worries about the forthcoming mission. The experimental trips had gone well, I recalled, first with machines, then with animals and now, for the first time, with a human crew who could report back on the experience.

"Happy?" a female voice whispered. "Only a few days left before ..."

I hushed her. "Let's just enjoy the time we have. I'm not worried." That was almost the truth. I knew there would be no physical effects. They'd learned that from the rats and later the dogs and monkeys on the short distances. They had even returned from a short run of less than half a light year with no physical effects. There was no reason that this longer jump of a full light-year would be any different. No reason at all.

For an agonizing moment I was horribly split, the David part of my mind with mild anticipation of what was to come and my conscious mind horrified at his imminent death.

Unknowing of the horrible fate that awaited, David continued to adjust his instruments, worry about what might happen, and thought about Jocelyn's firm ass. I wanted to scream at him to abort the voyage, to stay the hand of the project lead.

Suddenly my heart was beating rapidly as I gasped for breath. "You were going into shock," D'vore said as he swam into sight. "I had to pull you out of there."

I looked around. No one seemed to be paying us undue attention. "David knew it was an experimental ship—a star drive," I whispered as if that had not already been evident. "We were going to jump a light year. I couldn't stop him."

The irrationality of that statement struck me immediately. It had only been a memory. There was no way I could have communicated to David; no way I could save him and the others. Idly I wondered what had ever happened to the Jocelyn of David's memory? It was so confusing, this memory of a memory.

D'vore brought me back to reality. "Do you recall anything else? How was the ship powered? Where did you get the design?" There was a note of urgency in his voice.

"I don't know. I was thinking of someplace called 'Bermuda' and a woman named Jocelyn. Something about animal experiments, but nothing more." I sat up. "That was the most detailed memory I've ever had about the ship. I have to get back in there. I need to find out more."

D'vore shook his head. "Obviously it gave you too much information for you to process objectively, but I am encouraged that it elicited useful memories. We can do more later, when you are better prepared for the emotional storms that might occur."

"No, let me go back."

D'vore refused. "I am as anxious to learn more as you, Case, but we have many more hours to probe. There is no need to be stressed. Take time to rest and relax. We will do this again tomorrow."

I wondered what D'vore might have given me. Too much, he'd said but of what? I recalled no injections. Was it some mental inoculation, like the ability to perceive what others could not? There were too many questions that I had not the energy to pursue at the moment.

That night I dreamed of nothing but my recent memories, as if the shocking clarity of David's thoughts had purged the demons for a while. It was the best night's sleep I'd had in ages.

When the next visit to the virtually reconstructed ship brought no new recollections I wondered if D'vore was somehow suppressing any further memories. It might be a blessing until after I'd scoped the entire ship.

I moved past David's chair and discovered other similarly arranged alcoves, each with its bank of instruments, each with its form-fitting chair. I noticed tape marks where sheets had been pasted against the panels, clips that might have held a sheaf of papers, shelves that might have held reference works or instructions.

At the end of the corridor was a larger alcove whose panels swept the entire width of the area. Two chairs sat before the panels, each commanding half of the instruments. This, I imagined, was where the project lead and pilot sat. Yes, there were the gaping holes where the view panels must have been. Somehow I knew those were the attitude control handles and there were the instruments that advised the pilot of her local position, acceleration, and direction. If I sat in her chair would I recall what she might have thought? Would I share her thoughts as I had David's? Would I be able to withstand the mental embrace of a woman's thoughts, dreams, fears, and hopes?

No, I didn't want to attempt that this visit so I turned and headed toward the other end of the corridor. That, I'd realized, was where the drive most likely would reside and recalled that …

… the engineering on this ship, with this engine had not been settled science. The theory did not account for all the effects and there was still much to be understood about multi-space travel on the scientific level. Gaylord had mentioned some obscure anomaly deep in the mathematics, but assured everyone that they needn't be overly concerned.

Those quibbles aside, there was enough known to build the

*drive and enough solid engineering to make it work, even though
some aspects not quite understood. Only at a power level well
beyond what they would apply would the math break down.*

Multi-space travel! I realized that someone in the crew must
have known about seven-space navigation. That must be why
learning math had come to me so easily. But the memory hadn't
felt like it was that well explained. More like it was a theory
grasping for concrete reality, somewhat soft around the edges
with more guess than solid exposition.

Why would they chance it if so much were unknown, I
wondered?

I had ample time to chase each momentary memory down
to its source as I sat among the huddled masses in the hold. I
would close my eyes and let my mind wander where it would,
bringing recent and old memories into fragmentary focus and
then seeing where that would lead. In most cases the trail
ended after only a few associations and often interrupted by the
painful realization that I would never see Provance again. I tried
to suppress these sad thoughts, but was not always successful.

At times I cried.

I began recalling the crews' faces and occasionally matched
those to a name, although my certainty of those associations
was largely absent. Some of the remembered people wore
strange clothing, quite different from anything I'd encountered
recently. Two appeared identically clad in dark blue, with
flashes of bright color on their breasts. Once I recalled a tiny
golden crescent in a sky dotted with stars and, associated with
it, a chorus of chirping noises and the smell of grass.

When someone stirred beside me it brought back the
memory of Provance's thin form in our shared bed, the feel of
her skin under my fingers and, with that, the glimpse of my
distant past dissipated as morning mist.

One night, roused from sleep, I clearly recalled the control
panel with its mysterious candle, only this time the flame was
flickering at a slow, steady rate. I could remember more details
of the dream this time—a rectangle of light inscribed with

numbers and words that kept changing as I watched.

"First stage charge building up," someone said quite close to me. "Check the primary coils."

I saw my hand reach out and touch the rectangle–a screen, I recalled. It was called a screen! The numbers changed. "Looks all right," I said in a high-pitched voice, a woman's voice.

"Twenty minutes to go," a loud voice shouted. "Strap in." I fastened toggle to clasp, settled back, and watched the flickering candle.

I could recall no more of the incident, although I still remembered the details and sequence, candle, screen, voices and all. This was a longer set of memories than any I'd experienced since that memory of Paris, or was it Parras? Perhaps, as D'vore had promised, the integration of my mind was continuing and that, one day soon, that integration would be complete. Or was it that whatever he had done to enhance my memories persisted long beyond my virtual visits to the ship?

Other memories flitted through my half-wakened mind–the taste of a bitter drink, the smell of flowers, a roaring sound and feeling or vertigo–but no more sequences of actions, no more crisp memories of the interior of that ship.

Finally, when the stink in the hold had reached a point that it was nearly a visible miasma, Lustal was given permission to return to the station. The crew quickly emptied the mass of refugees from the hold and began loading cargo as quickly as possible. I was asked to prepare an alternative routing to Solifugoe through seven space. The one their navigator had prepared a week before was now dated and therefore worthless.

"That is a job for your own navigator," I advised the captain. "I'm here only by accident."

D'vore intervened. "Excuse him, captain, he's been under considerable stress from the emergency. Give us a few moments, please." I would have protested such an outright lie, but D'vore's painful grip on my arm tightened every time I tried to speak.

It was a strong signal to remain quiet. Then, while Lustal was momentarily preoccupied, D'vore hissed. "As I said before, this is our ship, Case . I never intended us to board the *Schyys.*"

"But you said ..."

"I lied. *Schyys* was bound elsewhere, not Solifugoe. My comments on joining *Schyys'* crew were a ruse, a way to keep Provance in the dark—a stratagem that seems to have worked quite well. Had I not done that I am sure that she would have been the richer and you would be in the hands of the Penchon."

While I stood in stunned silence, appalled at this admission and half unbelieving the justification, D'vore continued. "Now, do as the *Pletopt's* captain asks and give us a good plot for Solifugoe. You can scream at me later if you wish."

I could tell by the sudden increase in air pressure that any objections I might have raised were too late. The ship had been sealed for immediate departure.

"You have obligations," D'vore said harshly. "Forget the woman and focus on finding your home."

The voyage to Solifugoe was as long and boring as any other. Now that they were underway I found few of *Pletopt's* non-human crew to my liking. The sleek aliens were of modest size, somewhat small in frame, with delicate, almost effeminate features. I would have called them attractive save for their tiny slit eyes and sharp teeth.

"Evolved from carnivores, I believe," D'vore explained. "I recall that their progenitors hunted in packs, surrounding and bringing down larger prey so that all could feast. Eventually, when the mega fauna disappeared, they had to depend on intelligence and thence evolved to their present form. Much of their instinctive heritage remains, as it does among you humans."

"Humans evolved far beyond their animal past," I responded with some heat.

D'vore's voice dripped with disdain. "So your group behaviors, your desire for communities, your fawning needs for appreciation and confirmation have nothing to do with your ancestry? Come now, Case, don't try to put the human races above the rest of the universe. All grew from beasts and each stays true to their origins."

"I imagine that your race is included in that condemnation?" I replied bitterly, resenting D'vore's supercilious tone.

"Of course we are. Listen; every creature in the universe possesses threads from a broad tapestry of inheritance. We may evolve, we may differentiate to meet our environments, we may even alter our physical bodies to something new and strange, but always we are the victims our past in thought and action.

"Yes, even my race must have evolved from some earlier form of less intelligence and capability, although I cannot imagine what that must have been since I no longer recall any specific details."

"But you are learning more of yourself," I answered. "You are becoming more than the simple medician I first knew. I have seen your powers and understanding grow even in the short time we have been together."

D'vore shuffled uncomfortably. "Yes, it feels that way to me. I can sense the changes in myself as well as those of his physical body whenever some new part is added."

"So you are learning what you will become," I insisted. "Perhaps that knowledge will help me find my home?"

"I don't think so. It isn't a conscious acquisition," D'vore replied. "Sometimes when I am offered something that feels as if it needs to be part of me, I find I simply cannot resist. I have no idea of why I need all the materials I collect nor what use I will eventually make of them. Perhaps it will become clearer when we reach Oroenoe, but until the moment comes I will not know."

That sounded like my own slow and jerky acquisition of memory. Even though I could "see" items in the ship's image, they had no relevance until a fragmentary memory appeared and became part of my own experience. Did D'vore's physical attachments similarly unleash unconscious abilities?

It was something to think about.

The *Pletopt's* two human crewmen seemed to express that same aversion to others that I had encountered before, no doubt because of my lack of *chaura*, which I began to suspect was something like empathy, but developed to a more sensitive and inclusive level. During most of our social time the two pale humans huddled together, arms about each other, sharing whispered secrets and an occasional laugh. Whenever they passed, they touched. Even in the mess they sat close, despite the availability of room to spread out.

Neither chose to sit near me.

PART FOUR ANSWERS

During the long and boring voyage I continued to struggle with doubts and suspicions of D'vore's motives and finally concluded that, despite the emotionally tearing consequences of the brutal separation from the deceptive Provance, D'vore may have believed he was acting with the best of intentions and, by the time *Pletopt* neared Solifugoe, we'd resumed our tenuous relationship; outwardly acting as if nothing untoward had happened, but inwardly I was justifiably apprehensive of what D'vore might be capable of doing.

As ever, there was some concern among the crew about the accuracy of my navigational skills and how closely the ship would come to disaster when real space resolved itself. There were the usual bets, with astronomical odds should they fall to mischance, but all concerns melted away when *Pletopt* emerged well outside of the Solifugoe system, even though it meant we had to glide at an agonizingly slow pace toward our dark target.

Solifugoe was so far from its primary that I wouldn't have been able to identify its star without referring to the ship's Index Stellarium. Consequently, the planet's dark continents and even darker seas were notably photon deficient as it spun a few thousand kilometers beneath the station. It was a fitting scene for my dark thoughts as I continued to struggle with my conflicting emotions over lost Provance.

The ambient temperature in Solifugoe's tropical regions, I learned from the WOFAT, never rose above freezing even at the warmest periods. Warmed internally from the planet's fires, the only habitable realm was far below the rime of ice that covered the planet from pole to pole and near the hot springs that spewed sulfurous gases into the water. I wondered why there was a human presence on a station orbiting such an unwelcoming and inhospitable world. What could possibly draw people to this gloomy place?

Upon docking and after unloading, the crew departed to enjoy what few pleasures Solifugoe station had to offer during the brief time before *Pletopt* departed. For most of the crew enjoyment involved a round of drinking and eating foods far richer and diverse than any *Pletopt* had available and, I suspected, some tended to more intimate pleasures of the flesh.

We passed a mobile tank containing two bifurcated aliens swimming in the murky interior. I watched with amazement at their wrinkled, blubbery hides as they gracefully glided by. "Native Solifugoes," D'vore whispered. "Highly adapted to their environment. They would be poisoned by the excessive oxygen and lack of pressure in this portion of the station."

I could not imagine how anything other than the most basic of life could have arisen on such a cold and inhospitable world, much less an advanced race of obvious intelligence. In fact, I doubted that they could have evolved at all in such a foreboding environment. "Aha! These aliens must have come from another world," I exclaimed with a sudden flash of insight. "Yes, and the human presence here means that there must be something to be gained by ..."

As soon as the words left his mouth I realized the fallacy of my logic. "No, it can't be. Please tell me they aren't *human?*" I choked on the words. Never could I have imagined that so different a creature could be a member of my own race.

"Oh yes," D'vore replied with obvious amusement. "The Solifugoes are just another variant from the common tree that unites all human species, albeit a slightly more extreme variant, I will admit. I doubt you would find another bed mate among them, although I understand their seed and eggs remain cross-fertile with most humans."

I suspected that statement as a joke, nevertheless, once the figurative scales had been stripped away I saw the telltale signs of the human frame that lay beneath the heavy layers of blubber and how their broad and stunted flukes were articulated like my own knees and ankles. "I'd think it would be impossible to make so many alterations."

"Genetic engineering assisted by natural adaptation," D'vore explained.

"Impossible! It would take centuries and centuries," I guessed.

"More than centuries. A small bit of adaptation here and there, coupled with some genetic tinkering, was all it took to initially allow them to survive the depths. Since then, they've adapted lateral lines, echolocation, and a refined sense of time and position to live as they do in their flowing, three dimensional world." As if that wasn't amazing enough, he added. "I believe the slow adaptation process took over two hundred thousand years. You should examine the WOFAT's history tab if you are interested."

The willingness of these supposed colonists to struggle over such a long time period defied my wildest imagination. Two hundred thousand years was a length of time I could not emotionally grasp. The first adaptation must have occurred when Neanderthals roamed the Earth and my own precursors lived in scattered tribes.

Neanderthals? Precursors? Tribes? Where had those words come from? I had only a vague idea of what those terms might represent, but that was trivial in light of a more important insight: implied by those memories was the concept that my Earth had a continuous record of evolution from earlier forms clear back to the dinosaurs, whatever they were. If the creatures of Earth had developed independently, as I'd apparently believed, why were all those I'd all-too-briefly recalled so close in appearance to these other varieties of humanity? Parallel evolution and biological compatibility would require such fantastic coincidences that the possibility of independent development bordered on the impossible. There was the slim chance that my ideas about evolution were false, but it hadn't felt that way.

Only my Earth held that answer.

We spotted the captain of *Pletopt* standing nearby as we applied for berths on any ship going to Oroenoe, our penultimate destination.

The captain followed us when we left the registry. "I must chat with you, medician," Lustal insisted. "Come, let us share a table." It glanced with displeasure at me and then added, in a wiggling gesture of apology–"no offense intended, navigator."

"There is a bit of interesting information from the latest WOFAT update," Lustal confided as it fiddled with a cup of blue liquid that reeked of kerosene. "It seems that the Penchon are anxious to locate a certain medician and its human companion. They are offering a reward."

It felt as if a knife had been thrust into my breast but, before I could say a word, D'vore reached over and grasped Lustal by the throat. "No need for that," the imp squeaked. "I only mentioned the offer as a curious fact. I have little need for reward and less desire to contribute to the Penchon organ banks." When D'vore did not release his grip it squeaked, "I'm merely curious as to why they might have such an interest. The two they seek have different identities than yours; that is, different from the ones you carry." The little alien twisted, trying to free itself. "I do find it curious that there might be two medicians traveling with human companions–so curious that I wonder if there might be something amiss with the navigator's identity as well."

"There's nothing wrong with our identities," I blurted before he realized how ridiculous such a declaration sounded now that Lustal realized who we were.

"It makes we wonder why a medician would be traveling with a human companion." Lustal looked at me. "Tell me, navigator, what makes you so valuable to this creature. Do you tell it jokes, relate interesting stories about your home, or divulge knowledge that it might not otherwise obtain? Or does the obligation go the other way? You do not appear wealthy enough to have a personal medician."

The imp's questions were getting too close to the truth. "I had an accident and do not remember my way home. D'vore repaired me and is helping me."

D'vore loosened his grip but did not release his hold. The imp took a deep breath. "Is that so? I wonder how, in a time when no one is truly lost, when identity and movement are common records, you can't know your way home?"

"I lost my memory." No sense saying more.

"Indeed? You appear to be different from any humans I'm familiar with, therefore you are either a variant or you come from some place uncommon."

"Earth," I replied. "I do remember that much. D'vore thinks it might be a lost colony."

"*Arth*, is it, and unknown as well? Hmm, I imagine that finding a source of fresh supplies unknown to the rest of the human community would be of great interest to the Penchon, would it not?"

"That's a very dangerous supposition," D'vore warned as he once again tightened his grip. "One would say, decidedly *dangerous.*"

"And expensive," Lustal squeaked hastily. "Listen medician, I have no love for the Penchon, but one must be careful not to earn their enmity."

"Then why did you bring it up? What purpose in warning us?"

"I saw how you ministered to the wounded and was much impressed," the imp replied. "You seem to have an impressive skill set, far above what one would normally expect for a ship's medician."

D'vore answered without modesty. "I have acquired templates that allow me to treat any being that shares this biome."

Lustal leaned forward. "All? Would that include my people?" When D'vore nodded, the imp squirmed and turned to me. "How extensive were your injuries, navigator?"

"He is a man of parts," D'vore admitted. "It was a difficult reconstruct." He said, ever the one for understatement. "He was assembled from various crew members who did not survive."

"That would be remarkable, if true." The imp looked at me. "Yet I find it believable. Humans must be far more biologically flexible than my race."

"You are going to ask if I can repair your withered limb." Lustal appeared taken aback and, but did not respond as D'vore continued. "I believe I can, but it would take considerable resources. Besides, what would be in it for us?"

"I might be willing to redirect my ship for Oroenoe. We still need a medician on board." Two of its appendages strained helplessly against D'vore's grip. "I might even," It glanced warily at me and added, "be willing to continue using your companion as my navigator."

"That is a generous offer," D'vore said.

Lustal lifted its withered brown appendage. "For years I have searched for a way to eradicate this shame. Even the Penchon swear they cannot replace this. It seems that they have no way of providing my races' delicate parts–some strange biochemistry, they say. Lucky for us but bad for me."

"Surely there are other medicians ..." I began.

"No medician I've approached over the years has admitted having the skills to repair this limb. I was about to give it up, to doom myself to a shameful life until you said you *might* be able to do it. Medician, if you can construct a human from damaged parts then I believe you have the skills I need, that I want."

"And what if I do? Will you help us get to Oroenoe?"

"*Pletopt* is a small freighter of little note, but profitable for, ah, certain clients. As such I have great liberty in where and when we go. If you can repair me I will allow your navigator to divert it to Oroenoe."

I didn't know whether to trust the imp or not. "What proof do we have that you can keep your end of the bargain? We have only your word."

D'vore lifted the imp. "I do not know if I can do as you ask. I will need to examine you and, if I still think it possible, might attempt surgery. I can also," he added with menace, "ensure that you will never speak of us again. Trust must run both ways—agreed?"

Lustal shook. "You will do it then?" The pleading was plain in his voice.

"I make no promises, but let us go to your ship where I can examine you." Without waiting for acknowledgement he began walking away, dragging the imp along by the forearm. To anyone watching it would appear that the hulking D'vore and the tiny alien were unusually companionable. I followed.

Pletopt's surgery became D'vore's examination room. It only took one glance to watch D'vore spread wide his array of arms and begin fondling Lustal's brown limb. Neither Lustal or D'vore uttered a sound during the examination.

"It will be difficult, but not impossible to give you four useful appendages," D'vore concluded. "I would suggest that we begin after we are underway. Only then can I trust that you will not have an opportunity to betray us."

"A fair bargain."

As soon as we returned to *Pletopt*, Lustal ordered the crew to prepare the ship as I gathered the needed supplies. I had worried that D'vore's shopping list would include another grisly body part from a Penchon abattoir but that was not the case . Instead his list included strange drugs, assorted tools, and objects of less familiarity. The material filled two small crates along with some ordinary boxes of small parts, several sacks of non-descript powders, and two delicate and intricate machines whose functions and purposes I could not discern and whose names I could not pronounce.

As *Pletopt* prepared the drive for Oroenoe I asked Lustal what had deformed its arm. "How did ...?"

"My race are arboreal and our world a complex tangle of forest and jungle," Lustal replied. "I was once a happy youth, sailing through the world, searching for a niche could call my own, a place to take a mate or two, and where I could ensure the continuation of my line.

"But such was not to be. I stumbled upon a pylos, a poisonous creature who preys on smaller animals. Normally it would have raced away, but my appearance startled it. It struck out immediately and bit me on the forelimb. I nearly passed out from the pain, nearly falling to the deadly ground. But fortune smiled and I managed to get to a nook where that danger could be avoided.

"I tried to get to help, but with only three limbs useful and the fourth a growing agony, I could only cover a short distance before I collapsed. They found me the next day and managed to nurse me back to life, such as it was, since the poison had destroyed the muscle tissue, numbed the nerves, and rendered me a shameful cripple, a reject.

"I cried for someone to repair my limb, a medician to restore my wholeness, but there was none willing. The underlying structure, they said, was inadequate to the task. 'Go to the ground,' my family suggested, dooming me to a certain death, but I refused and instead chose the life of a cowardly exile, shamed to never return home.

"Over the years I prospered and failed, traded what I could, and made a few fortunate friends. In the end I own half of this freighter, and one third of the cargo value. The crew shares a third and the other owner the rest. It is enough for me to survive and live in hope that I would eventually find someone to help me."

I was moved by the imp's tale, although I was not entirely convinced of its truthfulness. The story seemed too pat. It was too smooth a transition from cripple to successful trader with a ship of its own to be credible. There were obvious gaps in the captain's history, and I was not sure Lustal wished to fill in the blanks, especially regarding its "friends." Perhaps I would learn the truth of its words when D'vore completed his surgeries.

I could not understand the lengthy and complex surgery. My function was only to provide the objects D'vore requested, take away things he no longer needed, and dispose of assorted portions of Lustal's withered limb, dripping with clear fluid and smelling of fish. I could not help but watch D'vore's tiny limbs flickering, cutting, rearranging, stitching, and performing a hundred other delicate operations that I had neither the words nor skills to describe.

The operation went on for hours and continued as I, unable to remain awake, gathered a few hours of much-needed sleep on the deck, only to be troubled by further memories of Provance and my undying need for her presence. I woke with tears in my eyes and an ache in my heart as D'vore continued to work.

When he finished, Lustal, naked and unconscious, lay on the table, three limbs to the side while, across its trunk lay a metallic arm. Its appearance, in all but color and material, was identical to the other limbs.

"One final thing," D'vore said as he reached down to remove a tiny machine from Lustal's forehead. Lustal shuddered for a moment and then its eyes fluttered open. "Is it done?"

"It is done," D'vore answered and, in answer Lustal twitched the new limb, tentatively at first and then with greater vigor. I feared that its reaction would be similar to Sylvestra's horror at having such an alteration when the imp lifted it for examination. Instead, Lustal beamed, its face turning a brilliant rose color as its eyes grew wide.

"Ten times stronger than the others," D'vore advised. "I'd be careful until your new shoulder muscles adapt."

"I will no longer be despised," Lustal whispered as it cautiously moved the limb back and forth. "I am a whole being once more. I can go home. I can earn a mate." Even though the imp was alien in voice and appearance I sensed the joy in its words and tried to imagine how it must feel to once again be given life when a return to home appeared lost.

Would that D'vore had done the same with me so simply.

It was only later that I noticed that D'vore was only using one arm to pack away the surgical materials. "What is wrong with your other arm?"

D'vore shrugged. "As I said before, I have little attachment to my limbs and felt that it would serve Lustal better than me. Don't worry about it, Case . I can get another."

Just the same I was shocked. What was this creature that so willingly gave of himself to help others? Had I misjudged him yet again?

To say Lustal was joyous was an understatement. It crowed about the change, bragged about renewed strength, and talked endlessly of what it could now accomplish and the mates it could capture. The only relief I had from the imp's endless recitation were frequent conversations with D'vore.

We usually spoke of the many things that I had seen since my "awakening," but little outside of my direct experience. We had more than enough questions about what we'd seen or heard to keep them occupied for hours at a time.

"You seem distracted," I said at one point when we wandered

too deeply into some aspect of interstellar trade that was well beyond any hope of comprehension. "Is it the loss of your metal arm?"

"Hardly," D'vore replied. "No, instead I ponder my circumstance. We are much alike in some respects, Case . Like you, I sometimes glimpse partial images, faint memories of senses, dimensions, and movements that I don't understand." He grew silent for a long time and then said wistfully. "Could these be sketchy memories of what I was before they found me, memories of my past? Although I clearly know what I am, I do not fully understand what that signifies. Nor can I recall any specifics of the supposed misfortune that left me so crippled."

I wondered if this insightful behavior was some new phenomenon spurred by his own recovery? What did D'vore mean that he had no clear memories of his own past? More suspiciously, I wondered if the admission implied that the D'vore was acting as an agent of more than one player?

"I've been wondering about your *resources*." There was no sense wondering about D'vore's motivations if a simple question would provide an answer. I just hoped that I could tell if D'vore was lying. "Why has ThripoBlastenav," I again struggled to gargle correctly, "been so helpful? What have you done to earn all the support he's provided?"

"I have wondered the same thing, Case . I doubt that carrying unknown packages was worth all the help ThripoBlastenav has given. Perhaps supporting your quest has something to do with the enmity between Penchon and Human, or something dealing with trade relations, social interaction, or the price of zebbles on Roam? I don't even know who or what brought us to ThripoBlastenav's attention. Perhaps it was the Pittul, the Penchon, the blue hats, or the Carhera station overseers. It is a puzzle, as is my irresistible impulse to help you find your home. It merely provides me with means, and not a view into its motivations."

His revelations sounded stranger by the moment. "Are we participants in some scheme, mere pawns in a larger game or were we more central, the bishops or knights in a grand contest?" Again, unbidden and unknown words of some forgotten game rolled easily off my tongue.

"I do not know the references you mention, but that is an excellent question. I just wish I had an answer. There are too many unanswered questions."

"Such as whether the Penchon killed *Tollembol's* crew?"

"The Penchon are alien. I would not presume to understand their logic." D'vore replied haughtily.

"And why would they keep the wreckage? What was so important to them about that twisted pile of metal that ties me to my past? What if that wreckage contains some clue to Earth that we hadn't found, some remnant of what I was?" I stopped and wiped at a tear. "I guess it's too late now. I guess I'll have to be satisfied with visiting the virtual model."

"I am changing," D'vore confided on our next meeting.

"Changing how?" I asked with some trepidation. "Are you in pain?"

"It's as if there were something at my core, trying to escape the confines of my body." This was disturbing. D'vore was the ship's medician and if something were to go wrong with him there was no one else who could help.

His comment about something growing inside bothered me. What if it meant that he had become pregnant? Had I been mistaken about D'vore's sex, that is, if such a term was appropriate for so strange an alien? "Is it physical?" I hesitated being more specific, besides, what would I do with the answer anyhow?

"No, it is not a physical pain. It's as if there's a desire that wants to be released but does not yet have the strength to manifest. I fear how that might manifest; it is most disturbing to think that I may not be able to control myself. I am sorry, Case, but until I can trust myself again it is best you let me be."

Although the idea of D'vore giving birth had been momentarily frightening at best and horrifying otherwise, I was relieved to hear that the discomfort was not a physical manifestation. "I will let you be," I answered. "Rest."

Despite my doubts about D'vore's motivations I'd become somewhat accepting of the medician's continually changing form and puzzling behaviors. I occasionally thought of the alien as a friend, with all that implied, but could not honestly say that D'vore shared those feelings, nor any other human emotion. Did he consider me a mere acquaintance, a pet, or an accomplice in whatever scheme he followed? Try as I might, I could think of no reason why D'vore would value me more than he would any other random human aside from the accident of my creation. Insofar as I could tell, there was nothing unique about me, not after that masterful reconstruction–or should I say creation–of my body. D'vore knew me as no other and probably better than I knew himself.

Rather than continue to bedevil himself, I resolved to wait until D'vore recovered from whatever ailed him. Only through D'vore could I hope to return to Earth, to learn the fate of all those lost loves, and lay a flower on the graves of those who were lost but whose souls remain in me.

It took days before D'vore climbed out of his fugue state. Nothing appeared to be resolved nor had he determined what was causing such distress. "One must surrender to what they cannot control," he advised. "Or at least wait until one can understand it enough to discover what control can be applied."

"So, are you reconciled to these unsettling feelings?"

"Let us just say that I await developments," D'vore replied with what I took as an attempted at humor.

"I think I've been away from that virtual ship for too long," I said.

"I understand. But this time why don't you examine the rear of the ship," D'vore prompted as I "stepped" through the virtual hatch. "Perhaps we can learn something of the drives this time."

I was amazed as the ship had materialized before me, but accepted the illusion willingly. Instead of following my previous path forward, I turned left to face a hatch held firmly in place with three dogs, put a hand on the first dog, twisted, and then the others, until all three were loose and the hatch opened. I had to duck to pass through and step onto an open catwalk. As I made my way along the walk I let my hand brush the huge coils on either side, to caress the thick cables that festooned the overhead, to linger on the panels beside each coil. It was fascinating how the faint tactile impressions affected me. Apparently D'vore's simulation went well beyond simple sight.

"Do you know what these are?" D'vore whispered as I approached a collection of small cans.

"I think these are the starter coils," I answered, dredging up a faint memory. "The main drive must be further back." Once again I was surprised how the answer came so easily.

Five steps further along the catwalk was a complex device that filled the entire width of the ship. On three sides, symmetrically arranged about the main axis of the ship, were segments of equipment. Each of the three segments was connected to the others through a shared wreath of colored wires and had a silver cylinder with a thick black cable at its head. Beside these cylinders were blue blocks from which gold tubes emerged. Crammed beside each blue box were eight black cables with brass heads snaking their way into the space behind.

In the center of the array was a flat silver disk with a three-armed device, each arm connected to the segments by black cables as thick as my thigh. Three cans with pistons surrounded the flat disk and, in the middle, was a black lump of fused metal whose surface glinted with silver particles.

"I suspect this is the source of your problem," D'vore said. "Can you recall what it might have been?"

There seemed no sense of the arrangement. It looked so different from the drives of the ships I'd been on that it was hard to believe that it could have controlled seven-space travel.

Modern ship drives required at least seven controllers, while I'd been told that safety dictated that thirteen would ensure reasonable accuracy of reaching one's intended destination. Three controllers seemed ridiculously few. How could this ship have possibly expected to reach its destination with any guarantee of success?

"I think that might have been the emitter." I examined the black lump. "The segments send the impulse from the coils once they build up sufficient power and discharge it into the emitter. Those silver cans must equalize the power flow." In my minds eye I could recall the general schematic, a block diagram that linked function to function and seemed to have vague hints of equations that made little sense. I quickly scribbled the partial equations on a pad and sketched what he could recall of the diagram before I began to wonder where the pad had come from.

A second later I was on the deck, exhausted and with a roaring headache. I looked about for the pad, but it was nowhere in sight. Had it only been a mental construct or reality?

D'vore appeared excited. "A most interesting discovery," he crowed. "One would not have thought that you have an operational drive with so few controls. It seemed a rather crude lash-up; almost as if there had been no previous knowledge of drives."

I wondered about that. "Maybe that's the reason for the accident and why the ship was destroyed. The Rift probably wasn't our planned destination, but just some random point where we emerged."

"Yes, considering the primitive nature of the drives' assembly I would imagine that was the case. There are also some errors in these few equations, but I do not know if they are the result of your incomplete memory or actually were based on an erroneous theory of seven-space transport."

"Primitive? To me the layout looked more like advanced engineering."

"Obviously another fact of how far your world is removed from human civilization. But put that aside and rest your mind for a while. Find something else to preoccupy you while I consider these notes. We'll conduct another examination later."

As much as I wanted to discover what other facts might bubble from memory, another visit so soon would only increase my splitting headache. D'vore was right. I had to do something else.

Which was why, hours later and relieved that the navigational path I had mapped for the ship conflicted with no earlier visits, skirted no danger areas, and placed *Pletopt's* arrival at a safe distance from Oroenoe, I began recounting what had brought me to this point, the wonders I had seen, and, as ever, Provance.

Dwelling on her loss was senseless, yet I could not stop myself from wanting to hold her once again, to hear her voice, to smell her sweet breath and touch her soft hair. It was as stupid as picking at a sore, each attack made the hurt the worse, but I could not stop doing it.

Thinking about Provance was painful, especially the realization that I had not understood the depth of my feelings until far too late. It mattered little what D'vore said about her disinterest. Over time I *knew* I would have proven myself worthy. All that I'd needed was more time to express the depth of my feelings and, once I'd done that, I was positive that she would return my love. Ah, Provance, what might have been? We could have visited your beloved Parras had we time.

Suddenly there was something about the combination of Provance and Parras that nibbled at the back of my mind. No, it wasn't my Provance, nor even Parras the world, but some similar sounding words that brought back a recollection of sunny days and fine food, a man chatting with a young brown woman to his right, and an offer of some sort.

"Doctor LaPlatte, we really would like you to be a part of this project. Your mathematical insights on the development of the FTL drive have been invaluable. What do you want that would make that a reality?"

I looked at the woman and then back at Harry Dufont. "I want to be a member of the crew."

The woman jerked as if struck. "You can't be serious," she said. "What about our children? Besides, not wanting to haul us all to frozen damn Norway I certainly don't want to see you risk your life on some damn experimental lash-up."

I shrugged. "That's your problem. I am not going to pass up the greatest advance in human history."

After she slammed her napkin down and stalked away, Dufont turned to me. "That was a pretty brutal thing to say to your wife."

"I don't care. This mission is too important."

"I heard you were a real cold son-of-a-bitch," Harry said with

apparent distaste. "I see they were right, but the offer still stands.
You will be part of the crew."
   "Excellent," I replied. "Now, shall we order dinner? I'm
starved."

The memory remained clear as I jerked awake from my nap. I
was horrified by the callousness of that fragmentary memory,
especially LaPlatte's complete lack of emotional attachment to
Simone. My own recollection of how I'd felt toward Provance
had been quite different, which made me immediately thankful
that this LaPlatte individual had not contributed greatly to my
emotional makeup. If nothing else the callous mind of LaPlatte
had driven any dreams of Provance from my mind.

The recollections seemed to flow so freely as forays into the
virtual ship became more frequent. Perhaps they stemmed from
an increasing confidence and the sense of who I was apart from
those whose components I contained. For certain I was now less
fearful of them and their memories. And, with the loss of fear
perhaps I would be more receptive to their memories.
   Sensing there were no more memories in the drive
compartment, I moved forward, intending to sit in each chair
and elicit whatever thoughts emerged.
   The simplest instrument panel was midway along the ship,
the location where I'd imagined a flickering candle. But there
was no evidence of a candle here, nothing but a single blank
screen, a keyboard, and a control stick for the telescope. Why
would the ship need a telescope, I wondered, but that question
evoked no answer.
   After moving forward to what I assumed was the command
section and sat in the left-hand chair. Before me were three rows
of lights. I wondered why the yellow ones should be illuminated
before I realized that illuminated lamps were a memory, not
what I actually saw. Yes, I now recalled that the lights would
tell me that everyone was ready for engagement. I recalled the
clanging bells as the ship rocked from its release.

"Ready," came a chorus of voices as the lights began to blink from

yellow to green. A single red switch was at my right hand. In my mind's eye I imagined flicking the guard away and exposing the toggle beneath. I hesitated for a moment and said a brief prayer. The engineering on this ship, with this drive was not settled science. There was still much to be understood about seven-space travel on the scientific level. There was enough settled science to build the engine and enough solid engineering to make it work, but there were still aspects not quite understood. Gaylord in particular was worried about some obscure bit deep in the mathematics, but the project lead had assured everyone that they needn't be overly concerned—everyone knew that Gaylord was being unrealistic about the drive. Nobody could ever achieve the degree of precision he demanded.

The final light—power—blinked green. No hesitation, no doubts, no excuse to delay a moment longer. "Engaging," I said as my thumb touched the toggle pressed it forward and ...

Then I was again lying on the deck while D'vore rested a cool hand on my forehead. "I'm afraid you attempt too much with each trip," he cautioned.

"I pressed the activation switch for the drive," I said slowly, trying to recover this latest memory before it faded, much as a nightmare does when awakening. "Then I felt something horrible."

"You screamed and collapsed. You panicked. Something about whatever you perceived or remembered sent your heart racing and your respiration soaring. I was afraid you were going into shock."

"I can't remember what it might have been, only that it was unpleasant. Perhaps the next time I'll be able to handle it better." But I did not believe it. Would I remember death on my next visited? Would I have to suffer each crewmember's agony as I recalled their memories of the ship being destroyed? I shuddered at the thought. "But I don't think I want to do that very soon."

On recovering from my session with D'vore I found Lustal's alien crew in a state of agitation, their ears alert and teeth bared.

"There are vermin about," Lustal reported. "Two sightings, but not enough to determine what they might be."

Vermin were a common feature on ships, as they had always been throughout history. I could recall tales of rats and mice on seagoing vessels and cockroaches taken into space, although the context of those tales gave me no clue as to when and where. I tried to imagine what strange creatures might snuggle aboard interstellar craft–mouse and rat equivalents from a hundred planets or creatures spawned in alien stations?

The crew relentlessly searched the ship, the aliens prowling in pairs, one scouting ahead while the other stood ready to catch anything flushed from its hiding place. After a full day of this, which comprised the entirety of the ship, they could find nothing. I stood by, scorned by the more capable crew for my uselessly weak human senses. They did discover mice aplenty and seemed to take delight in eating them immediately, often battling over the treat. There were other things as well, small and brown, quick and scaled, which they ate with equal delight.

What the crew also uncovered was evidence of poor maintenance work, unrepaired damage and equipment missing components. None of the missing items were essential to the operation of the ship or the maintenance of the life support. There were missing parts of an entertainment device, a portion of the food preparation equipment, and a small hole in the spare parts storage locker among a hundred other items.

The raw emotional reaction to David's death haunted me for days as I immersed myself in navigational duties. Most dealt with merely verifying the location where *Pletopt* might emerge. It was a trivial task but it gave me time to enhance my knowledge of seven-space navigation and become more familiar with the ship's stellar charts. I vaguely recalled a far different method of navigation, of using primitive instruments to determine stellar signatures and rather simpler charts of the sky rather than the million-volume data deck *Pletopt* used.

One of the ways I recalled was simplifying positions by observing the constellations rather than painstakingly search through the observable stars. The configurations were, for the most part, vastly different at each destination, as was the case for Oroenoe. One of the unique clusters nearby that location was called the Lion, with three sets of stars forming the legs and another four the head. It looked like something I'd known before, but it wasn't a lion, it was a … bear? There were others, many others. I quickly sketched those I could recall before memory faded. A pair of bright stars, a string that resembled a tail, and a small cluster looking like a metal drinking cup.

I grew excited as I reviewed them, energized that I might be recovering the location of lost Earth. I entered the rough shapes of the constellations into the ephemeris and set the equipment to search for a system that would reveal stars in such configurations. Although I did not recall how the separate images related to one another perhaps by finding a single match would lead to the second and thereby reveal some hint of my origin.

The equipment gave no immediate results, which I did not realistically expect, so I let it run and prayed that it would soon produce the needed match.

Perhaps it was thoughts of constellations and stars that prompted, in the moment between sleep and wakening, another image of a night sky

… resplendent with stars and the one wobbling in the sighting ring—Polaris. "It's interesting," I said as I lay the sextant down on the deck. "For thousands of years we've been using Polaris to guide us at night."

"So what's so special about the north star, Jos?" David replied.

"If the dinosaurs were smart enough to discover navigation they wouldn't have a fixed north star. We wobble around, the sun moves, and they would have seen a far different sky filled with different constellations. One might have been the Great Lizard, Big Egg, or some mythical creation of theirs."

"Now you are really getting weird. Dinosaur astronomers indeed."

"The night sky is only stable on our time scale," I answered. "Over geologic time periods it changes ever so gradually as the system moves around the galactic ring. If our race continues long

enough they'll never see the sky like this. They'll have different constellations to name."

"If they care anymore or even use names as we do. Besides, the human race will be replaced by something else by then. Evolution proceeds, you know."

I batted him on the arm. "How do you know? The dinosaurs were around for quite a few million years while we've barely made a couple hundred thousand."

"But mammals are what we're talking about, not the human race. The dinosaurs are still with us as birds so who knows what the mammals will become?"

"Lemurs, most likely. A return to our roots." David sat down beside me. "Why don't you tell me about the stars now? What are those two called?"

"Castor and Pollux," I replied.

The clarity and completeness of the sudden flash of memory left me breathless. It was as if I had been Jocelyn and that wonderful moment on the boat's deck only moments in the past. I wondered if Jocelyn could have imagined on the deck of that ancient sailboat how complex stellar navigation could become when time itself became a factor? She had been right: The stars moved all the time. It was only against a limited life span that they appeared eternally the same. Constellations would change over time as the stars moved through the heavens but certainly not in the short time since I'd left Earth.

Three sleep periods later the ephemeris produced no results that matched two of the diagrams and, of the three that matched at least one diagram, none could be seen from any habitable location. Either the memories had played me false or my ship had improbably come from someplace completely unknown and so far off the paths of commerce that even remotely similar patterns could not be found.

"I very much doubt that the humans of the diaspora could have gone so far to colonize your distant Earth," D'vore responded when I voiced these thoughts. "From the degree of genetic drift the Pittul mentioned, your group must have deviated from the human line long before humanity possessed any ships capable of such vast jumps."

That answer did not satisfy me. "But why is there no known system that could have such constellations? Why should my memory be so clear?" He had no doubts in this regard since I could easily bring to mind childhood visions of a night sky dotted with stars as my scoutmaster pointed out the constellations with a flashlight.

"I must admit that is a puzzle, but there may be alternate explanations."

"Such as?"

"Perhaps the early settlers were captured by aliens and transported to some distant system, someplace away from known space."

"*Aliens*? You can't seriously expect me to believe there are races *unknown* to your Carhera, can you?"

"They may not know everything, Case . The universe is vast and much remains outside their knowledge."

"Alien involvement might explain the lack of Carhera knowledge, but it doesn't address how my ship got to the Rift," I argued. "Didn't you say a ship of that size and configuration couldn't travel very far? Didn't you say the drive appeared too primitive to make a long jump through seven space?"

"Yes, all true. Could it be that you were released from another ship?"

With a shudder, I recalled my ship's deadly red toggle, and David's brief prayer. "No, I clearly recall us being disconnected from one of our own ships."

D'vore appeared to be excited. "I think you must continue to explore the wreckage. Your improving memory may help us discover more clues."

While that was good advice I was not ready to revisit the ship. The fear of enduring multiple deaths was still too threatening. "Later," I insisted. Then, hoping to still a rising fear, I changed the subject. "Let's talk instead of ships and stations, planets and stars, humans and aliens, but mostly let us just talk as friends."

I badly needed a friend.

Sleep came uneasily that night. Idly, I seemed to float with languid movements along the spine of the virtual ship, sensing the thoughts of those phantoms so alert in their alcoves, all braced for whatever might come, half afraid, excited, and each bothered by their individual concerns on their part of the mission.

Phillip Mellorez thought the coils had stabilized after running hot for half and hour. This had happened before and they had changed out everything on the circuit from output through the regulator to the busses on the drive mounts. The generator output showed fifty amps on the twelve-volt circuit with less than a half percent fluctuation. One of the three drive coils appeared to be sucking more power than the others, but that could easily be instrument error. In any case , it was well within the allowable limits. Just the same he asked Obinna to check the connections to make sure one of them hadn't jiggled loose again.

"Everything all right back there?" David asked over the link. Bolsteri was the lead on the project and bristled when anyone called him "captain."

"The voltage spiked at one point, but now appeared right on target," Phillip answered. "I've got Obinna checking the connections one last time and then I'll wait a bit to see if we have another fluctuation before we engage. I'll go green when I'm satisfied, captain."

"I'll hit the kill switch if it isn't ready in ten minutes," David snapped. Phillip could hear the irritation in David's voice, but whether that was from his use of the offending title or the stress of the forthcoming launch was not apparent. He stared at the readings, tensed for any further fluctuations that might cause a problem and waited for Obinna's confirmation that everything was all right.

The dream changed and I was once again in the Penchon ship, but Provance was there, along with a host of Pittul and we were driving a car to Florida as …

Melika Cohen fiddled with the joystick, adjusting the attitude of the ship to roughly point at Polaris, the north star that her ancestors had used to navigate across the oceans and cross the desert. What would grandfather Saul say if he could see her now? For that matter, what would any of her mixed ancestry say about her flying a fucking starship? What would the African hunters on the Serengeti that were certainly somewhere along her line make of this huge hunk of metal suspended in space? She doubted they could even have imagined such a thing.

"Turning nav to you," she said into the mike once she had Polaris centered and pressed the button. In the back Jocelyn would have her computers doing the fine-tuning on their alignment. She twitched the joystick to confirm that she was now in control. Nothing for her to do now except wait for the big bang, the shift, or whatever the physicists were calling this great leap of half a light year. Once they were there all she had to do was turn the ship around, let Jocelyn find the sun and, after the jump back, goose the ship to the station where a cold beer and warm bed awaited.

Wakefulness left the dream memories intact. Once again the feelings, the conversations were as if they had just occurred. Was this sign of my increasing mental integration, that I should retain such explicit memories? What or where could this Florida have been? Which part of the dreams could be discounted and which believed?

"Variable stars?" D'vore mused. "If you could recall any further details we might be able to use that knowledge."

That had already occurred to me; the Cepheid's were the most reliable navigation points in the universe, but with only their names, and those in a language D'vore did not recognize, they might as well be black holes.

"Best you rest for a while and let the thoughts settle," D'vore said.

Absence from explorations of the virtual ship allowed more dreams to haunt me. I continued to see people's faces and overhear snippets of conversation that were never clear in meaning or context. Like common dreams, the details vanished like the summer fog the moment I became fully awake, leaving only useless and momentary fragments behind.

D'vore was no help interpreting these unconnected, partially recalled sequences and, I had to admit, were not terribly clear when I tried to explain. "Being able to recall your dreams may be evidence that your mind is finally integrating its memories," he suggested. "The travels to the virtual ship may be helping.'

"But I feel no different that what I was before. If I am integrating shouldn't the crews' personalities come to the fore? Shouldn't I start to feel different?"

D'vore let out a low chuckle. "You may not be aware of changes, but I have watched you grow since you first awakened. Then you were confused, unsure, awkward in movement, and swimming in ignorance of self. Since then you have become assured of your body and more stable in mood and behavior. You are finally becoming the man I hoped you would be."

I grinned. "You've changed as well."

"True, insofar as to my external integuments, but my mind remains confused and driven by impulses I cannot fully understand. I mirror your confusion, Case, but as I gather more parts of whatever I am, the confusion seems to lift."

"As does mine when I explore the ship and find the memories."

"Perhaps it is time to return and discover what new recollections await you."

D'vore's suggestion was so logical that I did not hesitate. Was flattery all he needed to overcome my fears? It seemed so superficial, but even knowing that, I felt not a momentary pang as the ship grew around me.

Without hesitation I made his way to the navigator's alcove, sat in the chair, let my mind relax in hopes of trying evoking the memories of whoever had been seated here when … No! I warned himself not to think of death but recall instead those moments leading up to the execution of the mission, the moments before *she* toggled her readiness from yellow to green.

I was certain the navigator must have been a woman,. The memory of the panel was somehow different through her eyes. Recalling that she must have been several centimeters shorter, I scrunched down in the seat, bringing my eyes to her level. Jocelyn, that was her name, and she knew she was simply backup to the automated computers. As soon as they arrived, the system would start analyzing the star field, looking for spectral signals that uniquely define each star. From its database of a million visible stars it had enough emission signatures to compare with whatever they saw. In addition, the computer could calculate the angular displacement of any triplet to pinpoint their location within a few light-seconds. At the same time, other machines would be searching for the one specific signature of a dim yellow star that shone down on Earth.

Jocelyn was concerned should any of these marvels fail, worried that she would have to find the variable pulsars that were her specialty and figure out, after weeks of observation with their radio telescope, their location. The optical scope and its associated light amplifier, a simple spectroscope, and a precise clock would help, but it was her knowledge, her skill, and experience with the pulsars that would get them home.

The detail of her memory was astounding; so crystal clear and precise. I realized that she had also known the ship was experimental, the first test of the drive with a human crew. There was uncertainty in where the ship would emerge due to an incomplete understanding of the mathematics. Hadn't Gaylord said so? He might have reasons for doubt, judging from his certainty.

I tried to wrest more insight of Jocelyn's memories, to her thoughts and feelings, to grasp the whole of her as I slouched in her chair waiting for more memories to emerge. "I am done," I said after nothing further happened.

"There was a machine, a computer," I told D'vore as soon as the ship dissolved. "It had records. It contained all the data we need to find our way to Earth. We need to find it."

"Case," D'vore reminded. "You were dealing with a simulation, a virtual reconstruction, not something physical. Were there a physical record it would be in the wreckage itself, and we have no way of recovering that."

I was crushed. The image of the ship, my explorations, and memories had combined to make me almost believe I had been dealing with something real. Once again I regretted the loss of the Penchon ship and the torn metal it housed.

"Jocelyn, the woman recalled someone named Gaylord who might hold the key to what happened. She thought he might know more than her."

"Perhaps if you could recall whatever this Gaylord said was wrong with the mathematics, or even recall the math itself, we could use that to calculate the error envelope."

"I doubt that." my frustration was increasing with each memory. "I only seemed to recall worthless observations."

"Nothing is worthless, Case . I am certain that someone would be able to wrest knowledge from whatever you dream. I record every detail and impression, so leave nothing out."

Additional forays over the next few watches gave rise to no new facts, no new numbers. A few stray data points surfaced as I sat idly at the navigator's alcove. On the bare metal to my right was a scratched table filled with meaningless names and numbers, all in a language unlike the one I recalled with such certainty: delta Celphei, Eta Aquilae, Zeta Geminorum, and Beta Doradus were written in a neat hand along the side and along the top of the table, while pairs of numbers filled the intersecting boxes. It looked like something Jocelyn might have written in an idle moment. Try as I might, I could recall nothing of what those words and numbers represented nor why they were significant enough to be written down.

I did recall Jocelyn confirming angular measurements on a screen with those in a large book filled with dates and measurements. Three and a half days was one entry and four point four another.

"Thus far I've recalled some names that might be stars and a table of numbers, but there is no context, no explanation I can think of," I complained. "Jocelyn was an astronomer–I've found out that much, so the table has some significance."

"I doubt the names of stars she used would be much use to us," D'vore replied. "I suggest that you examine that scribbling more closely. We may find it means nothing, but we might be able to use it to narrow the possibilities of revealing the location of Earth."

Arrival at Oroenoe was a moment's disorientation and then a long and boring dive to the station where, with a great clashing of metal, abrupt changes of direction, and a final, jarring crash, *Pletopt* finally docked. The air pressure changed shortly after and, in time, Lustal informed us that his obligation was at an end. "To home, I must," he declared. Whether that meant abandoning his ship, selling it, or something else, I had neither the time nor interest to find out.

Lustal did not bother to thank D'vore. I was somewhat surprised at the limits of Lustal's gratitude, but that might be because he did not appreciate the value of travel when compared to D'vore's medical miracles. How could Lustal equate the restoration of his life with the trivial cost of transport, much less the discounted services we provided during the passage for which, I hastened to add, they'd received nothing?

Lustal lost no time in off-loading the cargo and despite a half-hearted request for me to continue as navigator—a desire strongly influenced by my free contribution of navigational skills to date, no doubt—I wished him well on his homeward return and followed D'vore onto the dock.

Oroenoe had the same dismal docking bays, the same smell of heated engines, sweating bodies, and exotic cargoes, the same dull paint splashed randomly on every surface, obscure signage, most of which I could not read, and a crowd of aliens, alien humans, and human-like aliens, although, truth be told, I could not distinguish among the lot save by my own opinionated prejudices regarding proper size, shape, and color. I found the variegated crowd to be interesting, but no longer startling; such was my slow acceptance of this unfolding universe.

The glamor of interstellar travel that Jocelyn had dreamed was far different than the reality of stinking cargo decks redolent with smells of hot lubricants, exotic spices, and the effluent of alien and human workers. All about us were seemingly random stacks of cargo containers along with the grime and grit of a thousand worlds. Everywhere was the overwhelming din of machines, voices shouting in myriad human and alien languages, and the dull crash of cargo being handled not very kindly.

When D'vore abruptly departed, I worried that he had some other purpose having nothing to do with me and wondered again about our relationship. Were we traveling companions, joint seekers of the truth of our origins, or something else entirely?

D'vore's revelation about his inner needs and lack of memory still concerned me and made me worry that neither of us truly had free will, but were moving like marionettes on someone's strings. Who was our puppet master, or were there many? Not only did I not know the answer to that question, but didn't have the faintest idea of how to obtain it.

The humanity at Oroenoe station presented a broad range of bizarre, acceptable and infrequently lovely forms. The variety and novelty of the passers-by held me fascinated as I took my place at what I thought to be a bar, but could have been a clinic for all I knew. That it offered refreshment and a comfortable place to sit was all I needed to know.

No sooner than I was seated a short woman with cinnamon hair served a drink and scooted away before I could ask what it might be. The drink had a rather pronounced invigorating effect and, by the time I had drained the second cup that mysteriously appeared as I watched a lovely blue-black woman stroll languidly past, I felt much more optimistic than circumstances should have allowed, a condition that resulted in D'vore finding me a few hours later embraced with a refreshingly flexible female of green eyes and rose hair who smelled of hay and sunshine and was fascinated by my ignorance of social mores and her own status.

"You amuse me," she'd said as the two of us had drifted from one place to another, sipping various exotic drinks, and winding up in a secluded nook where we quickly confirmed our all-too-human bono fides.

Her passion reminded me so much of Provance.

"Ahem." The sudden noise made me turn. It was D'vore. He had once again modified his appearance, but to an extent far beyond any other. He appeared larger in both length and girth. His head had become flattened and less egg-shaped. I could only guess what other changes had been made under D'vore's voluminous cape and chose not to. Clearly, D'vore was abandoning any human pretense and becoming something new and strange as he tried to regain his true self.

"We have a problem," D'vore said simply. "The stationmaster wants to know why the WOFAT says that the Penchon are interested in a medician and human pair."

"What's the matter?" my newfound friend raked my back with her nails. "Have I become so uninteresting?" That she was clearly ignoring my conversation with D'vore's hulking presence puzzled me.

"My friend has just arrived."

She peered over his shoulder. "I see no one."

"Then who did you think I was talking to?"

She pushed me aside. "I did not hear you speak." She sat up and gathered her clothing about her.

"Can't you see him standing there?"

She backed away. "There is no one there, sweet man, and I certainly would have noticed, considering how closely we were intertwined."

I clearly recalled rolling over and seeing D'vore standing in the narrow confines of the alleyway. I just as clearly recalled him speaking. But how could I still be lying naked on the ground and standing at the same time?

"She cannot see me," D'vore said. "Nor was your upright posture of a physical nature."

There were so many startling concepts, abilities, and implications in that simple statement that I was stunned.

Somehow, without interrupting the flow of my pleasant activity, D'vore had made me experience actions and words that had no real-world existence. It was probably the same technique he'd used for my explorations of the ship, but well beyond D'vore's stated capabilities.

That idea called my entire perception of reality into question. This was frightening and immediately called into doubt every waking thought, every dream and chance encounter since I'd awakened to see that silver orb hovering over me.

"If you can control my mind then how can I ever trust what I am seeing when you're about?" I said aloud, or at least seemed to do so–how was I to know?

"If I could control your mind isn't it possible that I might have controlled your companion's mind instead?" D'vore replied as he stepped aside to let the woman race by and send one frightened glance over her shoulder.

D'vore hadn't denied or affirmed the possibility of mental control, damn it, which still left me wondering.

"As I started to say, the stationmasters are curious as to why we carry false identities and even more so in the reason the Penchon are so eager to find someone remarkably like us."

I slipped into my clothing, alarmed that D'vore might have confided too much. "Why did you tell them anything? Was the admission your idea or theirs? Are you certain that your willingness to tell them was your own choice?"

"I thought nothing of it," D'vore replied. "It hardly seemed information we should withhold if we are to research the records for your Earth." He shrugged. "As to your question, I did not feel compelled in any way. Rather they seemed genuinely concerned that the Penchon would be so interested in a medician, something the Penchon have little need for themselves."

"You said something else," I reminded him. "When you first arrived." D'vore's ambiguous answer about mind control was still uppermost in my thoughts.

"Yes. I am certain that Lustal's ship brought the Penchon's search update here from Solifugoe, just as other ships are carrying it to other worlds. By announcing their interest on the

WOFAT, the Penchons' statement of interest will expand as each outwardly bound ship spreads the word so that, within the next week I wouldn't be surprised if our descriptions extend far beyond any reasonable distance we might have traveled. Once such an inquiry is introduced to the WOFAT it takes on a life of its own. I have no doubts that their interest will be perpetuated until a countering confirmation is propagated to cancel it, if ever."

The idea that the entire universe, if not the Penchon themselves, were now looking for us filled me with dread. Why were they so interested in me, a creature D'vore had scavenged from the remains of a doomed crew? There was nothing about me that anyone would find unique. In fact, I was probably the least unique person in the entire universe. A persons with no special abilities or secret talent. I was just a man lost in space, a man seeking home among the stars, a man who could not remember his origins or the manner of his many deaths.

"It would be best were we to depart for the library as quickly as possible and before the stationmasters become even more involved."

"Why should that concern us? We've done nothing wrong."

D'vore shivered. "Everyone fears another Human-Penchon war. The resources available by both races are now more than sufficient to completely destroy both races. It would only take one singular event, a spark to ignite a war that would spell the eradication of one race or the other. Restricting our movement might be in everyone's best interest."

"I find 'compete destruction' hard to believe. Aren't both races fairly widespread? Dispersion would protect at least some."

"That is true," D'vore answered. "But only if you assume that only humans and Penchon would be involved. There are enough alliances and relationships involved on both sides to ensure that any conflict started would quickly become a multi-species war that could easily extend to other races."

I tried to imagine a galaxy-wide war, one where information traveled so slowly that it could never be extinguished completely. The Carhera might suppress one conflict, but as news of the war propagated outward at the speed of ship transport through WOFAT, more worlds would become alerted. It was a concept too great to grasp, so huge that my mind could only grasp the edges of what such a conflict might mean. Not only worlds, but entire systems might be extinguished.

The thought that an individual like me could be the spark to ignite such a gigantic cataclysm frightened me to the core. "What can I do?" I pleaded, hoping the answer would explain everything. "What do you want me to do?"

"I want only to see you safely home," D'vore replied. "I have only your best interests at heart, Case ." D'vore sounded sincere, but how could I trust his words? How could I trust anything, including my own perceptions of a world when I no longer knew what was real and what was being manipulated?

I provided for my own quarters, a narrow tube containing a bed and little like the commodious one I'd shared with Provance. There was barely room enough for my few personal items.

That memory of Provance triggered a momentary pang of regret for my poor lost love, followed immediately by the realization that my emotions had probably been cunningly manufactured by a self-serving bitch who had used me for her own ends. The mixture of loathing for how Provance had misused me was mixed equally with my gnawing lust and desire. Manufactured or not, my feelings had been genuine and heartfelt. I still missed her. I still hated her.

Rest was filled with strange dreams, but none that seemed to involve ship or crew. Instead they were of concrete tarmac, colored scrawls on whiteboard, reams of paperwork, smiling women and men, black, brown, and tan, tall and short, young and old. In one sequence I shared a conference room with several men. One, an older man with white beard, thick eyebrows, and unkempt hair stood out and I knew at once that he was Doctor Howard Pierce Gaylord, Nobel Laureate and project maven. He was ...

... *standing on the far side of the table, peering down at a huge schematic spread along its length. A pile of as-built documents sat on top with a sheet blazoned with red circles on the top. "Here and* here," he said with absolute assurance, pointing at the red marks, "are the mistakes I found in this spec." He tossed the stack across the table to land before me.

"It's exactly what you specified," someone said from my right. "The resonance coils are tuned as precisely as possible."

"Only with five figure accuracy," Gaylord sneered and pointed at the offending stack of papers. "We need to better than that— tuning to even seven place accuracy wouldn't be sufficient for complete safety."

"That sort of accuracy isn't technically possible. Even with the gold-plated components and precision machining we specified the contractor couldn't get any better accuracy. They had to use micro plating and Nano-techniques to hone these coils as fine as they are. What you ask is impossible with today's technology."

Gaylord looked over the tops of his glasses. "You cannot get an acceptable product from whoever makes the lowest bid, Joseph. I would suggest that management of this project find a decent company with better tools and who is willing to ensure the precision we need." He threw down his red pen. "Until these are produced to the accuracy I want you will get no further help from me. I will not be party to a suicide experiment." He turned toward me. "Phillip, are you willing to risk your life on something done this sloppily?"

"Be reasonable, David," I protested. I realized for the first time that I was recalling this scene through the memories of Phillip Mellorez, the ship's engineer. "I trust the engineers on this. If their QC people say these coils are acceptable I'm willing to take the risk."

"There, even the crew's engineer agrees with me," the man on my right continued. "Besides, there is no more reliable company that the one we used and, even if there is, we don't have the budget."

"Then there will be no Gaylord drive. There will be no experiment that sends people to God knows where."

After that brief scene the dreams became more ordinary, more related to current circumstance than of past lives. D'vore had repeatedly assured me that this was a welcome sign of greater mental integration, of finally becoming a unique individual instead of an amalgam of piece parts and faded memories. It marked a birth of sorts, the beginning of a life. From this point on I would have to make a place in this grand society.

Upon awakening I began to wonder about the reason for the accident. Again and again I tried to reason out what might have caused the drive to malfunction. Had it been an unexpected power fluctuation, some fault in construction, or was it the consequence of that small error possibility that so bothered Gaylord and LaPlatte?

It could be any of a dozen reasons or a combination of them. Gaylord's concern was that the destination would be displaced in space, as had been noted on earlier experiments with the chimps. What if he had been wrong? What if, as he'd earlier dismissed, the displacement had also been in time?

Everything in the physical universe is constantly in motion but in seven-space everything remains fixed in time and place along all seven axes of reality. A specific "point" in seven-space has a specific location independent of the four-space motions around it. It also has a fixed time point for everything that has ever happened or will happen. By that logic, the displacement in space that had Gaylord so concerned might not have been simply a change in location but a shift in time—the ship appearing in the proper location while the rest of the universe moved. That would make it appear as if the ship had moved, wouldn't it?

I understood that was exactly what happened on the longer jumps and resulted in the back and forth time shifts that had so confused Spiknuck, that had made Jaycea choose a suboptimal path to Vizzon, and made my encounter with the Penchon at Sluggard so confusing.

The fused lump could only mean that the drive had overloaded and twisted the ship both physically and along the time vector.

What if I had moved in *time*?

D'vore was skeptical about the possibility of a time shift. "That might be possible but, even so, your home system would still be within a reasonable distance. The stars move at a different pace than we ephemeral creatures but, insofar as our time horizons are concerned, they remain relatively fixed."

"But what if the time displacement was so great that Earth moved further away? A quick estimate meant that it would take at least ten thousand years for any system to shift even a tiny fraction on its galactic orbit. Even so, most of the stars within a reasonable range of where *Tollembol* found me were not places a human could survive even if their primaries were slightly off the main sequence."

"The closest human planet was over a two thousand light years away," D'vore countered. "Far too distant to be crossed by a ship of that size."

"But it's ridiculous to even think that my ship could have jumped more than two thousand years. Hell, even a jump of a dozen years seems impossible! No, Earth has to be closer!"

"True. The time displacements we encounter are never more than a few weeks, two months at most on the long voyages," D'vore said as he considered the problem. "As you said, there are two variables—time and distance. If the time is not possible then it must be a question of distance."

"So we should consider that I may have jumped contemporaneously from someplace beyond known space?"

"Perhaps, but if your ship, the first such vehicle, had been an experiment that long ago then where are your people?" D'vore countered. "They would have been discovered by now."

"Unless, as you say, they abandoned the effort to build starships when mine failed," I concluded dismally. The idea that the vibrant society I recalled had turned their backs on the universe and been confined to a single, solitary world was unthinkable. I felt in my heart that such an attitude couldn't be sustained. The people of memory had seemed more resilient, adaptable, and flexible. I was certain that they would have found a way to expand and grow within their own system even if reaching the distant stars was denied.

D'vore must have read my thoughts. "It is logical that there would have been other experiments, other ships. If you are correct about the spirit of your people then they would not abandoned the effort, but I am afraid there can be no other possibility. Perfection of a star drive leads inevitably to contact with the Carhera and, since it is unreasonable that your people haven't made contact long before now, there could not have been any time displacement."

"Right! So It has to be nearby–someplace no one has looked," I said hopefully.

D'vore shook his head. "It is unlikely that your system lies hidden, Case . Even if no one physically explored the system, simple orbital mechanics would have revealed its presence long ago. Planets might go unseen, but you cannot hide a star. No, Case, there must be a solution we have not considered, something still hidden in your mind."

That was unacceptable. "What if my ship traversed only a few light years? Could it be hidden in the Rift itself?"

"No one has been able to enter the Rift," D'vore protested.

"So the possibility that someone could represents a threat to the Carhera. Maybe that's why the Penchon are after us. Maybe that's the real reason for ThripoBlastenav's interest."

This possibility gave me further reasons to fear for my own future: Once anyone else had the knowledge supposedly buried in my mind, their continued value would be minimal. Worse, the danger that others might also gain access would make him superfluous and, regrettably, disposable.

Maybe the Penchon weren't my only concern.

D'vore woke me. "Three Penchon ships have docked."

"Is the *Qalyub Gudlag* among them?"

D'vore paused. "That would be … No, it is not."

That gave me scant comfort, even if it implied that it had either been destroyed in the explosion or had given up pursuit. Neither mattered considering that the damned Penchon were nearby. "We can't hide and, even if we do manage to evade them for a while, now that they know our identities we'll be discovered when we try to get transport down to the Library."

"Perhaps I can ask." D'vore paused, "ThripoBlastenav to protect us."

"How can you do that?" The suggestion was ridiculous unless D'vore had some way of communicating that hadn't been revealed. My earlier suspicions of D'vore's motives were renewed. "If you can call in support then why the hell haven't you done that before?"

"I'll explain later, but first we must find a way off this station," D'vore replied. "Now come!"

I threw my few possessions into a bag and followed.

The place we found was an empty room, lighted by a glowing overhead that threw dim light into the far corners. A little trash was scattered about a few dew-encrusted containers standing at one side. These were cool to the touch so they couldn't have been here long. I worried that whoever had put them here would return but after too many hours of no activity, that worry dissipated.

I napped fitfully and trusted that D'vore would return with food and clean water, but mostly that he *would* return. Without the alien's help I was defenseless against the Penchon and whatever forces were driving events. Where was he?

Slowly, with little stimulation, I drifted effortlessly into the dream state, where memories of those who were now part of whatever I'd become dwelled.

Jocelyn worried that she was their only backup should the computers fail to identify their destination. She knew it was an irrational fear. Half a light year was a trivial distance from the sun and the computers should have no difficulty in locating it. Even if for some strange reason they couldn't or wouldn't find it, it would still be a first magnitude star, outshining all the rest— something she could find with a naked eye. Besides, even if they didn't emerge from seven space where they planned and couldn't see the sun, she still had the variable pulsars to determine her position. All she'd need to calculate their precise position was to unfurl the radio telescope and confirm the Cepheid's' periodicity and angular differences. It might take weeks to sort how far they were off the center point, but she was certain that her knowledge, her skill, and her experience would get them home.

And just to be sure that she recalled all the facts she scribbled a little reference table on the bulkhead next to her chair. It was a way to pass the time and besides, it looked kind of neat.

Her computer pinged to report that Polaris was centered and that the ship's attitude was stable. She kissed her fingers and planted it on the star chart she'd taped to the bulkhead beside her. That done, she switched the toggle to green and looked through the eyepiece of the optical telescope at Polaris. What would it look like when the drive engaged, she wondered? Would she see any change at all or just a momentary blankness? If she blinked, would she miss the shift?

I started as I abruptly became David Bolsteri and ...

... was watching the readiness lights change, one by one, from yellow to green. Deep in the bowels of the ship the computers were doing all the work, monitoring every aspect of this experiment, watching the power levels, ensuring that life support was operating properly, and monitoring the life signs of every member of the crew, including his own racing heart. His function was only to give it permission when everyone was ready. I rested my thumb on the toggle and waited for the last yellow light from engineering to glow green. Once I gave the go-ahead It was the computers that would decide on the exact moment for the jump through seven space.

The final light blinked to green. I pressed the toggle.

I sat up, completely awake, chilled, and drenched in sweat. My heart was hammering hard even though there had been no horror associated with pressing that toggle when all thought, all life had ceased.

I tried to analyze what I could recall. What could have gone wrong? Half a light year was a trivial distance in seven-space, yet used as much power as a voyage ten times as long. Why had our crew seemed so cautious? Hadn't we put a year's supply of rations and water on board, just in case we had to limp back to where we could be rescued? But the idea of rescue was ridiculous, since at maximum acceleration we could only travel a quarter of the distance before our supplies ran out. The only reason would be to let us survive long enough to get the ship back to where it could be examined, once the dust of its crew had been cleared away.

Obviously the ship had gone far beyond that miniscule half a light year's distance. But what had happened to twist the ship into a crush of metal, plastic, bone and flesh? Was it a power fluctuation, a loose connector, or a poorly understood application of half-understood seven-space phenomenon?

Once again I regretted the actual wreckage. Examination of the physical wreck might reveal a cause, but who knew if that could be?

After a night without food or water my stomach rumbled and my mouth was foul and dry. I scoured for a source of water and, more importantly, someplace to relieve myself. A puddle that had accumulated beneath the thawing containers slaked my thirst despite its bitter, metallic taste. In a distant corner I emulated my Penchon pursuers and deposited waste on the deck.

"I have arranged for us to travel to the Library and, for that, we may yet survive," D'vore announced without preamble when he returned.

I suspected that D'vore's "resources" were not being charitable. They wouldn't be doing all this without expecting a return. Or had D'vore once again given away something of value? Since we had nothing to trade but our bodies and untouchable obligations, there could only be one thing they might value.

"You told them about my dreams. You gave them the information we discussed, didn't you?" I wondered what other information he'd traded. "Damn it, I trusted you!"

D'vore hesitated. "I am well and truly your friend, Case, and want only to see you safely restored to your home."

His non sequitur puzzled me. "Some things you've done make me doubt that."

"I have done what was necessary for our continued safety. Your story was the only thing I could use so we could resume our search."

I was relieved but wondered why D'vore's "resources" couldn't search the records themselves? "I assume that you have some reason to trust whoever you spoke to?"

"Trust is not a word I would choose." D'vore seemed ill at ease, a strange manner for one that was normally so confident. "I have not been a free agent in all this, Case, but I have always remained loyal to your search. In all the time we've been together I have done everything needed to protect you."

I was less than surprised at this revelation. "Surely you must have some idea of what is going on. You wouldn't be doing this if you didn't have some suspicions."

"I've long wondered at the forces at play, actions underway, and discoveries waiting to be made," D'vore admitted. "It seems obvious that we are both actors in a greater drama. I don't know the extent of this play or my role, only that I have no choice but to help you solve the puzzle of your home before we can leave the stage. Until then I will not be allowed to become my own self, just as finding your Earth will release you."

At last I felt my suspicions confirmed. ThripoBlastenav had been using our mutual needs for identity to drive us. The question remained if something more than simply finding lost Earth was involved, more than escaping the wrath of the Penchon, more than ... whatever it was, I could not imagine. I wondered, almost as an aside, whether I was one of the lead players, a supporting actor, or just the guy who gets killed at the end of the second act? Considering the power of the alien playwrights involved, I thought the latter all too likely. "I'm sure that ThripoBlastenav didn't arrange transport simply to repay you for recounting a few of my dreams. What else is involved?"

"There has been no change in our original purpose. We are to continue to examine the ancient records for some hint of a lost colony, a missing ship, or some other indication of your origins. Once we have located Earth I am certain that someone will take you home."

"And you? What happens to you after that? Are they going to release you or just chain you with a new set of obligations?" Despite the appeal of reaching Earth I felt a twinge of loyalty for this alien creature who had, in a sense, given me birth.

"I have been assured that finding your origin is all that will be asked, but I have no other choice than to believe that." D'vore sounded honestly puzzled. "Ever since I can recall others have been guiding me, assisting me, helping me build my knowledge. I have no more idea of their motives than you, no more awareness of the forces around me than one of these crates. You have spoken of free will, of freedom and neither of those has applied to me in all the time since my misfortune."

I could sense the pain in his voice and felt shamed. Up to now D'vore had been my salvation, aide, and one who provided answers. To discover that he was as afloat in the mysterious affairs of others shocked me.

"You said the Carhera have been directing you since your misfortune? I thought it was the Penchon who captured you, who brought you back to functionality, and who sold you to *Tollembol*. Isn't that what you told me?"

"I never said it was the Penchon who rescued me, only that they gave me my skills."

While that might be true, it was beside the point for what I wanted to find out. Whoever was controlling D'vore had a purpose in placing him on *Tollembol*. It was just too much of a coincidence that a medician with his surgical skills and knowledge should just happen to be aboard at a time and place to recover the crew's fragments and bring me to life.

I quickly explained this logic to D'vore. "That's too damned many improbable events for my liking. Someone had to have known about the wreck in advance." The instant the words left my mouth another thought occurred. "What about your own 'misfortune?' Was that an accident or could someone have engineered that as well?"

D'vore shook his head. "It does not matter. As far as I was concerned it all happened in the normal flow of my travels. It was only after your wreck had been detected that I was told of it. I knew nothing in advance." He paused. "Perhaps the ThripoBlastenav is simply taking advantage of your situation—an interesting pursuit quite apart from anyone's original intentions. But this discussion might be fruitless. We could pursue those ideas forever and still come to no conclusions."

I didn't want to drop the subject so easily. "Even so, someone seems to be expending a great deal of resources to find out about the ship. There has to be some purpose for that, some reason. I doubt they are doing this out of charity. They have to think they are gaining something."

"Again, their motives and goals might be unknowable. We are both driven by our need to solve the mystery of our origins. We have no choice but to pursue our own goals and hope that things will become clear. I doubt we will ever understand the greater game that is being played."

Over the next few days we moved, seemingly at random, following instructions D'vore mysteriously and silently received. When D'vore tried to explain by using terms that had no meaning for me such as "radiant thomage" and "residual etherics" I imagined some sort of radio transmission and thought no more of it.

We moved from the warehouse to an empty ship and remained there for days. There were no crew aboard, and the only being I saw the entire time was a red-scaled alien who pointedly ignored us as it checked the certificates posted on the outer hatch.

Lacking anything better to occupy our time D'vore suggested further explorations of the ship's image, to which I immediately agreed. Perhaps the vivid dreams of the previous week would help me forge new associations with what I'd observed. I certainly felt more of a connection to the crew now that I'd experienced them in my dreams. Yes, exploration would be a good use of my time. Maybe I could discover more about Jocelyn's variable stars.

As I walked the virtual passageway from hatch to command console I named each crewmember as I passed their alcoves. There, in the left-hand seat, sat David Bolsteri sat and, to his right, Melika Cohen, the pilot. Immediately sternward were Fedor Albert, the life support specialist and, across from him, Vladmir Crebenitza-computers. In the next pair of alcoves were the engineer, Phillip Mellorez and Jocelyn Bell, the astronomer.

I sat in Jocelyn's seat and tried to imagine looking through her eyes at the critical moments leading up to the accident. What would she be thinking, doing in preparation besides scratching that strange table on the bulkhead? Was there something he had missed? He gazed at the panels, wondering what they might have shown, what she might have seen, but no more memories were evoked.

Above the main panel was where I recalled she'd posted a star chart. He could see the discoloration where it had been taped and recalled the dream of the flickering candle.

Why was the memory associated with a candle and the star chart? What was there about that dream that had seemed so important? I looked closely at the place the candle might have sat, if indeed there had been such an anomalous item on this ship. There was no puddle of melted wax, no hole where a candle would fit, and no sign that anything other than the chart could have been there.

Immediately below that spot were the controls for the radio telescope. I recalled the table as he leaned closer to read the faded, pairs of numbers: 3.5-4.4, 3.6-4.4.3.7-4.2, and 3.46-4.08. Could these be coordinates of some sort and, if so, what did they mean?

Jocelyn had seemed to be one who, if she had been a man, would have been a belt and suspenders type. That said, why would she write such a table? Surely these names and numbers were readily available from the computer so why bother?

I tried to reason through it. The Jocelyn I recalled had been a cautious, deliberate, detail-oriented scientist, someone who left nothing to chance. It followed that, should something go wrong she would be prepared. If they did not end up where they intended the computer could figure out where they were. If it couldn't, she had the optical telescope and the spectrometer. Only in the direst circumstances would she need to use a radio telescope and, if that circumstance turned out to be a computer failure, these might be the coordinates that would identify the location of Earth.

But what could they mean?

"Because of the proximity these are obviously settings for the telescope," D'vore guessed. "I would assume the numbers refer to angles."

"Angles would be numbers between zero and 360, wouldn't they?" I doubted that there would be any system where the angles would be measured finer than that. Besides, why have them paired? If these were settings then what was the zero point—straight ahead, the telescope's rest position or some known star that would be observable regardless of where they emerged? I was missing something, something that might be important.

"Wasn't your Jocelyn a specialist in pulsars?" D'vore asked as soon as the ship dissolved.

"Pulsars have regular beat," I replied slowly. "Maybe she could use their timing to calculate a specific location?" And there were *four* coordinates. Could the paired numbers beside each strange name indicate the location of Earth? "We need help to figure out what this table means?" After chiding D'vore for sharing his dreams I felt a hypocrite by asking for help. Nevertheless, there was no way I'd ever figure out this table alone.

"Perhaps, but first we must get off the station and that means keeping away from the Penchon until we can reach the next planet-bound transport." He led the way from the room down a narrow passage. "We must be cautious."

"Why can't ThripoBlastenav" protect us, for God's sake? I can't believe that ..."

"My resources cannot act openly," D'vore answered, leaving the question of whether he was talking in general or about someone in particular. "The ramifications of your tiny ship extend well beyond humanity's petty concerns. The seeming ability to transit vast distances is important. It is a discovery, that would seriously affect a great number of races."

We raced from our hiding place, surprising a few random aliens and humans in the process. D'vore indicated a narrow passageway half the width of the others. "Maintenance cutoff," he remarked, which explained nothing. We entered a box-like room with no apparent exit—a dead end?

Without warning, the box began to slowly rise. I watched the narrow corridor sink as an unpainted gray wall replaced it. "This is a maintenance riser," D'vore explained. "It will take us up into the superstructure of the station, but don't worry" —he must have seen my look of apprehension—"it has the proper environment for you to breathe."

He was partially right; the air was breathable but the temperature was far from comfortable. "It's freezing up here," I complained as I avoided the icy spots on the narrow walkway across the open superstructure. Two meters below was the roof of the human portion of the station and less than a meter above my head was the base of some other environment. D'vore's head scraped the overhead while I only occasionally bumped my own. Below were conduits and piping, hoses and wires, huge boxes containing who-knew-what. The sound of humming fans permeated the air. I had never given much thought to how the station managed to operate so well but seeing its raw bones gave me an appreciation of the building effort that had been involved.

D'vore halted. There was a short ladder leading down to a hatch.

"What's that?"

"Access to someplace safe," he replied as he moved a few meters further. "You go first. I want to ensure we are not being followed."

I cautiously stepped onto the flimsy ladder, unsure that it would bear my weight, let alone that of D'vore. It was only three steps and then I had to twist about, turn a handle, and lift a hatch. Through the opening I saw a longer and apparently sturdier ladder. I stepped through and began to descend.

"Screee!" came a piercing cry. Talons clutched at my legs. Something climbed past me to block the hatch. Two Penchon had me by the shoulders and another my left leg. "Screee, screee," they screamed as I was dragged back and down. The Penchon at the top of the ladder jumped through the hatch, followed by two of his comrades.

Their hold was so tight that I could not move, so close to them that their acrid stink filled my lungs. Their shrill cries blocked out any other sound. A hood was thrown over my head as bounds were placed around arms and legs, trussing me like a prize pig being carried to market. No, not a market: It would be a Penchon ship where I would become components of their parts inventory after they drained me of whatever knowledge they thought I possessed.

When the hood was removed I saw that I was in a cell not unlike my quarters on *Qalyub Gudlag*. The amenities were almost identical, except there was no bucket in the corner. "You could at least untie me," I demanded.

"Scree, screee!" they answered, but did nothing.

An agonizing hour later, long after my arms had gone thankfully numb, a Penchon, holding one of their obscene translators, squatted on the floor. "We wish of interest to know," it began, "the where of your kind."

"Bite me." I hoped that his interrogator did not take the phrase too literally. "I don't know." I wondered if they had captured D'vore as well. The Penchon were probably better adapted to scurrying about the overhead than D'vore. Had they already rendered him back to a bare torso and stored his trunk with the cargo?

"Source of ship, of interest as well. Carhera experiment fulfilled?"

"Experiment?" I hadn't the faintest idea of what it was talking about.

"Carhera ship *Tollembol* involved. What role yours? Where they find you?"

I thought that question interesting. "Are you saying *Tollembol* was one of the Carhera's vessels? I didn't know that." Yes, and I certainly didn't think I'd any role except being the ship's fool, a role that I seemed to have been playing ever since awakening.

"Lie! We have reports that you were with surgery unit so you must be important. Where *Tollembol* find you?"

So it came down to wanting to know the location of Earth after all. But they were mistaken: *Tollembol* had not found me by making contact with an unknown human colony. "At the Rift," I replied honestly and then added a small bit of misdirection. "They rescued me when my ship escaped the Rift."

If I had suddenly turned into D'vore my interrogator

wouldn't have been less surprised. It rocked back and opened its wings in astonishment. "Screee, screee, screee," it babbled while the translator was echoing "Yes," "As suspected," and "Gack" in equal measure.

Finally it regained its composure. "How possible? Where in Rift? Coordinates?"

"I don't have the faintest idea. All I know is that I was apparently rescued and treated to recovery."

That, it turned out, was exactly the wrong thing to say. As soon as the translation device finished screeching its translation, four Penchon dragged me to a chamber looking suspiciously like D'vore's surgery and stained with several interesting shades of brown. Dried blood, I imagined, no doubt from previous victims.

Overcoming my screams and resistance, they thrust my arms into restraints and locked both ankles to the sideboards. As I lay immobile other Penchon began a detailed nightmare of examination. Scaly hands probed and prodded, squeezed and palpitated, penetrated and explored areas I would rather remained untouched. The worse part was the stench of their noxious breath.

They strapped instrument after instrument on my head, arms, legs, and torso and shined bright lights into my eyes. They stuck moist rods up my ass and down my throat and thankfully, used different instruments for each. Finally, after what seemed an eternity of agony something pricked my arm and blessed unconsciousness overcame me.

I awoke unbound, naked, and chilled. I immediately patted my body to make certain that I still had my original parts and that all were in their proper place. Aside from a couple of punctures in my bicep I seemed to be all right, albeit very, very thirsty. My throat felt especially tender.

A Penchon entered, but without its organic translator. "You are recovered. Excellent. Do you need water, food?"

"Water would be nice," I replied automatically and realized I could suddenly understand the Penchon. More surprising was that when I replied it had been with an unholy screech. "What?"

I began. My throat hurt.

"Small modification and implant," the Penchon replied. "We did not understand why you do not have such."

Now *that* was an interesting statement and raised another question I would like D'vore to answer. "What else did you do to me?" I was fearful that other liberties had been taken with my body or mind.

"Much had been done already. Other needed modifications and improvements might create problems. We did not meddle much, but you need time to rest and recover. Interest high that you are a patchwork human with parts from a line we have not sampled."

I shivered at the mention of "sampled."

Unlike my earlier experience on a Penchon ship, I did not have freedom of movement but had to wait alone in the cell save for the infrequent visits by an interrogator. I could not tell one from another, not that it mattered greatly.

The solitude between sessions gave me ample time to reflect on what had brought me here. Had D'vore known of the waiting Penchon and led me into a trap? The idea that D'vore might have betrayed me reawakened my periodic distrust of his motives. Had D'vore been working for the Penchon? Had he been using their supposed pursuit to goad my memories of Earth's location?

No, that made little sense. Neither did it make sense that the Penchon had not captured us during their earlier encounters. In each case D'vore had opportunities to betray me, yet had not.

No, there was no way he had been working with the Penchon.

The ambush may have been a surprise to him as well. I hoped that he'd managed to evade his pursuers or had overcome them with his great strength. That thought gave me a surge of hope. If D'vore had gotten away he would probably be working free me, unless of course, this ship had departed and was now underway to a Penchon world where I would be dissected, analyzed, and disposed without consequence.

That grim thought did not help my outlook at all.

Since the red glow of the cell gave me little indication of a daily cycle I let the natural rhythm of my body dictate a routine. It must have approximated the Penchon's cycle as well for interrogations occurred shortly after I awoke and eaten the dry rations they provided. There might have been some sort of surveillance that cued this, but I doubted that mattered. There was nothing I could do about it.

On the third or fourth "night" I dreamed I was LaPlatte and once again on our ship, staring at the screen and reading the equations, trying to find where Grayson's so-called erroneous assumption might lie.

"Only two more hours until we're at full power," Mellorez barked over the intercom.

Two hours and there was no more I could do. All of my checks had been completed earlier, during the run out to the launch point. Gods, I can't just sit here and twiddle my thumbs. There must be something I could do to keep busy and quell the butterflies in my stomach. I glanced over at Florence. She was scribbling something on the bulkhead next to the telescope housing with a pencil. A pencil for God's sake! Why did she do that when she had the entire astronomical database right there on the screen before her? Must be nerves.

Further forward Bolsteri and Cohen were whispering to each other and flipping switches on their panels. He doubted they were discussing the affair Albert and Lyle had suspected. More likely they were being the cool professional pilots going down their extensive checklists. Besides, with their age difference why would they have an affair; she was at least ten years older than him, closer to my wife's age?

I had to do something to calm down and take my mind off of what was about to take place. I'd sacrificed so much to be here, to participate in this historic trip. I flipped up the reference work. Perhaps going over the math would take my mind off the reality for a while.

The maths that dictated the drive's design had been examined by the handful of physicists versed in six-space theory. The engineering had been checked multiple times and then tested time and again until they were assured that no mistake had been made. The animal trials, the short runs of a quarter light had happened without incident, as had the half-light tests. Even the full light year automated trial had been successful, although it had exhibited the same imprecision of arrival location as the others–a navigational error that seemed directly proportional to the distance traveled.

That was why Florence was along—to discover how much error they had to correct to get back home. Of course, she was simply backup should the automated astronomy programs fail. Everyone agree that a failure was an unlikely possibility but "Belts and suspenders" as the mission chief kept saying as the reason an astronomer was aboard.

Nevertheless I worked my tortuous way through the assumptions that defined current physics theory of the six-space reality underlying the universe. Six-space theory hadn't yet led to a general theory of everything, but it stood a better chance of eventually getting there than that much-maligned string theory ever did. Better, this theory was consistent with Einstein's theories and, now that they had perfected the drive, gave us a way to verify it.

The derivations were simple, once you accepted the assumptions and, no matter how much I would like to find out where something might have gone awry, my focused concentration produced no new revelation. The assumptions were correct, the math was solid, and the drive should work as designed.

"Five minutes," Bolsteri said in a voice not unlike that of an airline pilot announcing that the passengers could release their safety belts and move about the cabin, not that we were about to flash a light year away in an instant.

Well, going over the math had certainly made the time fly by after all.

I woke with a shock. Six-space math! That was the basic assumption they had gotten wrong. The drive design had been based on an imperfect understanding of the seven-space reality of the universe. That was why there were so few controllers on the drive housing and possibly the reason the drive had malfunctioned!

No, that couldn't be: The drive had been tested extensively so even a flawed and imperfect theory had been close enough to work. It must have been something else that caused everything to go catastrophically wrong. Something LaPlatte might not know about.

Learning of yet another error was exciting news. I had to tell D'vore, but to do that I had to get away from the Penchon without revealing that knowledge.

I just wished I knew how to do that.

The interrogator showed up as usual and settled itself on the deck. "Are you well? Your sleep seemed disturbed."

Well, that certainly answered my question about their surveillance, I thought, which now meant I needed to worry about talking in my sleep.

"This confinement does not agree with me," I screeched in reply. "Where are you taking me?"

It shrugged, a rippling movement that shook its wings. "No place. We still seek the surgical unit and the data it carries regarding you."

So, they hadn't yet found D'vore and, more importantly, he'd indicated that this ship hadn't yet left Oroenoe. I felt a brief glimmer of hope that a rescue might still be possible. D'vore certainly wouldn't have abandoned me, not when his own future depended on my memories. No, I was certain that something would be done to free me.

"I am Catsclaw," the Penchon announced abruptly. This was the first time one of them had introduced itself. I wondered if this was an attempt at friendliness or if it simply wanted to put discussions on a more personal level? Did the Penchon have that much knowledge of human psychology? There was no way I could know and, lacking any knowledge of Penchon behavior,

I thought it best to accept.

"And I am Case Pasticher." I almost stuck out a hand.

"A human of assorted parts who appeared in WOFAT at Toril. One of our qalyub gudlag reported picking you up from life pod along with a medical unit."

"The medician and I escaped together. Don't read more into it than that; I wasn't important. Wait a minute; did you say one of your qalyub gudlag?"

"Yes. We have many such scouts." The news stunned me . Why hadn't D'vore mentioned that? Why was I allowed to believe we were being pursued by a single ship? Had this been another scheme to goad me along, to keep me under control?

Catsclaw grew impatient. "You to tell why Carhera have surgical unit continue to accompany you."

"No, I'm just along for the ride. D'vore was just delivering something outside of the usual channels. It had nothing to do with me."

"The Carhera have little need of couriers. Also, why would they rebuild you, a costly proposition?"

"Are you seriously suggesting that I'm part of some Carhera plot? That I'm some sort of agent?"

"Gudlag report is that wreckage of ship was not familiar. Strange design. Was associated with *Tollembol*'s destruction? Why only one pod released? Why just you and surgical unit?"

"I have nothing to with any wreckage," I objected. "I was just ..."

"*Tollembol* had no record of you as crew. You must have come from wrecked ship, but how? Damage was extensive. How would you survive?"

Catsclaw was getting too close to the truth and I could think of no way to divert him from that line of questioning. Suddenly I had an idea. "What do *you* know about the Penchon destruction at Toril? What caused the explosion?"

Catsclaw tilted its head to one side. "Blast did not affect Penchon. Why you think so?"

That answer was stunning. I had assumed that a Penchon ship had been destroyed in the explosion. Wasn't that what D'vore had hinted? Try as I might I could not recall D'vore making any direct statement about the Penchon ship's destruction, but then, I still wasn't very good at recalling details. "One of your qalyub gudlag still has my wreckage?" I blurted.

Catsclaw's steady gaze intensified. "Is true then; you and wreckage connected? Wreckage severe and you a human of unknown parts. Assume you were repaired by surgical unit and therefore must be important to Carhera."

"It was a clone ship, not Carhera."

"It is the same. *Tollembol* was Carhera retrieval ship."

Now it was my turn to be taken aback. That revelation was interesting and not a little shocking since it implied that *Tollembol* been there specifically to collect the wreckage. But that meant that someone had prior knowledge of the instant our ship would appear. Hadn't D'vore said that organic remains would only have a few minutes before they deteriorated to uselessness?

"Assumption is that *Tollembol* intercepted and destroyed your ship then constructed you to discover origins. Why they do this?"

This information really worried me. What if that was true and *Tollembol* had captured my crew? I recalled thinking that it seemed to be a military vessel so it might be possible that *Tollembol* had destroyed the ship, interrogated the crew, and then dismembered them so they could construct a willing dupe D'vore could manipulate.

Catsclaw's revelations were shaking the foundations of everything that had happened. I had no way of knowing what had happened in those two years of recovery, if indeed it had been that long. God; all I *knew* were what I'd been told by *Tollembol*'s captain and D'vore without knowing if they were being truthful.

Once again it threw my relationship to D'vore into question: Had D'vore been working on my behalf or simply guiding me along? How could I find out? How was I to know whom to trust?

"Can offer aid," Catsclaw offered. "Can make new identity for you to evade Carhera interest. But need your knowledge first."

"I know why, you bloody ghoul," I shot back. "That's why you've been pursuing me–to find more humans to harvest, isn't it?"

"Penchon are honest traders in organics. Why is this a problem?"

"Because, because ..." I sputtered into silence. How could I explain what was so wrong about what the aliens did by rendering bodies for their parts? Was my emotional reaction the same as when I first learned of D'vore's use of human parts, a reaction that defied conscious analysis? Could my revulsion stem from some buried instinct? "It's just wrong," I blurted, ruefully acknowledging that the same technology had given me life.

Catsclaw appeared to be taken aback. "Why wrong? We harvest and build with other species' organic parts. You raise animals for consumption. Which is wrong?"

"I don't know. It just doesn't feel right. Was that what the war with humans was about?"

"War was mistake. Systemic conflict on trading rights, misunderstanding on both sides and then conflict. We no longer want our worlds plundered so we pursue honest trade."

"In body parts, you mean. I've seen your abattoirs where you render humans captured during the war. I've heard stories."

Catsclaw rose and spread its wings. Its head jutted forward as its claws extended on widespread arms. I leaned back; half afraid it was going to attack. "Lies! We do not *harvest* humans," Catsclaw let out an earsplitting shriek. "We harvest cells and grow human parts."

I wondered if that might be the truth? Judging from its reaction, Catsclaw believed it was. I had heard differently from Jaycea's crew, who, I recalled with some chagrin, were hardly reliable witnesses where assessments of aliens or even other humans were concerned. Had my understanding of the Penchon's activities been wrong as well? Gods, what else could I have misunderstood and how in hell was I ever going to discover the truth?

Catsclaw had turned to leave. "Lost control is bad. We talk later," it screeched and left a trail of droppings near the hatchway.

The next day Catsclaw left the hatch wide as it left. I tentatively stepped into the corridor; half expecting other Penchon to force me back. Instead I saw Catsclaw standing close. "Is gesture of trust," it said, waving at the hatch. "Come, I will show you what we do."

Thus began my informed exposure to Penchon technology. What I had supposed to be an abattoir on my first visit turned out to be the processing and packing portion of the ship's manufacturing process. In the dim red light Penchon were feverishly working to feed the mass of tissues and move the finished products to the abattoir. In an area I'd not seen in my exploration of the *Qalyub Gudlag* were the tissue tanks and composing machines quite unlike the cool machines, glass vessels and tanks of fluids I expected, but that type of hard-edged equipment would only be found in a human lab. The Penchon did things differently.

All about were flexible masses that could have been animal or vegetable, colored in various shades of brown through red. Each one surged and moved as it accepted raw tissue and exuded muscles, skin, and even fully assembled arms and legs, which were quickly whisked away to a waiting container. I was glad that none of these limbs were remotely human.

"We serve many races," Catsclaw explained and waved at a fresh appendage. "These are for Blutturi hospital on station."

With this new understanding the place no longer seemed something of the nightmares that had haunted me for months.

Catsclaw led me through the tree-like control tower, the warm recreation rooms, and the passageways that had so baffled me so that, in the end, I began to feel comfortable about the Penchon and wondered again which version of the past I should believe–the version Catsclaw suggested or that related by D'vore. Just how much should I trust my captors?

Worse yet, how much could I trust D'vore or whoever or whatever he was working for?

Catsclaw led me to an opening to the docks. There were no other Penchon about. "You have a decision to make, Case Pasticher," Catsclaw said. "You can help us or you can continue to support the Carhera's mysterious project."

I was incredulous. "After all the trouble you've taken to find me you are offering me freedom? Why should I believe you?"

"Is a gesture of trust. Also, we now have all the information that your body can give us. I doubt if your mind contains any other trustworthy data. Most reconstructed are given false memories to anchor them emotionally. I suspect the same is true of you."

Suddenly Catsclaw took my arm and tugged me back.

"I thought I was free." Then I saw a group of Eglaners advancing, their posture and expressions indicating they were not in a friendly mood.

"Look at the bloody human with that stinking animal?" one shouted and pointed. "Helping the filthy beasts are you?"

"Fucking traitor to his own kind," another cried. "Damned ghoul."

"They are angry over a small trade dispute," Catsclaw said as it backed away. "And I suspect intoxicated as well."

I wondered what sort of "trade dispute" would make Eglaners this angry. Then I remembered the lack of empathy expressed by Jaycea's crew for anything non-Eglaner. It wouldn't take much to push them over the edge to physical violence, and having a bit too much to drink might do it. Yes, it could well be Dutch courage driving them.

"That's right, hide in their filthy ship, you bloody traitor," the Eglaners shouted and, after several minutes of shaken fists and more obscure curses, the group drifted away, possibly in search of more to drink.

Catsclaw's revelations and unexpected offer left me with no anchor, no bulwark of truth that I could use to bring about some resolution to all my questions. Were the Penchon truly benign, as Catsclaw contended, or had it been lying? Should I cooperate in hopes that the Penchon would protect me? Cooperating seemed to be my best option for the moment and the only one that would allow me to shake D'vore's leash, but the question remained was how I could trust that the Penchon didn't have even more sinister motives?

I debated: Was I the victim of a Copenhagen complex, unconsciously befriending my current captors? No, I felt certain I was being rational and making decisions based on the facts as I knew them. I'd formed no emotional bond to the ghoulish Catsclaw, for which I was thankful, but at the same time, I could not deny that there was a ring of truth to everything it had said.

But wasn't that equally valid for most of the statements by D'vore?

Faced with two versions of the "truth" I struggled over who was the most believable. This was no longer a decision of which I trusted the most, but how best to ensure my own survival and, at the moment, that meant working with the Penchon.

In the morning I would be honest with Catsclaw and pray that it had been as honest.

Screams and blinding light awakened me from a sound and dreamless sleep. There were screeches of Penchon fury and loud human voices. "This is a violation," If heard a Penchon screech. "You have no rights."

"No bloody damned god-damned traitor is going to help you filthy beasts," a gruff voice replied. "Where the hell are you hiding the bastard?"

"We have called the stationmaster. Leave at once."

"Down this way," someone yelled. "They got something in … watch it!" Sounds of a scuffle followed, punctuated by Penchon screeches and human screams. Something heavy hit the hatch and made the walls ring.

Silence.

I held my breath. These couldn't be the rescuers that I'd hoped for just a day ago, before I changed my mind about the Penchon, not with the cries I'd heard. Could this be a ruse to bring me back under Carhera control? No, they'd said 'traitor' and I hardly thought that meant they were here to help. Either possibility could be true but there was nothing I could do except wait for the conclusion of whatever battle raged outside.

There were scrabbling sounds at his hatch and, a moment later, it burst open. It was a battered Catsclaw, one wing drooping and ichor dripping from its chest. "Come quickly. We will protect."

I had to step over a blood-soaked body–human, I noticed. The smell of alcohol was strong enough to momentarily overcome the pervasive ammonia miasma that I'd become so used to. Whether the man was dead or merely unconscious I could not tell and Catsclaw didn't say. There were two limp Penchon lying nearby.

Catsclaw moved faster than I could run, even in this lesser gravity. It abruptly turned a corner but I was moving too fast to make the turn. I'd taken half a step back when I heard a shot. Catsclaw cried just as a voice crowed. "Got the butcher right in the gizzard."

I stopped. Whoever had shot Catsclaw would find me in seconds. What should I do? Was there anywhere to run? Should I could find Penchon protection? My burning desire to get away from this violence intensified with each microsecond's delay. I continued moving in the direction I'd been heading.

Panic gave me speed and, after several random turns, always away from the sounds of the fight, I spotted an open hatch and dashed through, slamming it closed as I looked warily about, expecting to be discovered.

I was in one of the ship's cargo bays and there, barely seen through the packed crates on the opposite side, was a half opened loading bay and beyond it, the station's dock.

I raced across the space, dodging around crates, stopping only at the edge of the opening and hesitated before taking another step, unsure of what might await beyond. There was no one standing guard when I tentatively stuck my head out to look around.

Twenty paces to my right were the three Eglaners who'd shouted at me yesterday. They were being confronted by six Penchon screeching warnings and waving a variety of weapons. The three looked uncertain. I guessed that each was waiting to see if another would take the first aggressive step. It looked like it would be a fairly even match, but I was damned if I wanted to waste the time to find out which group would prevail.

Ten meters to my left was a row of stacked containers that might conceal me, but first I had to cross an open space, which raised the danger that one of the men would glance my way.

The alternative was to huddle indecisively and that could prove fatal. I took a deep breath and raced across the open space, fearing a cry of discovery at any moment.

Once I was across and hidden from the ship, I kept moving, unwilling to look back. I kept running but eventually had to stop to catch my breath. I had come at least halfway around the station's periphery.

I debated whether I should try to find D'vore or not. Part of me opposed this idea. Why should I let D'vore dictate my every move? Hadn't I already been too damn passive? No, contacting D'vore, even if I knew how, would not be a wise course of action.

Maybe I should try to reestablish contact with the Penchon once the furor died down to indicate that I was still willing to cooperate, as I'd intended. But then, I had been their captive and that had definitely influenced my choice.

No, now that I was free I had to reassess my options and figure out how to get down to Oroenoe to find this library of records that might reveal Earth's location, that is, if any records existed.

The problem with that plan was my complete ignorance of how to arrange transport. Worse yet, I had no idea of how to would find the library once I somehow managed to reach the surface. Aside from my shipboard existence I was completely ignorant of this civilization's conventions, practices, and customs. I'd be like some ignorant grunting savage plopped into a modern city.

No: that was wrong—I *was* an ignorant savage!

The realization of my own inadequacies meant that, like it or not, I once again had to depend on either D'vore, my untrustworthy guide to this strange universe, or the Penchon. It was a bitter decision, but of the two D'vore was probably my better choice.

But how was I to find him?

In the end it was D'vore who found me wandering aimlessly near where we'd been hiding before being captured. I somehow hoped to find the small bag I'd left. It had only some personal items and the tiny favor Provance had given me.

"It is good that you were not injured in the Eglaners' rather misguided attack," D'vore said as a greeting. "That unruly crowd of rogue humans would have easily precipitated a serious incident had the blue hats not become involved."

"Serious incident?" I saw Penchon shot and at least one dead Eglaner. I gritted my teeth. "Glad to see you as well. Did you send that group after me?"

"Not at all: I was contemplating a more direct method of gaining your release, one that would once again obligate me to the Penchon. Whatever happened was beyond my control."

I wondered if being a sacrificial offering was the only bargaining strategy D'vore knew? Did he have so little regard for his own welfare that he would voluntarily return to the Penchon? It was a gracious offer, if true, and made me wonder if I would have made the same sacrifice. But, I realized I would not, and was very uncomfortable with that realization.

At the same time I wondered if D'vore really understood what the Penchon wanted or if he was still under the assumption that he was simply a surgical unit?

I recalled poor Catsclaw saying they wanted the data D'vore contained. I had assumed at the time they meant data about his presence on *Tollembol*, but what if their interest lay in other, completely different information–something I might have unknowingly revealed?

No, I didn't want to think about that possibility. The very last thing I needed at this point was to add another level of complexity to my already over-complicated life. Better to assume the Penchon had suspected that D'vore knew more about the situation than I had provided. It was simpler that way.

"I learned too late of the Eglaners' anger," D'vore continued, completely unaware of my internal debate. "As soon as the station was alerted to the confrontation I knew that it concerned you, a fact that was confirmed by the station administrator as they rounded up the miscreants and who, I am afraid to say, are now even more interested in us than before."

"They wanted to kill me, not rescue me. They called me a traitor for being with a Penchon while I was talking with Catsclaw about helping them."

"Helping them?" D'vore sounded incredulous. "I was under the impression that now, after they had pursued you for so long that you would never do that."

"It's too complicated to explain," I replied but stopped there. I wanted D'vore to know as little as possible about my discussions with Catsclaw. "But forget about that. Look, is there any way we can get to the library before anything else delays us?"

D'vore shrugged. "If you will recall, I made arrangements before you were detained. If we rush, we may make the next transit to the surface."

The transport hub was not too distant, and, by sticking to the less traveled corridors and evading any blue hat, Penchon, Eglaner, or Carhera, we managed to reach a small vestibule where a bored, blue-skinned human waved us aboard. "We'll be leaving on time," he said. "Have a nice decent."

Expectations were that the trip to the surface would be in some sort of streamlined craft that would scream across the sky in a blaze of flaming light and swoop gracefully onto Oroenoe's surface. Instead we were shoved into a box-like room after being placed on gurneys that locked into slots in the walls and then forced to wait for seeming hours until my bladder wept in protest. Around us were other humans, some resembling the attendant, and a few aliens. None gave me the faintest bit of attention.

Finally, the blue-skinned attendant closed the hatch and, with a stomach-churning lurch, that embarrassingly removed the distress of my bladder, the box began to drop at an alarming rate, rocking as if in a maelstrom. With every screech of tortured metal I worried that something had gone terribly wrong. Had the station simply dropped us into the atmosphere? Were we going to perish when we hit the surface? When I realized that no one else was screaming I assumed this strange manner of descent was normal and stopped worrying.

As we continued to fall, the rocking movement was replaced by a steady, vibrating rolling. It seemed we were still falling, but at a decreasing rate, or so my stomach reported. Eventually I could detect no motion whatsoever.

Had we landed?

The hatch abruptly opened and bright sunlight poured in. In short order the passengers were released from their gurneys by more of the blue humans. I staggered a little, my legs too weak to hold me upright.

"Gravity is somewhat higher than you are used to," D'vore explained. "Your legs should adjust in a few hours."

With that reassurance I staggered forth and looked back, curious about this thing that had brought us down.

It didn't look like any ship I'd ever seen. It was just a simple metal box, albeit with a strange golden ring girdling its midsection. There were no visible drives, no wings, nothing remotely ship-like about it. It was inconceivable that this ridiculous thing could have flown from orbit; yet, here it was, safely grounded under a pale sky.

I felt uncomfortable standing in the open with neither bulkheads nor overhead to set the limits of vision. The lack of confinement felt disturbing and completely at odds with my fragmented memories of Earth's open spaces. What horizon I could see beyond a row of blazingly white buildings seemed impossibly far away. The few trees in sight were unlike anything in my dreams, with the bulk of their foliage near the base and a single, slender spine projecting from the peak.

As we made our way toward the buildings I became aware of the dirt and grime and the grim-faced workers of varying blue hues scurrying about. There was an overwhelming stink of wastewater and rotting vegetables in the air. Small animals looking nothing like dogs ran freely about making mewing sounds as they sniffed at every feature of the landscape and rummaged in the detritus of the port.

I could make no sense of the language blaring forth from every direction while D'vore seemed completely fluent as he inquired about the library. "We're to wait here," he instructed after a brief conversation with a human in a tan uniform.

I perched on a small seat and stared with wonder at the tall screens that covered every wall, each displaying line after line of script in dazzling colors. I had no idea of what the scrawl might convey, but did notice that each of the screens used a different set of characters. One of them scrolled from bottom to top and right to left. Another flashed blocks of characters in a clockwise fashion.

"Departure times, trading data, and news," D'vore explained when he noted my interest "Boring and totally irrelevant for our mission. Ah, here is our guide."

The guide was a simple metal pod that floated a meter above the ground. It led us silently to a station where, moments later, after entering a capsule that comfortably embraced us, and whisked, after several moments of uneventful travel, to another platform where a tall blue human waited.

"We welcome all who come in the name of honest inquiry," the tall man said solemnly as he led us up a flight of stairs and into a vast dome ringed with cubicles, one of which, on the fifty-third level and halfway around the dome from where we'd entered, turned out to be ours.

There was no instrumentation that I could see, no screens, no interfaces for eyes or ears, nor cap for his skull. It was simply a bare room with three chairs.

"Curious," said D'vore an instant before a translucent, multi-limbed alien appeared on the empty seat. "You may call this image 'Librarian,'" the alien announced pleasantly. "How can I help you?"

"Gak!" I replied after a single glance at the Librarian's assortment of writhing limbs. I was puzzled by the alien display. "Why not represent yourself as human?" I asked the machine image. Aside from the horror of all those wiggling appendages I was impressed with the beauty of the alien's iridescent scales that shimmered like oil on still water

"You assume that I am an artificial interface," the Librarian replied. "I assure you that I am not. I merely occupy a biome that is incompatible with yours, hence the need for this virtual interface."

I had no way of knowing if this was the truth or whether the Library's machinery was being clever. It mattered little either way. I could live with the artifice, if that's what it was.

"What is the nature of your inquiry?"

"I want to locate a system named 'Earth,'" I replied. "We think it was an early colony that was lost somewhere near the Rift."

"Such a search would not be cheap," the Librarian replied.

"I assure you that ThripoBlastenav will pay whatever is necessary," D'vore replied.

"That has been confirmed." The Librarian nodded and looked away absently. "The records indicate that over a thousand early human settlements or traces of such have been identified. Twenty apparently met with disaster, one hundred and ten failed, and all of the rest have been accounted for. There are no 'lost' colonies."

"But that cannot be true," D'vore interrupted. "There are no known humans with his biological makeup–his kind were obviously separated from the rest of the humans over three thousand generations ago. Here, let me upload his medical data."

Librarian churned its limbs and change colors. "I fear your guess as to the age of the deviation was somewhat modest. The separation has to be at least a million years ago. We will refine the number later, but for now, I need more data."

I summarized all that I had dreamed of my past and was interrupted frequently by D'vore providing illuminating information about our experiences, my tiny ship, and somewhat immodestly described his massive recreation of the ship's original appearance. "I have given the library a complete copy," D'vore mentioned as an aside. "The addition of that information will more than pay for any obligations we might incur."

My belief that Librarian was a computer interface was reinforced by the speed with which it responded to that information. "Your suspicion that this table you describe contained coordinates of some sort has been affirmed and, although we do not know the relevance of the names, we do have some confidence that the smaller numbers appended to them might represent a timing interval.

"Using the most common human time measures as a guide we deduced that those periodicities could be the signatures of a few hundred variable stars. However, just to be certain, we also identified those that deviate from the rough approximations in your table by less than ten percent.

"Using those that most closely matched these intervals," the Librarian continued without pausing for breath, "We projected points equidistant from each set of four to determine possible locations."

Since that information had been conveyed in one continuous, rapid-fire string I had difficulty parsing it. Did Librarian really mean there were hundreds of locations where I might find my lost Earth?

Librarian continued, again without pausing for breath, if indeed he breathed but then, how else would he speak? I was more certain than ever that Librarian was a computer. "Of all the possible locations only a few are near any known system and more than half are confirmed to be empty space.

"Of the remaining possibilities, only a dozen locations could possibly define a volume small enough to serve as guidance. There are some systems not too distant from these convergence points and only three are known to be inhabited by humans who trade frequently with the Carhera and other members of the human race." An image appeared in the air. "This is the sole planet that most closely resembles your description."

The planet floating before me somewhat resembled the blue and white marble of memory. "Earth," I choked and felt tears course down my cheeks. My search was over at last. I could finally go home.

Only after closer examination did I realize that the differences between this planet and my own were vast. The planet was mostly white with small rivers of blue tracing the outlines of nothing I recognized. I doubted that an ice age could have occurred in the few years since I was found, still …

"Wait! If this planet is already known it can't be his Earth," D'vore protested.

"There are no other solutions," Librarian protested.

"Then your basic assumptions must be wrong," D'vore argued.

"In that, we need more information than has been provided,"

Librarian replied and had I not known it was a computer, I would have thought it had been offended.

"This is futile," I complained. "It's as if I came from another universe."

"Unlikely," Librarian replied immediately. "It is more a matter of not finding the complete solution set. Perhaps you can recall some other information, some snippet of data that might clarify the issue?"

"Isn't there some other solution?" I pleaded. "I couldn't have appeared out of nowhere. My ship had to come from a planet else how would I exist?" Catsclaw's disturbing suggestion that my memories might be false came to mind, but I didn't want to confuse matters further with suppositions I could neither prove nor disprove.

It took an enormous amount of time before Librarian answered that question–almost half an hour. "This has been a most interesting exercise," it continued as if the previous conversation was only seconds before. "Your numbers seem to be the points of tetrahedral system whose centroid solution, interestingly, was also invented by an ancient human named Aler."

"Euler', "I corrected without thinking and then realized what he had just said. "Wait, if you know Euler's name then there must have been some contact between the Carhera and Earth."

"A coincidence of names," D'vore argued.

"Too much coincidence for me. This has to mean there was some contact. But if so, why were the Carhera withholding the information?" Wheels within wheels, I thought and mentioned my suspicions to D'vore only after we'd left the Library.

"What I don't understand is why you would help me if the Carhera have known Earth's location all along?"

"You can't be certain," D'vore answered. "The similarity of names might be an accident of language. Mere coincidence, as I said earlier."

"But what other explanation might there be? Why should I know the one name Librarian produced, the one man whose mathematic developments led to seven-space navigation? The coincidence is too much for my liking. There must be something else we haven't discovered as yet."

"Perhaps the answer still lies within the ship. There could be other memories waiting for you to awake them."

I was thinking the same thing. Exploring the virtual ship had produced results earlier and anything that might clarify the situation would be welcome. "Then let's do it!"

We obtained penitent quarters in the Library's visitors' complex. My room was scarcely more spacious than the escape capsule where I'd started this mission and as before, its small size did not impede D'vore's creation of a fully realized virtual ship.

I took a deep breath and entered.

In the days that followed we tried to decipher the mystery of the drive. "Gaylord, the theoretician, was the only one who could have in-depth knowledge of the drive," I recalled. "None of the crew, insofar as I remember, had bothered to acquire very much knowledge about the drive's detailed workings."

So that left the nasty and unfeeling Etoile LaPlatte, the bastard who left his wife and child to go on this ill-fated jaunt, as the only one whose memories might contain some of that detailed knowledge. He had been the physicist who had guided the construction of the drive.

"Maybe I can tap into LaPlatte's recollections of events preceding the launch. If he knew anything then there might be the possibility that I could figure out what went wrong."

"You said he was sitting at the third alcove," D'vore reminded me as we prepared for another virtual exploration of the ship's image.

"A seat I am not looking forward to filling," I answered. "I disliked the last time I touched his memories."

"Nevertheless, he might hold the key to what happened. He might provide an insight to the problem of the drive."

I reentered the virtual ship and hesitated as I stood behind LaPlatte's chair, one hand on the back, and tried to recall what his specific role had been. A glance at the board surrounding the chair gave him no clue. There were three holes that must have held screens, a panel of colored buttons, and a row of switches. Nothing that would indicate what part of the mission he managed.

I sat and waited but no memory came to mind: No recollections, no sudden memories of what LaPlatte might have been thinking in those last few moments. I stroked the buttons, pressed the switches, and stared at the three empty sockets, hoping for inspiration, wishing for something to be revealed.

But there was nothing. "This is useless," I said and then imagined LaPlatte talking to Cohen, the pilot.

"We're just as likely to be sitting here with egg on our face as jumping a quarter of a light year," I said. "This just doesn't feel right to me."

"Anything specific?" Cohen interrupted, worry clear in her voice. "Jesus, if there's anything less than perfect ..."

"No, no! Nothing like that. It's just that I've been thinking about what Gaylord said and getting worried."

Bolsteri's voice cut in. "Look LaPlatte, if you want to abort just say the word."

I considered the options. Would I blow a couple of billions just for the sake of vague doubts at this late date and look like a prize idiot when I couldn't explain my reasons? Yeah, Nicole would love that—seeing me embarrassed in front of the whole world. Probably justify her wanting the divorce, the bitch. "No, I'll give it a pass." I leaned forward and pressed the button that would give my assent to the launch.

I dismissed the fragmentary memory as useless. I'd already known of Gaylord's protests, his theatrics, and his demands for precision beyond technological capabilities. I had learned nothing new. "Let's end this," I pleaded.

"But only for another day," D'vore answered.

The Librarian began speaking as if it had not noticed the day's break in our conversation. "As I was saying, I have decided to use your angular supposition to see if it may prove helpful. It is only a matter of calculating various sightings to see which variables produce a result as we hold the angles constant." At once the chamber became a star field, the possible variable stars clearly indicated.

I sat gape-mouthed as the time regressed, imagining the millions of calculations and thousands of star charts that had to be involved to make this flow so seamlessly. Time flew as the point of view moved ten, twenty, thirty, and then a hundred light years and then beyond. I stared in growing horror as the distance increased and still no stars appeared in the target area.

At a thousand light years there was still no resolution. I felt a gnawing fear that he might never again return home; that hope of regaining Earth was fading quickly. What if this whole scheme was simply an accident of poor memory and misinterpretation? Worse, what if the Carhera, as Catsclaw had suggested, had created me out of whole cloth and imparted false memories? Still my eyes remained fixed on the cascading star field; there was still the chance that my unknown, hidden Earth might yet appear.

I watched the stars shifting, one after another of the variable stars moving away from any hope of solution until less than half a dozen possibilities remained. We had moved six thousand light years—an impossible distance. Such a distance was beyond the possible range of any Carhera ship and therefore clearly beyond the capability of my tiny vessel.

Nevertheless, the Librarian plunged ever deeper, driving the galactic map further and further, swooping in and out at it adjusted orbital viewpoints to keep the few variables in sight, getting further and further away from the Rift. I wanted to call a halt since we were so clearly getting nowhere, but Librarian persisted, unwilling to stop until it had reached a solution, regardless of what that might mean.

At eight thousand light years four of the five remaining variables began to form a pyramid and, in the center of that geometric shape, a system appeared. At ninety thousand light years one of the variable stars deviated too far from possibility and blinked out of existence. I held my breath, amazed that there should be any solution that satisfied the criteria.

A single system filled the target area and, at ninety-five hundred light years, the angular alignment of variables closely matched the numbers I'd seen so casually scrawled near Jocelyn's station. There was no mistake. This was the position Jocelyn had described. But what did it mean? It was beyond belief that this could be Earth's home.

"This is a G-class star with four populated planets," Librarian announced with what I took to be smug assurance. "The residents now call in Atil; which means Home."

"How far away?" I asked, afraid of what the answer might be.

"Tracing the speed that this particular system has been moving and using its distance from the galactic center as radius and accounting for the perturbation above the galactic plane we conclude that it has taken one million, two hundred, and three thousand years of regress to reach its current position from this point."

It was too far to be possible. This could not be Earth. There had to be another solution, I prayed, but knew my hopes might well prove baseless.

D'vore insisted that I not give up hope, even if the stellar regression strategy hadn't proved fruitful. "Your Jocelyn might have written those numbers for some reason unconnected to the flight," he suggested hopefully. "Perhaps it had something to do with her research in variable stars."

"Could it be Earth?"

"Unlikely, but we could still find our way to Atil to see if we could discover some remaining trace from your era," he suggested. "Surely some vast enterprise, a soaring tower, a critical highway, or one of your mighty cities would remain, albeit in greatly changed form."

"Ridiculous. Atil can't be Earth, and even if it was I doubt anything would be left," I scoffed, unwilling to believe there was any possibility that our ship had jumped an impossible nine thousand light years.

D'vore persisted. "Even if nothing remains on Atil there might be something on the surface of an airless moon that you might recognize."

I was getting pissed. "That's ridiculous. It's a waste of time and energy. We have to look elsewhere."

Despite my protests, D'vore continued to research Atil. The bitter facts were disheartening. Glaciers covered most of the planet, encompassing it in a mantle of ice that left a narrow belt near the equator that contained little dry land. What few humans populated the chill and scattered artificial islands had forsworn the physical in hopes of achieving mystic heights. Consequentially, Atil's main commerce was pilgrimages from the many branches of humanity seeking enlightenment and peace while providing sustenance for these latter-day monks.

I could neither understand the precepts of their beliefs nor generate any interest, particularly when I learned that, while a few pilgrims found enlightenment, many more were disappointed and, more probably, were I a judge of human nature, felt the poorer for it.

Any cities, tracts of open countryside, or even the graves of Atil's ancestors were entombed below miles of ice, that is if they hadn't been ground into the geologic record as the glaciers had proceeded on their slow, but steady march.

"A visit to Atil would be an exercise in futility, fraught with more wasted hope than the answers I want," I complained. As much as I was disappointed that Atil could not be my lost Earth I was heartened to think that there remained a solution. It was impossible that our little ship could have crossed such an immense gulf of space.

With these thoughts in mind I went through the motions of daily life, taking food, sleeping, and aimlessly wandering through the extents of the Library while lost in an all-embracing fog. How would I ever find a home? Was he doomed to wander as an atavistic remnant of a lost world?

Nights did not give me sweet surrender. Occasional dreams of earlier lives were now tinged with a bittersweet overlay, the knowledge that these memories were of a time and place that might never be found. Imagined was the sorrow of all those husbands, wives, children, and coworkers when the ship had not returned. I no longer felt the need to revisit the virtual ship. Now that all of the clues proved useless there seemed no need of further investigation.

D'vore disagreed and was not hesitant about saying so. "If not for your own benefit then do this for me," he pleaded. "While the facts of your home are no longer your concern, the Carhera's interest is the how and why of the accident. We must learn how your ship reached the Rift."

"Who is this 'we' you mention? I thought your interest was only in helping me discover my origins." Despite the wracking disappointment that filled my mind, I was not so debilitated that I could not detect the false notes in D'vore's voice.

D'vore hesitated. "We owe it to those who have aided us since your recovery."

"Which is interesting in itself," I replied. "Why would ThripoBlastenav help the two of us, with little to offer save some scattered memories and a bit of wreckage? For that matter, what was the motivation of *Tollembol's* captain to have you rebuild me or save the wreckage of my ship? Why were the Penchon so willing to transport me and then so inept about catching us?"

There was no reply. "Need I mention the string of coincidences, the suddenly opened berths on star ships, and the endless parade of spare parts you seem to acquire and discard with alarming frequency?" I continued. "I've asked this before with no answers. What the hell is going on?"

"There are perfectly logical reasons for everything you mention," D'vore answered.

I doubted his seeming sincerity. "Yes, you've given me a reason for every action we've taken since my awakening. Yet, when I think back at the whole of it, the sequence of events seems highly improbable." Both Jaycea and Provance had thrown doubt on D'vore's honesty about my recovery and that interpretation lay beneath everything that had happened since. If I doubted D'vore's tale of the discovery of my ship and the remains of my crewmates, then everything else fell apart.

"I thought I had explained at every step. I've kept no secrets from you."

I continued to push ahead. "Really? It's highly improbable that *Tollembol* would just *happen* to be close enough when my ship appeared, close enough so you'd be able to recover fresh body fragments. Even if it happened that way, what were the odds that the ship would have someone who could knit together a whole person from those few fragments and, more amazingly, recover memories from the dead crews' brains?"

"I told you how I happened to be on the ship," D'vore replied. "That I should have the medical knowledge was a fortunate happenstance—at least as far as you are concerned. I don't see what you are driving at; without *Tollembol* discovering the ship and restoring you none of what followed would have happened. The coincidence is only the result of its own occurrence, nothing more than a mental artifact, I assure you—an imagined conspiracy; mere coincidence."

His comments didn't mollify me. "Then there's the curious reason the Penchon would collect the wreckage and *Tollembol's* crew. Despite your claims that they were scavengers, nothing of what I've learned indicates that they would have any interest in a shipwreck."

"I cannot attest to the motives of a Penchon," D'vore answered. "Nor can I explain what they were doing so near the Rift."

"That's another curious happening. Why would they have been close enough to discover our escape pod—the *only* escape pod?" Suddenly the string of coincidences was near a breaking point. "Then there's the amazing willingness of your mysterious ThripoBlastenav, who just happened to be at the very station where the *Qalyub Gudlag* berthed, to become our benefactor."

"I told you that was in exchange for my acting as courier for ..."

"No! What possible reason could he, with hundreds of races and vast resources to chose from, resort to using a broken-down medician and a confused human as couriers? What is really going on?"

"It is truly amazing the complex web of rationalizations that the human mind can build," D'vore began calmly. "You are overwrought, Case . Perhaps your mind is still not stable enough to ..."

His patronizing tone infuriated me. "Don't give me that line of bullshit! I know that something is going on, something that you won't tell me and, by all that's holy, if you won't tell me then I'm going to leave you and find my own way around this crazy universe." I realized that was no idle threat. I really was fully prepared to walk away from D'vore and his Carhera friends and try to survive in this horribly complicated universe into which I had been so unwillingly thrust.

"I cannot let you do that," D'vore murmured. "You are too valuable."

"Valuable? In what way—I've already told you how little I recall of the drive. What else do you want me to remember?"

"Consider the time, Case . Consider that there was no way the Carhera could not have known of an Earth so close to the center of human space. How is it possible that none of the races of humanity vary greatly from you in mind or form? Don't you find it curious that your drive is a cruder version of the technology humanity uses to span the stars? As you said before, when the coincidences become so numerous the obvious cannot be ignored."

"No! I told you that it's impossible. There must be some other solution."

D'vore cut me off. "I think that despite your protests, Atil is indeed your Earth. It is the only conclusion that can be drawn from the facts."

"But that's impossible," but I felt a hint of hesitation, as if my denial was failing. "It's too far away. Gods, it would take a ship a million years to cross that distance!"

"If your ship had come from the dawn of time, the very beginnings of star flight," D'vore bore on. "Then the immense time span might be appropriate for the development of sixteen differing branches of humanity."

I wondered if that could possibly be true? Hadn't *Homo Sapiens* evolved from *Australopithecus* in just two million years? With a shock I wondered how I knew that fact, but continued with that line of thought. Assuming continued advances in genetic engineering and the effects of encountering different environments on distant planets, the diversity of human forms could easily have separated during a million years. It made sense, logically, but I was still unconvinced.

"Consider those million plus years, Case," D'vore continued patiently. "All this humanity may be the heirs of your time, descendants of the people you've remembered in your dreams. Don't you see, Earth must be where it all began. Atil must be the forgotten source of humanity."

"No, no, no!" If that were true then all hope would fade.

"Case, your ship somehow spanned a million years and more and that is more of a wonder. Now do you see why it is important to learn how this happened?"

I struggled to think of some way to disprove what I was hearing.

"One more fact," D'vore added. "The Pittul asserted that your mitochondria were ancient, even if they vastly underestimated the amount of drift. That bolsters the truth of a voyage from humanity's distant past."

It was an astounding conclusion. One I could hardly grasp. "I have to think about this for a while. It's rather too much to absorb right now."

"I understand your distress," D'vore answered, misunderstanding my feelings. "Such a huge leap across the ages is quite unprecedented. I suspect we should return to the station where you may be left alone."

Once again his compassion surprised me.

While I struggled with D'vore's unbelievable conclusions I wandered the bustling station. At one point suddenly realizing that I was standing on the deck of a station built by a galaxy-spanning civilization thousands of light years from Earth, surrounded by aliens and stranger humans, and looking at ships that had ranged from distant systems and planets.

The sights and sounds of the station had become so ordinary that they failed to elicit more than a modicum of wonder any more. How could he have become so blasé that he failed to be awed by what mankind and the thousands of alien races had achieved? After seeing and understanding all this, what would it now take to impress him more?

I was more surprised that I had not fallen into an emotional slump now that my search for Earth was over. Although a faint doubt remained about Atil really being Earth, there was nothing I could do to disprove it. As unemotional and rational as D'vore's answer might sound, I had to accept it. As D'vore had said, I had become a person in my own right, divorced from those crewmen who composed me, and freed from those memories of a distant and lost past.

It was time to live the rest of my life.

Much later D'vore found me. His excitement was palpable, as evidenced by a nervous twitching of his entire form. "ThripoBlastenav has offered to rebuild me so that I will be free to leave these crowded spaces; that might help me become what I once was." I sensed that there was something that D'vore was leaving unsaid.

"It sounds as if it would be everything you've wanted. Was there a price for his largess?"

D'vore shifted uncomfortably. "There were conditions. I must ensure that we have gotten as much information from your memories as we can. To get what he offers we must solve the mystery of how your pitifully underpowered ship managed to bridge so much time and distance."

I already knew that was what everybody wanted. I'd long ago lost any illusions that ThripoBlastenav, or anyone else, was being charitable, expending so much resource and time simply to get me back to Earth. "So the only thing that's changed is that you've resorted to emotional bribery. I hoped better of you."

D'vore was taken aback. "No, no Case . We are still in pursuit of the truth for your sake."

"Is that *all* he wants?" Obviously, ThripoBlastenav wanted the secret of the drive before anyone else: Knowledge of the drive might enable humanity to reach beyond the bounds the Carhera had imposed and allow the human race to trade with distant civilizations, to share the wealth of an entire galaxy.

On the other hand, the secret of the drive might easily enable humanity to settle some old scores and move against the Penchon, if not others. I had no faith in humanity's benevolence. The human race hadn't a particularly noble history, as witness the many wars of my memories and what I had learned of humanity's attempted genocide of the Penchon. Would humanity's first use of the drive be to build ships that could be used to perform genocide of galactic proportions? I would not put it past my descendants, nor could I deny that they would similarly wipe out any race that stood in their way once they had the technology in their hands.

But any idea of humanity threatening the five hundred known species and succeeding was beyond ridiculous. The Carhera could easily amass vast energies and technologies beyond humanity's imagination. Humanity would be squashed like bugs if they even tried. No, dreams of galactic conquest were not a viable future for humanity.

At the same time, my fellow humans might be able to gain a little trade advantage from the knowledge. Sure, the secret of the drive could be sold for a profit. It might also be used to improve trade among the human races. That outcome would be far more likely than the nightmares I'd imagined earlier.

None of which answered the question of what good a drive that bent time so much might be.

"The drive, the drive," I complained. "Damn it, what is the good of a stupid malfunctioning drive that jumps thousands of light years if it also loses a million years? Anyone employing it will leave behind all they knew, all they loved. Even if they didn't care about that, what benefit would there be for anyone left behind? There would be no trade advantage, not over such a long time period. Besides, the ship would be ancient technology whenever it appeared. I can't imagine who or what would want a one-way trip into a distant and unknown future, much less why!"

D'vore listened patiently. "Despite what you say, Case, such a capability has enormous value. There are races to which lost time is not a factor. They dream instead of traveling across the great gulfs that lie between galaxies.

"Did you know that in a few billion years our own small galaxy will collide with giant Andromeda? In less time than that the approach will create adverse gravitational effects? There are races who wish to be as far away as possible when that begins."

I wondered if D'vore had gone insane. "Surely you don't

expect me to believe that anyone has that long a view, for God's sake! That collision's a billion years in the future, not a decade or so—A fucking BILLION years!"

"Three billion four hundred million of your years before the outer mantles of dark matter interact," D'vore corrected. "Somewhat later for the hydrogen envelopes."

"Nevertheless," D'vore continued as I struggled to grasp those incredible time scales. "There are also races for whom deep time presents no problems. For them, if that same mischance that cast you forward could be tamed, then the entire universe would be open. It would be a noble enterprise, Case, one that I'm certain your short-lived human race can scarcely grasp."

Planning a few billion years in advance seemed a serious waste of time. I doubted any species or race would survive over that long a time. Hell, there were even stars that wouldn't last that long! The idea of jumping millions and millions of light years to an unknown destination where you'd encounter God knew what, seemed ridiculous.

At the same time, I had to admit that I somewhat liked the idea of jumping ever further into the future, being able to discover new things, to go beyond where no one had gone before, and thereby ensure that a small bit of their race would continue in him. A million years, for God's sake! I could grasp the spirit that would compel those who wished to journey far, but I just didn't want to do it personally.

Once was enough.

With something of a mild shock I realized that I had finally and fully accepted the fact that I had indeed come a million years in my own future! With that realization and acceptance I was awed by the sheet immensity of what had happened and, almost immediately after, an emotional abyss opened as I realized how alone I'd truly become and how distant all that I remembered were from recovery. There was no hope of returning, no chance of standing over the empty graves of my brave crew members, no way of offering solace to their loved ones and family.

Yet, strangely, I did not feel a great deal of sorrow. Instead, a sense of wonder began to emerge at what humanity had accomplished after the ship disappeared. Despite the disappearance, there must have been later experiments, and probably more losses before the drive technology was finally tamed. Then, with a working star drive humanity must have exploded from the solar system. It would have only been a matter of time before they came to attention of the Carhera, took their place in the galactic society, and allowed my descendants to become the sixteen.

Yet, I still wondered if all my memories hadn't been colored by some induced artifice. Were my recollections in the virtual ship influenced by contemporary interpretations? "How reliable were my memories of the crew?" I asked. "Have I been unconsciously changing them? Might there be some alterations caused by my restoration—an implanted memory of some sort?"

"I assure you that if there were any alterations they were not of my doing," D'vore replied testily. "I do understand your concerns, however," he hesitated and once again I felt that he wanted to say more.

"And?" I prompted.

D'vore sagged. "I have on occasion wondered about my own memories."

The abrupt admission disconcerted me. "How so?" That D'vore, my anchor since awakening, should express such a fundamental doubt worried me considerably.

"I cannot clearly recall anything that happened before I recovered on a Penchon ship," he continued. "All of the knowledge of my own past came from them and, of my kind, I know only what I've gained from the WOFAT. My earlier memories could have been implanted during my restoration. What if I, like you, am a chimera stitched from assorted fragments? What if I was created artificially simply to act as a companion for you?"

"That's ridiculous. What would be the purpose of doing such a thing? You said yourself that you had been recovered years before *Tollembol* came across my ship. It seems inconceivable that my rescue could have been engineered that far in advance."

"Indeed. Nor can I think of any motivation the Penchon might have had in instilling a medician's skills—they certainly didn't need them for their own kind. Neither did my sale to *Tollembol* make logical sense. There was even less need for a medician on a clone ship."

"So you suspect that there might be something more to this than even you know?" Up to this time I had imagined D'vore very much in control of his own fate. It was disconcerting to realize that the alien's history was as suspect as my own.

"Even if I were truly a Centul, who normally dwell in the cold dark regions, then why should stations and ships seem so familiar? I am very concerned, Case, that I had not thought deeply of this before you questioned your own memories. It seems that neither of us can trust our memories or motivations."

"How *would* we know?' I countered. "All we can do is act as if we are in control of our own destiny. To do otherwise is to freeze into inaction and I don't want that to happen."

"You are right, Case . We both should move on."

That raised another question. "Do we know if anything was really in those containers you carried?" I'd been curious about the purpose of those mysterious packages.

D'vore considered. "Do you suspect that they were simply an excuse to explain ThripoBlastenav's help? That is definitely a possibility and, like you, I've wondered why he would choose me for such a role."

We considered these new questions, wondering if either could trust our memories or understand what lay behind everything that had happened.

"I'd like to discuss these possibilities of motives and subterfuges, but I really feel that we need to focus on what we'll do next," I suggested. Until now the search for lost Earth had driven us from station to station, but from this point onwards we had to survive. "What happens after I reveal all I can recall about the drive?" I asked. "I mean, you've been promised some sort of restoration, which is fine, but what happens to me? Where would I go? What could a backward savage like me find to do?"

"You are hardly a savage, Case . You have adapted well and have even acquired a few skills that should stand you in good stead although I doubt you will need to rely on them. You are a valuable historic artifact in your own right. You could provide valuable insights regarding humanity's pre-Diaspora days. I imagine that you might never lack for comforts once others learn of you."

"I'm not sure I want to be a museum specimen," I replied. "Nor do I think I can provide any more information than I've already revealed. My dreams aren't something I can willingly draw upon. They seem to well up of their own accord."

"But with training you might ..."

"What good would it for anyone today to learn what a son-of-a-bitch Etoile LaPlatte was, about Jocelyn's affairs, about Melika's love of beer, or what a pain in the ass Gaylord was? The only things I know about them are related to their roles. Outside of that, I recall little, not an inkling of what drove them, what made them happy, or how they related to the rest of the world.

"Those few flashes of the Earth I do recall are random and probably duplicate scenes that could exist on a dozen planets— mountains, deserts, sunsets, oceans, a restaurant, and the inside of a sailboat. What good would those descriptions do for anyone?"

D'vore was a little taken aback by my anger. "I am certain that there are aspects of your personality, quite aside from the vast amount of medical information they would be able to gather ..."

That inflamed me even more. "No, I won't be some damn bug on a pin either. The Library has all the physical data on me that you provided and I'm certain that the Pittul and Penchon have managed to broker their data and samples to anyone who might be interested. There would be nothing more to be gained by further tests or examinations. Listen, I just want to be left alone so I can find my way. Is that too much to ask?"

D'vore remained silent until I had vented all my outrage. "You have experience as a navigator now, Case . You would have no problem obtaining a berth on a ship. You could go places you'd never imagined. See sights that might amaze you."

"Going where? Being a gypsy navigator is as unappealing as a museum exhibit. Thank you but I've seen enough stinking cargo decks and aliens to last me for a lifetime. I just want to find a home, D'vore. I want to be among people I can relate to. I want to be part of something." Almost, I said I wanted to find Provance and restore our relationship, but did not. D'vore would not understand. Besides, how could I possibly find her, even if she wanted to be found?

Even if she cared.

"You will find your way," D'vore whispered. "Give it time, Case . Give yourself time while we search for the drive's secrets."

"No! I am not going to do a damn thing until I'm assured of a future that won't put me on exhibit, become a medical specimen, or be questioned endlessly by historians about things that have no relevance to me. I want to know what getting the drive's secrets will mean to Case Pasticher. I want to know what the hell I'm getting out of all this time and effort. For all I know, are they going to turn me off since I'm not a real person?"

"You are upset. I assure you that …"

Whatever he was about to say was lost to me, so great was my rage. "Go to hell! I want nothing to do with you, ThripoBlastenav, or your damned Carhera!" I stomped away, heading where I knew not, but unwilling to admit that I had nowhere to go.

Nowhere.

Despite my resolution to think no more of the lost treasures of Earth my dreams continued unabated. For the most part they were jumbles of recent incidents, random visions of undeclared vistas, and scenes from my travels. I wondered if there might be some unresolved issue surrounding Gaylord that put him in that most recent dream about a meeting during the initial planning phases when the engineers were still converting mathematical theory into practical equipment. Yes, I recalled Gaylord saying something about the calculations and …

Gaylord was sitting across the table, a disorderly pile of papers before him as the project leader droned on and on about another delay in getting the drive tuned for launch. Something about tight parameters that they were asking about. "I think your specifications are too tight," the project manager, a man more interested in meeting schedules and cost than any scientific benefits that might result. "They are beyond our contractor's capabilities to produce.

"They are tight for a very good reason," Gaylord replied. "I believe that the errors we saw on the test flights were caused by not being sufficiently precise. Tightening them to get accuracy in the tenth place in the settings will reduce possibility of error significantly."

"Quantum effects make that sort of precision impossible," the PM replied. "Whenever we adjust one unit the other one drifts out of phase. We've done everything we can think of to get the cans precisely synchronized without success. We have to go with eight place accuracy."

Gaylord shuffled his papers. "We are risking taking a misstep unless we get the numbers right. Look here," he produced a paper covered with tensors. "As the mass increases to the amount we contemplate for this ship the error bars increase exponentially. A slight change to this," he pointed at a scrawled line, "would give us and error of nearly four nanoseconds."

"Which is less than one meter," the PM replied. "Yes, we did run the math as you suggested. Look, I appreciate your insistence on precision, but your desire for perfection is beyond our capabilities at this point. We will have to be satisfied with what we have."

"In that I am off the project," Gaylord shot back. "There is too much unknown about this theory to chance the amount of error you are going to introduce to the experiment. I will have no responsibility for this foolishness." With that he gathered his papers and stomped out of the room.

"How many times is he going to do that?" Jocelyn asked.

"He'll be back," Mellorez, the engineer looked up from the specifications for the coils and replied. "He always comes back."

I woke with the dream intact and, more importantly, with Mellorez's crystal clear memory of the coil specifications and design details. These were the critical pieces that would enable anyone to replicate the entire drive assembly and build a long-range, long-time ship. This was what ThripoBlastenav wanted.

It didn't take much deduction to realize that Mellorez and the others must have gone ahead and used the flawed coils that Gaylord correctly declared would not be safe. Then when the coils overloaded, the ship went light and calendar years beyond the imagination of its creators. A pity Gaylord would never learn the truth or its amazing results.

The specifications and designs that I'd dreamed answered the question of what the melted coils had originally looked like, but it did not explain why the ship had been destroyed upon its emergence. What forces had been unleashed that would torment metal and plastic to such an extent? Were those forces a consequence of the crude drive's malfunction or something else? Could the destruction of the ship have happened as a result of brushing the mysterious Rift? I imagined all those questions would remain unanswered until a similar drive was constructed, but with intentionally flawed coils.

The idea of anyone deliberately replicating such an insane leap amazed me. There would be no way to contemporaneously discover the results of the experiment. If successful, the ship could be cast forward untold eons into the future. How many *Tollembol's* would have to be arrayed across the galaxy for how long a period to detect where and when their experiment would emerge? Who in their right mind could undertake such a massive and long-term project? The resources required would be astronomical, even on a modest scale.

I dismissed those thoughts as I tried to decide what to do with this new information. Would it be best to give it to the Librarian so it would be widely available? Would my best course be to seek ThripoBlastenav and wrestle some sort of payment out of him, which was doubtful considering how much obligation I'd already amassed. What about the other players–the Carhera, Penchon, and any one of the sixteen varieties of humanity–all products of my loins so to speak?

The possible courses of action flew about my head as I debated the consequences of each choice. I knew so little of the political, social, and technical powers that I didn't have the tools to make a decent decision.

What to do?

I wrestled with the problem for hours, and wished that D'vore were still around so we could talk it out. Despite our differences I still needed the alien's knowledge of how society was organized, how to best use the system, or how to contact our supposed benefactor.

I wondered what would happen to D'vore? Would ThripoBlastenav interpret their separation as a failure, that he had not been able to discover the secret of the drive? And what would happen once D'vore was gone? Would they give him back to the Pittul or some other group to discover what else he might disclose?

No, I realized that wouldn't be necessary now that I had the final piece of the puzzle. Once I delivered the coil designs and specifications my usefulness to all but a few historians would be minimal. All I had to do to avert that was to disclose what I knew.

But how, and for what advantage?

The only way to find a solution would be to find D'vore and discuss what actions would be to our mutual benefit. Despite misgivings, I still believed him to be my only friend. Yes, I would find D'vore and apologize.

I thought that finding such a unique being as D'vore would be easy, given the limited confines of Oroenoe station, but could not find him in any of the common areas nor around the loading docks despite making three circuits and examining every nook where the huge alien might find refuge. I checked the Registry to see if D'vore had signed on another ship, but that proved fruitless: There were no open medician berths available.

D'vore could have gone to one of the volumes of the station that were inhospitable to humans. Would he have done so and why? Hoping that he hadn't left the human enclaves, I decided to seek the help of the blue hats. Seeking their help was so obvious that I regretted not considering it earlier, before my fruitless search.

The closest blue hat office was a quarter way around the rim. I half expected the centaurs I'd seen earlier, but found a different group, including one human closely resembling Brews—an Eglaner, I guessed. That was surprising, given what I knew of their attitude toward any non-Eglaner.

"I am trying to find someone," I announced.

"Aren't we all," came the Eglaner's laconic reply. "Just ask the WOFAT, friend."

Simple enough, but I had not the faintest idea of what it entailed since I'd depended entirely on D'vore to do all the communicating. "Could you tell me how to do that?"

The Eglaner looked surprised. "Are you saying you can't contact it or won't? Religious issues or phase related? Derelict perhaps?"

I wondered if the blue hat suspected I was a vagrant. "I have funds. I don't know what the other things you mentioned mean. Look, could you show me how to use the WOFAT?" I looked around for something that might be an interface to the repository.

The blue hat tapped his head. "Use your link, friend. Use your damned link to connect and ask for the locator."

I gulped. "I don't have a link, whatever that is. Look, just tell me who I can ask about my friend and I'll go away."

The Eglaner stepped back. "Everybody has a link, friend. How the hell do you manage to get around if you don't?"

I was confused. I'd given little thought to the way food and quarters were provided. No one had ever asked for payment, which, now that I thought about it, was damned strange. Had D'vore been taking care of those details? Had I been far more dependent than I liked to admit?

My distress must have been obvious. "Are you all right, friend? Sit down over here for a bit and tell me what's going on."

Perhaps it was the tone of the Eglaner's gruff voice or my frustration that prompted me to spill out everything that had happened since leaving the Library. It took the better part of an hour and, at the end, I was exhausted.

"If that isn't the strangest tale I've ever heard," the blue hat concluded. I noticed that five other blue hats had gathered around and were now chattering in a variety of languages. "I admit you don't exactly look like any human I've ever seen before," my interviewer said, "which makes your tale credible. Here, let me see your tab." He reached out a huge hand. His voice softened, cajoling me as if I were a small child. "C'mon now, I'll need your tab to help you."

"I told you who I am," I protested. "Why do you need to know more?"

The Eglaner grinned. "We can use your tab to check on your friend and maybe get the answers to a few other questions. Come on now; your tab." This time his voice was more authoritative. The hand was still extended, waiting and so, not knowing what else to do, I handed it over.

"Navigator, eh?" the blue hat mused after a brief examination. "I see that you had a berth on an Eglaner ship before but there's no history before that. Looks like you just popped out of nowhere," he chuckled a little before his eyebrows rose when he took another look at the tab. "What's this? You have a Carhera minder?"

He had to mean D'vore. "Yes, he's been helping me. That's the one I'm looking for."

But the Eglaner wasn't paying any attention as he turned to hand the tab to an alien with rose skin and too many legs who garbled something and departed.

"We have to verify," the Eglaner said, but very, very politely. "Why don't you rest while we locate your minder?"

"He's not my fucking minder," I protested, even though, in truth D'vore had been such since that first awakening. But it mattered little what he was called so long as they could find him. I just wanted D'vore to help me understand what we should do with the secret of the coils.

I lost track of how long I'd waited. A number of humans and aliens moved in and out of the station, some of who sent inquiring glances in my direction, but none stopped to satisfy their curiosity. Occasionally some of the officers would drag some bedraggled batch of beings through the room and take them behind a gray door in the rear. Whether that led to the holding cells, a magistrate, or something for which I had no concept, none of them returned. Nor did anyone come through the door in my direction. I suppressed my impulse to see what lay beyond, supposing that boredom was the source of that idea, just as counting the number of fastenings around the doorframe, guessing the weights of the blue hat aliens, and trying to classify the humans he saw. There was little else I could do. I had to depend on the blue hats. I dozed for a while.

I was abruptly shaken to find ThripoBlastenav looming over me. "Why did you not continue your research?" it demanded. I supposed it was upset because of its pale rose mantle coloration.

"I found Earth," I said simply as I swung my feet to the deck and wiped sleep from my eyes. "There seemed little more to do."

"I know that you found Atil, which is not of consequence. I demand to know how you reached the Rift from that pathetic planet."

That rankled me. How dare this insect impugn Earth, the source of all the human races across the galaxy? How dare he trivialize everything that had been accomplished by the human race? I was appalled to think that I had actually considered giving him the secret of the drive, the coil design, and erroneous equations. Well, ThripoBlastenav would pay for that insult by damn. "I've told D'vore and the Librarian everything I could recall."

ThripoBlastenav drew back and let its mantle fade to deep purple. "I know what you have told them, but I am certain there is more. Humans are well known for their duplicity and I doubt that even a primitive such as you would be any different." It hesitated. "Perhaps I should have one of my human agents question you to see where you are lying. You are quite transparent, I'm told."

"There are some things I need to talk out with D'vore," I answered. "Perhaps that will trigger some memory. It worked before," I added hopefully.

"That failure? Your D'vore is no longer available," ThripoBlastenav replied. "It is being reconfigured for a new role."

It had been my worst fear, that the God-damned aliens were sticking D'vore in a can again, treating him like a piece of disposable and expendable machinery. I'd seen the same indifference among the Eglaners, from Provance, and virtually everyone I'd come in contact with. Was there so little compassion left in this future that everyone could so casually treat another this way?

"I need D'vore," I demanded. "There's no one else who can …"

"Ridiculous. You've anthropomorphized a medical unit programmed to support you in the search for answers. Trust me, the thing has no separate identity save that we choose to give it."

"You're wrong! D'vore has dreams and desires. He wants to be complete. I know that deep inside he is an individual as worthy of friendship as anyone else."

ThripoBlastenav was silent for so long that I wondered if it had gone to sleep. "Interesting and surprising," it said at last. "Apparently the medician was able to establish an emotional bond. That was far beyond my expectations, but not unwanted. I imagine that was what made its data extraction so productive."

"Obviously not productive enough to suit you," I muttered. "When did the objective change from a search for Earth to how the drive was constructed?"

"We believed that your ship came from within the Rift initially, some hidden system, but you proved otherwise. I must say that a jump of thousands of light years is impressive."

"And worth a fortune if you could figure out how it was done," I added dryly. "That is, if you didn't mind losing a few eons in the process."

"There are races where such considerations are irrelevant," ThripoBlastenav replied. "It might make crossing the galaxy possible."

"I thought you things already controlled most of the galaxy."

ThripoBlastenav turned orange—Laughter? "The Carhera control only a minuscule portion of the galaxy, even though to humans that might seem immense. It is a tiny fraction of that traveled by the greater races and even they, mighty as they may appear, are spread over no more than four or five percent of the whole.

"Which is why the secret of the drive is so critical," I shot back to hide my dismay at finding how insignificant my small world had been. "With that knowledge you can reach beyond the greater races, establish ties to worlds unknown, and gather knowledge you can only dream of." I paused. "What would you be willing to give for that secret?"

"Haven't we done enough for you, human? Had it not been for my intervention you would be nothing more than a vacuum-desiccated bit of flesh. Without me you might be a part of the Penchon inventory. Without me ..."

"I know what the Penchon really are," I interrupted. "Despite everyone's lies to fed my paranoia."

"It was necessary. We could not let you disclose something that would give the Penchon an advantage. I chided D'vore for letting that happen; a failure on its part that will not happen again, I assure you."

"Which means I need to talk to D'vore, have him walk me through the ship again and see what more information I can glean."

Suddenly the ship surrounded him. "You do not need that thing to experience the ship. It is a simple matter to realize it whenever I wish."

I tentatively took a step forward and tripped over something unseen. As I fell the virtual ship tilted as well. I could feel that I was lying on the deck, but as far as I could see, I was still standing where he'd been when the ship materialized.

The ship went away. "I need D'vore to read my muscle impulses," I said as I kicked the chair I'd tripped over. "I can't explore the ship without his help."

"That would be impossible. He is being installed ... elsewhere." ThripoBlastenav turned and moved away.

The thought that D'vore might once again be rendered was alarming. The D'vore wasn't some damned tool. He was a living, thinking individual who was trying hard to find his place in this universe. The vivid image of D'vore's legless and armless trunk in that Penchon container was forever seared in my memory.

Yet, what could I do to save him? The equations and coil

designs might be a bargaining chip, but I hated the idea of giving those to ThripoBlastenav, who represented Gods knew what. There had to be a better way. There had to be some way I could bargain for my friend.

I located ThripoBlastenav near the repair bays–a quadrant where ships were repaired, refitted or, in the worst case, decommissioned. It appeared to be watching the reconstruction of an old and battered ship that lacked any visible designation. It hardly seemed something that would interest such a powerful being.

"D'vore doesn't deserve punishment just because I couldn't remember something." I said the moment ThripoBlastenav acknowledged my presence.

"A tool is only useful when it fulfills its purpose," ThripoBlastenav responded. "I am amused that you seem to have anthropomorphized this tool. I assure you that it does not reflect such human feelings as you imagine. It is simply a medical machine following my instructions to help you recover whatever information you might recall."

"That's not true. He isn't some brainless machine. He's a living, breathing creature with hopes and dreams. All he wants is to rejoin his brothers once again. All he wants is to be a whole person."

"Nonsense, both of you are flotsam that are to be used as productively as possible. Were it not for me the D'vore fragment would have drifted for eons, useless and unthinking. It is a mercy that we gave it life. It now has an obligation to be used as we see fit.

"But it seems that our investment in this enterprise is at its end. Despite an enormous output of capital and incredible amounts of trouble you seem to have only vague notions of what went wrong, despite a paltry few technical facts about your crewmates. I'm afraid that the D'vore has not been as productive as I hoped."

I hesitated. "What would it take to spare him? What could I know that would let you free him?"

ThripoBlastenav raised its mantle. "Oh, you think you have

some little fact you didn't see fit to provide earlier, something you withheld from your "friend?" Didn't you say you had a trusting relationship?"

"He was, he *is* my friend," I protested. "But there were some issues ..." Best left unsaid what had happened. "Nevertheless, I recently recalled something critical." I waited; hoping the creature would rise to the bait.

"I can think of nothing that might be of sufficient interest to satisfy all outstanding obligations. What is this new information–an uninteresting bit of history regarding pre-Diaspora humanity or some little known fact about the crew? Perhaps you've had a sudden insight into the romantic habits of the female astronomer? Ah, that got a reaction. How foolish of you to think that we did not have access to records of all your dreams."

"What if I knew the coil designs?" I said. "What is that worth to you?"

The alien's mantle flared crimson. "There is no indication ..."

"A late revelation," I interrupted. "And keyed to the equations themselves ..."

ThripoBlastenav composed itself. "Those might be a few of the key elements that we were hoping to obtain. Perhaps that information might have value."

"I want D'vore freed of the obligations s you promised him."

"Ridiculous. There can be no obligation to a mere tool. Besides, the thing is of no use to you now. What would you do with it? How would you support it? "

"I wouldn't support it. I want him freed, not transferred to me as a personal slave."

"What do you imagine that your precious D'vore will do with its so-called freedom?" ThripoBlastenav asked. "How do you propose to guide him in his fruitless quest to reclaim his identity?"

"As I said before, D'vore is his own being, capable of making his own decisions about his life. Is it a deal?"

"Only if I deem the information worthy."

I stared at the alien for a long while, hoping the brief delay would make what he'd held seem more meaningful. I hoped that ThripoBlastenav would be true to its word, but there was little I could do if it was not. A lone human can hardly stand up to the might of a galactic society. My only hope was that the stakes, while high on my side, would be trivial on theirs. Once again I had to trust.

"There are two elements to the solution of the drive," I began slowly. "The technology of building the coils is easily within the grasp of anyone, human or otherwise. That is the technology that I give to you in exchange for D'vore's freedom." I handed over the scrawled pages of what I recalled.

ThripoBlastenav sneered, or at least that's how I interpreted its shift of color. "Hardly a valuable contribution, I'd think, but not quite useful enough."

"The second page contains equations that describe what my people mistakenly believed to be a theory of star flight, equations far different than humans use to build these modern drives." Unsaid was that the same understanding of the physics also applied to the Carhera star ships.

"I fail to see the relevance of their failed understanding."

"*Flawed*, not failed," I corrected. "These ill-formed equations represent a different approach to interstellar flight, a difference that might be the key to what went wrong."

ThripoBlastenav riffled the pages quickly. "So I see." Earlier I would have been astounded that the alien could have absorbed so much material that quickly, but I had frequently underestimated nearly everyone's abilities. "It seems that you have bargained in good faith." ThripoBlastenav removed a chain about its trunk. "Here, this will free your friend when you choose. I must warn you however, when you do so it becomes *your* responsibility."

It started to turn when I raised my voice. "What I didn't mention was that this same data was put into the WOFAT. I imagine that it will shortly be propagating across the galaxy as quickly as ships may travel. It won't take long before others take the chance at the long jump and risk losing a few years in the process." I smiled. "If I were you I'd start trying to understand this as quickly as I could."

ThripoBlastenav stared in crimson splendor for a long while. "More clever than I expected, aren't you?" It shrugged, a ripple of orange that crossed the mantle, something I did not know if that meant anger or laughter. "It seems we both bargained in bad faith." It waved an arm at a nearby observation window and stalked away.

The bay around me was as busy as ever, humans of many forms racing about among the aliens as if nothing untoward had happened. It seemed strange that something so significant should have passed just moments before with such little notice

I was puzzled by ThripoBlastenav's last remark. Was there something I'd missed in the exchange? I stared at the chain. How the devil was I supposed to use this, and where was D'vore? Maybe I should contact the blue hats and ask them to help me one more time.

I hoped D'vore would use his freedom to escape the Carhera's grasp and become his own entity. I wasn't going to hang on to him. No, freedom was what the D'vore deserved and I would grant it when we bid farewell.

I wondered if D'vore would offer thanks for his emancipation, but knew I had no right to expect human behavior from the alien. I was pretty certain I could survive without D'vore's help. My navigator's tab would ensure passage on any ship and allow me to visit many of the current human habitats, talk with academics interested in ancient history, or even take the time to recount all the memories of a time when humans knew only one race, one planet, and had a pitifully limited view of the universe.

But where would I find something that might pique my interest? Would it be a ship bound for distant worlds? Could I find a companion who would fill the empty emotional space vacated by Provance? Could I, a remnant of forgotten Earth, hope to find another friend like D'vore?

I glanced at the old ship. Was that another relic of the past that was being given new life? How much of its former self would it have when they replaced the drives and made it a tool for others? I continued to watch as the technicians and machines refurbished the old ship's skin.

I jerked as the chain sent a small shock up my arm and he heard D'vore's voice. "I acknowledge your command."

I whirled about, half expecting to see D'vore in another of his endless modifications. There was no one nearby. "Is this another of your mind tricks? Where are you hiding?"

"You are looking at me, Case ."

"You mean you're on that old ship–or are you one of its machines?"

"I am not on or in the ship, Case . I *am* the ship."

I struggled to get my mind around how our conversation could be possible if D'vore was the modified ship. It helped to imagine that somewhere, deep within the hull was the segmented blue-black core of D'vore I'd once glimpsed in that Penchon container.

"But besides being this ship I am still part of you, Case, just as you are still part of me," D'vore continued. While I was absorbing that bit of news D'vore let out a low chuckle. "This link has only a limited range so you need not worry about it being permanent. As soon as I am sent away the link will be broken, so don't worry, you'll be shy of me shortly."

"Were will you go?" It was hard to think that this old ship could make it out of the station, let alone range the galaxy.

"Wherever ThripoBlastenav wishes," D'vore answered.

"I own you now," I replied. "Not that I want to. Tell me how to free you from this control and you can do whatever you want."

I began to worry when D'vore didn't respond. Had he once again misunderstood the situation? Was D'vore no more than the tool ThripoBlastenav had claimed? Had the alien failed to uphold his end of the bargain and …

"It is done, and I thank you," D'vore interrupted my thoughts. "I am now my own agent, as are you, my friend." I wondered if the alien had absorbed a bit of humanity over the past year or so. It seemed that way.

"The cold dark continues to call to me," D'vore continued. "I think I will use this configuration to travel to the galaxy's distant edge and contemplate the intergalactic gulf. Perhaps by the time I reach it some race will have perfected your long drive and provide me an opportunity to travel further."

"And deeper into time," I added. "Time's arrow is a one-way journey, my friend. Take it from one who knows." I could almost feel D'vore relaxing his grip—a strange sensation. "I will be sorry to see you go. Life will be rather dull without you, I think."

"Perhaps we can help one another," D'vore hinted. "I could use your perspective just as you could use my knowledge. In honesty, I do not wish us to part. In your terms you might say that I have formed a deep attachment to you. Most of your body came from my organic parts–there weren't enough useful fragments so I had to improvise. You are my son, in a way."

And he, a sort of father, I imagined. "Yes, I feel a bond as well, but neither of us can go back to what we were. This is where we must part, where we each must take a different path." I waved farewell at the ship.

"Not necessarily, Case," D'vore replied and all at once I found himself staring at a distant window where a man was waving an arm. I glanced down and saw that I was sitting in open space on the outer skin of D'vore's ship.

"This is impossible," I shouted. "There's no air!"

"Which is why you shouldn't hear that exclamation," D'vore chuckled. "Relax. You are in no danger. You are merely a virtual instantiation of yourself, one that can utilize rather interesting capabilities."

The man in the window had turned to walk away. "How is this possible? I can't be in two places at once." I patted to assure myself that I was real.

"Your original remains as he was, independent of you, of this instance," D'vore explained. "I have no doubts that he will find his place among humanity, grow old, and eventually die. This instance of Case, on the other hand, is a copy I've made so that we may become more than either D'vore or human."

"But, but ..." I sputtered into confusion as I tried to think that I could be in two places, only I was in only one while the other, the "real" I ... No, no, no. I couldn't deal with this.

D'vore interrupted. "Of course, it is your choice whether this instance of you persists. If you find the duality unacceptable you have only to say the word and I will remove you from my mind, although with great regret. Without you it will be very lonely on the long journey."

"How *long* a journey?" I was pretty sure that "long" did not refer to distance.

"Several thousand cycles at least," D'vore replied and I easily translated that into my own terms–a quarter million years at least. "How did I do that?" I asked, astounded that it had not taken any conscious effort on my part to calculate the time span. "A quarter of a million years is longer than I'll survive, for God's sake!"

D'vore chuckled. "Hardly. While your physical instance might deteriorate in a few short years I assure you that this instance of you will live as long as I."

"And probably die of boredom," I sneered, reconsidering the offer of being trapped with anyone, no matter how interesting, for that long.

"I doubt if boredom will be possible, Case . Not only do we have the entire contents of WOFAT available, but you can now recover every detail of your own memories–every thought, every dream, every event you've experienced since you awakened. What is more, you can relive every moment of your short life with every emotion, every smell, every sensation intact."

The wonder of this supposed ability was astonishing. I would be able to relive my time on *Tollembol* and *Qalyub Gudlag*–but with new understanding.

I grew excited to realize I could once again meet Provance *for the first time* and experience the awakening of love. I'd be able to relive my time with Halo, but this time I could better understand her agony at my crude advances.

In short, I'd once again learn how I came to be myself. What is more, I might even be able to recover the full memories of each of the crewmembers, allow them to relive their lives, their excitement, their joy and sorrows, and even their untimely deaths.

"But it wouldn't be real," I concluded. "It would only be virtual. Worse, I'm only a simulation."

"You cannot return to Earth, Case . That is forever beyond

you. Neither can your physical self rediscover the pains and joys of your own mortality. By the way, that physical copy of you is now registering for a berth on an outbound ship."

"But to have nothing but the opportunity to live a few short months again and again doesn't sound like a hot prospect either," I shot back. "If that's all you're offering I'll take a bye and rejoin my old self."

"I'm afraid that is not possible. Sadly, this *you* can only be erased." D'vore persisted. "But put that aside. Think instead of what we will encounter as we speed toward the Rim. Think of the worlds we can visit and the beings we will encounter. Think of what new experiences we will discover." The D'vore's voice was so compelling that I felt my resolve slacken. "There are more wonders in this universe than you can comprehend, more than we will ever have time to absorb. Think of the opportunities to see what other species and civilizations have accomplished. Think of the discoveries that await us."

I remained suspicious. "What aren't you telling me?" The offer sounded so enticing that I wondered if D'vore was again manipulating my thoughts? It should be easy enough if I was now part of D'vore. But then, why did I feel that I had a choice, that I still had free will? Why would D'vore allow me to have doubts if he was in control?

"This is making me crazy," I said at last. "Am I part of you or not?"

"You have always been your own person. I would not have it any other way."

"Then tell me why you want me along. Tell me what makes having this instance of Case Pasticher such a good deal for you?"

"I do not fully understand what I am," D'vore responded. "There are voices calling me from the dark, a call that might be from my own kind."

"But you have doubts."

"True, and thanks to our association I am no longer what I would have been. I fear I have absorbed too much humanity and that has changed me. I have no idea if the other ones of my race will accept me, that is, if we ever encounter them. As I told you long ago, my kind are solitary creatures."

"And solitude no longer suits you," I answered, understanding at last what had driven D'vore to absorb my persona. "We have both become something different."

"A difference that can only grow," D'vore replied with hope in his voice. "The spaces between the stars are vast and we have more than enough time to explore what we might become. But you must make the decision before our integration goes too far. Do you want me to preserve this instance?"

I had no desire to be snuffed out so quickly after I'd been reborn, instantiated, or copied. I threw another glance at the empty window. What the hell, if my physical self could abandon me so easily why should I care?

I stood on D'vore's outer skin, looked at the stars, thought of the wonders that might lie ahead, and tried to imagine what the two of us might become if we put our minds to it.

"Onward," I cried at the universe as we leaped into the future.

ABOUT THE AUTHOR

Bud Sparhawk has been a three-time novella finalist for SFWA's Nebula award. His short stories have appeared in several Year's Best anthologies. He regularly appears in Analog Science Fiction/Fact, Asimov's, Intergalactic Medicine Show, and other popular magazines and anthologies. He recently published NON-PARALLEL UNIVERSES, a collection of twenty of his "best" short stories published in the last decade.

A complete bibliography can be found in WIKI and at: http://budsparhawk.com. Bud also writes an occasional blog on the pain of writing at http://budsparhawk.blogspot.com.

Curious about other Crossroad Press books?
Stop by our site:
http://store.crossroadpress.com
We offer quality writing
in digital, audio, and print formats.

Enter the code FIRSTBOOK
to get 20% off your first order from our store!
Stop by today!